W9-AZF-102

## "I wouldn't blame you if you wanted to quit."

Charles's words jerked her attention back to him as she buckled her seat belt. "Quit? Because someone's accusing you of something for which no one has any proof? I don't think so."

She jumped when his palm hit the steering wheel. "I won't let whoever is doing this send me running with my tail tucked. I won't."

Charles turned, eyes narrowed as he drilled her with the intensity of his gaze. "I didn't kill Olivia Henry. I don't know who did. I just know *I* didn't."

## Books by Lynette Eason

Love Inspired Suspense

*Lethal Deception*
*River of Secrets*
*Holiday Illusion*
*A Silent Terror*
*A Silent Fury*
*A Silent Pursuit*
*Protective Custody*
*Missing*
*Threat of Exposure*
*\*Agent Undercover*
*\*Holiday Hideout*
*The Black Sheep's Redemption*

*Rose Mountain Refuge

## *LYNETTE EASON*

makes her home in South Carolina with her husband and two children. Lynette has taught in many areas of education over the past ten years and is very happy to make the transition from teaching school to teaching at writers' conferences. She is a member of RWA (Romance Writers of America), FHL (Faith, Hope, and Love) and ACFW (American Christian Fiction Writers). She is often found online and loves to talk writing with anyone who will listen. You can find her at www.facebook.com/lynetteeasonauthor or www.lynetteeason.com.

# THE
# BLACK SHEEP'S
# REDEMPTION
## LYNETTE EASON

*Love Inspired*

If you purchased this book without a cover you should be aware
that this book is stolen property. It was reported as "unsold and
destroyed" to the publisher, and neither the author nor the
publisher has received any payment for this "stripped book."

Special thanks and acknowledgment to
Lynette Eason for her contribution
to the Fitzgerald Bay miniseries.

Recycling programs
for this product may
not exist in your area.

™ LOVE INSPIRED BOOKS

ISBN-13: 978-0-373-44489-2

THE BLACK SHEEP'S REDEMPTION

Copyright © 2012 by Harlequin Books S.A.

All rights reserved. Except for use in any review, the reproduction
or utilization of this work in whole or in part in any form by any
electronic, mechanical or other means, now known or hereafter
invented, including xerography, photocopying and recording, or in
any information storage or retrieval system, is forbidden without
the written permission of the editorial office, Love Inspired Books,
233 Broadway, New York, NY 10279 U.S.A.

This is a work of fiction. Names, characters, places and incidents are
either the product of the author's imagination or are used fictitiously, and
any resemblance to actual persons, living or dead, business establishments,
events or locales is entirely coincidental.

This edition published by arrangement with Love Inspired Books.

® and TM are trademarks of Love Inspired Books, used under license.
Trademarks indicated with ® are registered in the United States Patent
and Trademark Office, the Canadian Trade Marks Office and in other
countries.

www.LoveInspiredBooks.com

**Printed in U.S.A.**

But we had to celebrate and be glad, because
this brother of yours was dead and is alive again;
he was lost and is found.
—*Luke* 15:32

To my wonderful in-laws, Bill and Diane Eason.
Thank you so much for your love and support.
I couldn't do it without you!

# ONE

Demi Taylor jumped as something scraped against the window behind her. Her book fell to the floor. Heart thumping, she bolted from the couch and spun to look at the window. She'd had it cracked to let in the sound of the ocean crashing on the cliffs just below the house but the blinds were closed and blocked her view.

Which was good.

If she couldn't see out, no one could see in. Quickly, she moved the blinds, shut the window and latched it. Heart still racing, she simply stared at it for a moment as she told herself to calm down. Absently, she shoved up her wire-rimmed glasses back on her nose.

What would someone be doing anywhere near that window? Or was she just being silly and it was a tree branch knocking against the pane?

After all, this was her first week on the job as nanny to Charles Fitzgerald's children and she wasn't used to the night sounds of this house. A shiver danced across her skin, raising goose bumps and her blood pressure.

She walked to the front door and checked the lock.

Secured.

Pulling the curtain covering the small window to the left, she parted the blinds and peered out into the dark night. The motion-activated floodlights weren't on which meant no one had moved in front of them.

She breathed a little easier, her heart rate slowed and she could almost laugh at her jumpiness.

It was only eight-thirty. Her new employer should be home any minute. She'd agreed to stay late while he made a house call, but she wasn't sure she liked it.

Ever since waking up in the hospital three weeks ago with no real memory of who she was, or where she belonged, Demi quickly found out she didn't like the dark.

The fact that no one had come forward to identify her even after her face had been all over the news and in the paper was a bitter pill to swallow. Starting over in Fitzgerald Bay, Massachusetts, had seemed like a good idea last week and getting a job almost immediately had seemed like a dream come true.

Now, doubt assailed her.

She peered out again. The inky blackness made her shiver. Charles and his family lived in the Fitzgerald Bay lighthouse keeper's residence, but even the lighthouse beam didn't reach far enough to cut through the dark.

All Demi knew was that darkness brought flashes of pain, screams, angry words and what she thought was a memory of heavy fists. But that was all she could pull from her shuttered mind before the pounding headache drilled into her, forcing her to abandon her efforts to remember.

No, she didn't like the dark. Add in the weird noises and her adrenaline had stayed spiked since Charles had left three hours ago. A fine tremble set in and she clenched her fingers into fists.

She stood still, eyes closed.

And listened.

Maybe it was just her imagination.

At night, in her small apartment above The Reading Nook

bookstore in town, she often thought she heard footsteps outside her door. Lurking, hiding.

But every time she checked, no one was ever there.

Maybe—

Another scrape against the house made her jerk. Then a muffled pop caused her to gasp. What was going on?

This was *not* her imagination.

She made her way into the kitchen and closed the blinds. Standing next to the window with the blinds now shut, she thought she heard a footfall, a rattle.

And another pop.

A muffled curse.

Her breathing quickened once again and her heart picked up speed.

Someone was definitely near the garage.

What should she do? Get the kids? Hide?

The phone.

She needed to call the police.

And Charles.

Trembling, knees almost knocking, she slapped the light switch on the wall and threw the room into total darkness.

A shudder ripped through her as she thought about the children sleeping down the hall. What if the person was trying to get into the house?

She had to protect the children.

Fighting the fear threatening to cripple her, she groped for the handset of the cordless phone on the counter beside the refrigerator.

The cool plastic slid into her palm and she felt for the digits. 9-1-1.

Lifting it to her ear, she waited, heart thudding so hard she wondered if she'd be able to hear the dispatcher.

"9-1-1, what's your emergency?"

"Someone's outside the house," she whispered. "Charles Fitzgerald's home. I think he's trying to get in."

"Ma'am, stay on the line. Can you get somewhere to hide?"

"No. I'm responsible for two children sleeping in two different rooms. If I wake them to hide… The noise they would make… No."

"Someone is on the way, ma'am, just stay on the line."

Demi did as the woman said, while the garage door drew her attention. It was closed, yet she peered out anyway to find the space empty. But the door…

It moved. Rattled.

Sucking in a deep breath, she said, "He's by the garage."

"Help is coming." A pause. "Is Dr. Fitzgerald there?"

"No, I'm his nanny. I'm staying here with the children while he made a house call."

Another pause that seemed like a lifetime. Then, "I've alerted Detective Owen Fitzgerald, Charles's brother, that there's trouble at your location. He's on his way."

"Thank you." Still the fear churned inside her.

More rattling made her spin. Gasp.

Then silence.

Demi stilled.

Was he gone?

She pulled away the phone from her ear and listened. Nothing.

She crossed the kitchen, the moonlight streaming through the blinds lighting her way.

A sound from the direction of the foyer diverted her attention in that direction, and she padded silently toward it. Was he now trying to get in the front door?

Quivering from head to toe, she gulped. Forced herself to keep it together. She had children to protect. She just prayed she'd made the right decision to let them sleep instead of grabbing them and hiding.

*Please don't let them wake up,* she breathed silently.

Where were the police?

"Please God," she whispered. Then wondered why she found herself praying. She didn't know if she even believed in God. But she wanted to. Wanted to believe He would help her, keep her and the children safe.

Another few seconds passed as she stared at the front door. *Think, Demi, think!*

A weapon. She definitely needed a weapon. All she had to do was keep him away from the children long enough for the police to arrive.

But what could she use?

She looked at the block of knives on the kitchen counter and shuddered. The heavy crystal vase would have to do. She grabbed it, ready to hurl it at the head of whoever dared come through the front door.

Then she heard the faint sound of retreating footsteps, moving as though they were in a hurry. She rushed on silent feet to the door and pressed her ear against it.

The distant sound of sirens reached her ears.

Help was on the way.

They must have scared him off.

Relief flowed through her and she nearly dropped the vase from suddenly weak fingers.

Then realized she still held the phone in the other hand.

Demi set the vase on the table, lifted the phone to her ear and said to the 9-1-1 operator still on the line, "The police are close. I can hear their sirens."

"Yes, ma'am."

"I think he left. I heard him run away." Her sentences felt choppy, short. Like she was having trouble stringing coherent thoughts together.

"Don't check, just stay where you are until the police get there."

Demi didn't bother telling the woman she had no intention of opening the door.

The first police cruiser with the Fitzgerald Bay logo on the side finally pulled up to the house.

An officer opened the door and climbed out, weapon drawn, gaze darting.

And then Demi spied Charles's truck pulling up beside the officer.

Demi opened the front door and everyone froze as she stepped outside.

Charles saw his new nanny standing in the doorway and thought his heart would stop. When Owen had called to tell him Demi had dialed 9-1-1 because he had an intruder at his house, his only thought had been to get home and make sure everyone was safe. He couldn't help the terrifying thought that he'd find Demi murdered in his house. Just like Olivia, his former nanny who'd been found dead on the rocks at the base of the lighthouse that was on his property. But Demi wasn't dead. She was standing in front of him, safe and sound.

"Are you all right? The children?" He rushed to her, the limp he'd acquired while serving in Iraq not slowing him one bit. He took in every detail of her appearance. She looked scared and couldn't hide the fine tremor he could see in her hands but, at first glance, she didn't appear hurt.

Her frightened green eyes blinked wide behind her lenses. Her honey-blond hair lay in disarray as though she'd run her hands through it several times. His heartbeat didn't slow.

She nodded. "I'm fine. The children are fine, too. They never woke up."

Owen approached, followed by Charles's other brother, Deputy Chief of Police Ryan Fitzgerald. Charles introduced them and Ryan asked, "Did you get a look at him?"

Demi shook her head. "I peeked through the blinds, but never saw anyone. He was mostly near the garage door. I did hear some popping sounds, though, and the motion lights never came on."

Owen spoke to the officer next to him. "The garage is around the side of the house. Check it out, will you?"

"Sure." The man's badge read Mike Hughes.

Officer Hughes took off around the side as another patrol car pulled up. Charles groaned when he realized it was his baby sister, Keira, and her partner. Looks like the entire family had gotten the word. But Keira would be the worst. Even though she was the younger sibling, she'd want to mother him. Since Olivia's death and the suspicion that had shadowed his every move, Keira's mothering had turned to smothering.

She climbed from the vehicle, concern etched on her pretty features. "Charles? I was just getting ready to go off duty when I heard the address over the radio. What's going on?"

"We're just about to get to that," Owen said.

"Tell me what I can do to help," Keira offered. "Do I need to stay with the kids?"

"No," Charles assured her. "Demi said they never woke up. They're still sleeping."

Keira ignored him and headed for the front door obviously needing to make sure of that for herself.

Officer Hughes appeared around the corner, a flashlight held at his side. To Demi, he said, "The popping sounds you heard were the lights being broken." To Owen, he jerked his head toward the garage. "I think you need to come see this. And you might want to bring a camera—and another flash-light."

Charles looked at Demi. She said, "I'll stay here out of the way."

He nodded and followed his two brothers and the officer around to the side where his garage was.

As he got a good look at it, he gasped.

In bold red letters, someone had spray painted across the landscape of his garage door.

*MURDERER!*

# TWO

Demi took Officer Hughes up on his offer to listen for the kids. She and Keira followed everyone around to the side of the house to see what all the excitement was about.

She saw the garage door and flinched as though she'd been slapped. Her heart shuddered in pain for the man staring in disbelief at the vandalism. Who would do something like that? Demi hadn't known Charles very long, just long enough to be interviewed and accept the job. She'd heard the rumors. Been privy to the whispers as she walked through town. People wondered how she could work for a suspected murderer. But after meeting Charles, Demi knew in her gut that he hadn't murdered anyone. If she thought he was capable of that, she wouldn't be working for him.

Owen stared at the vile accusation and looked ready to snap someone in two. The set of Keira's jaw said she was right there with Owen.

"What's going on here?"

Demi turned to see Aiden Fitzgerald, chief of police and head of the Fitzgerald family, stride toward his children. She recognized him from the family photo Charles had sitting on his mantel.

"Dad?" Charles frowned. "You didn't have to come out here."

"When I hear someone's trying to break in my son's house, I do." He looked at the garage door and Demi thought she saw him pale when Keira turned her light in his direction. "Someone decided to play dirty tonight, I see."

It wasn't hard to pick up on the fine thread of steel lacing his words.

Charles shook his head. "They egged my house last month and just a couple weeks ago I found all of my tires slashed." He sighed and shrugged. "Don't stress about it, Dad. Until you catch whoever killed Olivia, this stuff is going to happen."

Olivia Henry. Demi had heard the story straight from Charles's mouth. A young woman had come over from Ireland several months ago and Charles had hired her as his nanny. When she'd been found dead on the cliffs at the base of the lighthouse, the town had been rocked.

And then the accusations and rumors had started about Charles's involvement with Olivia.

He'd told Demi in no uncertain terms that there had been nothing between him and Olivia except an employer-employee relationship.

Demi believed him.

"Maybe so," Owen stated, "but that doesn't mean we're just going to sit back and take it."

Keira grunted. "I'm going to check on the kids again."

She disappeared around the corner of the house and Charles simply watched her go.

Demi thought Charles looked weary, battle worn. Not beaten, or defeated, just tired. She ached for him. Wished she could somehow take his pain away. The lump in her throat surprised her. But she couldn't help it. She cared.

She hadn't counted on the spark of attraction that had arched between them when he'd interviewed her.

When Fiona, her landlady and Charles's other sister, had

suggested she apply for the nanny position, she'd mentioned he was having trouble finding help because he was a suspect in the murder of his previous nanny. Demi had at first refused. But Fiona had been adamant about her brother's innocence and Demi had finally agreed.

And she'd been captivated by the hurting father accused of a murder he didn't commit. After speaking with him, she had no doubts about his innocence or she wouldn't be there.

Charles's gaze landed on hers. "I'm so sorry."

"It's not your fault," she reassured him.

Stepping to her side, he placed a hand under her elbow. "Come on. They'll take care of all this. Let me take you home." Right now, she depended upon Charles for most of her transportation to and from his home. She'd love to drive, but had no way of getting a driver's license. Not without some way of identifying herself.

"After she gives a statement," Owen said.

Demi said, "I've told you everything."

"Go through it one more time, if you don't mind," Ryan suggested as he tucked his phone in his back pocket.

"Sure."

They walked back into the house where Keira paced in front of the fireplace. She looked up. "The twins are fine. Still sleeping. I told Officer Hughes he could take off."

"Demi's going to give a statement," Charles said. "Then I'm going to take her home. You said you were just getting ready to go off duty. Do you mind staying with the kids until I get back?"

"I can do that."

Aiden stepped into the house. "I think we've done all we can do here. I'll have a cruiser drive by on a regular basis tonight. We'll talk more tomorrow."

Charles nodded and Demi saw his jaw tighten. "Thanks, Dad."

As Aiden left, Owen flipped his notebook closed. "I'll catch up to you later."

Demi followed Charles out to his car, her heart chugging with dread. Would he tell her that she no longer had a job?

Then certainty filled her.

No, he wouldn't do that. He needed her. Just like she needed him. Or at least the job. She didn't need *him*.

When she'd arrived in town, she'd had a small bag packed with clothes and some money provided by the sweet nurses who had cared for her after her accident.

Fortunately, she'd run into Fiona Fitzgerald Cobb who'd had a vacant apartment above her shop and was willing to take a chance on someone who didn't have a job and couldn't remember her name.

Getting the nanny job had proven easier than remembering her name. Charles had been desperate. Careful who he hired, but still desperate.

He started the vehicle but didn't move to put it in gear. "I'm afraid I've allowed you to land in a hornet's nest by hiring you. I wouldn't blame you if you wanted to quit."

Charles's words jerked her attention back to him as she buckled her seat belt. "Quit? Because there's a jerk out there trying to intimidate you? Because someone's accusing you of something for which no one has any proof? I don't think so."

The relief on his face made her want to reach out to him, soothe his worry and pain.

She jumped when his palm hit the steering wheel.

"I won't let whoever is doing this send me running with my tail tucked. I won't." Charles turned, eyes narrowed as he drilled her with the intensity of his gaze. "I didn't kill Olivia Henry. I don't know who did. I just know *I* didn't."

Demi gulped. Olivia had been murdered by a blow to the head. And if Demi understood everything she'd managed to pick up from snatches of muttered conversations, not much had been found to prove Charles innocent.

But nothing with substance had been found to prove him guilty, either.

She let her gaze run over him. Dark hair, flashing blue eyes. Honest blue eyes. Hurting blue eyes. But definitely not the eyes of a cold-blooded killer.

Demi said, "I believe you, Charles. I believed you when you offered me the job and explained your situation. And I believe you now."

He closed his eyes and leaned back his head against the headrest. "Thank you for that." He paused. "I'm sorry. You don't deserve this."

Demi couldn't help it. She reached out and curled her fingers around his and squeezed. "It's okay, Charles. I promise. And for the record, I don't think you deserve it, either."

He returned her squeeze then let go to grasp the steering wheel. "I'd better take you home and get back so Keira can get some sleep."

He backed from the driveway and Demi noticed Ryan standing in the doorway watching them leave. The frown on his face made her blink and she wondered what he was thinking.

After the heavy conversation back at his house, she was ready for a lighter topic. But that wasn't to be when Charles asked, "Any changes in your memory?"

"No." She glanced out the window. "I just continue to have flashes of some things, but nothing I can put my finger on. And if I try too hard, I get terrible headaches."

"Then don't try. It'll happen when it happens. That scab on the edge of your hairline looks pretty bad."

Self-conscious, she raised a hand to touch it. It had mostly healed and she thought it was looking better.

He must have caught her look because he was quick to say,

"Hey, I'm sorry, I wasn't saying it looked bad...bad. It was just a medical observation. I just meant that it was obvious that you suffered a pretty traumatic injury."

"Oh." She lowered her hand to clasp it in the other one.

The car slowed and he parked in front of The Reading Nook. The quaint bookstore owned and operated by his sister, Fiona. Demi's apartment was upstairs above the store.

Before she could get out, he said, "Wait a minute, Demi."

She turned expectantly.

He tapped his thumb on the steering wheel then said, "You know, when I interviewed you, the fact that you had amnesia put me off a bit. I mean, how could I trust my children to someone who can't even remember who she is?"

She lifted a brow. "Are you sorry you did?"

"No, of course not." His quick response reassured her. "But I do have a confession to make."

Her brow lifted. "What's that?"

He cleared his throat. "I have to be honest. I had Owen run a background check on you. On the name you gave me, anyway."

She tilted her head. "I figured you probably had. You're not the type to just hand over your children to someone you haven't looked into."

He nodded. "Nothing came up, of course. But more importantly, your fingerprints weren't in the system."

"The nurses in the hospital gave me my last name. I remembered my first name, but that was it." She let out a deep breath. "When I came to in the hospital, the police also tried running my fingerprints. Again, they came up empty, but assured me that might be a good thing. At least I'm not in the criminal database."

At the feeble joke, Charles felt himself smiling.

Another shrug. "I don't blame you for doing a background check on me."

He let out a long sigh. "Good, because I was going crazy feeling like I was lying to you. Part of me was afraid you'd be furious."

"No. I would have done the same thing if the roles were reversed." Her soft voice pulled him to her. Delicate features framed with honey-blond hair drew him like bees to honey. Her emerald-green eyes wanted to ensnare him. Innocence and gentleness radiated from her. He'd definitely made the right choice in hiring her.

"It's only been a week, and the twins already adore you," he said.

A gentle smile pulled at her lips. "The feeling's mutual."

There was something about her that he liked. Trusted. Wanted to know more about.

But not tonight.

"Come on, I'll walk you up." He climbed out of the truck and walked around to help Demi out.

"So, Fitzgerald," the voice to his left said, "is this your next innocent victim?"

# THREE

Charles whirled. "Burke, what are you doing here?"

"Just enjoying a little walk. Reveling in my freedom, taking in the taste of the night air." His gaze hardened. "Wondering why criminals are allowed to roam free, given another opportunity to prey on more innocent women."

Burke Hennessy. A lawyer and his father's rival for mayor. Burke and Judge Ronald Monroe, who was rumored to be considering a run for mayor, were two peas in a pod. Fitzgerald Bay would be in major trouble should Burke win the election.

Charles held his tongue long enough to get it under control. Then he said, "Knock it off, Burke. This is Demi Taylor. She's the children's nanny."

"Yes, I'd heard you managed to talk someone into taking the position." Burke smirked and eyed Demi. "Be careful about following in Olivia's footsteps. Especially if they're along the edge of some steep cliffs."

Charles felt his fingers curl into a tight fist. With effort, he loosened it and forced a smile. He would not sink to this man's level—or do anything to mess up his father's chances to beat Burke in the election. "Nice to see you, too, Burke. Now if you'll excuse us…"

He placed his hand on Demi's rigid back and tried to usher her into the rear entrance of the bookstore.

Burke stepped in front of them, anger smoldering just beneath the surface. Charles felt the tension in his shoulders escalate. Burke jabbed a finger at him. "You know you should be in jail. If the main suspect was anyone else not related to the almighty Fitzgeralds, that person would be rotting in a cell right now."

"And if there were any proof that I'd killed Olivia, I'd be there, family or no family. But there's no proof because I didn't kill her. Get out of the way, Burke. Now."

Demi walked away from the two of them, pulling her keys from her purse. Charles swallowed hard. Was she scared? Repulsed? Had she decided Burke was right and that she was placing herself in danger by just being in his company?

He remembered the look in her eyes when she'd said she believed him. No, it was something else.

Turning his back on Hennessy, Charles followed Demi. He saw her hands shaking as she unlocked the door and slipped inside.

"You haven't heard the last of this, Fitzgerald!" Burke hollered.

Charles didn't bother to turn around and waste any more time or breath on the man. "Demi?" She stopped on the steps and looked back down at him. The fear in her eyes cut him. "Hey, I'm so sorry."

"No. Don't apologize. It wasn't you," she said with a shudder. "I had a flash of something. Of violence and anger and… and I just had to get away from that man."

Charles hurried up to her and put a hand on her shoulder. "I understand. I was in a bit of a hurry to get away from him myself."

"Is he gone?"

"Yes, I think so. I didn't stick around to make sure."

She took a deep breath and lifted a brow. "Too busy trying not to smash his nose?"

Charles jerked then gave a surprised laugh. "You noticed?"

"Oh, yeah. I noticed." He felt some of the tension leave the shoulder under his hand. She bit her lip then said, "I'm sorry I was such a wimp. I didn't mean to just walk away and leave you to deal with him, I just…"

He placed a finger on her lips. Her soft lips.

He pulled back his finger and rubbed it with his thumb even as he said, "No need to apologize. Burke's a pain with a loud mouth, but he's harmless. The trick is to just ignore him."

She nodded and finished the trek up the steps. At the top, she turned down the short hallway that led to her apartment.

Charles caught her before she got to the door. "Demi, I want to make something really clear."

"Sure, what is it?"

He raked a hand through his hair. "The rumor is that Olivia and I were romantically involved." A frown creased her forehead and he resisted the urge to smooth the shallow lines. "We weren't. She was my children's nanny and I trusted her with my children. She was a pretty private person, but I'd like to think we were becoming friends. There were no romantic feelings between us whatsoever."

Her eyes stayed locked on his for the longest time and he wanted to squirm under the scrutiny, but he didn't. He just stood there as she decided whether she believed him or not.

Finally, she smiled. "I believed you the first time you told me that. Tonight hasn't changed anything."

Key ready, she reached out to unlock the door when Charles stopped her again, his hand on hers. "Wait a minute. It's open."

Demi gripped the keys tighter and pulled back. "That's weird."

"You probably just didn't pull it shut behind you hard enough when you left earlier."

The doubt on her face said she wasn't buying it.

And after the night he'd just had, he wasn't sure he was, either.

Demi stared at the door. "Maybe Fiona needed to get in for some reason." But why? And why would she leave the door open? "The furniture was delivered last week. Maybe they had something else to bring up...or...or...something."

And what about Chloe, the stray cat she'd taken in the day she'd moved into the apartment? Chloe had followed Demi up the stairs and sat outside the door meowing until Demi had finally let her in. Chloe had made herself at home and some of Demi's loneliness had dissipated.

Had Chloe slipped out the open door?

Worry for the cat and other emotions swept through her. Unexplainable fear.

Breath-stealing panic.

Something flashed in her mind. A clenched fist, a harsh yell. Pain lancing through her head. She blinked, raised a hand to her forehead, felt the scar.

Then the image was gone, leaving a pounding headache in its wake.

"Demi? What is it? What did you remember?"

"Fear," she blurted out. "Just a horrible fear, but I don't know the source. I don't know why!" She lifted a hand to her head and pressed as though she could push the headache out and the memories back in.

He pulled her to him while she shook. His arms held her, comforted her. Offered her shelter.

Swallowing, her breath hitched as she gathered herself and pulled away to face the door once more.

"I'm okay." Her hand reached out to push the door open.

She appreciated Charles's comforting presence behind her. "You're probably right," she said, hating the tremble in her voice, but unable to do anything about it. "I'm sure I just didn't close the door tight." From what she could see, all looked normal. Except...

"Chloe?" she called softly. "Here, kitty."

Demi stepped inside for a better look in the kitchen. "Everything looks fine in here. But my cat usually greets me when I come in."

She moved to the small living area, Charles right behind her. It was just as she'd left it. The new couch hugged the far wall with the afghan Fiona had given her bunched up against one end. The coffee table held the latest book she'd been reading. Her morning's coffee cup sat on a coaster on the end table.

Normal.

But where was Chloe?

Her pulse slowed and her breathing evened out. But sorrow hit her. If Chloe was gone, Demi knew she would miss the cat who, for the most part, had been her only company in the evenings for the past week.

She walked the few steps to the bedroom and peeked in. All looked fine. Just as she was about to check under the bed for the missing feline, her gaze landed on the closet door.

It was shut.

"What is it?"

Charles's voice in her left ear made her jump. He'd picked up on her sudden stillness.

"The closet's shut." She pushed her wire-rimmed glasses up on her nose.

"And that's a bad thing?"

"It was open this morning when I left to take care of the kids."

Why could she remember that and not her last name? Regardless, she distinctly remembered leaving it open. Heart thudding, sweat broke out on her upper lip.

Her front door had been cracked open. Had someone been in the apartment? Someone looking for something? For her? *Go, get away. Run.*

Fear resurrected its head and cut off her breath. But why? Why did she feel this fear that seemed to come from nowhere? There had to be a reason. *Why* couldn't she remember?

"Maybe we should just leave," she said. "Something's not right here."

He placed a hand on her shoulder and the comfort it offered made her shiver. "Let me just check the closet for you."

"No!"

And the images hit her again. A flash of blood, a heavy hand on her face. Someone screaming. Was that her?

She gasped, her breaths came in pants and that sweeping fear that came from a place she couldn't explain nearly consumed her.

Shaking with the urge to flee, she stepped back never taking her eyes from the closet door.

"Demi." His gentle voice forced her gaze to his. Gulping, she saw concern, caring…a warmth that thawed the ice freezing in her veins. "Let me check," he insisted. "It's fine. Really. If someone was in there, I feel sure he would have made his presence known by now."

Pulling in a deep breath, she nodded. Then firmed her jaw.

Walking to the end table, she picked up the lamp and stepped back to the closet door. "All right, I'm ready."

"What are you doing?"

"If someone's in the closet, I'm not leaving you to fight him alone."

The tightness along his jawline that never seemed to

ease, finally did. He smiled and nodded. Then his expression turned hard again as he eyed the closet.

Charles walked to the closet and swung open the door, even as he crouched in a defensive position ready for whatever might come at him. A cat darted out, startling him.

His pulse pounded and he realized how tightly wound his nerves were. Of course after what he'd come home to tonight, it wasn't a surprise. And then Burke's confrontation in the alley…

He watched Demi set the lamp back on the table then lean over to snag the cat and hold her close. "Silly cat, how did you get locked in there?"

"Is the window open? Maybe there was a draft and it blew the door shut."

Demi walked over to the only window in the small room and pushed back the curtains. "No. It's closed."

"Well the cat didn't close herself in the closet." He shrugged. "I don't know. It is kind of strange, I'll admit, but maybe someone from the bookstore wandered upstairs, found your door and opened it to see what was behind it. Seeing that it was an apartment, maybe the person didn't quite shut the apartment door well enough and the draft caused the closet door to shut."

Demi lifted a brow at the weak suggestion. Charles grimaced. "Yeah, I'm not really buying that, either."

Demi's frown deepened. "I suppose something like that could have happened. But I'm pretty sure I locked the apartment door when I left earlier." Reaching inside the closet, she flipped on the light switch.

He could see the sum total of her wardrobe. Four or five shirts. Three pairs of jeans, two pairs of shorts and a sweatshirt and a light windbreaker. On the floor, there were a pair of sandals and some pink slippers. She wore her only pair of tennis shoes.

The sparse selection stunned him. He thought about his ex-wife and her bursting-at-the-seams closet. He'd always been tripping over her shoes that seemed to multiply daily.

And then there was Demi.

Charles felt his heart ache for the fragile-looking woman who'd been victimized twice in one night.

Demi saw the pity in Charles's eyes and turned away from it. She wasn't ashamed of her lack of material goods and she didn't need anyone feeling sorry for her. Straightening her back, she firmed her jaw. Another look around confirmed what she'd originally thought. "Nothing's missing."

"You're sure?"

For some strange reason, Demi felt like giggling. "Trust me, I'm sure. I have no jewelry, no fancy clothes, nothing. There's nothing worth stealing."

Charles's stare made the back of Demi's neck heat up. Ignoring the sensation and praying the flush didn't spread to her cheeks, Demi looked around. "Everything looks fine. I guess no one was up here after all." She frowned, not understanding how this could be when the closet door was shut. "I'll ask Fiona if she came up here. If she didn't, then—" she lifted her shoulders in a shrug "—I have no explanation."

"Is there any reason someone would want to break into your home?"

"No." She paused. "At least I don't think so…I mean…" she stammered to a halt. How would she know? "I don't really know."

"Of course there is," he muttered answering his own question. "Someone who might be mad that you're working for me. Maybe this is just the beginning."

Demi came to his side. "Stop it."

He looked at her. She frowned at him and he could see the frustration in her eyes. Charles sighed. "You're right. I don't need to be having a pity party. But I hate to think of you being in danger because of me." He paused. "Will you be all right to stay here alone?"

Her chin jutted out. "Of course. Nobody was here. I'm just being jumpy after what happened at your house." She glanced at the clock on the wall. "You'd better head home. I'm sure Keira is tired from working all day and is ready to spend some time in her own house."

Charles rubbed his chin, wanting to protest. But he knew she was right. Again. "Okay." He walked to the door then turned. "Tomorrow's Saturday." He found himself fidgeting with the doorknob and forced his hands to his side. "I know it's your day off, but...ah...how would you feel about spending it with me and the kids?" He wanted to spend more time with her. Getting to know her better was at the top of his priority list. At first he tried to tell himself it was because of the kids, but if he was honest, he'd admit he wanted to get to know her better...for himself.

Demi swallowed. Hard. Excitement swirled in the pit of her stomach even as she wondered if spending the day with her boss—her very attractive boss—was a wise thing to do.

Probably not.

"Sure," she said. "I'd love that."

His shoulders relaxed and when he smiled, his blue eyes crinkled at the corners. "Great. I'll let Brianne and Aaron know. They'll be thrilled."

*What about you?* she wanted to ask. But bit her lip in time to keep the words from spilling out.

"Nine o'clock?" he asked.

"I'll be ready."

She shut the door behind him and made sure the lock

clicked. She would definitely be ready to spend the day with them, but wondered if she would get any sleep at all.

Looking around, seeing nothing out of place, she wondered what she was missing.

Because no matter what she had said to the contrary, she felt sure someone had been in her apartment.

# FOUR

Saturday morning dawned a little overcast, but no rain fell yet. The thought of the day to come sent a twinge of excitement through Demi, spurring her to toss back the covers and pad toward the bathroom. She had something to do today besides sit in her apartment spilling her guts to Chloe and bemoaning the fact that her memory hadn't returned yet.

Self-pity was no fun. It was time to start making plans for the future, start to live again and try to either get her memory back or accept that it was gone for good and move on.

Of course she wanted her memory back, but if that wasn't meant to be, she was determined not to let the amnesia negatively affect the rest of her life.

At least that was the pep talk for this morning. Tonight, when she was all alone once again, she would have to figure out how to keep the despair and frustration at bay.

Briefly, she thought about the Bible she'd seen on the shelf in the bookstore. Maybe she should turn to God for comfort. Making a mental note to think about that, she went into the kitchen for her morning cup of coffee.

And realized she didn't smell it.

Another thing she'd discovered since getting out of the hospital was that she loved coffee. Any kind, flavored, black, with cream. It didn't matter.

The last thing she did before bed was set the timer on the coffeemaker Fiona had given her as a housewarming gift.

Only she'd been so distracted last night, she'd forgotten to set the timer.

She filled the carafe then opened the cabinet to pull out the canister of coffee.

When she pulled off the top, she gaped.

A piece of paper sat on top of the ground coffee.

Wariness flooded her. How did this get in her coffee can? Reaching in, she pulled it out and read, *Stay away from Charles Fitzgerald. You don't belong here.*

Knees suddenly week, she dropped the paper back into the can, slapped on the top and gasped, her lungs deflated.

Flashes of a hard fist. Shouted angry words. Pain in her head.

She cried out and sank to the floor, hands gripping her hair. Her head throbbed, but she forced herself to think, to remember.

"No!" The word echoed, the pain in her head intensified and tears slipped down her cheeks. Heart thudding, head pounding, she whispered, "Please, stop. Stop."

For the next few minutes she sat there and emptied her mind of every thought. She couldn't force it. And she had to pull herself together for Charles and the children.

Twenty minutes later, a fine tremor still shook her, but she took a look in the mirror as she ran a brush through her hair. The excited anticipation of the day had waned because of the message still in her coffee can—and the disturbing flashes that resonated in the corners of her mind.

But the thing holding her together was the thought of being with Charles and the children.

That gnawing in the pit of her stomach agitated her as she realized she'd been right. Her instincts had been dead-on when she thought someone had been in the apartment yesterday.

But who?

And what should she do with the odd—and scary—message? Was it from someone who was warning her away from Charles because of what happened to Olivia? But what a weird way to do so.

Should she report it to the police? But what could they do? And why say she didn't belong there? Why would someone go to all the trouble to sneak into her apartment and leave that in her coffee can?

The coffee can.

A strange place for a note. Why put it there?

Unless the person knew her. Knew her habits.

A chill swept through her.

The person had to know that she loved coffee. That she would be in that coffee can first thing this morning. Or soon anyway.

Or was it simply coincidence? The coffeemaker sat in plain sight on the counter. It would be a short thought to realize there would be coffee in the cabinet somewhere.

But *why?*

Her head started to ache again. Determined to push the incident out of her mind until she felt ready to deal with it, she focused on the excitement she'd felt when she first woke up and remembered what she was doing for the day.

She muttered, "You really shouldn't be so excited about spending the day with Charles and the kids. He's your employer, nothing more."

She flushed as she said the words out loud because she knew they were a lie.

She'd been attracted to him the minute she'd looked into those blue eyes and seen compassion—and a spark of something more as he'd questioned her during the interview for the nanny position.

Wishing she had some lip gloss or lipstick made her flush hotter and she rolled her eyes at her reflection. Shiny lips hadn't gotten her the job. Trustworthiness and capability were the qualities Charles had been looking for, and she'd assured him that she had both. He was obviously a good father who was very careful about whom he left his children with.

As well he should be.

But today wasn't about work even though she looked forward to caring for the children during their time together. Most of all, she wanted to get to know Charles a little better. Spending the day together would allow that.

She didn't mind the idea one bit.

But someone else did. Someone else thought she didn't belong here. Here in town? Here with Charles? Here in The Reading Nook?

Again, who?

Standing at the window in her bedroom, she glanced down in the small alley that ran behind her building. It was a shortcut to the other street and had a lot of traffic most days.

She'd stood in this spot many times since moving in. Just watching, wondering about the lives that passed under her window.

Today, the foot traffic was light.

A solitary figure in a hooded sweatshirt, hands tucked in the front pockets walked slowly. Then paused in front of the back door that would lead into her building. She watched him reach out, his arm moved in a twisting motion.

What was he doing?

Seeing if the door was unlocked?

Fortunately, she and Fiona kept it locked unless there was a delivery expected. Tensing, she waited to see if he could get in. Was he the one who'd broken in and left the note?

When he dropped his hand and turned to walk off, she breathed a sigh of relief.

Chloe wound herself around Demi's left ankle, distracting her from her thoughts and unanswered questions. She picked up the cat and carried her to the bed. Setting the animal on the coverlet, she asked, "Shorts or jeans?"

Chloe commenced cleaning her left front paw.

"Right. That's what I thought, too. Jeans it is."

Pulling up her hair into a ponytail, Demi dressed in her thrift store jeans and a flowered top. She opened her purse and grabbed a ten-dollar bill that she stuffed into her front pocket.

She picked up the cell phone Charles had insisted she have the first day she'd reported for work and stuck that in her back pocket. Then she snatched her light jacket from the closet. Unable to bring herself to close the door, she left it cracked open.

Demi stepped out into the hall and pulled the apartment door tight behind her. She double-checked the lock, doing her best to push yesterday's and this morning's incidents from her mind. Shivering at the unpleasant memories, she pocketed the key and slipped into her jacket.

Once down the steps and outside, she looked around for the man who'd stopped at her building and tested the doorknob. Seeing no one, she told herself to relax.

Since she was much too early to meet Charles and the twins—and there was no way she was touching that coffee in her cabinet—Demi decided to have breakfast at the Sugar Plum Café. Excitement at seeing Charles again swirled through her. And yet she couldn't help wonder at the reasons behind the invitation. Did he just want extra help with the twins? Or was it possible he was interested in her as a woman and a potential date? She grimaced. It would do no good to ask questions she didn't have the answers for. "Just take it one day at a time," she whispered.

Clouds hung low and gray, but the sun peeped out behind them so she hoped the rain would hold off long enough to enjoy the day with the Charles Fitzgerald family.

After several glances up and down the street, she crossed at the intersection, then followed the short road past the park. Splashing through a puddle left over from the night rain, she finally found herself in front of the café. The white structure with the large porch was welcoming. And yet, she couldn't shake the feeling that someone was watching her. Waiting for her.

But who? And why?

The man she'd seen trying to get in the building? Demi scoffed at herself. He was probably someone who wanted to go to the bookstore and thought he could take a shortcut by going in the back door.

Surely that was all it was.

But what about the note?

Still feeling a hovering sense of foreboding, Demi shivered as she stepped inside and took in the atmosphere. One of comfort and refuge with tables and chairs and couches. The display of pictures tacked to the walls was mind-boggling. Everywhere one looked, a picture smiled back.

Several patrons sat alone, working on laptops. Tempting smells made her empty stomach rumble and she headed straight for the glass-front case display. An assortment of cakes and pastries called to her. She wanted one of each, but she'd only been working for one week and her funds were still tight.

"Can I help you?"

Demi jumped and turned to see a pretty woman in her late twenties. Her brown eyes sparkled friendliness. Victoria, the owner of the Sugar Plum Café.

After checking the prices on the menu posted on the wall, Demi chose the cheapest option. "I'd love a cup of coffee, black, please."

"Sure thing." In a few minutes, Victoria returned and handed her the cup. "So how are things going?"

"Pretty well."

"Charles hired you to be the children's nanny, didn't he?"

"I guess it's all over town by now."

"Indeed. I'm just glad you're not buying into all that nonsense about Charles killing Olivia."

"No. I'm not buying into it."

From what Demi understood, Olivia had come to Fitzgerald Bay from Ireland three months before her murder, a stranger in town, but one who quickly made friends with Victoria and her daughter, Paige, when she'd stayed at the inn.

Curiosity lifted Victoria's brow. "So, you work for my future brother-in-law, but I don't really know anything about you. Do you have family around here?"

Victoria was engaged to Owen Fitzgerald, Charles's younger brother and a detective with the police force.

"I…" What could she say? *I don't know? I don't remember?* Demi forced a smile as she handed over three precious dollars. "No. I'm just looking for a new start. Fitzgerald Bay seemed like the kind of place where I could find that."

"You're right about that. Why don't you have a seat over there by the fire? It may be May, but it's still chilly here first thing in the morning so I keep the fire going."

Demi nodded. "Thanks. I'll do that." She started toward the comfy-looking chair by the flickering flames.

Once seated, she grabbed the abandoned newspaper on the table before her and opened it. Of course the front page story was still about Olivia Henry's unsolved murder. The first murder in forty years in this town. But there was nothing about the incident at Charles's house last night. She shivered and set the paper back on the table.

The fire crackled and the warmth felt lovely. Soon, she'd warmed up enough to shrug out of the light jacket one of the nurses had given her before she'd been discharged from the hospital three weeks ago.

Everything she now owned in the world had been given to her by another person. The familiar fear filled her, coming from a place she couldn't define. She just knew it was very real. A mental picture of the note in her coffee grounds added to that feeling. Someone had been in her home. Warning her to stay away from Charles.

She couldn't fathom it. But *who? Who?*

And should she report it?

But what would she say? What could the police do about it? She continued to toy with the idea. Maybe she would tell Charles about it and see what advice he had to offer. Then again, if she told Charles, that would just add to his guilt about hiring her. What if he fired her because he thought it would keep her safe?

She shuddered. Jobs in Fitzgerald Bay were few and far between. She couldn't afford to lose the nanny position. No, she'd just keep quiet about the note and hope Olivia's murderer was found soon.

Demi briefly wondered if she should pray about everything. Did she even know how?

*Dear God, please give me my memories back. I need to know who I am. I need to know why I'm so afraid and constantly feeling like I need to watch my back... Please....*

Closing her eyes, she did her best to bring forth memories from before she woke in the hospital.

And couldn't do it. Not even one. Just the feeling of fear whenever she tried to remember.

And the headache.

And now the note in her coffee can. The headache worsened. Quickly, she tossed her thoughts in another direction.

Fitzgerald Bay. A small close-knit community that was friendly to outsiders. At least that's what the website advertised when she'd been narrowing down her choices.

And now she had a place to live and a good job. She was doing all right for someone who'd had nothing and no one three weeks ago.

She glanced at the clock on the wall behind the counter. Eight forty-five. She still had a few minutes before she needed to walk to the park. Demi leaned her head against the cushioned back of the chair and stared out the window while she sipped her coffee. Her mind spun, wondering, desperate to remember who she was, where she was from, if she had relatives that missed her. She swallowed hard against the tears that sprang to the surface.

"Hey."

Demi jumped and did her best to hide her whirling emotions from Victoria who stood before her holding a plate of sandwiches and some delicious-looking pastries.

"Oh. Sorry, I was…thinking."

Victoria set the plate on the table beside Demi and said, "Help yourself."

"What? Oh, no, that's okay. I have money." She flushed and wondered if she looked like a charity case.

Victoria shrugged. "I just thought I'd give you a sampling of what we serve here. Maybe tempt you to come back."

Now Demi felt embarrassed. And hungry. "Well, thank you." She snitched a croissant filled with chicken salad and took a bite as she tried to push the depressing thoughts from her mind. "Wow. This is delicious. I'll definitely be back."

They laughed and Victoria said, "It's my own chicken salad recipe. Pretty good, huh?"

"You could win ribbons with this stuff." Demi quickly polished off the first sandwich and took a sip of coffee.

Victoria laughed. "I knew I liked you." She settled into the chair opposite Demi. "So, how do you like working for Charles? I know it's been only one week, but you must have some impressions."

What was the woman fishing for? "I'm very grateful he hired me. The children are definitely a handful, but very precious."

"I know. They're great. And Charles is a wonderful man regardless of what you might hear said around town."

"Oh, come on, Victoria, how can you say that?"

Demi and Victoria turned in unison to find the owner of the voice. A young woman with her blond hair hanging around one shoulder planted her hands on her hips. "Charles might be guilty of murder."

Victoria sighed. "Meghan Henry, cousin to Olivia Henry, meet Demi Taylor."

Demi gave the adamant young woman with the pretty hazel eyes a tremulous smile. "Hi."

"Hi. I'm sorry, I shouldn't have interrupted your conversation, but I'm just very concerned for you. For anyone who has anything to do with Charles Fitzgerald." And she did look worried, a genuine kind of worried, not the fake kind of worried most people in the town had expressed in order to pump her for information about the Fitzgeralds.

Frowning, Demi exchanged a look with Victoria then said, "I appreciate your concern, but Charles has been nothing but kind to me."

Meghan sighed. "Well, I would watch my back if I were you." She slipped her purse over her shoulder. "I'm in the cottage on the beach, the one just up from the lighthouse. If you ever need anything, please come see me."

Again, sincerity rang in Meghan's words and Demi wasn't sure what to think. "Well, thank you. I appreciate that."

"Be careful, okay?" She glanced between her and Victoria. "See you around."

With that, she left.

Demi raised a brow at Victoria who sighed. "I hope you won't take what she said to heart. I don't believe for a minute that he murdered Olivia."

"I know. I don't believe he did, either."

"Good." Approval radiated from the woman. "He's needed some help for a long time. His father's housekeeper, Mrs. Mulrooney, is wonderful, but she can't keep up with two rambunctious toddlers. I'm so glad Charles found you."

Demi felt a smile slip across her face. "Thanks. It was actually his sister Fiona who told me about the job." She looked at the clock again. "And now I've got to run. Nice to meet you."

"You, too. I'm sure we'll be seeing a lot of each other."

Charles gave the swing a push and felt his heart lighten at his children's laughter. His eyes drifted from his kids to the direction he knew Demi would come from.

He'd had a hard time falling asleep last night as her image kept appearing in his thoughts—in between wondering who'd vandalized his house. He preferred thoughts of Demi. She was beautiful, had a gentle spirit about her—and she scared him to pieces.

She'd been in his life just a short time, but already, he felt as though he'd known her for a while. And while it was true he didn't know as much as he'd like due to the amnesia, he liked what he knew, what he'd observed.

He also knew that if he had any brains at all, he'd find a woman old enough to be his mother to care for the children simply to cut down on the wagging tongues. Unfortunately, no one in that age category seemed to be in the market for a job that taxing. Or one that had anything to do with him.

Him. A murder suspect. He couldn't wrap his mind around it. But apparently the townspeople didn't have any trouble believing it. Everywhere he went, he felt eyes on him, knew they were wondering if he was a killer. His medical practice had suffered as had his confidence in most of those he used to call friends.

His gaze went to a young couple strolling hand in hand along the park path as though they didn't have a care in the world. He remembered those days. Sometimes he missed them. Then he looked at Brianne and Aaron and wouldn't change the past even if he could.

His eyes went back to The Reading Nook bookstore.

But Demi had him thinking more and more about the future and what it might be like to find the one he was supposed to spend the rest of his life with.

A feeling of someone watching pulled him from his thoughts. Glancing around, Charles spotted two women on a park bench near the sandbox. They stared at him as they talked.

Christina Hennessy and Dolores Nunez, nanny for Burke and Christina's toddler. Distaste curled through him. He didn't care for Mrs. Hennessy much, not simply because she was Burke's wife, but because she was such a fake. Probably why she and his ex, Kathleen, had gotten along so well.

And still, she didn't take her gaze from him. Out of a morbid sense of humor, he lifted a hand and waved.

Her right brow rose and she deliberately ignored him, turning her gaze on the nanny.

Why the woman needed a nanny was beyond him. She didn't work and didn't seem to have any responsibilities that he could see.

Speaking of nannies, Demi surprised him and stepped out

of the Sugar Plum Café instead of The Reading Nook and headed his way. He tried to forget about the pair across the park.

But the hair on the back of his neck rose as he continued to feel their stares. He reminded himself not to let their snide glances and whispered words affect him.

But a small part of him wanted to stomp across the park and demand they cease their nasty gossip. Instead, he took a deep breath and watched Demi approach. The concerned frown on her features told him that she'd picked up on his expression. With effort, he loosened his jaw and relaxed his shoulders.

Only to tense up again when Burke stepped into view. The man glanced at him and pursed his lips as though seeing something distasteful.

He said something to Christina and the nanny, then practically shouted, "Come on. It's not safe for Georgina to play here. Apparently, they don't screen the people who use this place and will allow murderers around small children."

# FIVE

Demi couldn't read the expression on Charles's face, but the smile he shot her looked forced, the frown lines between his brows deeper than yesterday.

Burke said something that Demi wasn't close enough to catch, but apparently Charles heard it—and didn't like it. She saw the fury on his face and the rock-hard tension in his body. She had a feeling he was exercising extreme self-control at the moment.

Burke held his daughter as he and the two women left the park.

Charles relaxed and occupied himself by pushing the twins on the swings. They each sat in the little side-by-side bucket seats, legs dangling. Sweet laughter reached her ears, chasing away the frown she knew was on her face.

A twinge in the vicinity of her heart made her wince. What about her own father? Where was he? Was he missing her? Worried about her? Or was he even alive? She had the same questions about her mother, but no amount of trying could bring to mind a face that she could call family.

Drawing in a deep breath, she stuffed her sorrow away and pasted a smile on her face. "Good morning," she called.

Charles turned and his answering smile flashed her way. It seemed a little less forced than the previous one. "Hey, there. We got here a bit early and this was the only way I could corral them."

Demi let out a laugh. "Looks like fun."

"They seem to like it, but even as petite as you are, I don't think you'd fit in the seat."

His appreciative gaze made her pause. Was he flirting with her? Sure looked like it. Did she mind? Warmth centered itself in her midsection. No, she didn't mind a bit. "You're silly." She stepped next to him, placing herself behind Aaron. "Let me take one so you don't have to dance back and forth between them."

His eyes lingered on her a moment longer and his expression seemed to soften even more. "That'd be nice. Thanks."

Demi waited until the little boy came back toward her then gave him a gentle push. He squealed and laughed, his black hair blowing in the wind. As he approached her again, he held out his hand and yelled, "I gots Dino!"

Demi laughed and caught the swing, pulling Aaron to her so she could study the plastic dinosaur clutched in his fingers. "He's the best-looking dino I've ever seen."

That sent Aaron into more peals of laughter. She let the swing go and Aaron swooped into the air.

She looked at Charles who stood watching her, the strangest expression on his face. "What?" she asked.

He shook his head and cleared his throat. "Nothing really. You're just good with them." He smiled. "So, how are you this morning?"

"I'm…" She started to say fine, then decided to be honest. "I had a rough night." And a crazy morning. "But I suppose that was to be expected after that scare I had at your house, then thinking someone was in my apartment." She didn't bother to mention the man she thought had tried to get into the building through the back door. And she didn't want to say anything about the message in her coffee can. Not yet.

She didn't want to ruin what had the potential to be a wonderful day.

"I'm sorry."

Demi shrugged and gave the swing another push. Aaron crowed, "Higher!"

She complied then looked at Charles. His blue eyes sparkled when he watched his children. Instead she asked another question burning in the back of her mind. "Do you mind me asking where the twins' mother is?"

He went still for a moment then let out a sigh before giving Brianne another push. "No, it's not like it's a secret or anything. Kathleen left me when the twins were about six months old." He shook his head. "Her parents spoiled her and she always was rather flighty, I suppose, but…" He shrugged. "She seemed to love me and I…well…I was enamored with her." He pulled in a deep breath. "And then after the babies came, she just couldn't handle it. I was in the process of hiring a nanny to help her out. One day Kathleen was there, the next she was gone. Months later, she sent me divorce papers and a note that she was living in Mexico fulfilling her dream of becoming an artist and wanted to get married to another man, an artist who understands her."

All Demi could think was that the woman was insane. She'd given up all this for…that? "I'm so sorry. That must have been a terrible time."

"It was." Pain flashed across his face. "But you know, I don't really hurt for me anymore. It is what it is. I just hurt for them." He nodded toward the kids. "It's going to be hard explaining her desertion when the time comes."

Demi bit her lip. "Yeah."

"Then again, if that's the kind of person she's decided to be, maybe they're better off not knowing her." He paused. "Would you like to take the kids down to the beach?" Charles asked. "It's too cold to get in the water, but we could build a sand castle and let them run around, burn off some energy, maybe get some ice cream."

Brianne heard him and grinned. "Ice cream."

"I like chocolate," Demi said. "What's your favorite?"

"Ice cream, Daddy!"

Charles groaned. "Now I've done it."

"What?"

"I'll have to let her have some ice cream or I'll hear about it all night."

"Ice cream! Now!" Brianne shouted.

"Hush, Bri, not so loud. We'll get some in a little while. Why don't we go play in the sand?"

"No sand. I want some ice cream."

Charles tossed Demi a wry look. "We might be eating ice cream a little earlier than I planned."

Swings, the park, the beach and now ice cream? Shivers danced up her arms. This day was feeling more and more like a date.

She looked at him, wanting to ask him to clarify if this was a date or if they were just…hanging out. Instead, she simply said, "That sounds nice."

Ten minutes later, the twins were in their car seats in the back of Charles's truck. The red king cab with the leather seats was plush and roomy. Demi inhaled the new-car scent and smiled. "How long have you had this?"

Charles closed his door and cranked the engine. "A couple months."

"I like it."

He flashed her a grin. "I do, too."

Small talk filled the short ride to the beach, interrupted occasionally by Aaron and Brianne's two-year-old chatter.

Charles looked in the rearview mirror and frowned. His eyes flicked back to the road in front of him. Then up to the mirror.

"What's wrong?"

"That car's coming up behind us pretty fast."

Demi glanced in the side mirror and spied a dark-colored sedan gaining on them. "Maybe he's in a hurry and will go around."

Charles let his foot off the gas and slowed.

And the car kept coming. Demi shifted, uneasy. "Charles?"

Charles's fingers flexed on the wheel. The narrow two-lane road didn't leave a lot of room to maneuver and she wondered what he was thinking.

Another look in the mirror showed the car about twenty feet behind them. Ten.

"Charles! He's going to hit you!"

"Hold on." He pressed the gas pedal. Aaron, picking up on the tension, started to cry.

The truck growled to life, responding to the burst of speed instantly. The sedan fell back, but soon gained lost ground.

"I don't want to go too much faster, there's a curve just ahead," Charles said.

"Can you turn off?"

"Hang on, he's coming faster."

Demi felt herself jerk forward, then slam back. She yelped. Brianne cried out and Aaron howled.

Charles went faster. "Call 9-1-1. Tell them where we are."

The curve ahead was sharp, the guardrail offering flimsy protection against a speeding vehicle.

Demi clutched the door and held on while her heart thumped in terror. She held the phone to her ear with effort. The operator came on. "We're on Lighthouse Lane headed toward the beach! Someone is trying to run us off the road!"

Tires squealed as Charles took the curve. Her seat belt cut into her shoulder. From the side mirror she could see the car following behind.

And then they were on a straighter part of the road.

With another curve just ahead.

From a side road, Demi could see flashing blue lights.

Brakes squealed from behind them and she saw the car backing off. It did a quick three-point turn then sped back the way they'd just come.

Charles slowed the truck. Sweat dripped from his forehead and his face had lost color, as he pulled to the side of the road and stopped.

From the back, Demi heard a giggle. She turned to see Brianne gripping the front of her car seat. "Do it again, Daddy."

Aaron's eyes were wide, but he'd stopped crying. When he saw Brianne smiling, he chuckled.

Charles let out a breath and leaned his forehead on the steering wheel.

Demi swallowed hard. "You did a good job, Charles."

"Thanks." He paused. "You okay?"

"Yes. We're all okay."

A Fitzgerald Bay cruiser pulled up beside them. Charles rolled down his window to greet his sister Keira who exited her vehicle, walked to the window and demanded, "What happened? I saw that guy trying to run you off the road." Her anger with the man was a visible thing. "He could have killed you!" She looked in the backseat and paled. "And the kids are with you."

"We were on the way to the beach. He kind of came out of nowhere." Charles shook his head. "Did you get a plate?"

"A partial. He went flying past me. By the time I turned around, he'd disappeared. I called it in for someone to see if they could chase him down so I could make sure you all were okay."

Charles swallowed. "Someone really has it in for me, don't they?"

"Unfortunately, it looks like it, yeah." She pursed her lips.

"Who was Olivia so close to that her death would drive someone to want to hurt you, to get revenge?"

Charles shrugged. "I have no idea. She didn't talk about her life that much. I did a background check and she was clean. She took care of the kids and pretty much kept to herself so I'm not sure who she was close to."

"What about her cousin, Meghan?" Keira asked.

Charles gave a slow nod. "She was really upset about Olivia's death, but I can't see her coming after me like this."

Keira shrugged. "You never know. I'll make a note for Owen and Ryan to check her out." On a small flip-top notebook, she wrote something then slid it back into her front pocket. "Be careful, Charles. It looks like someone isn't very happy with you."

After consulting with Keira, Charles and Demi decided not to let the incident ruin their day.

And while Demi couldn't say she was relaxed, at least the person who had nearly run them off the road was gone for now.

But a shiver ran through her as the thought occurred to her that he would be back. Somehow, deep in her gut, she felt that it wasn't over. When they'd decided to keep their appointment with the beach, Keira promised to drive past the area often. "If whoever tried to run you off the road is watching, he'll see the cruiser keeping an eye on you."

"I don't know if that's necessary, Keira."

She shrugged. "I don't, either, but it can't hurt."

"Guess not." Charles looked at Demi and she offered him a reassuring smile.

Now at the beach, Demi climbed from the truck and while Charles unbuckled Brianne, she went ahead and released Aaron from his car seat.

Then the four of them headed down the pier. Brianne

seemed to have forgotten about her demand for ice cream since the incident with the car.

Charles limped slightly and again, Demi wondered what happened. Before she could be nosy again, his brows pulled tight into a frown as he gazed at the cliffs and rocks under the lighthouse.

Wondering at the expression, Demi looked where he did. The white lighthouse with the red roof matched the building next to it. Charles's home. It sat at the top of a cliff overlooking the ocean. Just yesterday, she'd stood at the window and stared at the view. She'd been in awe of such beauty. "What a great place to raise kids."

"I think so." He shot her another smile, but it didn't reach his eyes and the frown between his brows seemed even more pronounced. "The path to the beach is this way. Be careful, there are a lot of rocks."

Demi held on to Aaron and followed Charles, noticing that he carried a picnic basket in one hand while holding tight to Brianne's small hand.

Once on the beach, Charles opened the large basket, pulled out two towels and handed one to Demi. "I decided not to bring the chairs. We can use these. We won't stay very long. I'll have to get the twins back to the house for their nap."

The wind whipped her ponytail around her face and tugged at the towels. Demi followed his example and planted herself on one. He'd placed them close together so that her shoulder nearly touched his.

As her gaze scanned the area, she caught sight of the cruiser sitting at the top of the rock. Keira stood looking down at them. Peace settled on Demi's shoulders for the first time since finding the note this morning.

His musky cologne wafted to her and she inhaled, deciding she could get used to that smell. "It's chilly for May, isn't it?"

"Chilly and windy."

Brianne and Aaron each grabbed a bucket and shovel from the basket. "Daddy, you help me?" Brianne asked. "I want a castle for a princess."

Charles shook his head. "In a minute, Bri. I want to talk to Ms. Demi, okay?"

Brianne cocked her head and turned her shy smile on Demi. "You come help me?"

She would have been happy to dig in the sand with the little ones, but took her cue from Charles. "Why don't you get started and I'll help you in a few minutes."

"Okay." Brianne joined her brother and the two started digging and flinging the sand.

Demi watched the little ones as she waited for Charles to say something. When he remained silent, she turned to look at him. His eyes were on his children, but even only knowing him such a short time, she could tell his thoughts were elsewhere. "What are you thinking?"

He blinked. "Nothing much."

She didn't believe it, but didn't feel it was her place to push him. The hair on the back of her neck lifted and she shifted. Uneasiness shivered through her and she looked toward the cliffs again. That feeling of being watched just wouldn't leave her.

Keira was still there, now perched on the hood of her cruiser, talking on the phone. Her presence offered comfort. So where was Demi's edginess coming from? Someone after *her?* Or were these incidents all related to Charles, and she was just caught in the middle?

The latter, more likely. That's what everyone seemed to think with the incident at his house or the one on the road just now. But what about the break-in at her apartment?

Something just wasn't right, but Demi couldn't figure out exactly what it was that was making her so uneasy.

If someone was watching Charles right now, he didn't seem to notice.

He handed her a sandwich, breaking her train of thought. "Do you like ham and cheese?"

"Love it. Thanks." She unwrapped it and took a bite as she watched the kids. Even though she had her eyes on the children, she was extremely aware of the man beside her—and the fact that her back was exposed to a number of hiding places in the rocks behind her.

"This is the first time we've been down here this year," he said suddenly.

His quiet words surprised her. She heard the strain behind them. "Really? Why?"

He turned his gaze to her. "Because of what happened to Olivia, of course."

"Oh." She looked around again. "Is this where it happened?"

"Not exactly, but pretty close. She fell—or was pushed—over the cliffs. She was found down there on the rocks below our house and the lighthouse. They found a rock with blood on it and are running tests to see if they can find any DNA on it. We're waiting for those tests to come back."

"I'm sorry you're having such a rough time."

His eyes softened and he lifted a hand as though to reach out to her. Then must have decided against it as he snagged a bottle of water. "Thanks."

Demi wondered if now would be good time to say something about the note in her coffee can. Opening her mouth to do that, she was interrupted by Charles's phone ringing. "Just a sec." He found the device and said, "Hello?" She watched him listen. Then he said, "That's fine, we're not staying much longer anyway."

He hung up and told her, "Keira needs to leave in a few

minutes." His lips quirked in a small smile. "She said she'd feel better if we'd leave when she did."

"We can if you like."

"Not yet. The children are loving this." His gaze met hers. "And so am I."

Demi flushed as she caught his unspoken message. She decided to change the subject. "So what's your family like?"

His smile widened. She hadn't fooled him one bit. "You've already met a few of them. Fiona, your landlady, is my sister, and Victoria, who owns the Sugar Plum Café, is my sister-in-law-to-be. Probably one day soon. She's engaged to Owen, a detective. The rest of the crew are also with the Fitzgerald Bay Police Department as you found out last night. My mother died a few years ago and Dad's the chief of police and running for mayor against the oh-so-subtle Burke Hennessy. My granddad, Ian Fitzgerald, is the current mayor, and is stepping down. I have three brothers and two sisters."

Demi sighed. "I'm envious. I have no idea if I have any family anywhere." She looked at the cliffs where Olivia died. Clouds moved in and hovered, obscuring the sun. Demi shivered.

"Are you cold?"

"A bit."

"Daddy! Come play!" Brianne insisted.

Charles quirked another smile at her. "I guess we can warm up while we help them dig that hole to China." He looked up as Keira's cruiser pulled away. "Then I guess we'd better head home and let two little ones get some shut-eye."

Demi grabbed a shovel and sank beside Aaron. He grinned up at her and said, "Dig."

"Say please, Aaron," Charles reminded his son.

"Puleeeeeeze," Aaron said with a grin.

But even as she sank the shovel into the soft sand, she couldn't help watching behind her. Talking with Charles and spending time with his family had been a wonderful diversion from her less-than-pleasant thoughts. However, the feeling of being watched never fully left her.

The cliffs were steep, the rocks sharp and dangerous. She felt a deep pang of sympathy for the woman who'd died there. Turning, she concentrated on digging.

The sound of a low growl snapped up her head. A dog stood on the rocks watching them. "Charles?" she whispered.

He turned and she heard his indrawn breath.

"It's a German shepherd." He kept his voice low and she heard the tension running through it.

"He—or she—doesn't look very friendly." Demi gripped the toy shovel as though she would be able to use it as a weapon. Slowly, her eyes never leaving the dog, she moved between it and the children.

The animal bared its teeth once more and Charles reached for a piece of driftwood. He flung it toward the dog with a harsh, "Get!"

The dog flinched, tucked her tail and ran off.

Demi let out her breath in a huff as she wilted on the sand. "I wonder if she has puppies around here."

"You're amazing."

"What?" Demi gaped at him. Why would he say that?

He nodded, his eyes serious and intense. "Your first instinct was to protect the children with no thought of yourself. I've never met…I mean other than family…I don't know of anyone that would have done that."

"Daddy, play!" Brianne called, oblivious to the danger she could have just been in. Charles gazed into her eyes a moment longer then turned to pay attention to his daughter.

Speechless and surprised at his praise, Demi still shivered

at the feeling of trepidation that swept over her. Especially when she thought about that note in the coffee can.

She swallowed hard and hoped that by being vigilant and watchful, she wouldn't be the next victim the cliffs would claim.

# SIX

Sunday morning, Demi woke early, tossed and turned until she heaved a sigh of frustration. Climbing from the bed, she decided to head to the beach for a walk. She'd so enjoyed the time with Charles and the kids yesterday that she wanted to feel the wind in her face and the sand beneath her feet before she had to get ready for church.

Within minutes, she was out the door on the bike that Fiona had said she could use anytime. It was a long ride, but she didn't care. Being outside was chilly, but exhilarating. Already she felt lighter, like her burdens were sliding from her shoulders.

At the end of the wooden boardwalk that led to the beach, she slipped off her sandals and dug her toes into the cool sand.

For a moment she just stood there, watching the waves crash against the shore.

To her left, she saw another person walking her way. Squinting, pushing up her glasses as though that would help bring the individual into focus, she watched.

A man with a gray hoodie.

Spinning on the sand, she headed back the way she'd come. Who was he? Had he somehow followed her?

Demi shivered and shot a glance over her shoulder. The man was closing in.

She considered turning around and confronting him, but the thought of Olivia Henry, and the fact that her murderer still roamed free, spurred her faster toward the walkway.

True, the man could be harmless.

Or, he could have a weapon.

No sense in finding out the hard way.

She hurried along, but couldn't help one more glance over her shoulder.

The man had stopped following and just stood there watching her walk away.

She wished she could get a good look at his face, but with the hood pulled up and low, it was impossible. However, she thought she saw him lift his hand in a small wave.

Demi gulped and continued her hurried pace along the walkway that would lead her to her bicycle. Another glance back told her that the man had started walking again, but at a leisurely pace, seeming in no hurry to catch up.

Would he come up to the walkway, as well?

No. Demi adjusted her glasses a little higher on her nose. He looked like he was leaving. She watched him turn and head back down the beach. Her pulse slowed slightly.

But she desperately wanted to know who he was. If he was the one who'd broken into her apartment and put the message in her coffee can, she wanted to know why.

But she'd never seen him anywhere other than the alley behind The Reading Nook and now. If it was even the same person.

Grasping the handlebars, she swung her leg over the bike and placed her foot on the pedal.

Only now she felt a shiver go through her at the idea of riding to her apartment all alone.

* * *

Safely back home, Demi dressed for church. Shoving aside the creepy encounter with the stranger on the beach, she allowed herself a small measure of joy. Yesterday she'd managed to put aside the note in her coffee can and just as she'd hoped, the day had been lovely—except for almost being run off the road and the dog scare on the beach.

However, she'd take what she could get at this point.

Spending time with Charles and the children had filled a void she hadn't been consciously aware of until she'd had to leave them and come home.

Worry bit at her. Would she feel this way if she had her memories intact? Or was she using them to make up for what she lacked in her life?

Unsure of the answer, she decided there was nothing she could do about it right now.

As she pulled the brush through her hair one last time, she gave herself a quick check in the mirror. The flower-print dress made her feel pretty and feminine and she wondered what Charles would think. She flushed and turned from the mirror. She didn't bother trying to tell herself she shouldn't care what Charles thought. She was attracted to the man and that was that.

And he'd invited her to church. She'd agreed and told him that she would meet him there. When he'd offered to pick her up, she'd hesitated then said no. She'd confused him, she could tell, but with all the rumors flying around about Charles, she didn't want to add fuel to the fire by being seen walking into church with him after having already spent yesterday with him.

She had a feeling she was only prolonging the moment, though. Word was already out that Charles had a new nanny and she figured the wagging tongues were going triple time.

And if she sat with him in church this morning…she might as well have let him come get her.

But she couldn't concern herself with that. Or listen to gossip. She was going to go to church and enjoy it.

She'd passed the Fitzgerald Bay Community Church located just off Main Street during her explorations of the town, and had given some thought to stepping inside, wondering if she would find God there.

Now was the time to find out.

"Demi? You ready?"

Fiona had promised to stop by and walk with her to church. Turning from the window, Demi determined to put her fears to rest and enjoy the day.

She crossed the room and opened the door to see Fiona dressed in a khaki skirt and a light pink pullover summer sweater.

"Good morning. Come on in while I get my purse." Demi grabbed it from the chair.

"Sean and Hunter left a bit early so they could have their 'man breakfast.'" Fiona laughed. "No girls allowed."

Together, she and Fiona descended the stairs. "That's so sweet. Hunter is like a father to Sean, isn't he?"

"Yes, after my first husband, Jimmy, died, I was crushed, but—" a real smile spread across her face "—Hunter has been an answer to prayer. He loves Sean like he's his own. And Sean returns the affection. God's been good to us."

"Even with all the crazy stuff going on?" She'd heard about the fire at the bookstore and the arsonist who'd been caught just before Demi's arrival in town.

Fiona smiled. "Even then."

Outside, they started the short walk to the church and Demi couldn't help glancing around, and back over her shoulder.

"Are you okay?" Fiona asked.

Demi jumped. "Oh. Yes, I'm fine. I'm sorry, I guess I'm just a bit skittish."

"Well, who can blame you after what happened at Charles's house Friday night? And then to come home and think someone had been in your apartment? I'd be skittish, too." She paused. "So you really think someone was there?"

Demi frowned. "Yes, I do. I just don't know why."

Fiona gave her a sympathetic pat on the arm and frowned. "I have someone coming today to reinforce the locks."

"Might not be a bad idea." In fact Demi thought it was a very good idea.

And then they were at the church. It was a lovely white-steepled structure with old-world charm. Demi hoped she would be able to find some peace inside.

Fiona led the way and Demi followed her down the aisle, watching as the woman spoke to nearly everyone there. She introduced Demi as a friend and her new tenant.

And then the man who'd been so snarly the other day, Burke Hennessy, walked up and gave her a haughty smirk. "You don't have much of a self-preservation instinct, do you?"

"What do you mean?"

Burke's voice carried through the chattering crowd. "I'm just trying to give you some advice, dear. Getting mixed up with the Fitzgerald family isn't the smartest move in the playbook. Charles is a murderer. His family's position at the police department is the only reason he's not behind bars."

Demi blinked at the man's audacity.

"Burke, enough," the pretty blonde at his side hissed. The crowd immediately around them had quieted and now watched the interaction play out.

"It'll never be enough, Christina," Burke continued. "Fitzgerald Bay hasn't had a murder in over forty years and—"

Fiona broke in, "Burke, not everyone believes the vicious rumors being spread about my brother. Leave Demi and Charles alone."

Fiona pulled Demi away from the man still watching, his eyes burning holes into the back of her. Demi shivered at the underlying menace in the man's voice.

By the time they walked to the middle of the church, Demi's mind spun with names and faces and Burke Hennessy's warning. Was he right? Was she being stupid to get involved with a man under the shadow of a murder investigation?

Her gaze landed on Charles—and the rest of his family.

His huge family, surrounding him, offered a buffer against the cold self-righteousness of members who didn't believe a man suspected of murder should be in a house of worship. But she was glad to see others treated Charles well, slapping him on the back and shaking his hand. Apparently they'd missed the exchange with Burke.

All eyes seemed to land on her at the same time and panic hit her. What if the Fitzgeralds didn't like her? Up to this point, the only time she'd had any real contact with his family was when she'd called 9-1-1 and they'd all shown up at Charles's house.

What if they thought she was crazy because of the amnesia? What if they didn't think she was good enough to take care of the twins? What if—

Charles lifted his head and caught her eyes. Pushing his way out of the circle around him, he held out a hand. "Good morning, Demi. Let me introduce you to the members of the family you haven't met yet."

Once again, Demi took in the names she knew she'd never remember, but was grateful no one seemed to find it strange that Charles had invited her. In fact everyone welcomed her with open arms.

Then the music started and Demi slipped into the pew beside Charles. She was glad she'd come, but she couldn't help glancing around the congregation.

She continued to scan the crowd, eyes probing, looking for any hint of recognition. But she saw nothing that triggered her internal alarm. She thought of the person on the beach. And then the one who'd tried to get into the building via the back door. Was it the same man?

She wasn't sure. All she knew was that the hairs on the back of her neck stood up. And somehow, she knew someone was here in this church...watching her.

Charles glanced at the woman beside him as his mind spun with ideas to help her. He was having a hard time staying focused on the sermon. A problem he had developed shortly after Kathleen left him. If it wasn't for the children, he wasn't sure he'd even bother to attend. Might as well figure out a way to help Demi in the meantime.

She seemed so fragile, so needy and yet he'd seen strength in her when her first instinct had been to protect the children from the dog—or protect him from whatever was in her closet.

Those were things he wasn't likely to forget any time soon.

And the children had been asking about her this morning as he got them ready for church. They'd already fallen in love with their new nanny. Charles knew that if she decided to quit because of all the things that were happening to her—things that were happening because she was involved with him and his family—the children would be heartbroken.

A little voice in the back of his head said he would be, too.

Then he'd seen Burke say something to her at the start of the service and figured it wasn't good. She'd looked spooked, then worried, but her expression had smoothed as the music had started.

Whatever had been bothering her at the beginning of the service seemed to slide from her shoulders and her mood lightened.

Was she a believer?

He made a mental note to ask her. Then scoffed at himself. She had amnesia. How would she know?

Charles leaned back and relaxed, glad to be in the company of his family. They shielded him from the dark looks the good people of Fitzgerald Bay shot him even in the church.

Movement from behind the pulpit grabbed his attention. Long heavy blue velvet curtains hung behind the pastor. One fluttered.

Then stopped.

Charles frowned as he watched for more movement. He looked for the air conditioning vent, but didn't see one.

Nothing else happened over the next several minutes and he started to relax.

When the congregation erupted in laughter, Charles jerked. He'd been so preoccupied with the movement of the curtains, he'd missed the joke.

He tuned back in.

Pastor Larch said, "And now we have a video that will show you a little bit of what our young people will be doing on their mission trip to the mountains of North Carolina."

The lights dimmed.

The curtains parted and the music started.

As the curtains pulled apart, Charles gaped at the words that were revealed on the lighted screen.

YOU DON'T BELONG HERE.

Beside him, Demi jerked and gasped.

The congregation muttered and pointed.

Aiden Fitzgerald popped to his feet as did Ryan, Owen and Keira. "Turn the lights back on!" Aiden shouted.

The sanctuary lit up.

Aiden, followed by several other members of the Fitzgerald Bay Police Department and leaders of the church, strode to the screen.

Charles joined them, heart thudding, listening to their speculation even as he studied the message.

Was it meant for him?

"Don't touch anything," he heard his father order.

Keira said, "Everyone back up, please. Can you all please return to your seats?"

But all Charles could do was stare. And it became very real to him that there were people in this town who not only thought he was a murderer, but hated him. Hated him enough to attack him in his own church. Hated him enough to vandalize his home and terrorize his family.

Anger bubbled just beneath the surface and he turned. He'd get his kids and get out. Turning, he saw Demi staring at the words, her face pale, her eyes wide. Scared.

His gut clenched. Would she now tell him that she no longer wanted anything to do with him? With his children?

The thought stabbed him in the heart.

"Demi?"

She turned her gaze on him, shook her head and walked toward the back of the church.

Ryan Fitzgerald, Deputy Chief of Police, came to stand beside him. "You think this was because of you, don't you?"

"Don't you?" Charles gritted out.

The uncertainty that flashed across Ryan's face was answer enough. Then Ryan shrugged. "Probably, but I wouldn't let it get to me. You know how people are, bro. Let it roll off your back."

"Not everyone feels that way, Charles," Pastor Larch said

from his left. Charles turned to see the compassionate gaze of the man. "Don't let this run you off. You belong here just as much as the person who left that message."

"Thank you, Pastor, but I think it's best if I just leave for now." He appreciated the man's reassurance, but the only thing he was interested in was getting his children and finding Demi.

Charles touched Fiona's arm to get her attention in the chaos. "Will you get the twins? I need to take care of something."

Concern reflected in her gaze, but instead of questioning him, she nodded. "Sure. We're going to Dad's for lunch." She looked again at the front of the church where the message still blazed. "At least we were."

"I'll be back in a minute."

He ran after Demi.

*He means me,* she thought. It was the same message as the one in the coffee can. *I don't belong here. He's right.* But how did he know that? And why make such a public display of it? To send her running?

Did she belong anywhere? To anyone?

Sobs crowded her throat as she made her way down the front steps of the church. She'd tried so hard to be brave, to believe the amnesia would go away and her memory would return.

But it hadn't.

Tears slipped down her cheeks and she ignored them.

Anger, self-pity and fear all swirled inside her. Why had she even bothered coming to church? Did she somehow think that by doing so she could make God happy and He would miraculously restore her memory?

Maybe.

Her sandaled feet slapped the sidewalk as she hurried

toward her apartment. She would have to use the phone in The Reading Nook to call Charles and—

Charles.

She stumbled to a halt.

And felt a heavy hand land on her arm.

Gasping, she spun and saw Charles.

"You s-scared me to death," she stuttered.

His grim mouth tightened even more. "I know. I seem to have that effect on most of the townspeople these days."

"I'm sorry."

His brows drew even closer together as he frowned. "What do you mean? Sorry for what? I'm the one who needs to apologize to you."

That stopped her. Drawing in a deep breath, she said, "Oh. Why?"

"I suppose after that little surprise in the church, you've rethought your decision to work as the children's nanny?"

"What?" she blurted out. "No! I figured you wouldn't want me anymore after...wait a minute. You think that message was for you?"

"Well, of course, who else..." Realization dawned on him. "And you think it was for you." His frown lightened a fraction. "But why?" When she didn't answer right away, he said, "I think we need to talk."

She glanced behind him. "Where are the children?"

"With Fiona." His gentle hand swiped the tears from her cheeks leaving a heated trail behind.

She flushed but hoped he would contribute that to the emotion of the moment. "Who would do such a thing?" she whispered.

"I don't know. I thought I saw the curtain moving before the lights went low, but I didn't think much about it." He swallowed hard. Looked away then back at her. "I have a confession to make."

"What?" Should she be worried?

But his eyes were kind. Gentle. And sad. He lifted his shoulders in a slight shrug. "I haven't been to church in a while. I got tired of the stares, the accusing looks, the mamas hiding their children when I passed by." He blew out a breath. "But today, I wanted to be there—" He met her eyes. "With you." He gave a wry smile. "I fought in Iraq, toe-to-toe most days with some pretty harsh guys. But going to church, facing those people intimidated me." Now he looked away. "I felt weak. And don't ask me to explain this, but going to church today, knowing you were coming, knowing there was one person besides my family who believed in me…" He pulled in a deep breath. "That made me feel strong."

"Oh, Charles." She stepped forward and wrapped her arms around his waist and offered him a hug right there on Main Street. In front of God and anyone else who cared to see. When she pulled away, the surprise in his eyes made her flush. "I'm sorry."

"Don't be." His voice was husky as though holding back some deep emotion. "I needed that."

"There you are."

They jumped as one as the voice echoed across the street. Demi turned to see Aiden Fitzgerald bearing down on them, one brow raised. He didn't say anything about the embrace he just witnessed. "We've got that mess taken care of back there. Now, can we put all this unpleasantness behind us and go eat? I'm starved." His father eyed Charles who still had a hand on her upper arm. "You're coming for lunch, right?"

"Sure, Dad, wouldn't miss it." Demi could hear the forced cheerfulness. "Who's cooking?"

"Keira and Fiona threw something together last night. Just need to heat it up."

Charles glanced at Demi.

"Demi's welcome, too," his father said.

"Thanks." He looked at her. "Will you join us?"

"I'm...um..." Uncertainty filled her. She should probably say no. But she wanted to go. "Yes, I'd love that, thank you."

"Great. You can ride with me and the kids."

"I just need to get my purse. I'm afraid I ran off without it." She ignored the embarrassed flush she felt climbing her cheeks.

"You get your purse. I'll get the kids from Fiona and meet you at the truck."

Demi nodded, excited at the prospect of spending more time with Charles and his family. And yet that excitement was tempered by the knowledge that while Charles thought that message was for him, she felt quite sure he was wrong.

Although she was unable to explain the reasons behind it.

# SEVEN

"Thanks for inviting her, Dad."

"No problem. She's a pretty girl."

Charles felt a flush at the back of his neck. "Don't go there, Dad. Lunch would be a great way for her to get to know the family. I mean she is the kids' nanny, so everyone should get to know her. And she should get to know them. I mean—"

His father gave a hearty chuckle and slapped Charles on the back. "You can stop that painful explanation any time now."

In spite of the morning's incident, Charles found a grin. "Right. I'm just going to get the kids from Fiona."

"Do you mind if I walk with you?"

"Sure, I never turn down an extra pair of hands."

As they walked, his father said, "I know you're anxious to hear about the DNA test results."

"I am."

"I called the lab yesterday and they said it would probably be another few days to a week. We should know something soon."

Charles's jaw clamped tight. He knew his family was doing everything they could to clear his name. And he knew that getting DNA results back in a reasonable amount of time was next to impossible. So he would wait. Maybe not patiently, but he would wait.

They arrived at the nursery to find Fiona gathering Brianne and Aaron. When Brianne saw her father, she squealed and opened her arms to him. He scooped her up, smelling her little-girl scent and thanking God for blessing his life with the two little ones.

"Daddy, I'm hungry. Want some ice cream," Brianne said.

"Me, too," Aaron agreed.

"Let's go eat some lunch first," Charles said. "Then we'll talk about ice cream. You have to eat veggies."

"No veggies." Brianne frowned. "No, no, no."

"Yes, veggies. Yes, yes, yes."

His father carried Aaron while Charles continued his dialogue with Brianne. At the car, he found Demi waiting, her smile welcoming, but the strain of the morning still stamped on her face. His father handed Aaron over to her and she helped him load the kids into their car seats.

His dad said, "See you at the house," then walked toward his own car.

As a result of Demi's presence, Charles couldn't help notice that the cloud of loneliness that Kathleen's desertion had caused seemed to lift. He watched Demi tickle Aaron under his chin and laugh. Aaron laughed back and tried to copy Demi by wiggling his little fingers under her chin.

Longing hit him. Hard. He wanted someone in his life. Someone who loved him, loved his kids. Someone like Demi.

As he climbed behind the wheel, he scoffed at himself. Someone like Demi? He'd known the woman all of a week and it made him nervous that he was thinking long-term about her because he wasn't sure he could trust his instincts anymore. They'd certainly been wrong about Kathleen. Could he trust them about Demi?

And what about the person that seemed determined to

keep flinging the blame for Olivia's murder in his face? And the fact that most people in town considered him a suspect? He looked in the rearview mirror at his children, then over at Demi.

His heart shuddered at the thought of something happening to them. In addition to keeping them all safe and clearing his name, he wanted to help Demi figure out who she was. But how?

Unable to come up with a satisfying answer, he thought about the Glock he had locked in his safe at home. Might be a good time to start carrying it again. It would be one step toward keeping everyone safe.

"Are you all right?"

Charles jerked. Demi looked at him, her wide green eyes waiting for his answer.

"Yes," he smiled. "Just thinking."

"About what?"

"A lot of things. But one thing was about trying to figure out a way to help you."

Interest brightened her face. "Like how?"

"Just an idea I've got brewing in the back of my mind. Let me put it to my brother Owen and see what he thinks. If he decides it has merit, I'll fill you in."

She frowned, but didn't question him as she settled back into the seat. The drive to his father's house didn't take long.

Inside, Victoria's daughter, Paige, volunteered to entertain the children in the playroom. Charles let her, watched Keira take Demi under her wing and then headed off to the den to find Owen talking with Ryan and Hunter.

Owen's large frame hogged one end of the couch. Charles got his attention and waved him over. Curiosity etched on his features, Owen followed Charles into the hall. "What's up?"

"I want to help Demi try to figure out who she is."

Owen knew about the amnesia. Word had spread quickly

that Charles had hired a woman with no memory. "What do you have in mind?"

"Demi said the police posted her picture in the papers and on the news for several days after she woke up, but no one came to identify her."

"Could be the wrong part of the country. Could be she doesn't have anyone."

Charles frowned. "That's a sad thought."

"Yeah." Owen glanced toward the den. "I know if one of us disappeared, Dad would stop at nothing to find us."

Charles knew that for a fact. "So what do you think about putting her picture back up on the news? See if we get a response?"

Owen shrugged. "Sure, we can do it." He pulled his phone from his pocket. "You got a picture of her?"

Charles grabbed his own phone. "I will in a minute."

"I'll let Deborah know it's coming." Deborah was the dispatcher. She'd see the picture was handled appropriately.

Charles went in search of Demi and found her in the dining room placing a huge bowl of mashed potatoes in the center of the table. Even growing up in this family, he was still amazed at the amount of food they put away whenever they got together.

She smiled when she saw him. He waved her over. "I need a picture of you."

Her right brow lifted. "Okay. What for?"

"We're going to put your picture back out there on the news one more time and see if anyone steps forward."

Grief flashed for a brief moment before she lifted her chin. "We already tried that. In the city where I was attacked. Springfield, Massachusetts. About a hundred miles west of here." She shrugged and swallowed. "I don't think there is anyone."

Charles felt his heart break for her. He placed his hands on her shoulders and said, "Demi, no one is completely alone in the world. Even if someone is the last surviving member of her family, there are still friends, coworkers, *someone* who would notice if she were missing."

"But no one did," she whispered. "That's what I'm saying."

"Then the right person didn't see the picture," he insisted.

"Are you always this stubborn?"

"Always," Owen said from behind him.

She glanced between the brothers and then shrugged. "Okay, if you want to try."

Charles snapped the picture and sent it to Owen's phone so that it got displayed on the six o'clock news that night.

"Owen," Victoria interrupted, holding out her phone. "Trevor Billings is on the phone. Wants to know if you can fill in and pitch the upcoming softball game. It's the special fundraiser game for the children's hospital and Kyle can't be there."

Charles watched his brother roll his eyes and explain to a confused Demi, "Trevor is the team's manager. He recruits us from church. Kyle is the regular pitcher. I pitched one game for him last season and now they're determined to get me on that team full-time. I told them I didn't have time for that right now. That I couldn't commit."

Victoria's gaze softened as she looked at her fiancé and Charles felt a pang hit him. Would he ever see that look in a woman's eyes again? He stole a glance at Demi and saw her watching them, a longing also written on her face.

Victoria said, "You need to take some time for you, Owen. You're going to burn out if you don't have a little fun. You can't spend every single minute working." Then she flushed and looked at Charles. "No offense, Charles."

He smiled. "None taken. In fact I agree with you. It's for a great cause." He said to Owen, "Go on, they need you. We may even bring the kids and cheer you on."

After another brief hesitation, Owen sighed and nodded his consent, but Charles thought he could see a gleam of anticipation in his brother's eyes.

Victoria smiled. "Great. I'll tell him that you'll be there."

Hours later, as Charles took Demi home, he asked her, "So, did we scare you off?"

She laughed. "No. You have a wonderful family."

"Thanks. I think so. Most of the time."

"And you didn't have to feed me supper. I could have come home long before now."

He frowned. "I'm sorry, I should have thought you might have something to do or things to take care of... I didn't... I mean... Did you want to leave?"

Another laugh escaped her and he decided that he could listen to that sound all day.

"No. And I didn't have anything to do. It was a lovely way to spend the day. Thank you."

Relief filled him. "Good. So, I'll see you tomorrow?"

"Eight o'clock sharp."

"Great. I have a nine o'clock appointment."

"I'll be there."

"I'll let you know if there's any calls about your picture on the news."

"Okay. Thanks."

As she started to climb out of the car, he couldn't stop himself from snagging her hand.

Startled, her eyes met his and he said, "Thank you for coming today. I'm sorry about the mess at the church."

She shrugged. "It wasn't your fault. And I enjoyed the time with your family."

Her hand felt soft, yet strong. And he wasn't ready to let go yet. But he did because he had to. He needed to keep their relationship more professional than personal. At least right now. He swallowed hard and wondered how he was going to be able to do that when everything in him wanted to get to know her better—and his reason had nothing to do with business. "I'll see you in the morning."

Demi bit her lip as she let herself into the apartment even as she wondered about the look that had been in Charles's eyes when he'd said goodbye. A longing.

And a distance.

Weird.

Her heart trembled at the thought of her face being on the news once again. If a silent phone followed the broadcast, she would be heartbroken.

So, the only way to avoid that was to refuse to get her hopes up. But she appreciated Charles's desire to help.

Speaking of help...

Her eyes went to the kitchen cabinet. She hadn't told him about the note. Each time she'd thought about it, there hadn't been a chance to bring it up without another member of the family overhearing. And in the truck, she'd simply wimped out. She didn't want to hurt him. Telling him about the note would be just another arrow in his already aching heart. He would feel guilty. Possibly even tell her that she needed to find another job.

She shuddered. She didn't want to find another job and she didn't want Charles worrying that he was putting her in any kind of danger.

So, she'd keep her mouth shut.

For now.

As Chloe wrapped a warm welcome around Demi's ankles, she felt her tense shoulders relax. She hadn't realized she'd been worried about coming home.

Facing her apartment all alone.

At least the door had definitely been locked this time, but she still worried.

Worry. Fear. Anxiety. Emotions she had become intimately familiar with over the past few weeks.

But excitement lingered, too. She had a job. True, she had no car and no driver's license, and it was a fifteen-minute walk to and from Charles's house, but that was no big deal.

As she puttered and cleaned a little, getting ready to relax for the rest of the evening—or at least try to if she could keep her gaze from straying to the cabinet that held the coffee canister—she realized she'd finished the last book she'd borrowed from The Reading Nook. Since she had no television, books had been her sole entertainment in the evenings.

She supposed she could just go to bed, but it was only eight-thirty and she was still wound up from the excitement of the day. Charles had been so attentive, his family kind and welcoming. And she almost wished she hadn't gone.

Being around the Fitzgeralds, watching their interactions, listening to their teasing, their good-natured arguing, had spiked a longing in her that nearly split her in two. What would it be like to be a part of a family like that? To know that someone would miss her immediately if she suddenly wasn't there?

Tears formed and she blinked them back.

She looked at Chloe who sat on the floor cleaning a paw. "I definitely needed a book to read."

Chloe looked up at Demi's words then went back to her business.

Since Fiona had told Demi to help herself anytime she found herself wanting something to read, Demi decided to take her up on that offer.

Making her way downstairs, she was grateful Fiona didn't bother to lock the door leading from the apartment stairs to the bookstore area. She supposed Fiona felt that locking the outer doors was enough security.

The dark interior made her shiver. But she knew exactly which book she wanted.

The Bible.

Fiona had a whole shelf of Bibles in every translation available. As Demi made her way through the store, she thought she saw a flash of light toward the back. She frowned and couldn't help the tremor of fear that shot through her.

It surprised her so much, she nearly stumbled. The darkness pressed in on her, suffocating her. Another flash of light near the window, then nothing.

More darkness. She couldn't handle the darkness. Her breathing quickened as she shoved down the fear that came from nowhere.

*Why am I so afraid?*

Gasping, she flew to the wall that held the light switch and flipped it.

Nothing happened.

She flipped it again. Down, then up.

Her stomach quivered and the images flared up again. The heavy fist, a flash of agonizing pain in her head. Angry words.

"Stop." She flinched at the harsh word then realized it had come from her. "Stop," she whispered.

The images faded, but the lights still didn't work.

Why not? They worked fine in her apartment.

A sliding scrape to her right froze her, heart pounding, blood rushing.

Was someone in the store?

After all that had happened since she'd arrived in Fitzgerald Bay, every nerve jumped into hyperawareness. Was that someone breathing? Should she call out? Warn the person she was there?

No, she had a feeling the person knew she was there. And she was right where he wanted her.

# EIGHT

Charles tucked the twins into bed and kissed them each good-night at least five times. He was exhausted. Thank goodness he'd had his family helping him today or he wouldn't have been able to function.

As much as he loved his children, they wore him out. Being a single father had not been the plan. But that's the way things had worked out and while he wished his marriage hadn't ended the way it had, he was grateful for the two beautiful children that had come from it.

He walked to the window and looked out. A police cruiser sat in plain view. Charles felt his jaw tighten. While thankful for the extra pair of eyes, he was frustrated at the necessity for it.

His right hand reached up to touch the weapon in the shoulder holster. It felt right. Comforting. Even as the need for it brought to mind the memories of his time in Iraq. A time he'd rather forget.

Now Olivia's death, the spray paint on his garage, the incident at church had him jumping at shadows and looking over his shoulder. Just like back in Iraq, he was now in a constant adrenaline rush.

He closed his eyes and did his best to concentrate on the good in his life.

As a result, he found himself looking forward to work tomorrow for the first time since Olivia's death and felt certain that had something to do with the fact that Demi's faith in him was salve to his wounded soul.

In addition to that, he hoped that with Demi's agreeing to be the children's nanny, people would stop looking at him like he was monster.

Last week at the office had been a little better.

Maybe this week he would continue to see an improvement.

Since Olivia's death, it had been only the sickest who'd been willing to see him. And some long-time patients who didn't believe the drivel they'd seen on the television and read in the newspaper. But those were few and far between. Especially with Burke spouting his nonsense.

Back on the positive side, he couldn't help the little leap his heart gave at the thought that he would see Demi in the morning for a brief time before he had to take off. Maybe they would even have a chance to share a cup of coffee together. He settled into the recliner to watch the end of the movie he'd DVR'd the night before.

Just as he picked up the remote, his phone buzzed.

He frowned when he saw the number was Owen's. Punching the talk button, he said, "Hello?"

"Just got a call from someone who said they thought they saw someone sneaking around Fiona's store. Do you know where she is?"

Charles's feet slammed to the floor. "No, did you try Hunter? Who made the call?"

"I don't know. Said they saw what looked like a flashlight bouncing around inside and thought it might be a prowler. And yes, I tried Hunter. He's not answering his phone and neither is Fiona."

"I'll meet you there." All of a sudden his fatigue was gone, replaced by racing adrenaline. Demi lived above that store. What if she went down there and ran into an intruder?

"No need, it might be nothing and I'll keep you updated."

"Mrs. Mulrooney can be here in five minutes. I'll be at the store in little more than ten."

He hung up and dialed his father's housekeeper. Charles explained his dilemma and she promised to come right over.

As soon as she stepped in the door, he said a hasty thanks and ran to his truck.

Demi clutched the phone as she waited in the dark, ears straining. She listened for the slightest sound, praying help would arrive soon. But how could it? The phone was dead.

She prayed that she was wrong, that she was just hearing things. That she was safe and no one was in the store with her.

A footstep to her right made her jerk.

Her heart tripled its erratic beat and she held her breath. She wasn't just hearing things. Just like she hadn't imagined the message in her coffee grounds.

She was on her own with no way to call for help. Her eyes darted in the dark, doing her best to ignore the desire to give in to the panic clawing at her.

In her mind's eye, she visualized the layout of the store. She was behind the counter where the phone was. To her left were the numerous bookcases, shelves filled with volumes.

A sitting area just beyond that.

Another footstep, closer this time, made her heart leap again.

Why wouldn't he say anything? What was he doing? Why did he want to frighten her?

"Who's there?" she called, her voice high, squeaky and scared. "What do you want?"

Now she heard his breathing, just beyond the counter. Why wouldn't he say something?

She had to move. Stay out of his reach until she could get out of the store. Right now, he stood between her and the door. If she tried to get back to the stairs leading to her apartment, she would be trapped by the locked door on one side and the intruder on the other.

Placing the phone on the floor, she took two steps to her left, gripped the edge of the counter and slipped around the side.

She caught motion to her right. The moon's light filtered through the blinds and now that her eyes had adjusted to the darkness, she could pick out shapes and shadows.

Which meant the intruder probably could, too.

Demi moved again. The shadow moved with her.

She ducked behind a bookcase and heard two more footsteps.

How was she going to get help?

*Click.*

What was that?

She didn't have time to dwell on that question as she could hear him coming closer.

Silently, she sidestepped around another bookcase, bumped her shin on a small table and sent it crashing to the floor.

It sounded like a sonic boom in the utter stillness of the store.

Breath hitching, Demi moved around the table to seek refuge behind another shelf.

She thought she heard a curse, muttering.

Then bright light filled the store through one of the windows and she saw the man standing next to one of the cushioned chairs. He froze like a deer caught in the headlights.

But she couldn't see his face.

He had his hoodie pulled up and she could only make out his profile.

Then he spun on his heel and headed for the back door of the store. Relief pounded through her. Anger followed swiftly behind. She was so tired of being a victim.

Should she try to stop him?

Her eyes darted, wondering how she could do it without getting hurt. By the time she decided she couldn't, he was gone anyway, out the back. The same way he'd probably come in.

But how had he gotten through a locked door?

Charles followed Owen as far as his brother would allow. "Stay here until I give the all clear, you understand?"

"Yeah, yeah, go."

Charles watched Owen place a hand on his weapon as he approached the front door to The Reading Nook. Everything in him itched to head in after Owen. Fighting in Iraq had prepared him to be in the thick of things. He'd willingly taken a backseat to the investigation into Olivia's death, letting his brothers do the job they'd been trained to do, but not knowing if Demi was all right was killing him.

He crept closer, watching as Owen drew his gun and stepped inside. A cold sweat broke over Charles as flashes from his days in the military, going house to house, searching for the wounded in the midst of the rebels and terrorists popped through his mind. Not knowing if you were going to be offered a drink or a bullet had kept his nerves on edge, his senses honed.

This was how he felt now. Would Demi be all right? Or not? Following a hunch, Charles did a one-eighty on his good leg and hoofed it around the side of the building.

Just in time to see a figure bolt through the back door of Fiona's bookstore.

"Hey! Stop!"

The person never paused, just kept pounding the pavement until he disappeared within seconds around the side of the building. Owen burst from the store, racing after the fleeing man.

Charles gave the brief thought to joining the chase, but knew with his injured leg, he didn't have a chance. Humiliation swept over him, but he managed to push it aside. Just because he didn't run as well as he used to, didn't make him less of a man. Besides, he needed to check on Demi. Her well-being was more important than chasing the man down.

Taking note in the direction the intruder fled, Charles turned back to the store and pulled open the door.

Stepping inside, he called out, "Demi?"

"In here."

Charles made his way through the darkened store toward Demi's voice. It sounded like it came from the small café area.

The lights came on and he blinked at the sudden brightness. "Whoa."

As his eyes focused, he took in Demi's frightened features. But she'd managed to find the fuse box and get the lights back on in spite of her fear. He went to her side and took her hands, feeling them tremble. "Are you all right?"

She nodded, eyes wide. "Someone was in here."

"I know," Charles said. "I saw him run out the back door and down the alley. Owen went after him. What happened?"

Pulling her hands from his grasp, she crossed her arms in front of her and rubbed them like she was cold. "I came down to get a book and heard something. The lights were out and didn't work. Then I heard…something. And he was there. Being quiet and watching.…" She shivered and swallowed hard. Charles felt his heart clench at her distress.

The back door slammed and they both jumped. Charles's hand went to his weapon, his pulse spiking.

Owen called out, "It's just me." When Owen joined them in the kitchen, he shook his head in disgust and said, "I lost him."

Charles asked, "Do you think this has anything to do with the message left in the church?"

"I don't know." Owen narrowed his eyes. "You and I haven't really talked much about that. You think it was meant for you?"

"And I think it was meant for me," Demi said before Charles had a chance to answer.

"Why would you think that?" Owen looked confused.

Demi bit her lip then motioned for them to follow her.

Charles frowned as she and Owen walked up the steps to her apartment. She opened the door.

"You didn't lock the door?" Charles asked.

She paused then looked over her shoulder. "I didn't think I needed to. I was just going down to get a book and then come right back up. I thought the back door was secured and..." Demi fiddled with her keys. "I should have locked it, huh?"

"Yeah." Charles nodded.

He drew his weapon, glad he'd decided to start carrying it again. At Owen's sharp look, he shrugged. He had an up-to-date concealed weapons permit. Might as well exercise caution.

Owen nodded and took the lead, Charles providing backup. Demi stepped aside, her fear in full expression on her beautiful pale face. Behind her glasses, her eyes looked huge.

A quick sweep of the small apartment revealed nothing. "Clear," he said.

"Clear," Owen echoed.

Demi's quiet voice cut into the relieved silence. "Do you

mind if I show you what I found yesterday morning? I think it'll explain why I think that message at church was for me."

"Sure."

Both men holstered their weapons.

Demi walked into the kitchen, opened the cabinet and pulled a coffee canister from the cupboard. She took off the lid and held the can out for the men to peer into.

Charles read the message on the piece of paper and felt his heart pick up speed.

Owen lifted a brow and looked at the two of them. "You found this yesterday?"

"And you didn't say anything?" Charles demanded. The words exploded from him. He couldn't help it.

She flinched and stepped back and Charles felt immediate remorse. "I'm sorry, I didn't mean to yell. But you really should have told someone about this."

"I meant to, I just…didn't. I wanted to think about it and try to figure out why someone would put that there. But all I get is a massive headache when I try to reason through it." She swallowed and met his eyes. "And I was afraid you'd blame yourself." Her eyes slid away. "And that you'd ask me to leave." She shrugged. "I didn't want to leave."

"Ah, Demi…." Charles sighed, guilt exploding through him. She'd been right about that anyway. He did blame himself for putting her in this situation.

Owen shook his head. "Have you touched this?"

"No." She grimaced. "I just slapped the top back on and determined to put it out of my mind for the day."

Owen asked, "Do you have a paper bag I can put this in?"

"I have a plastic grocery bag."

"It'll have to do."

Demi got the bag and held it open.

Charles reached for the salad tongs sitting in the container on the counter, pulled out the note and dropped it in. He looked at Owen. "You really think you can get anything off of that?"

"Thanks to new technology, fingerprints are easier than ever to lift. Matching them up is sometimes the problem. But we'll give it a shot." He looked at the can. "Let's throw that in, too. Has anyone besides you touched it?"

"Not here. Fiona gave it to me. I think she got it from the café, so…"

Owen nodded. "It's probably a long shot, but we can try. Let's put it in a separate bag."

Demi got another bag and placed the can inside.

Owen said, "Charles has told me some details about your past when he had me run a background check on you before hiring you. Of course, there wasn't anything to learn because it was on the name you were given in the hospital. Can you fill me in a little better?"

She took a deep breath. "I'm not sure. Like I said, I don't remember what happened." She dropped her eyes then looked back up at him. "I can tell you what I was told."

"If you don't mind sharing that. Start from the beginning."

Demi nodded. "I was found on a street after dark in a back alley in Springfield, Massachusetts. I had several bad head wounds. I had no identification on me and no one had reported me missing." Reaching up, she pulled the glasses from her face and looked at them. "They found my glasses next to me. One of the officers came to see me in the hospital and said it looked like someone had deliberately crushed them. He wanted to know what I'd done to make someone so angry." Tears filled her eyes.

Charles wanted to punch his brother for asking her to relive that. But if it helped them find a clue to her past, he supposed it had to be done.

Blinking back tears, she said, "The police put my picture on the news and asked for information about my attack. But again, no one came forward to identify me—or offer any information."

Charles felt his heart twist once again. "That must have been awful. I'm so sorry."

She nodded. "Beyond awful. I healed pretty fast physically even though I was in the hospital for a couple of weeks. When it came time for me to leave, I just wanted to get away. So I went to the library, did a little research and found Fitzgerald Bay. I got on the bus—" she spread her hands "—and here I am."

Owen clicked his pen and put his little notebook in his back pocket. "All right. I'll see if I can find anything in any of what you've told me to help track down your identity." He left with promises to stay in touch with any news.

Charles turned to Demi. "So someone was in your apartment that day."

"It looks like it."

In an unexpected move, he pulled her to him for a hug. He was almost surprised that she didn't resist. Instead, she settled her head on his shoulder with a small sigh.

His hand raised up to give her a comforting pat on the back but then he found himself cupping her chin tilting her head to look up at him.

Questions danced in her eyes along with a look he interpreted as wariness. Immediately, he let her go and cleared his throat. She was right to be wary, to be cautious. She didn't know who she was or whom she might belong to. The lack of a ring on her left hand didn't mean there wasn't a wedding license in some drawer somewhere.

He cleared his throat. "If you're all right, I think I'll take off."

He saw her swallow. But she nodded. "I'll be fine."

With one last lingering look, Charles let himself out of the apartment and waited until he heard the lock click into place.

Then he leaned against the wall and pulled in a steadying breath.

He decided coming face-to-face with Olivia's murderer wouldn't shake him up any more than his growing feelings for the woman behind that door.

# NINE

"I'm not seeing him, he's a murderer."

Charles Fitzgerald overheard the elderly woman's comment and closed his fist around the pen he'd just used to sign his name. Not exactly how he wanted to start his Monday morning.

Another unhappy patient.

There'd been a lot of them. As a result, the practice had suffered. He'd called in a favor from a med school buddy to come work with him and help keep the practice from going under. It worked, but left Charles with more free time than he liked. And now he had another patient refusing to see him because of this cloud still hanging over his head.

He'd hoped this week would be different. Apparently last week was an aberration. Things had started out wonderful this morning. The minute Demi had stepped into his house, the children laughed and chattered a mile a minute. She'd grinned and waved him on his way.

Arriving at the office with a smile on his face hadn't happened in a long time. Since Olivia's death and the string of accusations that had followed.

The smile had faded as the first person in the waiting room realized Charles would be his physician and mumbled he was feeling better. The man couldn't move fast enough to get out the door.

Things had been heading south ever since.

And now this.

If something didn't break soon in the investigation into Olivia Henry's death, his mind might be the first thing to snap.

Being under suspicion of murder for the past four months had gotten old fast. But it sure made clear who his friends were. And weren't.

"Ma'am." His secretary, Cecily Cross, couldn't have been more professional although Charles knew her well enough to hear the underlying thread of steel in her tone. "There's no evidence that Dr. Fitzgerald had anything to do with it or he'd be sitting in jail. He's a highly skilled doctor who has an open appointment. If you don't want to see him, we'll have to reschedule you with another appointment."

"I was told Dr. Hansen would see me."

"And I told you he called in and said he couldn't be here. He had a family emergency." Cecily's exasperation with the woman finally peeked through. Charles caught her eye and waved his understanding. He saw Cecily draw in a deep breath and get her thinly veiled indignation under control. "Fine." Cecily consulted the computer in front of her. "How about Wednesday morning at nine o'clock?"

The woman gave a disgusted moan, but nodded, "Very well. I suppose it's not an emergency. Please tell Dr. Hansen I'll be here at nine sharp and I expect him here, too." With a nod and a sniff of disdain, Mrs. Bertha Gold turned and toddled out the door.

Cecily eyed him from behind the desk. "You're too nice to people like that."

Charles sighed. "I can't do anything about Mrs. Gold and her attitude. I suppose until it's proven without a shadow of a doubt that I didn't have anything to do with Olivia's death, I'm just going to have to deal with that kind of stuff." He shrugged. "I'm getting used to it."

But he wasn't. The brave face he showed to the world hid his hurt and shame that people he thought were friends would believe him capable of such a thing. And truth be known, the longer this dragged out, the harder it was to keep the faith that the real murderer would be found.

Faith. Sometimes God seemed so far away. But, if Charles were honest, it was because he'd pushed Him away. The initial devastation he'd felt with Kathleen's abandonment had morphed into an anger that God hadn't stopped her from leaving. Now that Charles had healed from the hurt of his divorce, he wondered why it was harder to forgive God than it had been to forgive Kathleen.

Because Kathleen was human. She was supposed to make mistakes.

But God was perfect. And He could have stopped it all from happening. Just like He could reveal Olivia's murderer and end all the anguish Charles was now going through.

"Charles? You okay?"

He jerked, realizing he'd been standing there, staring at the door Mrs. Gold had exited. "Yes, sorry. I'll be in my office working on the files. Let me know if there's anything you need."

Cecily shook her head and muttered under her breath something about being innocent until proven guilty. Charles appreciated the woman's loyalty, but couldn't help wondering if he wouldn't feel the same way if the shoe were on the other foot. Would he be so judgmental if it had happened to one of his friends? He hoped not.

Back in his office, Charles picked up the picture of his children. Aaron and Brianne were his world. Thank goodness they weren't old enough to understand what was going on with their father.

His cell phone buzzed, interrupting his depressing train of thought.

"Hello?"

"Hey, it's Owen."

"What's up?"

"Just wanted to see if we were still on for a fishing trip sometime soon. I think we all need a break."

Charles shuddered. He didn't want Owen taking a break. He wanted to know who had killed Olivia. Forcing some levity into his voice, he said, "Sure." But he couldn't help asking, "Anything on the case?" No need to specify which one.

When Olivia had been found dead and he'd first been questioned, he'd been sure that the case would be wrapped up quickly and life would return to normal.

But it seemed like Olivia's murderer had been careful and clever.

Owen's heavy sigh didn't lift his spirits. "No. But we're working on it basically day and night. You know that. I called the lab ten minutes ago, pushing them to get us those DNA results. I feel certain that's the key in clearing you. Unfortunately, they're backlogged and we're waiting our turn in line. But they promised us no more than a week. A week, Charles, and you'll be cleared, all right? I've said it before and I'll say it again, we're going to get the creep who did this."

"I know. It's just…"

"No need to explain. I understand." Owen changed the subject. "How are the twins? I guess they didn't miss you last night."

"No, they were still sleeping when I got home."

"Well, Paige wants to see them again soon. She had a blast with them yesterday."

Paige. Owen's nine-year-old daughter. The daughter he'd just discovered and was building a relationship with.

"They're great. They love Demi and are perfectly happy with their little world. I'll bring them by the bookstore soon and Paige can read them a story or something while I have a cup of coffee or catch up on some sleep in one of those big comfy reading chairs."

Owen laughed then sobered. "Sorry it's taking us so long to figure this out, bro."

"Yeah, me, too."

"But hang in there, we'll get it done."

"I know." He paused. "Any calls after Demi's picture went up?"

"Yeah. We're sorting through them. When you do something like that, all the weirdos come out of hiding." Charles winced.

"So," Owen said. "Douglas and Merry are getting married in two weeks. Let's try to make the fishing trip before then."

"I'll look at my schedule and let you know."

Owen hung up and Charles dropped his head in his hands. Closing his eyes, he drew in a deep breath and prayed out loud, "Lord, I know I haven't been very talkative lately, but I'm thinking that's a mistake. Please help me out here, if You would. I really need a break somewhere."

Demi really needed a break. Not from the children or her job, but from her thoughts. "Hey, guys," she said to the kids who were digging in the sand. "What do you say we get cleaned up and go into town to get some ice cream?"

"Ice cream!" Brianne was the first to respond. Of course. Demi laughed.

"Dino, too." Aaron held out the toy to her.

"Does Dino want ice cream?" she asked.

He grinned and nodded.

"All right, let's go. Everyone on the bicycle." Charles had provided her with a double-stroller-like contraption that could be pulled behind her bicycle. She'd used it often last week when they got antsy or sleepy. Helmets on and strapped in, the twins sang a song about ice cream while Demi pulled out the cell phone Charles had given her and pressed the number one. Charles had programmed his cell number for her. He answered on the third ring. "Hello?"

"Hi, how's it going?"

"It's going."

Demi frowned at his tone. He sounded...frustrated. "I don't know how busy you are, but I thought I'd let you know that I'm taking the children up to the Sugar Plum Café for a scoop of ice cream."

"Are they wiggle worms today?" The frustration had disappeared to be replaced with a warmth that entered his voice every time he referred to his children.

Demi relaxed a bit as she swung a leg over the seat and got herself situated. "They are, but they're excited about the ice cream."

He paused. "I'll meet you there. I could use a break."

"Really?"

"Actually no. I've had a pretty long break already, but I need to get out of here. See you in a few minutes and be careful."

"Will do."

She hung up and looked back at her little charges all buckled in to ensure their safety. Blankets tucked in around them would keep them warm from the cool morning wind. "Ready?"

"Ready!" they yelled in unison.

Demi pressed the pedal and they were off.

Ten minutes later, she directed the bicycle into the parking lot of the Sugar Plum Café.

It was eleven o'clock and the lunch crowd had already started filing in. But she knew there'd be a spot in there somewhere for her, Charles and the children.

Unbuckling them, she took a little hand in each of hers and together they walked toward the door.

"Hey, wait up!"

Demi looked over her shoulder and felt her heart give a little skip when she saw Charles, still in his white lab coat, heading their way.

"Daddy!" Brianne pulled from Demi and launched herself at her father. He caught her in a hug and kissed the top of her dark head.

Aaron seemed content to watch their exuberance. Demi had a moment where her world spun around her and she pictured herself doing the very thing Brianne had done. Only she was throwing herself into Charles's arms to receive his kiss on her lips. A *welcome home, I'm glad to see you* kind of thing.

"Demi? You okay?"

His question burst her daydream and she could feel a flush creeping into her cheeks. Turning toward the store to hide the fire in her face, she said, "I'm great. Let's get that ice cream."

Once they got the children settled in high chairs with bibs and a large supply of napkins, they started in on the treat.

Brianne managed to get most of hers in her mouth. Aaron wasn't having much luck. Demi took his spoon to help him. She looked at Charles. "Has Owen run my picture on the news yet?"

He nodded. "Yes, Owen said they were filtering the calls. When they get something worth following up on, we'll be the first to know."

Demi bit her lip and slid another small spoonful of vanilla ice cream into Aaron's waiting mouth. "Good. I think."

"It will be."

"Did he mention that I have amnesia?"

"No, he didn't want to invite any troublemakers or people who might want to take advantage of you. Instead, they ran the picture with the story that you were looking for your family and if anyone recognized you and knew who your family was, they were to call the eight hundred number at the bottom of the screen. As it is, we may have to weed through some crazies."

Demi grimaced. She hadn't thought about that. When the police had run her picture while she'd been in the hospital, she hadn't even considered that scenario. The police must have made the judgment calls in that case, too.

"Well, if this isn't a nice cozy scene."

Demi froze as she recognized the voice of Burke Hennessy. She glanced up to see him bearing down on their table.

Charles's posture went rigid. Demi ignored Hennessy and concentrated on feeding Aaron, hoping the children didn't pick up on the sudden tension.

"What do you want now, Burke?" Charles asked.

"Don't you have patients to take care of, Dr. Fitzgerald?" He didn't give Charles a chance to answer before he said, "Oh, that's right. You're a murder suspect. I imagine not too many people in town are in need of your services these days."

Charles's face went red and his hand clenched.

Demi looked at the man who seemed to have nothing better to do than cause trouble. "Could you please just leave us alone?"

Burke snorted. "Hiding behind a skirt? Who taught you that, your dad?"

Charles stood. "Burke, I'd like nothing more than to smash your face, but I'm praying real hard that I have more class than that. If you want to take this outside, I'll go, but you might want to think twice about how that will look to your constituents."

Demi blinked at the lightning-fast speed at which Burke backpedaled, his hands held in a conciliatory gesture. "Hey, no need for that." Then he dropped his hands and his eyes hardened. "But you can tell your father that I'm calling him out in a debate. I've had enough of this Fitzgerald monopoly in the police department and the town. Tell your father I'll be in touch."

Burke spun on his heel and left, seemingly unaware of the eyes that followed him. Charles cleared his throat and seated himself in front of Brianne. His daughter frowned. "Bad man, Daddy. Don't like him."

Demi choked back a surge of laughter, not thinking it was an appropriate response. Then she caught the glint in Charles's eyes as he nodded to Brianne. "Very observant young lady."

Brianne grinned as though she understood and Demi's heart softened at the exchange. She glanced at the door where Hennessy had just left. "I admire your restraint," she said softly.

Charles nodded his head. "Me, too." Pulling in a deep breath, he let it out slowly. Demi watched him for a moment longer, wishing she had the right words to say. Having none, she stayed silent.

He looked up and said, "How do you feel about fishing?"

She shrugged. "I don't know. Why?"

"Because I think that might be just the thing to take our minds off everything that's going on around here."

"And your mind off Burke Hennessy?"

"Exactly."

"Sounds good to me." She smiled then shivered as her eyes caught Burke's staring back at them from outside the restaurant window.

His malevolent glare said he wasn't finished with them.

# TEN

Surprisingly, the rest of the week and most of the next passed without incident. Thursday rolled around with no more break-ins, no more weird messages. And nothing on Demi's true identity.

It made Charles nervous, but relieved, too. Maybe whoever had been causing problems decided to move on to something else.

The twist in his gut told him he could hope for that, but not to stop watching his—or Demi's—back just yet.

And the DNA results *still* hadn't come in.

Owen said that he and their father were nagging the lab, promising to leave them alone as soon as they passed on the results. So far there'd been no word. Charles refused to get his hopes up that they would come through any time soon.

He gathered his fishing equipment from his garage and turned to see Owen's orange Ford Raptor pickup pull into the drive. Victoria and their nine-year-old daughter, Paige, were with him.

Demi rode up on her bike just then and Charles found his attention centered on her. With windblown hair and pink cheeks, she looked about eighteen years old. He gulped then caught the knowing glint in Owen's eyes.

Feeling the heat creep up his neck he focused on loading

the equipment into the back of his truck. "Morning," he called over his shoulder.

Demi parked the bike and greeted his brother and Victoria. Paige hopped out and slammed the door. "Can I help get the twins ready?"

"They're already in their car seats." Charles offered his niece a grin. "It was the only way *I* could get stuff ready."

Demi smiled. "I could have come a little early and helped."

"I appreciate that, but they're in a good mood this morning so I handled it." He turned to Paige. "But you can entertain them."

The girl gave an eager nod and climbed in the car where she was greeted with two-year-old squeals of glee.

Charles felt the hair on the back of his neck spike and he glanced around. All morning, he'd felt the presence of someone lurking, spying, and the feeling was getting old. He didn't spook easily, but the thought of someone watching him and the children made him jumpy.

He stared toward the cliffs where Olivia had fallen to her death and shuddered.

"Something wrong?"

Owen's perceptive question made Charles blink and he forced a smile. "Nope. Not a thing. Let's go have some fun."

"I called Dad and told him we needed an extra rod for Demi. He said he had one hanging in the storage building behind his house and to stop by and pick it up."

"Sounds like a plan to me."

Demi stashed the bike in the garage and climbed in the vehicle with him. Paige decided to ride buckled in between the twins.

Charles cranked the truck and headed to his dad's house. The sun continued to creep higher in the morning sky and the day promised to be a warm one. They'd shed their jackets in a couple hours, relax and maybe catch a fish or two.

A perfect day made even better because of the woman sitting beside him. "I'm glad you wanted to come with us. It took a little longer to get this trip lined up, working around Owen's schedule and Victoria's need to find someone to cover the shop, but I'm glad you decided you'd come."

Demi smiled. "Sure. I don't know if I've ever gone fishing before, but the adventure sounded too good to pass up."

He laughed. "Yes, I'm sure *adventure* is the right word for it."

A few minutes later, they pulled into his father's drive. "Sit tight. I'll just go in and get the rod."

Demi nodded and Charles climbed from the vehicle.

Owen met him. "I want to get some tackle, too."

Together the brothers entered the building and Charles went for the rods hanging on the wall while Owen opened the steel cabinet attached to the back wall.

Charles found a rod he thought Demi could use and turned to find Owen holding something and frowning at it. "What's wrong?"

"These."

Curious, Charles walked over for a look.

Several pictures of a couple, one holding a baby, stared back at him. "Where'd you find those?"

"In Dad's tackle box on the bottom under a bunch of fishing stuff."

Owen flipped through them, his face paling with each one.

Charles took them and did the same. He swallowed hard. Several showed a man and a pregnant woman in various poses. In one, the man had his hand possessively on the belly of the young woman, a grin on his face. He flipped the picture over and read, "My little one. Boy or girl?"

And then there was the picture of the man and woman holding a baby. No names or a date on the back.

"Hey, what's taking so long?" Victoria asked from the door. "The natives are getting restless."

Owen turned to her and held out the picture. "Look at this."

With a question in her eyes, Victoria took the photo and looked at it. Then her brows pulled together at the bridge of her nose. "Why does this picture look so familiar—like I've seen it before?"

"Where would you have seen this?" Charles asked.

"I'm not sure, but…"

Charles's heart thudded, dread coursing through him. His eyes met Owen's. "Is it possible?"

Owen swallowed hard. "You thinking what I'm thinking?"

"An affair?" Just saying the words left a foul taste in his mouth.

"A what?" Victoria sputtered.

"This is Dad in the picture, Victoria," Owen said.

She squinted. "Really?" A pause. "I didn't see it at first, but yes, the resemblance is there."

"And the woman he has his arm around is not Mom," Charles said.

"Who's the baby?" Owen asked quietly. "You don't think…"

Victoria gaped as she took in what Owen was saying. "That doesn't mean that your father…"

"…had an affair or that we have a half sibling," Charles finished the sentence for her.

Owen looked at Charles. "That's true. We don't know who this woman in the photograph is." He paced from one end of the toolshed to the other. Then he spun and jabbed a finger at Charles. "Just like I don't believe you killed Olivia, I don't believe Dad cheated on Mom."

Charles sucked in another breath. "You think I want to believe it? There's no evidence pointing to me being a killer."

He shook the picture. "This just raises some questions, that's all."

Owen ran a hand down his face. "I don't know. I just… don't know."

"Looks like we have something to talk to Dad about. And soon."

"No," Victoria protested. "Not yet. Douglas and Merry are getting married this weekend. Don't ruin the wedding for them."

Charles paused, his heart thumping with adrenaline. This possibility of an affair, a half sibling, if it was true, sucked the air from his lungs. "I don't know. This is pretty serious stuff."

"I agree," Owen said. "I want some answers." He pulled out his cell phone and dialed his father's number. Charles waited impatiently.

Finally, Owen said, "Hey, Dad, give me a call when you get a chance, will you? We need to talk."

He hung up and rubbed a hand down his suddenly haggard face. Charles suddenly wasn't much in the mood for fishing.

Demi didn't mind waiting in the truck, but she wondered what was taking them so long in the shed. Tears spilled down Brianne's cheeks as she kicked her feet. "I want out!"

"Don't you want to go fishing?" Paige asked.

"No!"

Demi stepped from the truck, ready to release the child from her car-seat prison when she saw Charles, Owen and Victoria exit the shed. Charles carried the fishing pole while Owen tucked something into his shirt pocket.

Victoria looked shaken and pale.

What had happened?

Everyone climbed into their respective vehicles. Charles placed the fishing rod in the back and the troubled, tight look on his face worried her. After pacifying Brianne with a peanut-butter cracker, Demi looked at Charles. "What's wrong?"

He glanced in the rearview mirror. "I just need to process something before we talk about it, all right?"

Demi bit her lip. "Sure." He didn't want to talk in front of Paige.

But for her, some of the excitement of the day had dimmed in light of whatever had happened in the storage building.

They rode in silence, broken only by the chattering of the children and Paige's exuberance at fishing in the river. "It's going to be so much fun!"

"I think it's funny that we're going out into the woods to find a river to fish when there's a whole ocean with a pier practically in your backyard," Demi teased.

Some of Charles's tension seemed to ease from his shoulders as he shot her a forced smile. "It's a place with a lot of memories. I grew up going fishing in this little spot. You'll love it."

"I'm sure I will."

Ten minutes later, Charles pulled into a clearing. Demi could see the path that led down to the river. Stepping down from the truck, she helped get the children out of the car seats and grabbed a folding chair. The men loaded themselves with all the fishing paraphernalia and Victoria lugged a rolling cooler behind her.

Paige helped with Aaron while Demi took charge of Brianne. Bringing up the rear, she let Brianne study her surroundings. The little girl clapped her hands and walked to the edge of the path.

"Ladybug," the little girl said.

"Where?"

"There." She pointed to a leaf where the insect sunned itself.

"She's pretty, isn't she?"

"Pretty," Brianne agreed, her black pigtails swinging back and forth with the movement of her head.

A twig snapped behind her and Demi turned.

Empty space stared back at her.

Demi turned to Brianne who still watched the little insect with fascination.

A rustle in the bush next to her made her jump and spin.

She could see nothing to cause her alarm, but the hair on her arms lifted and her heart thumped a little faster.

A shivering sensation slid along her spine and suddenly she realized how far ahead the others had gotten. She picked up Brianne in her arms. "Come on, sweetie, let's go catch a fish."

"Want the bug."

"Maybe we can find another one."

"Want that one."

Demi carried the little girl who was willing to be distracted with the idea of catching a fish. As she walked the path through the overgrown trees, following where the others had walked only moments before, she cast a glance over her shoulder.

Still she could see nothing and no reason to be alarmed.

But another rustling to her left made her flinch.

She picked up her pace and within seconds saw Charles's broad back. Relief filled her as she set Brianne down on the blanket someone had placed on the ground.

"Are you okay?" Charles asked.

Demi smiled. She didn't want to sound silly about thinking someone had been behind her, so she said, "I'm great. When do we get to fish?"

The corners of his eyes crinkled. "Soon."

For the next half hour, Demi was able to put the creepy

feelings aside and concentrate on having a good time with the Fitzgerald family.

With her line dangling in the river, her eyes on Charles and Owen as each man held a child, helping cast and reel to the children's excitement, she felt peaceful, content for the first time in a long time.

Leaning toward Victoria, she asked, "I have a question."

"Sure."

"Brianne spotted a ladybug on the trail out here and was fascinated with it." Demi held up an empty plastic container. "I thought I'd go find her one she could keep for a few days."

Victoria smiled. "What a great idea."

"I'll be right back."

Demi walked into the trees, studying each leaf, still wondering how she'd found herself in the midst of such a wonderful family.

She walked a good ways then stopped, remembering the creepiness she'd felt earlier. The feeling of being followed and watched. She supposed she could attribute the noises to an animal in the woods, but…

Nerves rippling, she glanced around. No animals, no strangers, nothing. Just her and the privacy of the woods.

And a pretty little black-and-red ladybug sitting on the leaf near her nose. Smiling, she scooped the little bug in the container, picturing Brianne's excited glee.

She turned to return to the river, but stopped as she realized she wasn't quite sure where she was.

The uneasiness in the pit of her stomach returned. Had someone followed them? Followed her?

The longer she stood there, the more the ominous feeling grew. Spinning, she hurried in the direction of the river.

At least she thought it was the right direction.

As she walked, she realized she'd gotten turned around.

Sighing in frustration, she turned again and walked in the opposite direction.

Only to come to a small clearing that she didn't recognize. "Well, that's not right," she whispered to herself.

Heart thudding, Demi stopped and stood still.

The woods were never truly silent, but she couldn't hear laughter from those she'd come with. Closing her eyes, she focused her attention on listening.

And heard the faint sound of the water to her right.

Relieved, she took a step in that direction.

A branch snapped. A bush rustled. She stopped and stood still once again.

The hair on the back of her neck rose, her stomach twisted.

And she felt someone watching her.

At the edge of the clearing, just as she took her first running step toward the sound of the water, she felt a vise clamp around her upper arm and a hand slap over her mouth.

Fear scattered her senses. A scream gathered in her throat. Instinct kicked in and she tried to jerk away. But he was strong. Blood hit her tongue as she twisted against him. His hand slipped and she pulled in a breath.

# ELEVEN

Charles glanced at the shoreline one more time. His waders kept his pants dry but the mud sucked at the bottoms of his feet. He didn't care, he was having a great time, relaxing and enjoying the afternoon with his family—and Demi.

Marred only by the knowledge that his father might have had an affair. And a child.

Another glance in the direction Demi'd disappeared made him frown. He'd watched the exchange between Victoria and Demi and smiled when he saw her tromp into the woods. She was a trouper, willing to try anything, including roughing it a bit in his favorite fishing spot.

But she'd been gone awhile.

As the minutes stretched, so did his nerves.

He started envisioning all kinds of things that could happen. A snake bite, a black bear, a fox…a two-legged creature.

A restless worry hit him. He had to check on her.

Sloshing to the shore, he set his pole next to Victoria. She held a sleeping Brianne. The little girl had given up fishing and crawled in her future aunt's lap. "I guess that's why she was so cranky."

"Probably." Victoria shot a look toward the woods, her

brow furrowed and eyes troubled. "I hope Demi's okay. She's been gone a long time."

"I noticed. I'm going to—"

The sharp scream cut him off.

"Demi!"

He and Owen exchanged a startled look. Charles said to Victoria, "Watch the kids."

Running toward the sound of the scream, heart thumping in his chest, the waders slowed him down a bit, but determination to get to her side spurred him on.

Crashing through the undergrowth, he slipped, tripped and caught himself. "Demi!" he shouted.

"Charles!" Her piercing cry called to him.

Her voice had came from the left. He turned, ran about a hundred yards and nearly tripped over Demi in a small clearing. She was sprawled on the ground, holding her arm. Blood from a cut on her lip glinted in the sun. A plastic container holding a ladybug lay to her right.

He rushed to her and dropped to a knee beside her. "Are you all right? What happened? Are you hurt?"

She touched her lip and winced. "A man grabbed my arm from behind and slapped his hand across my mouth."

"Which way did he go?" Owen asked.

Charles looked up, startled. He hadn't realized his brother had followed him.

Demi raised a shaking hand and pointed to the woods behind her. "When I screamed, he still tried to drag me, but when he heard you shout, he shoved me away and ran. I turned to see if I could get a good look at his face, but he was too fast."

Owen exchanged a look with Charles. "I'll see what I can find."

He took off and Charles helped her to her feet. Leaning

over her, he studied her lip and said, "Let me take a look at that."

"It's fine. When he covered my mouth, I bit my lip."

Still, he moved closer and narrowed his eyes as he ran a thumb over the uninjured area around her lip. "It's a slight abrasion. You'll have a sore there for a couple days, but it should heal pretty fast."

He saw her cheeks heat and realized how intimate his touch could be construed. Clearing his throat, he dropped his hand.

Owen's approach broke the tension. Then fear flashed back into her eyes and she gulped. Grateful for his brother's return, Charles asked, "Did you find anything?"

Using a broken stick, Owen held up a small scrap of fabric about the size of a quarter. "I suppose this could be considered contaminating evidence but I didn't want to leave it out there. I found it hanging on a branch. It's possible it belongs to our guy. I've got a bag in my car. I'll send it to the lab when we get back."

Charles looked at Demi. She trembled and his gut clenched in anger at the person who'd done this to her. He couldn't help wonder if it was because of him.

Then again, the message in her coffee can said that might not be the case. "Maybe we should pack up and leave," Charles said as he rubbed a hand across his face, weariness seeping in. Would this madness never stop? What would it take to catch the person trying to terrorize him? And now Demi?

Guilt plagued him. Was this his fault? Had Demi's attacker somehow figured out that Charles was developing feelings for his new nanny and had decided to get at him through her?

He shuddered.

"No," Demi protested. "I don't want this to ruin the fun for this afternoon."

He noticed her trembling had stopped and her eyes glittered with something he hadn't seen before.

Determination.

Owen shook his head. "Let's get back to Victoria and the children. I don't want to leave them alone too much longer." He grabbed his cell phone. "I'm going to get someone here to go through the woods. I want to make sure this person isn't living out here."

Demi rubbed her palms together. "I think he followed us."

Owen raised a brow. "Why do you think that?"

She shrugged. "I just do." She kept her gaze on Charles. "I think someone's targeted us for whatever reason and is doing his best to scare us or torment us. Or…whatever."

So, she was thinking along the same lines as he was. But was trying to be tactful about setting blame anywhere. He clenched his jaw. They both knew where the blame lay.

Owen eyed her. "And you still don't have any memory of anything?"

"No. I'm sorry."

He nodded. "You guys go on back. I'll wait here for the team that's coming. I want to show them where to look."

Charles took Demi's hand. "Come on, I'll take you to the river." He looked at Owen. "I don't like this one bit. You need to come up with a plan to catch this person."

Owen pursed his lips. "Working on it."

Charles grunted. Owen may be working on it, but Charles decided if he had to, he'd take matters into his own hands.

Because no one was going to hurt Demi just because she'd had the misfortune to be in his life.

Demi was relieved to see the children playing a game of tag, unaffected by her recent misadventure. Victoria, however, looked strained. When she saw Demi and Charles heading her way, she jumped up. "What happened?"

"Demi was attacked in the woods."

Victoria gasped and grasped Demi's arm. "Are you all right? Here. Sit down and tell me what happened."

While Demi filled her in, Charles joined in the game. Then he gathered the twins and Paige, challenging them to a contest of who could catch the biggest fish.

Demi's heart melted as she watched him with the children. Her fear dissipated slightly. She could feel Victoria's gaze on her.

Keeping her voice low so Charles couldn't hear, she said, "Someone's really out to hurt Charles, I think."

"Why do you say that?"

Demi gave a slight shrug, wincing at the pull of a strained shoulder muscle. "I think the person who killed Olivia may get away with murder because no one is focusing on finding the real killer. Whoever is causing Charles and me all this trouble may think he's doing the authorities a favor."

"You mean, he thinks that if he pushes Charles hard enough, Charles will admit to the murder?"

A sigh slipped out before she could repress it. "Who knows? I think it's possible."

Victoria nodded, her eyes on Owen and Paige, the tender expression catching at Demi's heart. Then Victoria said, "It makes sense." She turned and caught Demi's gaze. "It's obvious Charles cares about you. Even in the short amount of time I've spent around you two, it's clear that he has feelings for you."

Demi gulped at the woman's observation. What could she say? It was true. And she definitely had developed feelings for Charles. Victoria gave her a small smile. "I think it's great."

"You do?"

"Sure. Charles needs someone like you in his life. He has

for a long time." She bit her lip then said, "Just try not to hurt him."

Demi let her gaze rest on Charles. She smiled as he did his best to keep a wiggling Brianne from slipping from his grasp and into the water.

"Hurting Charles is the last thing I want to do. I promise."

"I catch it, Daddy." Brianne set her little mouth in firm determination and did her best to cast her rod. Aaron copied his sister and Paige giggled.

As the three waded back into the water, Demi caught Charles's gaze, pulled in a deep breath and prayed nothing else would happen to destroy their peace of mind.

Owen stepped from the edge of the woods and Demi tensed. She stood and walked over to him. "Did you find anything?"

"Nothing. I'm sorry. Just that scrap of material that I sent with one of the guys to the lab."

She nodded and bit her lip.

A cry from behind made her whirl, wondering what was wrong now.

But it was a happy cry. Brianne giggled and clapped as her daddy helped her pull in a decent-size fish. Aaron cheered his sister's success and Paige gave a mock pout. "It's my turn to fish with Uncle Charles. He's the only one catching anything around here."

Owen shot her a look that promised he wouldn't forget about her. Then he raced toward his daughter and caught her around the waist. "I should toss you in the water for that comment, squirt."

Paige let out a squeal and Demi walked over to settle on the blanket next to Victoria who patted her back. "Don't worry, Demi, the Fitzgeralds will figure this out."

"I know." And she felt sure they would. In time.

But would it be before anyone else got hurt? Or worse?

* * *

Night fell and Charles paced the floor as he waited for his brother Ryan to come back on the line. Just as Charles had answered the phone, Ryan's other line had rung and he'd put Charles on hold.

So now he waited, impatience twisting inside him.

Demi and Mrs. Mulrooney, his father's housekeeper, had volunteered to tuck the twins in and Charles had let them with a grateful heart. Mrs. Mulrooney had been at the house, putting a casserole in his refrigerator when they'd walked in the door several hours ago.

Charles had to admit he didn't know what he'd do without the woman who was supposed to be his *father's* housekeeper, but she seemed to enjoy doting on him, too. The twins adored her and if she hadn't said keeping up with them was too taxing at her age, he would have been content to let her be the children's nanny.

But she wouldn't have been up for hours of fishing like Demi had been.

They'd finished the day, doing their best to put on happy faces for the children while catching a few fish, but there was no denying it had been tainted for the adults thanks to the attack on Demi.

Ryan finally came back on the line and said, "Owen had to take care of something and asked me to give you a call. They didn't find much in the woods where Demi was attacked other than some broken branches where it looks like someone was in a hurry to leave. No footprints on that ground, of course, but we sent the fabric Owen found to the lab. Hopefully we'll hear something before too long."

Charles blew out a sigh. Nothing he hadn't expected. "Thanks for letting me know."

"Sure. We're not giving up and we're running Demi's picture on the news again asking for someone to come forward if they know her or any family members."

"Good. I can't believe there's absolutely no one who knows her."

"Someone will turn up."

"Someone legit, let's hope."

"Yeah."

Ryan hung up and Charles realized he and Owen still needed to talk to their father. And he still needed to get Demi home.

Even though it wasn't dark yet, there was no way he was letting her walk or ride her bike home by herself.

She and Mrs. Mulrooney came into the den. Demi flopped onto the couch and Mrs. Mulrooney picked up her keys.

Charles stopped her. "I hate to ask, but would you mind staying with the children while I run Demi home?"

The woman smiled and placed her keys back on the small table in the foyer. "I'd be glad to. They're so tired I doubt they'll stir." She eyed the recliner. "Might catch me a little nap myself."

Charles smiled. "Thanks." To Demi, he said, "I'll put the bike in the back of the truck. Ready?"

"I'm ready." She rose and gathered her bag.

Charles took her home. He noticed she didn't have a lot to say on the ride to The Reading Nook or even when he followed her up the stairs. But he did notice her increased nervousness the closer they got to her home.

"I'm going to check out your apartment, just to be on the safe side. Is that all right?"

They walked together as Charles inspected the shadows, the little hallway and the area around her door. All looked fine. He breathed a little easier.

She opened the door and stepped inside to flip on the light switch. As light bathed the room, he watched her shiver as she looked around. "It's kind of creepy staying here now." Chloe wrapped herself around Demi's ankles and Charles noticed the way she took comfort in the cat's affection.

He finished the short inspection then said, "Everything looks good, but I think I'm going to call Ryan and see if he'll okay a cruiser to watch the store. After everything that's happened, I don't think it'll be a problem."

Demi lifted a brow. "Have my own bodyguard?"

He nodded. "Something like that. Tonight Ryan said he'd have someone watching my house. I think it would be a good idea if he did the same here."

Her eyes went to the cabinet, now minus the coffee can with the message. "It seems like someone has pretty easy access into my apartment, doesn't it?"

"Unfortunately. I think it's time to change the locks."

She nodded, her eyes troubled, scared.

Charles could almost see her brain processing the memory of the attack in the store and the one in the woods. He pulled out his cell phone and dialed Ryan's number.

His brother answered on the second ring. After making the arrangements, Charles hung up and said, "Someone's on the way. Ryan agreed it might be the smart thing to do."

She pulled in a deep breath, rubbed a cheek against Chloe's head then nodded. "As long as you think Fiona won't be upset with me. I don't want to chase away any customers."

"She'll understand. She'd much rather you be safe than sell a few books if that's what it comes down to. Besides, security is always a good thing."

Demi hesitated. "Well, it would be nice having him out there at night, but I don't think it's necessary during the day."

Charles touched her cheek, his concern for her safety embedded deep in his heart. "Demi, I know we've only known each other a short time, but I…" He stopped. What could he say? He was a murder suspect.

Her wide eyes told him to back off. She wasn't ready for anything more than friendship and a professional working relationship. At least not yet.

Then her expression softened and she took his hand. "Charles, I think you're a wonderful man and a great father. But until I know who I am—" she shrugged "—I feel like I'm living in limbo. I mean I don't think I'm married." She shook her head and looked at her ringless hand. "I really don't. Somehow, I think I would know that. But I don't know if there's someone else or..." She trailed off with a sigh. "I just don't know."

He frowned. But he understood. "I know. And until this murder case is wrapped up, I'm right there with you, although in a different kind of way."

She walked to the window and looked out. "But the fact is, if I don't get my memory back soon, I'm going to have to make the decision to live with it and move on with my life. I can't live like this forever," she finished on a whisper.

"I agree." He followed her and placed a hand on her shoulder, hoping to offer comfort. He swallowed hard and turned her to face him. "Once this murder case is wrapped up, if you haven't gotten your memory back, or even if you have and there's no one..." He stopped and closed his eyes as he searched for the right words. "Just...after...you know? Could we..."

"Yes. After," she said, then bit her lip.

Elation filled him. She wasn't shutting the door on a possible relationship with him. "Good. After."

He left it at that.

"And on that note, I'll say good-night."

"Good night, Charles. I loved spending the day with you and the children in spite of...well, everything else."

Charles ran a finger down her soft cheek then turned to leave. He paused and swung back to say, "I know this is short notice, but would you go to Douglas and Merry's wedding with me on Saturday?"

She gave a gentle smile. "It's not after yet."

Charles stepped forward and took her warm fingers in his hand. "I know. But go to the wedding with me, then we'll worry about after...after that."

When she hesitated, he groaned. "Am I pushing you too much?"

"No. Not at all. I'd love to go to the wedding with you." A pause and a sigh. "And then, yes, we'll worry about after... after."

Charles pulled her to him in a hug, breathing in her scent, enjoying the feel of her in his arms, next to his heart.

Then he set her back from him, looked into her eyes and said, "After."

# TWELVE

Early Friday morning, Demi stood at the window, sipping her coffee and pondering the fact that she had a police car sitting outside her home. Watching her.

Because she might be in danger.

Danger. She shivered.

This morning, that word brought back a sense of dread and fear she couldn't shake for more than a couple hours.

Although, she had to admit, she'd surprised herself and slept well last night after Charles had left. She'd expected to toss and turn. Instead, she'd felt safe, protected, because of Charles and his brother Ryan's willingness to put an officer outside.

And the fact that she now had shiny new locks on her door thanks to a friend of Charles's who'd arrived bright and early this morning to change them.

But she couldn't help wonder if it was a false sense of security. She also wondered if whoever was after her was watching and just waiting for the moment to make his move. Because he knew as well as she did that the time would come when she wouldn't have someone with her or her guard would be lowered. The police officer would leave soon and she would be alone again.

And what about riding to work on the bike? Would she be safe?

Her cell phone rang and she snatched it up after seeing Charles's number on the screen. "Good morning."

"Good morning." Just hearing his voice sent a different kind of shiver through her. Which worried her. Being attracted to him wasn't a bad thing. At least she didn't think so. However, she couldn't get the worry out of her head that she might have someone else in her life. Someone she might not be able to remember, but someone who remembered *her*.

Having no memory of herself was one thing. What if she couldn't remember someone she'd made a promise to? A husband. A boyfriend.

Was she betraying another man by having feelings for Charles?

The thought made her gulp. Just like she'd told Charles last night, she felt sure she would know that instinctively even if she couldn't actually remember it. Wouldn't she?

"Dad and Burke are meeting in the park at ten o'clock sharp to have some sort of debate that Burke's come up with," Charles said. "It was on the news late last night. Victoria brought Paige over this morning to play with the twins and said she'd just bring them to the park. Do you mind meeting me there? My secretary called and said I have two last-minute appointments but I should finish in time to meet you."

She heard the relief in his voice. "Really? That's wonderful."

"Yes, it is. So, see you at ten?"

"I may be a little late, but I'll be there."

Ten o'clock rolled around fast. Demi soon found herself in the park along with a horde of people. Word spread fast in this little town. Reporters milled, waiting for the two candidates. She wondered if Judge Ronald Monroe would show up, as well. She'd heard something about him wanting to throw his hat into the ring, but hadn't yet done so simply because Aiden and Burke had so many supporters.

Demi kept an eye on the parking lot across the street. She figured Charles would meet Victoria to get the twins and then stroll over to her.

She caught sight of Aiden Fitzgerald and the rest of Charles's brothers and sisters. All but Fiona appeared to be here in an official capacity.

Because of the strong animosity between the two candidates, security was out in force. Uniforms and plain clothes patrolled the area. Her eyes landed on Judge Monroe. He stood near the platform, looking thoughtful and troubled.

Microphones were set up behind two podiums, ready for the candidates to take the stage.

Demi saw Burke arrive with his wife, Christina, who held their toddler daughter, Georgina. He looked proud, confident and almost strutted as he approached the microphone.

Aiden looked determined, calm. In control. She had a feeling control was very important to Aiden and he would do anything to keep it—in all areas of his life. She wasn't sure why that stood out to her, but it did.

Charles strolled the children up beside her. Victoria waved as she and Paige headed toward Owen who stood near the stage. Demi waved back, a twinge of envy unsettling her as she watched Owen wrap an arm around his fiancée's shoulder and tweak Paige's nose.

However, when the twins saw her, their eyes brightened and Demi felt the envy subside. She dropped to her knees to greet each child with hugs and raspberries to their sweet cheeks. Their giggles rang in her ears.

Then she looked up at Charles and said, "I hope this goes well for your father."

His jaw went tight as he looked at the man. "Yes, me, too." He didn't sound like it, though.

"Something wrong?" she asked.

"Yes. Very wrong."

Concerned, she stood and laid a hand on his arm. "What?"

He sighed. "It's something I need to discuss with my father—a conversation I don't want to have."

"I'm sorry." She wondered if whatever it was had to do with what happened in the shed the day they went fishing. Ever since then, Charles's tension level seemed to rise whenever he was in his father's presence. He'd talked about needing to process something that day, too.

A voice from one of the podiums spoke, "As you are aware, we have two candidates running for mayor. Burke Hennessy and Aiden Fitzgerald. Burke has called this impromptu debate and we appreciate you all coming out."

He went on to introduce each man and then said, "I have a list of questions, given to me by various town members."

"This ought to be good," Charles muttered loud enough for her to hear.

It was crowded and people milled around her. A slender man in a gray hoodie caught her attention. He looked like the man who'd tried to get into her building last week. And the one she had seen on the beach. Curious, she moved toward him wanting to get a better look.

A hand caught hers and she looked back to see Charles watching her with a question in his eyes. She pointed. "I think I've seen him before."

"Who?"

"That man in the hoodie."

Charles followed her pointing finger. "I don't see anyone."

She looked and the man was gone. A shiver slid up her spine. Who was he? And why did she feel like he was watching her? That he was here specifically because of her? The strange sensation refused to leave her alone even when she tried to reassure herself that no one would try anything in this crowd.

Then her attention was back on the debate that had started without her even noticing.

Burke gestured with his left hand. "And how can we want a mayor who is so lax in his current position as the police chief? One who can't even solve the murder of the young woman, Olivia Henry?"

"Now, wait a minute," Aiden protested.

"No, you wait a minute," Burke blustered as he jabbed a finger at Aiden. "Your own son is a suspect in the murder. Clearly, because he's your son, an arrest has not been made." Burke looked out at the audience. "Is this who you want for mayor? A man who allows his judgment to be impaired because he doesn't want to arrest his own son?"

Several people in the audience murmured among themselves. Those around Demi and Charles stared at him. She felt his tension magnify tenfold. Wrapping her fingers around his, she squeezed tight, hoping he got her message of support.

Aiden countered with, "And do you want a mayor who will order the arrest of a man when there's no evidence to back it up?"

And so it went back and forth for the next thirty minutes. Demi was amazed at the difference between the two men. Burke was all bluster and puffed-up pride. Aiden kept his cool and answered with thought and wisdom. The red in his cheeks said he kept a tight rein on his temper, but even that was far more impressive than Burke's lack of restraint.

She knew who she'd vote for. If she could vote. She frowned. The lack of identity was troubling in more ways than one.

"Come on," Charles said suddenly. "I need to get out of here."

"What is it?" Demi looked up to see a muscle jumping in Charles's cheek.

"Burke Hennessy gets to me. I can't watch this anymore."

A loud crack interrupted the ongoing argument at the podium. Demi gasped as something stung the flesh of her upper arm. And then she was surrounded by screaming people.

Another pop and the ground puffed up right where Charles had been standing a split second earlier. She felt an arm wrap around her waist and yank her down.

And then she realized it.

Someone was shooting at them!

"The babies!" she cried.

"Head for the cars, duck behind one," Charles hollered in her ear.

"Everybody down! Down! Shooter!" an officer to her right yelled.

Terror thumped a steady beat in her heart, as she turned to see Charles hunched over the twins' double stroller and she knew he'd take a bullet in order to protect the children.

Gasping, hurrying, she made her way to the nearest car and hunched behind several other people. Charles shoved the stroller next to her and dropped to his knees beside her.

Trembling, she tried to reassure the crying children that everything would be all right. Terrified screams echoed in her head, rattling her. The screams sounded familiar, as did the fear now coursing a steady path through her veins.

Brianne held out her arms and lunged for Demi, but trapped in her stroller, she couldn't get free. "Out! Out! Now!"

"I'll take you in a minute, baby," Demi gasped as she peeked around the tire to see what was happening. Her heart thundered, her lungs felt starved for air.

Law enforcement officials swarmed the area. She thought she saw Ryan and Owen heading to the spot the bullets came from.

One more shot and Demi lurched back with a cry as the bullet pinged off the front bumper.

Charles shifted behind her. "Stay with the children."

"Where are you going?"

"Away from here to protect everyone. He's shooting at *me*."

Charles rushed from behind the safety of the vehicle, his limp more pronounced under the stress of the situation. He prayed that if he got far enough away from them, Demi and the children would be safe. That if the shooter couldn't spot his target, he would have no reason to shoot again.

The guy had shot twice into the crowd. The only reason he'd missed was because Charles moved and messed up his shot. The third time had nicked the car Charles'd been hiding behind.

He moved away from the crowd, his body taut, nerves humming. Who was the man shooting at him? One of Burke's hires?

Someone wanting revenge for Olivia's death and thought Charles was responsible? He kept moving, away from the crowd, his mind back in Iraq, prepared for anything.

His breathing came in pants, but his cool control never slipped. He'd been a medic, but he'd also trained as a soldier. He slipped into that mode now as easily as pulling on a comfortable shirt.

Darting behind a large SUV, he paused, heart thrumming, but his breathing was even, his senses on hyperalert.

He looked back to see Demi watching him with wide, scared eyes, but she held her body over the children.

The sight of her caring for them, protecting them as though they belonged to her, did something to his heart that he'd never felt before. Something he'd have to examine a little more closely at a later time.

Charles let his eyes scan the park, the buildings surrounding it. Numerous hiding places. But the shots had come from behind him. Probably from a higher floor where the shooter would have a good view of the park.

Already officers swarmed the buildings. More sirens sounded. Chaos ruled, but Charles didn't let that distract him.

He moved to the left, exposing himself for a brief second then slipped back behind his cover. Nothing happened. No shots rained down on him.

He let out a deep breath and wondered what that meant. Had the shooter been caught—or had he escaped?

Officers appeared, shaking their heads. He saw Ryan put his gun back into his holster.

Well, that answered that question. The shooter was gone. Escaped. Free to return and cause trouble at another time. Trouble that Charles may not be able to dodge next time.

Not allowing himself to dwell on that possibility, Charles raced back to Demi and the kids. He wrapped an arm around her shoulders and reassured himself that she and his children were still in one piece.

Then he noticed the blood on her arm.

# THIRTEEN

The stinging, burning sensation in her upper right arm started the minute she realized everyone was safe.

Wincing, she looked down to find blood. Her stomach clenched. Had she been shot?

Charles gently set her back. "Let me see."

Brianne and Aaron hollered and fought against their restraints while Charles probed the wound.

She winced. "It must not be too bad. I didn't notice it until now."

"Adrenaline. It can mask pain. I saw guys with limbs blown off and they didn't even realize it." She jerked and he grimaced. "Sorry. I shouldn't have said that."

"No, it's all right. It's a part of you."

His eyes caught hers. "Yes, I suppose it is. Not the part that I particularly like, but one I can't change."

Demi lifted her uninjured arm and reached up to wipe a smudge of dirt from his chin. "I wouldn't change one thing about you."

His eyes darkened and an emotion she couldn't identify flashed in them. He started to say something but Brianne's whiny cry interrupted him.

He turned from her and did his best to reassure the children before once again focusing his attention back on her arm.

"Are you all right?"

"Is she hit?"

The voices came from her left.

Demi looked up to see Ryan and Owen hovering, their concerned gazes on her and Charles. Charles spoke without turning. "She'll be fine. I think the bullet just grazed her. Either that or it ricocheted off something."

Ryan freed a screaming Brianne from her stroller and held her on a hip.

She quieted and lay a head on his shoulder. "Thank you, Unca Ryan."

"You're welcome, darlin'." He kissed the top of her dark head and Demi's heart twinged again. How close and loving this family was. Then she saw Ryan blanch as he said, "I think I know what it bounced off of."

His white face and grim tone alarmed her. Demi followed his gaze. And saw the metal handle of the stroller inches from where Aaron's head rested against the cushioned seat. She gasped and felt Charles's fingers tighten momentarily on her arm. She ignored the flash of pain as the horror of what almost happened hit her.

"Oh, Charles…" she breathed, tears clogging her throat.

"They're fine. They're okay." She didn't know if he was saying the words to reassure her or himself. Probably both.

"We've got officers searching everywhere," Owen said. "He won't get far."

"Did you see him?" Charles asked, his voice low.

A pause. Then Owen said, "No. Not even a glimpse."

The two brothers stared at each other for a brief moment before Charles rubbed a hand down his face.

Ryan said, "Just more proof that God shows up even when bad stuff is happening."

"Yeah." Charles's voice sounded tight, strangled almost and Demi knew he was picturing what could have happened.

"As far as we could tell, there are no casualties. No one hurt except Demi," Owen said.

"That's because he was aiming at me." Charles's quiet statement rocked his brothers, Demi could tell.

But as the thought sank in, Owen nodded and said, "I can see why you would think that."

"I don't think it, I know it." Charles sighed and said, "Demi, your arm needs a bandage and you probably need some antibiotics just as a precaution. Let's get over to my office and get that taken care of. We can sneak through the back alley. If anyone else connects that shooter to me, it's going to be crazy and I don't think I'm up to facing the media or a crowd of hysterical people right now."

Demi reached out for Aaron's hand and he clasped her fingers and said, "Want out."

"I know, darling. Just a little longer."

Ryan settled a protesting Brianne back into her seat. "We'll take care of this mess here. You duck out while you can. Like you said, if the media gets ahold of you, they're going to start asking questions about Olivia. You don't need that aggravation."

"No, I don't."

"Then get Demi taken care of and I'll fill you in on everything later. Let me have an officer escort you. If this guy is truly after you, we don't need to be sending you off all by yourself."

Charles's jaw went tight and Demi knew he didn't want an escort. Then she saw his eyes dart to his children. Then her. He gave a slow nod. "I won't argue with you. Might not be a bad idea to have some backup. Thanks."

"Good." Ryan nodded and spoke into his radio. He looked up and said, "Someone will be here in a minute."

True to his word, a uniformed officer soon rounded the corner of the building and joined them. Ryan filled him in on what was needed. The young man nodded.

Charles took control of the stroller. His eyes landed on the dent left by the bullet and Demi saw him shudder.

She cradled her arm as she followed him toward his office. As they skirted the crowd, Demi saw the faces of the people. Shock, anger, terror. Emotions ran the gauntlet and the media grabbed every available emotional moment.

The walk seemed to take forever and she kept expecting someone to jump out and start shooting at them again. It didn't happen and soon she saw Charles's office come into view.

Once inside, Charles asked his secretary, Cecily, to watch the children. She agreed. Her eyes on the officer accompanying them, she asked, "What happened at the debate? I heard sirens. Sounded like the entire police force was out there."

"They were," Charles said. "Someone started shooting into the crowd." Cecily gasped and Charles continued, "Demi was hurt. I'm just going to take a look at her arm."

Still stunned, the woman nodded and released the restless children from the stroller. They darted to the play area with glee. The waiting room was empty. Apparently, the debate had been the priority for the majority of the citizens of Fitzgerald Bay, sick or not.

Charles was silent, his eyes troubled as he went about patching up her arm. She left him to his thoughts, not sure what to say, still in shock at everything that had happened in the past hour and a half.

With gentle hands, Charles put the final piece of tape on her arm.

"Are you allergic to anything?"

She blinked and sighed. "I have no idea."

"Right. We'll use a broad spectrum antibiotic, so you don't

have to worry." He shook his head as he wrote the script. "Sometimes I forget…"

Demi smiled. "It's okay. Sometimes even I manage to forget for a little while."

"The wedding's tomorrow." He looked at her arm. "If you don't feel like going…"

"No, I'll be fine. I want to go."

Frowning, he said, "I just wonder if I should go."

"Because it looks like someone is out to get you?"

"Exactly." He shook his head. "My children, my family, everyone at the debate was in danger this morning because of me."

"You can't know that for sure."

"I'm pretty sure. There were three shots this morning. The first one missed only because I moved at the last second. The last two missed because of dumb luck, God looking out for me, I'm not sure which."

She looked at her wounded arm then back at him. "I prefer to think God's looking out for us."

His face softened. "Yeah, I'm getting to that point, too." Then his jaw tightened. "Well, today answered one question."

"What's that?"

"I thought Burke Hennessy might have been behind everything going on, but looks like he can't be held responsible for this incident."

"Unless he hired someone," she muttered.

Admiration glinted in his eyes. "Yes, there is that." Then he sighed. "I'll talk to Ryan about whether or not I should go to the wedding and let you know."

"Okay. But it would be a shame for you to miss it."

"Yes, it would. Douglas and Merry have been waiting for that day for a long time now." He reached up to stroke her cheek and she sucked in a deep breath. He swallowed. "Today was too close for comfort."

"I know," she whispered.

"I know we said we'd talk...after...but—" his throat worked "—I don't want to lose you, Demi."

Her heart clenched. What could she say? "I know, Charles. I don't want to lose you, either. I just..."

"I know." He gave her a small smile. "I'll be patient."

Her anxiety eased slightly. "Thanks."

"Yeah." He helped her down from the table. "Come on."

They walked back out to the waiting area where Brianne and Aaron still played. Brianne poured imaginary tea and Aaron fired his Dino from the top of the small television set. Dino landed in Brianne's cup and she hollered her anger while Aaron looked confused about what had triggered her wrath.

Charles immediately swooped in and picked up the little girl. Startled, Brianne squealed, then giggled, her ire forgotten.

But Charles's shadowed eyes hurt her heart and she wished there was something she could do.

Brianne said, "I want ice cream."

Charles allowed a glimmer of a smile to lighten his face. "I'm sure you do. I think after today we all might need some ice cream."

Brianne gave an eager nod. "Very good idea, Daddy. Yummy."

Just as they were gathering the children, Ryan stepped into the office.

Charles looked up. "Did you get him?"

"No. He got away."

"Anyone else hurt?"

Ryan shook his head. "Come with me. We need to talk."

Charles and Demi finished loading the protesting children into the stroller. Charles pushed and Demi followed Ryan out the door. The officer stayed with them, bringing up the rear.

Back on the street, Ryan led the way to the Sugar Plum Café where Owen and Victoria ushered them into an empty back room used to host large parties.

Victoria took charge of the children. "We're going to see Fiona at The Reading Nook."

Charles shot a look of gratitude toward his soon-to-be sister-in-law.

Owen looked at Charles. Under his breath and out of earshot of anyone else, he whispered, "I know this isn't the best timing, but we really need to talk to Dad about that picture."

"You're right, the timing stinks, but—"

Aiden opened the door and stepped inside. Charles clamped his lips together as his father said, "Have a seat. I've decided we needed a little impromptu meeting about what's going on with Charles." He settled into the nearest chair and looked at his son. "Someone appears to be of the mind to want you out of the picture."

Charles nodded. "I agree."

"Writing a nasty message on your garage door is a far cry from shooting into a crowd of people." He raked a hand through his salt-and-pepper hair as his blue eyes drilled his son. "There were three shots fired today. All of those were aimed at you."

"Yes, I noticed that."

Ryan pursed his lips as he listened to his father.

"I don't like it," Aiden continued. "I'm putting protection on you until we get this figured out. More protection than just a car sitting outside your house at night." He looked at Ryan. "Can you take care of that?"

"Consider it done."

Charles shifted and he grimaced. "People are going to accuse you of favoritism. Again."

"So be it. A car will be stationed outside your house 24/7.

You'll have a tail and security at your office. One of your brothers will be around when they can."

"Dad," Charles protested. "You don't have the manpower for that. Not to mention the fact that it could be political suicide. The people in this town aren't convinced I'm not a murderer. For you to make this move…it might not be smart if you have plans to win the election."

Aiden's eyes hardened. "Your safety and the safety of my grandchildren are far more important than any political race." His eyes clouded. "It's the right thing to do and I'm going to do it."

Aiden glanced at Demi—and at her bandaged arm. "That protection will cover you, too. This guy doesn't seem to care who's in the path of his bullets."

"What about Douglas and Merry's wedding?" Charles asked. "I hate to let this guy keep me away. Then again, I don't want to show up and lure him there, either."

Aiden drew in a deep breath. "I've already discussed this with Douglas and Merry. Bottom line is they want you there. Security will be tight not only because of what's going on with you, but because of Burke and his veiled threats."

"He's made threats?" Owen asked, eyes narrowing.

"Not blatant ones, no. But his nastiness just keeps getting worse as this election gets closer. He plays dirty. It wouldn't surprise me if Burke has some sort of agenda, a plan to use the wedding as a way to further his own political ambitions." Aiden waved a hand at Charles's questioning look. "How he could do that, I have no idea. I just want to cover every angle when it comes to making sure Merry and Douglas's day goes off without a hitch."

Charles's father pursed his lips. "The reception at Connolly's Catch is a private one. No one gets in without an invitation." He paused. "I'm even going to have a couple of guys on the roofs watching. No way is anything going to mess up this wedding." Then he gave a grim smile. "Actually with all the security at the wedding, you'll probably be safer there than at your house."

Charles's gave a slow nod and shot a glance at Demi. "Fine. We'll be there."

"It'll be the same setup for the rehearsal tonight."

Charles stood. "I'll be there for that, too, then."

Aiden walked them to the door. "Ryan, let's get that security detail going. Yesterday."

"Yes, sir."

As Ryan got on his phone, Charles looked at Owen. "Uh, Dad, could we have a word with you?"

Aiden paused and glanced between his sons. "What is it?"

Owen opened his mouth and shut it. Charles looked at Demi. "Do you mind waiting in the hall for a minute?"

She raised a brow. "Oh, sure." Once she left, the brothers turned back to their father and Charles tried again. "Dad, we came across a picture of—"

Aiden's phone rang the same time Owen's did and Charles clamped his lips on the words he'd been trying to force past clenched teeth.

"Excuse me, I need to take this." Aiden grabbed the phone, listened and said, "I've got to go. They've found some evidence on the shooter I need to look at."

"What kind of evidence?" Charles asked.

"I'll fill you in when I know." Aiden left and Charles felt a tide of frustration rush over him. As Owen listened to the person on the other end of his line, Charles went to find Demi standing in the hall, leaning against the wall.

His phone buzzed signaling a text message. He checked it then told Demi, "Victoria just sent me a text. She wants to know if she can keep the kids the rest of the day and bring them to the rehearsal tonight. Apparently Paige is having a good time reading to them. Why don't you take the rest of the day off? Enjoy some time to yourself." He glanced at the officer who'd been assigned to Demi. "Or with your shadow there. I'm going to be really busy with all of the pre-wedding stuff but I'll have someone come by to pick you up for the wedding tomorrow afternoon. It's at two o'clock."

"I guess that'll be all right. You don't need help with the children tonight?"

He shook his head. "They're in the wedding and I'll have enough family there to help me out if I need it." He touched her wounded arm. "Take the time. Rest. Do whatever it is you need to do."

Demi nodded. "All right."

"Great," Charles said. "I'll see you tomorrow at the wedding. I'll be saving a seat for you."

"Sure."

"Hold up, guys." Owen caught their attention and they turned as Owen said, "Thanks for the tip." He hung up and said, "We just got some info on Demi's identity."

Charles heard her indrawn breath and felt the sudden tremble in her hands. "Who was it?"

"A hotel clerk in Springfield. Apparently, he'd been visiting relatives here in Fitzgerald Bay and saw a clip of the news. He called it in yesterday. It took us this long to determine it's legit."

"So, he knows who I am?" The hope in her voice grabbed Charles and he found himself praying Owen said yes.

"No. Not really." Her hope deflated like a punctured balloon and Charles squeezed her fingers. "But he did recognize your picture. He said you'd been living at that hotel for about three weeks before you just disappeared without a word. You never checked out, you never claimed your things."

"My things?" she whispered. "I have things?"

Owen offered her a gentle, sympathetic smile. "Apparently. He said he had boxed them up in case something had happened to you and the police came asking questions."

"What else?"

"He said you registered under the name of Michelle Smith and always paid for the room daily. Never in advance. You were quiet, kept to yourself and seemed like a nice person."

"Michelle?"

"He didn't think it was your real name. He said he called you by that name twice and you never responded." He paused. "He also said you seemed like you were afraid all the time."

"Afraid? Of what?"

"That he didn't know."

Demi drew in a deep breath. "I need to go to that hotel. I need to see it, see the room. Maybe that will trigger my memory."

"I agree," Charles said, "but you're not going alone. I'll go with you."

"When?"

He rubbed his chin. He knew she was anxious to get to that hotel. He didn't blame her. "I have the rehearsal dinner tonight and the wedding tomorrow."

"I hate to ask you to take me on Sunday."

Charles looked at his brother. "Why don't we call and see when he's going to be there?"

"Good idea," Owen said. He pulled out his phone. "I've got the number right here." He put the phone on speaker.

"Springfield Hotel."

"This is Detective Owen Fitzgerald in Fitzgerald Bay. I spoke with you earlier."

"Yes, sir."

"When would be a good time for us to come by and pick up Ms....uh...Smith's things?"

"I'm getting ready to leave in a few minutes to go out of town again for a funeral. I'll be back Monday morning."

"We'll see you then."

Owen hung up and Charles lifted a brow at Demi. "We'll go first thing Monday morning. Is that all right?"

He could see the longing on her face and felt terrible asking her to wait a few more days, but he couldn't leave yet—and he sure didn't want her going alone.

"I could go myself, take the bus," she said. "I really don't want to put anyone out."

"No!" Charles shouted the word and she blinked. He calmed his voice. "Sorry, but I don't think that's a good idea. You need someone with you." He pulled in a breath. "Just... please...let me go with you."

After what seemed like an eternity, she finally nodded. "Okay. I don't really want to go by myself anyway. I suppose waiting a couple more days won't hurt anything."

"Great."

The look of hopeful anticipation on her face caused mixed feelings and emotions to swirl through him. At first he couldn't figure out what was wrong, then realization hit him.

Once Demi discovered who she was, what if she didn't need—or want—him anymore?

# FOURTEEN

Demi grabbed her light jacket from the closet and her keys from the kitchen counter. Hurrying from the apartment, she waved to the officer assigned to watch her. He stepped out of the cruiser. "Everything all right, ma'am?"

"Yes, I just decided I wanted to take a walk on the beach. Is that okay?"

Hesitation made the man pause before he said, "I think it should be. I'll follow behind you. As long as you're not out of my sight."

Demi thought about the numerous hiding places along the rocks near Charles's house. She thought about the shots that had been fired from the building overlooking the park. Would someone try to shoot at her if she went on the beach? But the person had been aiming at Charles, not her.

Squaring her shoulders, she determined the man wouldn't make her a prisoner in her own home. "I promise to stay within your sight. I just want to walk on the beach a little. Do some thinking."

"Come on, I'll give you a lift. It'll be safer than that bicycle."

She smiled. The whole town knew she didn't drive. Demi climbed in the cruiser and participated in the small talk until he pulled into the parking area with beach access. It was farther down from Charles's house, an area she hadn't yet explored. But she noticed the clear view of the beach. The officer wouldn't have any trouble keeping an eye on her. And she didn't plan to go far anyway.

Climbing out, she said, "Thanks. I won't be too long."

"Take your time."

Demi followed the path to the beach, noting she still felt like she was walking around with a big old target on her back. Although why someone would want to single her out to terrify, she couldn't fathom. The hotel clerk had said she'd seemed afraid, that she'd paid her bill daily. To her that sounded like someone who wasn't sure if she would be staying in the same place from one day to the next.

So was she running from someone?

Had she committed some crime and was running from the police? But her fingerprints hadn't turned up anything so she really didn't think she was a criminal.

Shuddering at the thought, lost in her thoughts, she almost didn't see the young woman until she was nearly upon her. It was the woman from the café, Olivia Henry's cousin, Meghan.

"Oh, hello."

"Hi." The tall woman with the hazel eyes and blond hair offered a cautious smile.

"Sorry, I was lost in my own world. How are you?"

"I'm fine." A pause. "How is the nanny job working out?"

"It's working out well, thanks."

"Oh." The woman fidgeted for a moment then asked, "Do you mind if I ask you a few questions?"

"No, I suppose that's fine. What kind of questions?"

"Don't you think it's possible that Charles killed her?"

Demi didn't even hesitate. "Absolutely not."

Meghan eyed her. "You sound very sure about that."

"He didn't do it. I know I've only known him for a few

weeks, but I have no doubts about him on that particular issue."

Meghan nodded. "I appreciate that."

"But you don't believe me?"

The woman shrugged, a sad, grief-filled movement that made Demi's heart ache. "I don't know. I've watched him from afar, I've heard the townspeople talk about him, so I've gotten conflicting information."

"I suppose you're keeping up with the investigation?"

Meghan's jaw tightened. "Every step of the way."

On impulse, Demi reached out and took the woman's hand. "I'm so sorry for your loss, but it wasn't Charles who killed her."

Meghan squeezed her hand then dropped it with a sigh. "Thanks."

Then Meghan turned and walked back the way she'd come. Demi watched her go and prayed they would find Olivia's murderer before too much longer. Certainly before the person had the opportunity to kill again.

Charles paced the floor at the church. Last night the rehearsal had gone off without a hitch. Security ensured no one bothered the happy couple and his children were fully entertained by the other children involved in the wedding.

The whole process brought back memories of his own wedding. A lot of flash, a lot of money and very little substance if Kathleen could walk out on him and their children so easily. Her unfaithfulness was a sore spot that still chafed if he thought about it too long.

Which he'd been doing ever since finding the picture of his father with another woman. And a baby. His mistress and child out of wedlock?

Did he believe that?

Strangely enough, he did. Even with no concrete proof

other than the picture and how close the couple stood, their expressions, the look in their eyes, Charles knew in his gut it was true.

His father had cheated on his mother.

The thought made his blood boil. Anger with his father wanted to surface, but Charles held it back. If he let it out, he'd cause friction at the wedding. And there was no way he was doing that. Especially without knowing for *certain* that it was true.

He and Owen would confront their father at the right time in the right way. And soon. After the wedding.

Right now, he kept an eye out for Demi, anxious to see her, to reassure himself that she was fine. Of course, if she wasn't fine, he would know about it, so he could relax. Right? At least that's what he told himself.

"Ready to do this thing?"

He looked up to see Ryan, Owen and his father standing in the door. Owen looked tense. He knew he was thinking about the photo. So was Charles. He kept his voice light. They had so many questions for Aiden. If he had an affair. Who the woman was. Did they have a half sibling? "I'm ready, but what about Douglas?"

"He's chomping at the bit," Aiden said. "Paige has your little ones under control for now. No guarantee on how long that'll last."

Charles laughed. "True." He looked at the gathering crowd. "Is Demi here?"

"Officer Bolton just delivered her safe and sound. She's sitting with the family."

Charles felt that weight slide from his shoulders. "Good, thanks."

"Now, let's go round up Douglas and get this thing done."

Within thirty minutes, Charles was standing up in front of the crowd, his eyes scanning, his senses alert. Even though he could see how tight security was, it didn't stop him from keeping a keen eye out for trouble. Every so often, his gaze would land on Demi and he'd feel a jolt in the vicinity of his heart.

Douglas and Merry had decided to place his mother's picture on the organ and Charles couldn't help staring at it, wondering if she ever knew her husband had been unfaithful. If she had, she'd obviously forgiven him and they'd worked through it. However, Charles felt his anger stir.

Forcing himself to pay attention to the service, he was relieved when the minister finally pronounced his brother lawfully wed and no one had disrupted the nuptials.

Breathing a sigh of relief, but not relaxing his guard, he felt the comfortable weight of the pistol in his shoulder holster. Until Olivia's murderer was caught, Charles wouldn't go anywhere without the weapon.

As the wedding party dispersed, Charles wondered what it would be like to be married to Demi. He could envision her in a white gown and—

Cutting off those thoughts for now, he promised himself he'd revisit them when the time was right.

As they waited for the photographer to set up his equipment, Charles motioned for Demi to stay. She nodded and settled back into the pew.

As soon as the pictures were finished, they would make their way to Connelly's Catch for the reception.

Finally, he saw his dad standing alone, taking in the merriment. The look on his father's face made Charles's gut burn with resentment. What right did he have to be so proud?

His eye caught Owen's. Owen's expression said he was thinking about the photo, as well. Charles leaned down and whispered in Demi's ear, "Excuse me a moment, will you?"

"Sure." Demi raised a brow as though to ask if everything

was all right. He patted her shoulder to silently reassure her and she turned back to listen to Fiona.

He hadn't shared with her about the picture and what he and Owen suspected. He wouldn't until he had the truth from his father's lips.

He slipped up beside Owen. "Before or after the pictures?"

"After. No sense in ruining them for Douglas and Merry."

Another pause then Charles asked in a low voice, "What do you really think? Did Dad have an affair? A child with another woman? You saw the pictures."

In an equally soft tone, Owen said, "My gut says yes."

And then there was no more time for talk. Charles posed and smiled until his cheek muscles spasmed. Brianne and Aaron finally tired and protested loud enough that the photographer agreed he had enough pictures and they could all be dismissed.

Driving the short distance to Connolly's Catch, Charles kept an eye on the surrounding traffic. Demi teased Brianne and Aaron, and Charles struggled with what he would say to his father. How did one confront one's parent about his infidelity?

"Charles? Are you all right? You've been awfully quiet."

"I'm... I need to talk to my father about something unpleasant and I'm not looking forward to it."

She grimaced. "I'm sorry."

"Yeah." He forced a smile. "Come on, let's get something to eat, I'm starved."

They got the kids and made their way into the restaurant. Tantalizing smells made his stomach growl even more, although it was a bit early for supper.

Music played. Douglas and Merry danced a slow dance in the center of the dance floor. The lovesick look on his brother's face made Charles glance at Demi. She took everything in, delight written in her eyes.

Soon, she might get her memory back. The question from the other day crossed his mind. As much as he wanted her to heal and know who she was, where would he fit in her life once she did? Disgusted with his selfishness, he forced the insecurity from his thoughts and caught Owen's eye.

Owen walked over, followed by Victoria. "What's going on?" she asked. "I saw that look you two exchanged."

"We're going to talk to Dad about that picture," Charles said.

Victoria frowned. "Let me see it again. I know I've seen it somewhere—" She broke off and paled.

Charles lasered in on her. "You remembered where you saw it."

She nodded, a slow nod that conveyed her reluctance to tell him what she was thinking. "Come on, Victoria. What is it?"

Her gaze darted to Charles's father who still stood apart from the festivities. "I'm pretty sure that's the picture Olivia gave me to hang on the wall in the café."

Charles felt his heart slam into his ribs. "Olivia? She has something to do with this?"

Another wide-eyed nod and a nervous glance at Aiden. "Olivia came into the café one day shortly before she died and handed me a copy of this picture. She asked me to hang it on the wall—"

At her pause, Owen pushed her. "Why?"

"To honor the memory of…her parents."

Charles froze. "Olivia's parents?"

"Yes," Victoria whispered.

Charles's gut churned. If what Victoria said was true, not only had Olivia been his nanny, she'd also been his half sister. He almost couldn't wrap his mind around it. One look at Owen's white face said his brother was having the same problem.

"I'm sorry," Victoria said, "but I'm absolutely positive that's what she said."

"And it's the same picture."

"Yes."

"Olivia knew," Charles muttered. "That's why she came to Fitzgerald Bay." He looked at Owen and Victoria. "She never said a word."

Owen ran a hand through his hair and drew in a ragged breath. "Unfortunately, if Dad knew who Olivia was—and I highly suspect he did—we now have another suspect in Olivia's murder."

"Let's go," Charles said.

The man was alone, still observing the crowd around him. Together, they approached. "Talk to you a minute?" Charles asked.

Aiden smiled. Then frowned as he discerned the seriousness of their expressions. "What is it?"

Owen simply reached into his pocket and pulled out the photo. "This."

Aiden looked at it. His face paled and Charles saw him swallow hard before he asked, "Where did you get this?"

"We found it in your tackle box the day we went to get that fishing rod for Demi."

Aiden swiped a hand across his lips and cleared his throat. "I see."

"Yeah," Charles said. "We see, too."

"Did you kill Olivia, Dad?" Owen asked in a low voice.

Their father jerked and choked. Shock made his pupils dilate. "What? No, I... No. How can you even ask that?"

"You certainly have motive." Charles kept his voice even while Owen pinched the bridge of his nose.

"Come with me," Aiden ordered, having regained some of his composure.

"Where?"

"Someplace private and we won't be overheard."

Demi watched Charles walk from the main part of the restaurant into a back room with his brother and father. They looked so serious she almost got up and followed, but decided it wasn't her business. Charles would fill her in when he could.

Leaning over, she said to Fiona, "I'm going to the ladies' room. I'll be right back."

"Sure."

Demi got up and made her way in the direction the sign pointed. As she walked, several people welcomed her. The small hall with the restrooms at the end was empty. Catching her breath, she started down toward the women's room and felt the hairs on the back of her neck lift.

Spinning, she saw no one.

But the feeling that someone was watching her was very strong. So strong she shivered.

Her eyes scanned the crowd beyond the hall and saw nothing that should concern her.

She turned back to enter the bathroom.

Then looked behind her once more.

A young man dressed in a pin-striped suit stood there watching her.

Demi pushed open the door to the bathroom and rushed inside. She let it close behind her, feeling her heart thump against her chest.

Who was he? Why was he watching her?

A noise in the stall behind her told her that she wasn't alone. Relief filled her and she took a deep breath as she washed her hands.

The occupant of the stall came out and smiled. "It was a beautiful wedding, wasn't it?"

"It sure was."

Demi decided to follow the woman out. She wanted the company.

As they left the ladies' room, Demi's heart slowed as she gazed on the empty hall.

As she and the woman in front of her passed a section of the hall that branched off, a hand reached out and grasped her upper arm.

A scream welled in her throat only to die a quick death when a voice asked, "Demi?"

Gasping, heart pounding, she spun to see the same young man who had watched her enter the restroom. He had stylishly messy dark hair and brown eyes. Hand over her heart, she said, "Yes?"

He held out his hands. "I'm sorry, I didn't mean to startle you."

"It's all right. Do I know you?"

He blinked and she saw the hurt in his eyes. "Well, I would hope so. I'm your fiancé."

# FIFTEEN

Charles watched his father pace the small room. On the other side of the door, the merriment went on. Charles wanted to be out there, enjoying the party with his brother, but he wouldn't rest until his father said what he had to say.

Aiden rubbed his eyes. "Okay, so you found the picture and put two and two together. That was twenty-three years ago."

"Yeah. So?"

"So, your mother and I had hit a rough patch. We'd agreed to a divorce. I thought that my marriage was over. I was lonely, grieving…" He stopped and shut his eyes while letting out a blustery sigh. "I made a mistake," he admitted in a low voice. "I was wrong. Horribly, irrevocably wrong. When Tara called to tell me she was pregnant, I was already back and working things out with your mother. But…I just couldn't leave Tara with nothing. I flew back to Ireland to make sure she and the baby were well taken care of."

"Did Mom know?"

Aiden swallowed. "No. I never told her."

Charles nodded. At least she was spared that.

"So, Olivia Henry was your daughter."

A heavy sigh. "Yes. And I see your point about motive. Trust me, I've thought about how all this looks, but I didn't kill her." He looked at Charles. "And I know you didn't, either."

"The rest of the family needs to know this."

"Why?"

Charles looked at his father, incredulous that the man had to ask. "Because, it's going to come out one way or another. Olivia's dead," he hissed. "You can't keep your relationship to her a secret much longer. It would be much better for everyone coming from you than to see it on the news."

Aiden paced from one end of the room to the other. He finally stopped in front of Charles and Owen. "Okay. You're right." His gaze hardened. "But I tell them in my own way, my own time. Let's see if we can get Olivia's murder solved before we drop this bomb on them."

Charles glanced at Owen who gave a reluctant nod. "Fine."

Owen stared at his father. "Those baby items that were sent to the station anonymously last month. You sent those, didn't you?"

Charles remembered Owen talking about receiving several baby items, including a baby's hospital bracelet, a receiving blanket and an uncashed check for ten thousand dollars made out to Olivia Henry. These items had led Owen and Ryan to the conclusion that Olivia had a baby somewhere.

And their father knew it.

Charles felt sick.

"Yes, I did. Olivia gave them to me. After she was murdered, I felt terrible and knew I couldn't just sit on that evidence." He paused. "Nor could I come forward and tell everything I knew. That seemed like the right thing to do at the time."

"The right thing—" Charles broke off and ground his teeth. Did his father even understand how that sounded? "The right thing?" Charles felt all the rage he'd been holding in ever since being considered a suspect and then finding that picture in Dad's tackle box come boiling to the surface. "The right thing would have been to walk away from a woman who wasn't your wife twenty-three years ago. If you'd done the *right thing* twenty-three years ago, we wouldn't be in this situation, would we?"

Owen stepped between him and his father who'd clenched his fists. Charles stepped away, appalled at how close he was to losing control. Drawing in a deep breath, he closed his eyes and turned his back to Owen and his dad.

Aiden's voice, gravelly with regret, said, "You're right. Everything you said is right. I'm sorry, son, and I'll make it right. I will."

"When?" Charles demanded.

His father glanced at Douglas and Merry. "I'll tell everyone at the next Sunday family dinner. Douglas and Merry don't need to know until they get back from their honeymoon. Agreed?"

Charles and Owen nodded. "Agreed," Charles muttered.

Demi stared at the unknown man in front of her. At a loss for words, she simply gaped.

He gave a self-conscious laugh. "Um…so, are you okay? I saw your picture on the news and couldn't believe it was you. I mean, I have so much I want to talk to you about."

She felt frozen, the man in front of her a stranger. And yet, her fiancé? How could this be?

Gulping, she finally found her voice. "I…I'm sorry. I don't know who you are. I have amnesia. What's your name?"

"I'm Alan Gregor, Demi. Come on. Amnesia? Really?"

"Is there a problem?" Charles's voice cut through her brain fog.

Whirling, she stared into his blue eyes. Eyes she'd come to love over such a short period of time. Not just his eyes, but everything about him.

Only she didn't have the right to love him. She'd already promised her love to another.

Grief nearly shattered her. She should be rejoicing that someone had finally come forward, but she couldn't get past the fact that she was going to lose Charles. And the children. And his crazy beloved family.

"I…" What could she say?

"Demi?" A hard hand gave her shoulder a gentle shake.

"Charles, this is…" A sob nearly broke through. Clearing her throat, she tried again. "This is Alan Gregor. He claims that he's my fiancé."

"Your what?" His face paled and she saw him swallow hard.

She drew in a shuddering breath. "He says he's my fiancé. But I don't remember him." Her voice shook. Charles looked like he'd been dealt a blow to his solar plexus.

She looked at Alan and bit her lip. "I'm sorry, I don't remember you."

Over his shoulder, she spotted Owen, a thundercloud on his face. Ryan and their father were right behind him. For a brief moment, Demi put aside the strange man who'd just rocked her world once again and focused on the approaching family. "Charles? I think something's wrong." She pointed.

He turned and immediately went tense. "What is it?" he asked his tight-lipped father. "What's wrong now?"

Aiden said, "Burke Hennessy's dead."

Charles froze. "Dead?"

"A heart attack is what it looks like," Aiden growled. "They'll do an emergency autopsy. We should have the report sometime tomorrow."

"Oh, no," Demi whispered. "Poor Christina."

"Yes." Aiden nodded. "She's the one who found him. Walked in and started screaming according to her nanny.

The nanny called 9-1-1. It's a shame. I mean, I didn't care much for the guy, but I didn't wish him dead." A pause. He looked at his sons. "The media's already all over this." Aiden zoomed in on Charles. "Word's already filtering down that the death is being covered up as a heart attack. They're speculating that you had something to do with it."

Charles flinched. "What? Why? How did they come up with that ridiculous idea?"

Ryan rubbed his eyes. "Someone said they overheard you threaten Burke."

"I never threatened the man," Charles ground out. "I told him to buzz off and stay out of my business, but I never threatened him."

"Well, you were here surrounded by witnesses when he died so I think it'll be easy enough to prove you didn't have anything to do with it." Aiden gestured toward a wide-eyed Alan. "Who's this?"

Alan held out a hand. "I'm Alan Gregor, Demi's fiancé."

In a dazed voice, Demi told what Alan had explained to her only moments before.

"How did you get in here?" Charles asked. "This reception was by invitation only."

"I…sort of lifted an invitation." He pulled it out of his pocket and waved it with a sheepish look.

Aiden nearly growled. "You had no business doing that. I should have you thrown out."

"I'm sorry, it's just that I was trying to find a way to talk to Demi, but she's surrounded by cops all the time and I…" He shrugged and looked down. "I'm sorry. I should have found another way."

"Yeah, you should have. What took you so long to come forward?" Charles asked.

Alan winced. "It's a long story."

"Why don't we all find a seat and you can fill us in,"

Charles murmured. Already he didn't like the guy. Demi looked like she'd been sucker punched. The white lines around her lips and eyes betrayed her tension.

"Ah, do you mind if I speak to Demi alone?"

The panic in her eyes was all the answer Charles needed. "Actually, I do mind. We've come to think of Demi as family, so until you check out, I'll just stick around. Unless Demi wants me to leave...."

"No, stay. Please."

The grateful look she shot him told him that his answer was the right one.

A flash of anger on Alan's face, quickly snuffed, made Charles a little wary. Then again, he supposed could understand it, too. If he'd just found his fiancée and another man was horning in...well, he wouldn't like it, either.

But it didn't stop him from following the two of them over to an empty table. The reception was winding down. Douglas and Merry would soon leave and Charles wanted to wish them well.

With one eye on the newlyweds, he focused the rest of his attention on Alan and Demi.

Alan cleared his throat and leaned in so he could be heard over the music.

"I didn't come sooner because I've been out of the country."

"What's my name?" Demi asked.

"Demetria Michelle Townsend."

He saw her lips move as she repeated the name. Then she whispered, "I was right. I remembered my name." She smiled, tears glittering in her eyes.

"Do you remember anything about what happened?" Alan asked.

"No. The police think I was attacked and left for dead. I was in the hospital after I was found for about three weeks.

When I woke up, I had no memory of anything except my first name."

"Oh, Demi, honey," Alan murmured as he reached over and grasped her fingers for a squeeze. Demi pulled away before Charles had to smash the man's nose.

*Lord,* Charles began to pray, *I know I've been distant since Kathleen left me and that was wrong. I know I want to pray a selfish prayer and beg You to get this guy away from her, but if that's not in Your plan, then I ask that You help me accept and deal with it because there's no way I can do that on my own strength.*

"...right, Charles?" Demi asked.

He blinked. "I'm sorry, I was thinking about something. What?"

"I said you planned to take me to the hotel where I was staying before I was attacked, but now that Alan is here, that might not be necessary." She frowned. "Although I do want to get my things."

"What hotel?" Alan asked.

So Demi explained that part of her story while Charles fumed.

Charles looked at Alan. "The clerk said she seemed afraid. Do you have any idea what she would have been afraid of?"

Alan's eyes went wide. "No, I'm sorry, I can't imagine." He looked at Demi. "In all your letters that you wrote, you never said anything about being afraid."

"Letters?"

Alan smiled. "Letters, cards, emails. You were so diligent in making sure I had a huge number of them." His eyes lowered and he cleared his throat as though his emotions were too much. "I don't know what I would have done without you, Demi."

The hoarse words rocked Charles back on his heels. He knew exactly how the man felt. While in the service, letters and cards from family and friends had kept him going. What would Charles do if Demi left him? Chose Alan over him? A coldness swept over him as he considered the possibility. Then he firmed his jaw. No way. He wouldn't let that happen.

But how could he stop it? *God, please, do something...*

"Tell us your story, Alan," Charles said.

Alan sighed and rubbed his eyes. "Right. Okay. I was a government contractor working over in Iraq when my colleagues and I were hit with an IED."

At Demi's blank look, Charles said, "Improvised Explosive Device. A roadside bomb. Generally homemade and designed to do as much damage as possible."

"Oh," she gasped. "I'm so sorry."

Alan shrugged, but the lines on his face said the memory wasn't pleasant. Again, Charles could relate. He didn't like that. He didn't want to feel anything but dislike for the man who wanted to take Demi away from him.

The man continued. "I was the only survivor. It took me weeks to recover. When I did, I tried to contact you, but got nowhere. I was sent home on medical leave and started searching for you. Just as I was about to go to the cops, I saw your picture on the news and saw that you'd been attacked in an attempted robbery. But no one told me that you had amnesia, not even the nurses I talked to at the hospital. They just said you caught a bus to someplace near the coast. It took forever to track you down."

Demi simply stared at Alan. Charles couldn't read her expression and that bothered him.

Alan said, "I couldn't understand why you hadn't contacted me, why the letters suddenly stopped. Why you weren't answering your phone." He shrugged and a sad smiled pulled at his lips. "Now I understand." He looked around the room, at Charles then back at Demi. "I know you've made new friends, have a new life here, but I'm hoping you'll at least give me a chance, get to know me again."

Demi stood abruptly. "I need some air."

Demi didn't know whether to run or laugh or cry. Finally, she had what she'd been hoping—praying—for. Someone who knew her. Knew about her. And what did she do?

Run away.

But she needed time, space, to deal with this. To wrap her mind around everything.

She hadn't even asked about her family.

"Are you all right?"

Demi spun at the sound of the voice. It was the officer who'd been keeping an eye on her. Clearing her throat, she said, "Yes, I just need some time."

"Sure." He backed up, but she noticed he didn't leave her alone.

"Demi?"

She turned.

Charles. Tears welled as his warm hands settled on her shoulders. She felt his lips brush the edge of her hairline. "It'll be okay," he whispered.

Looking beyond him, she saw Alan standing in the doorway, watching, hands shoved in his pockets, mouth tight, brow furrowed. She moved away from Charles. "I'm going home. Give my best to Douglas and Merry for me. I'm sorry," she stammered, "I just need to be alone for a while."

She could see Charles wanted to argue—or at least go with her. But she turned on her heel, putting her back to him and Alan.

The officer followed at a discreet distance.

Demi's mind whirled. She needed guidance, direction. But all her friends were related to Charles. Who could she talk to? Who would be objective about her situation?

"Demi, wait!"

Turning, eyes nearly blinded with her tears, she made out Alan's form coming toward her. The officer followed behind.

"Demi." He caught up with her. "Please. Don't go yet. Come sit with me. Talk to me."

She wanted to. Only because she had a zillion questions to ask him. She searched for Charles, but he'd already left. That made her feel sad—and grateful. He'd been willing to honor her request for time alone.

And then there was Alan. Who seemed so desperate to be with her. She couldn't begrudge him that. How would she feel if the roles were reversed?

Brushing aside her tears and telling herself to grow a spine, she straightened her shoulders and nodded. "Fine. Let's go to the café, okay?"

"Sure."

Demi led the way, her heart beating double time once again. With everything in her, she wished Charles was beside her, but knew that wasn't fair to him or the man who'd just shown up in her life.

They found a table and ordered coffee. Thank goodness Victoria was still at the wedding reception. Demi didn't need her watchful eye.

As it was, nervous jitters made her hands shake. She took a sip of the steaming brew and said, "Can you please tell me a little about my family? My parents? Brothers and sisters?"

He hesitated, then said, "You're an only child. Your parents are missionaries in…ah…Brazil, I think you said. You can go months without hearing from them."

So that was why no one had reported her missing!

"But what about friends? A church family?"

He shrugged. "You lived with your parents in Brazil but came home to take care of their house. That's how we met. I leased the house next door to your parents. I asked you to stay a little longer rather than return to the mission field so that we could continue to grow our relationship." His eyes softened and his hand reached out to touch hers. "We fell in love and when I asked you to marry me, you said yes. That's about it."

Her head began to ache the way it did when she tried to think too hard, or when she tried to force the memories. This time she ignored it. "My parents' house," she said softly. "Where is it?"

"In Springfield."

"Where I was found. Where I stayed in the hospital."

"Yes."

"And yet no one knew who I was?"

"No, I guess not," he said slowly. "But it makes sense. You told me you fell in love with Brazil and hadn't been back to the States for a few years although you said your parents came back pretty regularly."

"I was a missionary?" The thought just registered. No wonder she'd been compelled to seek out God. Warmth infused her. She believed in God.

"Yes. You taught school."

"I'm a teacher."

"A missionary teacher."

Visions of children swam through her mind. Dark faces, dark eyes, smiles. Then yelling, a hard fist and a scream. She gasped.

Alan's grip tightened on her fingers. "You remember something."

"Ah, no. Yes. I'm not sure." She blinked the images away and the headache faded.

"Come with me."

"What?"

"Let me take you home. Show you where you live, where we were going to live after we were married."

The excitement in his voice made her hesitate. She didn't want to go with him. She wanted to go with Charles.

Something in her expression must have registered with him. "It's him, isn't it?"

Demi didn't bother to ask what he meant. "I'm not going to lie to you. I've developed feelings for Charles." His eyes shuttered and his lips tightened. "But," she hurried on to reassure him, "I want to be fair to you, too. I... Oh, my, I think I just need some time."

He smiled. A forced smile, but at least he was trying. "All right, Demi, just don't make any hasty decisions without letting me know. Please?"

"I think that's a reasonable request. I can do that," she promised.

"Good. Good."

Demi stood. "I'm going to lie down. I need to process all of this."

# SIXTEEN

Charles slept little and when he woke Sunday morning, he was in a foul mood. Not only because he'd had almost no sleep, but because it was now 5:00 a.m. and he was wide awake. The twins still slept so he prowled the house on silent feet.

In the den, his eyes landed on his mother's Bible. The book held a prominent position on the mantel. His mother had given the Bible to him several weeks before she'd died, making him promise to live by it.

Regret pierced him. He'd read that book every day after her death, seeking solace and comfort in the word. But after Kathleen had left him, he'd lost the will, the energy, to do anything but get through each day only to fall into bed every night exhausted beyond belief.

Now, he pulled the Bible from its resting place. With a puff of his breath, he blew the layer of dust from the top.

Carrying the book to the recliner, he settled himself in the chair and opened the Bible. His mother's handwriting leaped off the pages. She'd taken copious notes over the years. His finger traced the words and wondered what she would have done, how she would have felt, had she known of her husband's infidelity.

She would have been hurt, betrayed, angry. Of course she would have felt all those emotions.

Would she have eventually forgiven? Probably.

Charles tried to find it in his heart to pray for Kathleen. To completely forgive her for deserting him and their children. To his surprise, the raging bitterness was gone, replaced by a sadness for the woman. A regret that he wasn't what she'd needed.

But a thankfulness that Demi had come along when she had.

His phone buzzed.

Owen had sent him a text: Call when you get up. Have news re: Burke's autopsy.

Charles lifted a brow. That was fast. His father must have pulled a few strings to get that done in such a short amount of time.

He punched in Owen's speed dial number.

Owen picked up on the second ring. "It was murder."

"How?"

"Apparently the man liked to drink at night. Someone slipped a lethal cocktail of prescription drugs in his drink."

"How do you know it wasn't suicide?"

"The ME found a feather in his throat."

"A feather?"

"As in from a feather pillow. Looks like someone doped him up good, then held a pillow over his face to make sure the deed was done."

"Wow."

"At least that's the speculation at this point. Tox screen was off the charts with all kinds of different drugs. I can't even remember the ones the ME listed."

Charles heard the weariness in his brother's voice. "You know we—the family, I mean—will be suspects, don't you?"

"Of course I know that," Owen snorted. "I've already

thought about that. I can just see the headlines now. 'Fitzgerald family poisons rival for mayor.'"

"I don't suppose there's any way to keep this from the media."

"Not a chance."

"Right." Charles glanced at the clock on the wall. "I'm still planning on taking Demi to the hotel. She wants to get her things."

"And it's an opportunity to spend some time with her, eh?"

Charles felt the flush start at the base of his throat. Glad he was on the phone and not facing his brother, he simply said, "Yes."

Silence.

Then Owen said, "You're worried about this guy, Alan, aren't you?"

"I am."

"I don't envy your position," Owen said. "Let me know if you need my help with anything."

Charles didn't hesitate. "I want a background check on this guy."

"Absolutely. Consider it done." His brother paused. "One more thing. We've decided to release a picture of the dolphin charm found near Olivia's body to the media. Let them show it on the news and see if anyone can ID it. We've kind of sat on this piece of evidence because we were trying to track down where it came from without alerting the killer that we had it. We're hoping the killer doesn't even realize it's missing. However, we're running out of options and leads on this case and feel like it's time to reveal it and see what happens."

Charles drew in a deep breath. "Keep me updated."

"Will do."

Charles hung up and wondered if life would ever get back to normal.

* * *

After church Sunday, Demi and the Fitzgerald clan gathered at the ball field. Aiden had ordered extra security for the game just to be on the safe side. He'd thought about calling it off, but Charles said he would come up against such opposition that he'd relented.

With conditions.

There would be guards around the perimeter, and fans would have to consent to bag searches.

It looked like the entire town turned out for this special fundraiser game to benefit the children's hospital. Charles pushed the twins in the stroller and Demi walked beside them, her heart warm from being with them. She tried not to think about how much she liked being a part of this family. Because she had no assurance it would last.

At the bleachers, she joined Charles on the bottom one so the twins could be kept in their stroller as long as they would consent to it.

Paige and Victoria sat behind them.

"I'll play with them if you want me to, Uncle Charles," Paige offered.

Fiona's son, Sean, darted past followed by a group of his buddies.

Charles looked at Paige and smiled. "Maybe in a little while. They're pretty happy right now."

"Okay."

And then she saw something that disturbed her.

Alan Gregor sitting on the next set of bleachers, turned so he could see her.

When she caught his eye, he smiled and waved her over.

Her heart hit her toes. She didn't want to see Alan today.

The thought sent guilt coursing through her and she forced a smile. "Charles, I'm going to say hello to Alan."

The instant frown on his face sent a new surge of guilt.

Guilt for...just being her and the uncertainty she'd brought into his life.

Biting her lip against the desire to ignore Alan and run back to her apartment—so she didn't have to deal with the stress of Alan's presence and Charles's unhappiness at the whole situation—she made her way over to the man who'd rocked her world yesterday and said, "Hi, Alan."

Delight lit his expression. "Demi. I knew you'd be here. Would you sit with me?"

Awkwardness hit her. "Well, I've come with Charles and the kids, so I guess I'll stay with them. But thank you."

Alan's shoulders drooped and he turned his head for a minute. Then he looked back at her. "Sure, sure. I understand." But she saw disappointment in his eyes and almost asked him if he wanted to join them. Then bit her tongue. She wouldn't do that to Charles.

And yet, Alan looked so sad. She said, "But I'd love to meet you after and get a cup of coffee or something. Maybe we could pick up our conversation and you could tell me a little more about—my life."

His shoulders straightened a bit and he smiled. "Sure, I'd love to do that."

Demi nodded and turned to catch Charles, his eyes questioning and shadowed. She swallowed hard and felt tears threaten.

What was she doing?

Keeping a tight rein on her emotions, she felt them testing her control.

Instead of walking back to Charles and the children, she turned left and headed for the building that held the restrooms.

She darted around the side and let the dam break.

Tears trickled down her cheeks and she leaned her head

against the rough brick. *God, help me, what am I going to do? What is Your will in this?*

She had no ready answer for her desperate plea.

A hand fell on her shoulder and she turned to find Charles standing there, compassion written on his face. "Ah, Demi, I'm sorry."

She wrapped her arms around his waist and buried her nose in his chest. "Oh, Charles, I don't know what to do. I don't want to have coffee with him. I don't love him. I...I want to be with you, to keep building whatever it is we're building with each other and selfishly, maybe, I'm not ready to give that up."

Charles froze and she wished she could bite her tongue off. Why, oh why, had she blurted that out?

Heat scalded her cheeks and she didn't dare lift her head from his chest.

But he didn't give her a choice. His hand came up and he tucked a finger under her chin. Slowly, she gazed into his eyes.

He licked his lips then said, "I want that, too, Demi. I'm just not sure what to do about it."

Demi gave an anguished, humorless laugh as her embarrassment faded in the wake of his confession. "We can't do anything about it right now. Not until I figure out what to do about Alan, not until something gives with my memories."

"And not until I'm cleared of Olivia's murder."

Demi settled her forehead back against his shoulder. "This is all so crazy. When will it end?"

"Soon, I hope. Soon."

"Everything all right?"

Demi jerked at the woman's voice. Turning, she saw a uniformed officer standing, watching them. "We're fine," Demi said. "Just getting ready to go watch a softball game."

They walked back to the bleachers where Victoria had

Brianne sitting in her lap. Paige sat in the dirt with Aaron as they ran his Matchbox cars through a maze Paige had drawn. Dino sat in the middle.

Demi's heart clenched. What would she do without this little family?

She felt Alan's gaze on her.

Glancing at him, she did her best to smile.

But shivered when he didn't smile back.

# SEVENTEEN

Demi listened as Owen and Charles went back and forth about the trip to the Springfield Hotel. They'd decided to wait until after Burke Hennessy's funeral, which would be in less than two hours. The medical examiner had released the body, declaring all the evidence the police needed had been gathered.

Owen said, "After the funeral, I think I'll have an officer follow you."

Charles hesitated. "Why? Burke's dead."

Owen lifted a brow. "Burke wasn't the one shooting at you during the debate."

"True," Charles said. "Very true. So he either hired someone or it wasn't Burke."

"Exactly why we don't need to take any chances. Why don't you take Ryan with you?"

"Ryan?"

"He's a cop. He has the time. With the attempts on your life, I think it's the safe way to go."

Charles thought about it. "I've got my weapon."

"Yeah, but if you shoot him, you don't have to do the paperwork."

Charles smiled at Owen's attempt to lighten the mood.

"Good point. All right, see if Ryan can go with us. Couldn't hurt to have him along."

"Good." Charles could hear the relief in Owen's voice. "Thanks, Owen."

"Just stay out of trouble or I'll never hear the end of it from Ryan."

Demi saw Charles's truck pull up outside of The Reading Nook. Hurrying down the stairs, she couldn't quell the anxiety churning in her stomach. Today after the funeral, she would hold in her hands things that belonged to her. She was one step closer to finding out who she was. True, she now had a name, but she wanted her memories back.

Hopefuliy, a visit to the hotel she'd stayed in before the attack would offer that.

And then possibly, a visit to her home.

Her home. What was it like? Would she see pictures of her family, friends? Maybe the school where she taught.

And she would get to spend the day with Charles even if it included a funeral.

She climbed in the passenger seat and Charles said, "I appreciate you going with me."

"I didn't really know Burke very well, but I don't mind going."

"I feel like a hypocrite."

"Why? Because you couldn't stand the man and you're going to his funeral?"

Charles gave a short humorless laugh. "Exactly."

"Then why are you going?"

He let out a long sigh. "Because it's the right thing to do. The man had his issues and I think his wife, Christina, is going to need all the support she can get. She won't want it from us now, but maybe later, she'll realize…"

Demi took his hand and squeezed. "You're a very kind man, aren't you?"

He flushed. "I try." He paused. "I have to admit I'm hesitant to show up. I know Dad wants me to go, but I'm not sure that's the wisest decision he's made considering Burke's animosity toward our family." He shook his head as he made a left turn to head for the church.

Upon their arrival, the parking lot was almost full. In spite of Burke's attitude toward the Fitzgeralds, he was a popular man in town. Everyone who was anyone in Fitzgerald Bay had come to pay their respects.

Demi looked around and couldn't help but wonder if the person who'd killed Olivia was nearby. She spotted Meghan Henry and waved. Meghan waved back, but frowned when she saw who Demi was with.

Demi felt her heart dip at the response, but there was nothing she could do about it. Only by the authorities catching the real killer and clearing Charles's name would everyone finally see their concerns and suspicions had been wrong.

She prayed that happened soon.

"That was kind of Mrs. Mulrooney to offer to keep the children for you," she said to break the silence.

He smiled, a pulling of his lips that didn't quite reach his eyes. "She's a great lady."

Charles made the appropriate response, but Demi could see his attention was on the people going into the church. He caught her arm. "Do you mind if we go in toward the end?"

"You want to sit in the back?"

"If you don't mind."

"Not at all."

As they waited, Demi watched the crowd. Several people noticed her and Charles standing there and she saw them make comments. She felt Charles tense and was glad neither of them could hear what was being said.

"Are you ready?"

"Whenever you are."

He took her hand and led her to the door. As they entered, she could see a few of the Fitzgeralds already seated. "You don't want to sit with your family?"

He shook his head. "I want to be able to see who's here."

Demi nodded and they found a seat in the back. She saw Aiden's salt-and-pepper head held high. Ryan and Owen flanked their father. Seated next to Owen was Paige then Victoria, Keira and Fiona.

Demi glanced toward the door and gasped as she recognized Alan. Charles leaned over. "What is it?"

"Why is he here?" she whispered.

Again, she felt him tense. "I don't know. Do you want me to ask him?"

Alan finally spotted her and made his way toward her. She gulped and shivered. What was it about him that made her uneasy?

She didn't have time to try and figure it out. Alan soon stood in front of her. He nodded to Charles, but didn't take his eyes off Demi. She asked, "What are you doing here, Alan? You didn't know Burke."

He shifted side to side for a moment then shoved his hands into the front pockets of his khaki slacks. "I know. But...I knew you'd be here."

Demi sighed. "Oh, Alan. Let's get through the funeral, all right?"

"Do you mind if I sit with you?"

"Sure." She looked at Charles who didn't look happy, but shrugged. They found their seats with Demi between the men. The tension surrounding them was thick; it had to be visible to anyone who looked at them.

The funeral lasted about an hour. A very long hour where Demi had to consciously remind herself not to squirm.

When it finally ended, Alan turned to her. "Could we go somewhere and talk?"

Demi bit her lip. "I'm sorry, Alan, we're going to take a little road trip. Another time, all right?"

"Oh, right. Sure." He gave them a tight smile and left through the side door.

Demi felt the tension ease as she looked at Charles. "I'm sorry about all this. All I want right now is to just to be sure about who I am."

He placed an arm over her shoulders. "Don't be sorry." She shivered at the intensity of his gaze. "But I'll tell you this. Even if you never remember anything, I already know who you are. You're beautiful and sweet with an open loving nature that's not easy to find. You have a strength in you that I don't think even you fully understand. But I see it and I admire you. Very much."

Her heart tripped over itself at his gentle words. "Thanks," she whispered.

"Anytime."

Demi's excitement knew no limits as she and Charles walked to his truck. There, they found Ryan leaning against the vehicle. When he saw them, he climbed into the back. Before he shut the door, Demi asked, "You're going with us?"

Charles said, "In light of everything going on, we thought it might be best."

In other words, they were afraid someone would follow them. She gulped. "Okay." Climbing into the front seat, some of her excitement faded.

But not all of it.

Buckling her seat belt, she turned to Charles. "Thanks for doing this."

He smiled at her. "No problem."

Ryan's phone rang and he talked in a low voice. She heard

something about a background check. Demi said to Charles, "Alan offered to take me. I...I didn't want him to."

Charles put the truck in gear and she felt his eyes on her for a brief moment before he said, "I'm glad."

"I wanted to be with you," she almost whispered.

"And you feel guilty because of that?"

Demi looked out her window and nodded. "Is that wrong?" she asked turning to look at him once again.

Charles sighed. "No, I don't think so. And not necessarily because you just want to be with me, although I'd like to think that's why." His wink made her flush but she couldn't help the smile. And felt grateful for it. Charles continued, "But you know me. You're comfortable with me. Alan? You don't know anything about him. Why would you want a complete stranger sharing what's bound to be an emotional experience?"

Demi thought about that for a moment. She had to admit he was right. But she also silently admitted that she wanted to be with him and not Alan because she was in love with Charles. Not Alan.

But apparently she'd loved Alan at one time. Hadn't she?

Confusion and frustration swirled. She'd wanted to know who she was. Now she wasn't so sure she could handle everything that knowledge came with.

Instead of blurting out her feelings with Ryan in the back, she simply said, "That's true."

The rest of the drive was made in silence broken only by Ryan's phone calls.

He finally hung up just as they pulled into the hotel parking lot.

Demi glanced around praying for a spark of a memory. It was a nondescript place, nothing fancy, but not a dump, either.

"Let's go see the clerk," Charles said.

Climbing out of the truck, Demi continued to push her brain. She had a flash, a different one this time. Of running down a dark alley, looking back over her shoulder. She could feel the terror spiking through her and she gasped.

Charles turned and gripped her hand. "Are you all right?"

"Just a memory, I think. I was scared and running from something."

He and Ryan exchanged a look. Together, Charles still holding her hand, they walked into the hotel. The empty lobby echoed their arrival.

The clerk looked up and smiled. "Hi, I'm Martin Fields. You the folks I'm expecting?"

"We are," Charles said as he shook the man's hand.

The clerk's eyes landed on Demi. "Sure, I remember you. Ms. Smith, right?"

"Actually, it's Townsend, but I guess I was registered under Smith."

Confusion flickered, but she felt quite sure it wasn't the first weird story he'd heard. Mr. Fields said, "I'll just get your things."

He disappeared into the back and when he returned, he was holding a laundry basket full of neatly folded clothes. A large cardboard box sat on top of the clothes.

Carrying both items to the dining area to the left of the lobby, he set it down on one of the tables. "You didn't have much and I'm not exactly sure why I kept it, but maybe it was the Lord's leading."

Demi smiled. "I'm sure it was."

Anxiety gripped her. She inspected the laundry. Lifted a blue cotton dress from the top and shook it out. A memory flashed, but it was gone before she could grasp it. Another dress stared up at her. She set the first dress aside and ran her hands over the flower print on the second dress.

"Demi?" Charles's voice reached her through the fog of her scattered thoughts. "Are you okay?"

"I wore this when I flew home," she whispered.

"You remember?"

"Not really...." She bit her lip. "And yet, I do. I remember hugging someone, a woman, in the airport. Then being on a plane." She frowned. "But it's so vague, just bits and pieces. Snatches here and there."

"That's more than you had just a little while ago."

"True." She looked in the cardboard box and pulled out a framed photograph. The woman wore a floppy hat and a long button up shirt. She had weathered skin and a big smile. The man beside her wore khaki shorts and a blue T-shirt. "My parents."

She knew it without question. And felt a longing to see them. Then wrap her arms around them.

A tear slipped down her cheek and she brushed it away.

Charles's comforting presence behind her gave her the strength to pull out the other items. A few toiletries, another picture with her, a young man in his early twenties. Who was he? A friend? A cousin? A brother?

She frowned and went through the rest of the pictures. Biting her lip, she looked up at the men. "I don't have a picture of Alan."

"You don't?" Charles leaned closer.

"No. I wonder why."

"Maybe you had it on you when you were attacked," Ryan suggested.

"Maybe." She opened a small bag and pulled out a small card. "My driver's license!"

Looking at it, she read the address. "Forty-five Lenox Lane."

"That's about twenty minutes from here," the clerk said. When Charles lifted a brow at him, he shrugged. "I rec-

ognize that street. I used to drive a FedEx truck before getting into the hotel business a year ago."

"I want to go home." As soon as she said the words, the
fear hit her. She began to shake.

"Demi?" Ryan asked.

Charles gripped her fingers. "What is it?"

"I can't go home. It's not safe there," she blurted out.

Charles looked at Ryan. "How far from her home was she
found?"

Ryan pulled out his iPhone and looked it up. "About thirty
minutes in the opposite direction from where we are."

The sliding glass door of the hotel shattered inward, spray-
ing them all.

# EIGHTEEN

More bullets peppered the area, and Charles felt his back sting. Had he been shot? No, he'd been shot before and this didn't feel like that.

Without stopping to think, he grabbed Demi and pulled her to the floor. Ryan tackled the clerk. Charles was only seconds behind Ryan in drawing his weapon and heading in the direction from where the shots had come.

He saw a flash from the parking garage across the street and another bullet slammed into the floor in front of him. He ducked and rolled.

"Stay here!" Charles yelled over his shoulder at Demi and the clerk. Not waiting to see if they obeyed him, he and Ryan reached the inside of the first set of sliding glass doors and huddled in the corner. He wasn't sure the shooter was finished.

Ryan copied him on the opposite side.

Warm outside air rushed over Charles, blowing in through the gaping hole in the second set of glass doors. On the street pedestrians cowered behind whatever shelter they could find. Screams still echoed.

"Stay down!" Ryan shouted. "Stay down!"

Someone had followed them. The thought made Charles's

gut churn. They'd been careful, took a winding route, watched their backs. How had they been followed?

And the guy shot into a hotel? Why? That was crazy, wasn't it? What were the odds of hitting a target shooting through two sets of glass doors?

The question puzzled him. But one thing was certain.

Whoever was after him was determined to rub him out of the picture.

But not if Charles found him first. His jaw felt tight enough to shatter. He looked toward the parking garage again. To Ryan, he said, "He's using a high-powered rifle and he's on the third floor of that garage. I'm going after him."

"No, you're not."

Charles glared at Ryan. He wasn't the law in this city, but he was still his brother. "I have to."

Ryan shook his head. "We need to wait for backup."

"By then he'll be gone. This has to end now."

Charles took off for the parking garage.

Feet pounding the pavement, he heard Ryan yelling at him to stop. But he couldn't. He had to find the shooter. His military training kicked in and he zigzagged across the open street to hit the parking garage where the shots had come from. He expected to feel a bullet slam into him and was almost surprised when it didn't happen.

Ryan's shouts still rang in his ears. But he couldn't stop now. He hit the parking garage full-on, weapon drawn. Fortunately, it was mostly empty.

Breaths coming in pants, he scanned the first floor, then headed for the second. Footsteps behind him made him spin.

"Ryan."

The fury in his brother's eyes didn't faze him. The sudden sounds of sirens in the distance didn't stop him.

The law enforcement officers descending upon the garage didn't deter him.

He wanted his life back and he was going to go get it.

Demi felt the hand on her shoulder and turned, thinking Charles had returned through the back door. Instead, she came face-to-face with Alan Gregor. "What are you doing here?" she nearly shrieked. "Are you crazy? Someone's shooting at us!"

"I know." Sweat dripped from his brow. "I knew you were coming here and wanted to be here for you. But I knew you were with…him."

"Then why are you here now?" She flicked her gaze toward the door where Charles and Ryan had disappeared. Still no sign of the men—or the shooter.

Alan was saying, "I wanted to be here for you, Demi. I… well, it was my place to be the support you needed. So, I came anyway." He licked his lips and swiped at the sweat running down a ruddy cheek. "But when I got here, I couldn't make up my mind whether I should come in or not. Then the bullets started flying. I had to get in here and make sure you were okay."

She couldn't be too upset with the man. It wasn't his fault she couldn't remember him. She thought it touching that he would risk his life to help her.

Sirens sounded, lights flashed. Law enforcement descended upon the hotel and the surrounding area.

He grabbed her hand. "Come on, let's find a better place to hide."

"No, I need to stay here. Charles and Ryan went after the shooter and I need to wait on them."

"And what if the shooter decides to come inside? What will you do then?"

He had a point.

Both men had left. But there'd been no more shots. Maybe they already had him in custody.

"The police are here now," she said. "I think we'll be safer in here than out there."

Alan's hands gripped her shoulders. "Come with me, please, Demi. I...I need you to."

His intensity shook her. Why was this so important to him? "Alan..."

Tears pooled in the man's eyes as they hunkered behind the overturned table. "I thought I'd lost you forever. Now I've found you and I need you to come with me. Let me keep you safe this time. Just...let me do that, will you?"

Her heart thudded. Compassion filled her along with the certainty of what she needed to do. She had to tell Alan she couldn't marry him. She needed to call off the engagement. But now definitely wasn't the time. And she wasn't going anywhere with Alan in spite of his apparent need to be her hero in this.

"Come out the back way," he was saying. "I think it's safe now."

She started to refuse, then paused. Officers would be out there. Maybe Charles and Ryan.

"All right," she agreed. "Let's go."

Demi let him lead her toward the back of the hotel. As they opened the door a SWAT member descended upon them. "Hands up, hands up!"

They threw their hands in the air and were led to a safe area.

Demi lowered her hands and Alan clutched one as he pulled the baseball cap lower on his forehead with the other. "They're going to want us to give statements."

Nodding, only half listening, Demi looked around, taking in the chaotic sights and sounds surrounding her. Where was Charles? And Ryan?

Officers separated them as they questioned them. Demi gave the details she could remember even while her eyes scanned the area. Was the shooter gone? Had he managed to get away? Or had Charles and Ryan been able to get to him? Now that she was behind the police-erected safety barriers, she couldn't see the parking garage.

*Please God, keep them safe.*

Charles watched Ryan slink toward where he was sure the bullets had come from. Charles hung around the building, watching Ryan's back. His brother had finally convinced him that while Charles had training as a soldier, he wasn't a cop and couldn't go around acting like one.

But he didn't like it. The waiting, the watching was as nerve-racking here as it had been in Iraq. The familiar tension tightening his shoulders and the rock in his gut—that had started while in the service—returned with a vengeance.

"Clear!" Ryan called. "But he was here." Charles joined him at the edge of the wall of the parking garage. Bullet casings littered the area. A French fry nudged the wall and Charles looked at Ryan.

"Where's the nearest trash can?"

"Over there."

Charles walked over, covered his hand with his shirt, and nudged the top off. It landed with a clatter. Looking inside, he saw several fast food wrappers and drink cups. "All of this needs to be gathered for evidence."

"The CSU team will get that."

Charles walked back to the where the shooter had made himself comfortable and pointed to the scrape on top of the wall. "Look. That's where he rested the weapon."

Ryan sighed and shook his head as he walked away to check out the rest of the area.

But something nagged at him. Again, he studied the surrounding area as the CSU team arrived. Ryan flashed his ID, indicated Charles was with him and the officers got to work.

Charles pulled out his phone and dialed Demi's cell number. It rang four times then went to voice mail. He frowned. Why wouldn't she answer? He tried again.

Again, no answer.

Had she been hurt and he hadn't realized it?

A restless need to get back to Demi washed over him. He looked around. There was nothing more he could do here anyway.

And still something wouldn't leave him alone. He looked at the French fry, the trash can, the wall the shooter had hid behind.

"He was waiting on us."

"What?" One of the officers looked up at him.

"He knew we were going to be here. But how?" Desperately, his mind tossed around conversations he'd had concerning the trip here. He couldn't remember who'd been around when they'd discussed it. But someone had found out and beat them here.

Ryan was deep in conversation with one of the SWAT members. He pointed at Charles who walked toward them.

"It's clear," the officer said. "Shooter fired several shots into the building. He was probably gone before we even got here."

"But why?" Charles asked, puzzled. "There was no way that bullet was going to come near me or anyone else."

"What was his purpose?"

"Who knows?" Charles ran a hand through his hair and looked around. "I thought it was because he followed us here. He thought he'd finally have a chance at me. But I don't think we were followed. I think he knew we'd be here." Charles explained his theory. "But you'd think he'd have picked a better spot. And why didn't he just pick me off as we walked into the hotel?"

"Because he's not after you."

"What?"

"He's after someone else. Demi."

Charles processed Ryan's words and horror hit him. "The shots were a distraction, is that what you're saying?"

"We've been concentrating so hard on who's after you that we've ignored the fact that someone broke into Demi's apartment and left the message."

"You don't belong here," Charles whispered, recalling the message. "Then someone believes she belongs somewhere else."

"And what better way to get to her than to get us out of the way?"

Without another word, the two men whirled and raced toward the now-cleared hotel building.

Charles burst through the shattered doors, the glass crunching under his feet.

His eyes swept the lobby.

Demi was gone.

# NINETEEN

Demi answered the officer's questions as best she could, but she knew she wasn't much help. He finally let them go and she looked for Ryan and Charles to no avail.

Where had they gone? She knew they wouldn't just desert her. Were they hurt? Had they found the shooter?

"Demi, come with me," Alan insisted. "My car's over here."

"No, I need to wait for Charles—and Ryan," she said. "I can't just leave. I have to make sure they're all right."

"They're fine. And it's hot out here. If you want to wait for them, let's at least do it in air-conditioned comfort."

He took her upper arm and urged her to go with him. Looking around, she still didn't see the two men she wanted to see. "I'm not worried about being hot. I'm worried about Charles and Ryan." She pulled away from his grasp and started to turn back the way they'd come.

Alan groaned and stumbled.

Demi stopped and spun to catch his arm. With a gasp, she asked, "Alan? Are you all right?"

"Everything all right?" Demi turned to see the officer who had questioned her. He stood there, his expression concerned. "Sir? You need some help?"

"I'm...diabetic," Alan said. "M...my medicine is in the car."

"I'll get one of the paramedics," Demi blurted out. She turned to go get help and he grabbed her arm, his fingers digging into her skin.

"No," he said. "Please, just help me get to the car and I'll be fine."

Demi cast another glance over her shoulder. Still no sign of Ryan and Charles, but she could no longer see the front of the hotel.

She looked back at Alan and thought he did look flushed. The sheen of sweat across his brow convinced her. "Okay, come on, we'll get your medicine and then I'll check on Charles and Ryan."

"Do you need any assistance?" the officer asked. "It's no trouble to get some medical help over here now."

"No," Alan insisted. "They're busy taking care of anyone who may have been hurt in the shooting. And really, I just need to get to my car and get my medicine. I'll be fine. I promise." He looked at Demi and licked his lips. "But we need to hurry. Please."

Torn, Demi knew she had to help Alan. "Sure. Sure. Let's get it and then I'm going to come back and check on Charles, all right?"

"Yes. Yes, that is fine. Thanks. It's in the glove compartment." He paused as they walked, Alan leaning heavy on her, his breathing ragged. "I'm sorry to put you out."

She took his hand. "It's no trouble." It was, but she couldn't refuse to help the man who'd gone to so much trouble to track her down.

"There," he pointed. "It's the Camry."

At the car, she opened the passenger door.

And felt a hard shove in the middle of her back. She landed

face-first in the driver's seat. "Hey!" Turning, she came in contact with the barrel of a small gun.

Fear exploded in her chest. "Alan?" Disbelief shuddered through her. "What are you doing?"

"Move over," he growled. "Get in the driver's seat."

"No! What…"

His hand came back and slammed against her cheek. She cried out as pain shattered through her.

Along with her memories.

Darkness pressed in on her, but she fought it, refusing to give in and pass out. She needed to think. To remember. To focus.

Her mind spun, her breathing felt forced. And in that instant, clarity hit her.

Alan had done this to her.

And then she didn't have time to think of anything but surviving another attack by the man who'd beaten her and left her for dead. Ignoring the pain, she strived to gather her wits.

"Drive!" His furious shout in her right ear made her flinch. She grabbed the wheel and maneuvered behind it, her cheek throbbing.

Reaching over her, he jammed the keys into the ignition and cranked the car. "Now go!"

Demi put the vehicle in gear, but her hands shook too hard to grasp the steering wheel.

Alan muttered to himself as he glanced out the window, checked the rearview and side mirrors. Demi sat in stunned shock as she tried to sort through the sudden surge of memories, knowledge—and terror. She blinked as she remembered her loving parents. The home she'd grown up in. Friends she'd left in Brazil.

But along with those emotions came a rage like she'd never felt before. She'd been living in the hotel because Alan had scared her. He'd been persistent. Too persistent. When she'd come home to find him in her bedroom one Sunday afternoon, she'd realized something was wrong with the man.

Terror zipped through her.

As did a desperation to survive so she could be with Charles. Make a life with him. Through teeth clenched against the pain, she asked, "Where do you want me to go?"

He jerked as though he had just realized they weren't moving. He looked around. "Shut up. Let me think."

She held her tongue. He started that crazy muttering again. "They're going to wonder where you are. They'll come to your house."

"My house?" She played dumb. "I have a house? Where?"

"But they don't know I was there, they don't know I was the shooter so they can't find me, they won't know where to look." His words jumbled together into one long sentence and it took an effort to not only hear what he was saying, but to understand it.

"You were the one shooting?" Hysteria bubbled near the surface and she pulled in a deep breath as they sat in the car in the middle of the parking lot.

Alan still muttered. "They never saw me, I made sure of that." He grabbed her bag, rummaged through it and then threw it in the back.

"What are you doing?"

"Shut up and drive."

She gulped and put the car in Drive. "You gave a statement, Alan. The officer saw me leave with you." Demi pulled into the traffic going in the opposite direction than where she thought he wanted her to go.

He hadn't noticed yet. He was still thinking. He grinned at her and she wondered why she hadn't noticed before now that his smiles never reached his eyes. He said, "The officer doesn't have any idea who I am. I didn't use my name."

More memories flooded her. After the bedroom incident, he'd sent her flowers. Bought her a puppy she'd insisted he take back to the pet store. As much as she loved animals, she had no place in her life for one. He'd been angry, yelled at her and called her ungrateful. Grabbed her, pulled her against him and told her that she belonged to him and she'd better get used to the idea.

Demi remembered the fear that had filled her at his words, the expression on his face—the bruises on her upper arms the next morning.

And knew he was dangerous.

Demi had decided to leave. To get away from the man until it was time for her to return to Brazil. So she'd checked into the hotel.

"Hey, where are you going?" Alan yelled now.

Demi cringed away from him, scared he would hit her again. "I don't know. You haven't said where to go. I'm just driving. I'll go wherever you want. Just tell me."

Her compliance seemed to calm him.

A little.

"Turn around. No, wait, just go to the next street and turn left. Then make another right."

"Where are you taking me? Why are you doing this?"

He sneered at her. "You're mine." Then his face softened and he reached out a hand to stroke her hair. "From the moment I saw you, talked to you in your parents' yard, I knew you were meant for me."

She gulped, tried not to pull away from the hand still caressing the back of her head and recalled the few conversations they'd had before he'd turned mental on her. He'd seemed kind enough, like an eager puppy who just wanted to be friends.

And then he'd asked her out.

She'd refused because she'd been planning to return to

Brazil and hadn't wanted to start any kind of relationship with a man.

But that wasn't the only reason. As kind as he'd come across, she'd also sensed something, read something in his eyes that had set off her internal alarms. She'd used returning to her parents as an excuse not to go out with him.

He'd taken it well, she'd thought. How very wrong she was. "What made you decide you wanted me? Why me?"

"You were so kind, so gentle. So good with the children in the neighborhood. I watched how they'd run up to you and hug you." He swiped a hand across his face. "And you baked me cookies."

As a friendly gesture. Nothing more. Initially, he'd seemed lonely, sad, and she'd felt sorry for him. "You said you missed your mother's cooking. I was just trying to be nice, to be kind."

"And you were." From the corner of her eye, she saw his jaw tighten. She turned right. He continued. "You were nice. So very nice. Then I asked you out and you ran like a scared rabbit. I was so mad at myself for messing things up." He tapped the gun against the side of his head and let out a humorless chuckle. "Then it came to me. It wasn't me, it was you. You just didn't know what you were missing. You didn't realize that I was perfect for you. So, I decided to show you. But you wouldn't give me the chance to do it."

"Show me how, Alan?" She remembered her version, but wondered what he was thinking, wondered how his twisted mind interpreted her refusal to date him.

"I tried to convince you to go away with me. Just spend some time alone so you could get to know me. Again you refused. Said you could never go away with a man, that it wouldn't look right and you had to avoid all appearances of impropriety because of your job."

And because that's the way God had directed her to live her life.

Three weeks later, Alan had found her at the hotel. How he'd tracked her down, she wasn't sure, but he'd caught her as she'd been coming back from doing a load of laundry.

Her laundry. At the hotel. It had been folded neatly. She gulped. He'd folded her laundry. After he'd left her for dead. She didn't remember the whole attack, but she did remember the first few blows, the exploding pain. The realization that she knew the person attacking her. She remembered thinking she had to fight, to stay awake—or she'd never wake again.

Nausea swirled, her thoughts scattered at the memory and she wanted to scream.

Instead, she bit her tongue, forced her breathing to even out and ordered herself to stay calm. "I'm sorry. That doesn't sound very reasonable of me, does it?"

Satisfaction spread across his face. "Now you get it."

"You put that message in my coffee can, didn't you?"

He snickered. "Yeah."

"Why? What was the point?"

He frowned. "To show you that you didn't belong with that guy."

"Charles?"

"Yes," he snarled, then mocked. "Charles. I followed you, watching you mooning over him, acting all lovey-dovey. Smiling at him, helping him. That should have been me!" His fist slammed onto the dash and Demi jumped, the car swerving to the left. With effort, she pulled it back onto the road and bit her lip to keep the tears at bay.

Alan growled, "You belonged to me. Not him."

"I didn't remember, Alan. I didn't know," she whispered. Anything to settle him down. "Why didn't you just come up to me and tell me all of this when you found me?"

"I didn't know you had amnesia. The news didn't say anything about amnesia," he muttered.

He'd been afraid to approach her. Afraid she would recognize him and turn him into the police. But he'd approached her at the wedding reception.

"When did you realize I had amnesia?"

"I overheard some of the guests at the wedding talking about poor Charles's new and clueless nanny. When I asked what they meant, they were more than happy to fill me in."

And allowed him to come up with a plan to kidnap her.

She turned her gaze back to the road. "Where to now?"

"Make the third left up here."

"Where are we going?"

"We need to make a quick stop."

A stop? Excitement leaped inside her. Would she have a chance to escape?

He smirked. "And don't even think of trying to leave me again. If you do, I'll go straight back to Fitzgerald Bay and kill every one of Charles Fitzgerald's precious family members. Including his two little brats."

Demi's heart sank. Would he really? Could he?

Yes, he would. She had no guarantee she could get to a phone fast enough to warn Charles and his family.

She was trapped.

"And then," Alan said gleefully, "we're going to my house—our house. The house where we'll live after we're married."

# TWENTY

Charles was ready to punch something. "Where is she?"

His question met with silence.

Ryan's phone rang and he answered it. Charles moved in so he could hear and Ryan complied by pressing the speaker phone button.

Owen's voice came over the line. "Get this. Alan Gregor was indeed in Iraq, but his time line is off. His statement that he was a contractor was true, but he disappeared days before that IED exploded on the convoy. No one died, either. He was listed as AWOL. When they finally located him, they placed him in a mental institution. He just got out a few months ago."

Charles felt the blood drain from his face.

Ryan said, "Send me Alan's picture. I might need it."

"Sure thing."

"What else you got?"

"Nothing on Alan yet, but we released the information about that charm that was found at the crime scene where Olivia was killed."

"And?"

"We're hoping someone will recognize it and be able to tell us who it belongs to."

"But nothing yet?"

"No. That piece of the puzzle is still missing."

Missing along with someone he loved. The silent admission didn't even surprise. Yes, he loved Demi. And she'd told him that she loved him, too.

At first, the words had rocked him, but even as he'd struggled to absorb what that meant, he knew without a doubt that he wanted a future with her.

And now she was missing. The fact that something may have happened to her sent terror shooting through him.

Charles did his best to calm his fears as he cut his eyes to Ryan. "We can worry about all that later. I have a bad feeling about the danger Demi is in and we need to find her now."

Ryan said, "Be prepared to get down here, Owen. Something's going on and I have a feeling things are going to get dicey." He hung up and looked at Charles. "Let's ask around, see if we can figure out who she left with."

After questioning several people, they finally hit pay dirt when they approached the officer in charge of the scene and showed him Demi's picture. "Have you seen this woman?" Charles asked.

"Yeah, she was here a little while ago." The man's name tag read R. Luther.

Excitement leaped inside Charles. "Did you see where she went?"

Officer Luther's eyes squinted as he took another look at the picture Charles had on his phone. "Yeah, she got in a car with some guy. I remember because the guy looked like he might have been sick, was leaning on her pretty heavy. Think he said he was diabetic. I offered to get some medical help for him, but he said he had a kit in his car and would be fine. I was needed over here so I left them to it."

Charles felt slightly better. "That sounds like Demi. If someone needed help, she'd be the first one to offer. But why would she get in his car? And why wouldn't she call me and let me know what she was doing?" He looked at Ryan, his heart still troubled. "She would know I would be worried about her. This is really out of character for her."

"Sorry, can't help you with that," Officer Luther said. He paused then rubbed his chin and said, "It was kind of weird, though."

"What was?" Charles demanded.

The officer shrugged. "I turned back just for a second look to make sure he hadn't passed out or anything and noticed she got in the passenger side then slid over to the driver's seat."

Ryan and Charles exchanged another look. Ryan said, "You're right, that's weird. I don't like the sound of that."

"I mean she could have been trying to help, get the kit, and he asked her to drive him to the hospital for all I know," Luther said. "But I remember thinking it was kind of strange. Then my boss called and I got distracted." He grimaced. "Sorry."

Ryan shook his head. "The only reason I can think of for that kind of maneuver is if he was forcing her to go with him."

Charles's relief morphed back into worry. He looked at the officer. "Did you see a weapon?"

"No." He frowned. "But that doesn't mean he didn't have one."

"What kind of car was he driving?"

The officer rubbed his eyes then said, "I'm not sure. Some kind of sedan." He sighed. "Look, I'm sorry, things were crazy over here and I had already talked to those two, my boss was calling…" He trailed off, glanced back where the car had been then said, "It was blue. I do remember that."

Charles felt his heart skip a beat. Then had a wild idea. To Ryan, he said, "Show him the picture of Alan."

With a raised brow, Ryan asked, "You think she could have left with him?"

"I don't know. But I do know that he's unhinged and he wants Demi. Can't hurt to ask."

Ryan complied. "Was this the guy she was with?"

Officer Luther nodded. "Yeah, that could be him. He had on a baseball cap, but yeah…it looks like him." Then he frowned again as he pulled out a little notebook. He flipped a few pages then said, "But his name wasn't Alan. He said his name was Christopher Holden."

"I don't like this," Charles stated. "Something's not right with this."

"I agree." Ryan nodded, his eyes troubled.

"We need to track them down. And fast."

Ryan's gaze rested on the corner of the bank's building. "We've got all the footage of the shooting from the video cameras. Now we need to watch them again and see if we can get a plate off the car Demi got into."

"Where was the car parked?" Ryan asked the officer.

Officer Luther pointed. "Over there in that lot across the street, somewhere around the middle. I watched them for a little while to make sure he didn't collapse and need more help. But they made it to the car fine."

Ryan nodded his thanks then said to Charles, "Let's go watch that footage." He snagged a uniformed officer. "Do you mind checking that parking lot for a camera?" He explained in detail the area he particularly wanted to know about.

Five minutes later, in the security office of the hotel, Charles stood behind his brother while Ryan scanned the footage, running it through to the appropriate time. And then he pointed. "There she is. Demi and someone exiting the building. But it's from the back."

"And now they're out of range. They're off the camera." Ryan slapped his thigh in disgust.

Charles felt his fear blossom. How was he going to find Demi?

Prayers formed on his lips even as he kept his eyes on the next camera.

The officer Ryan had sent to check on the camera in the parking lot came in, phone tucked against his ear. "I've got it. They're in a blue Camry." He looked at Charles as he bolted to his feet, ready for action when Ryan pointed to the video that was now being fed to the monitor he watched. He said, "It looks like he forced her into the car."

"We've got to get her. Now," Charles barked. "How are we going to find her?"

"I've already got a trace on her cell phone." He looked at Charles. "You got her a good one. The GPS is on and we're tracking them now. And I've got a helicopter on the way."

Charles felt the tightness in his chest ease slightly. Demi was still in the hands of a madman, but at least they had a way to find her.

Ryan listened a few more seconds then frowned. "They're stopped? Where?" He looked at Charles. "Dedham."

Charles said, "You need to get the local police to the location."

"On it," Ryan said.

Charles paced, feeling like he should be doing something. Why would Alan take her to Dedham? Dedham was a small town, even smaller than Fitzgerald Bay.

Where strangers would stand out. Alan had to know that the authorities would put Demi's picture on the news again once they realized she was missing.

"That's not right," he said. "That's not them. He wouldn't just drive thirty miles then stop."

"Maybe he's not done. Maybe he's just stopped for gas or something."

"No, it doesn't make sense."

"He's not going to act or think like a rational human being. He's unpredictable," Owen agreed.

Charles gulped. "Which makes him all the more dangerous."

"Exactly."

Charles felt helpless. He paced, his limp more pronounced. The way it always got when he was under a lot of stress. Ignoring it, he ran a hand through his hair and then finally stopped, dropped his chin to his chest and sighed. *God, please be there for Demi. I don't know what's going on with her or where she is, but please keep her safe.*

"How close are the local police?" Charles asked. He paced forward, then back in the small room.

Ryan relayed the question. "They're there. They've tracked her cell phone to a car." He paused as he listened. "But it's a black Honda driven by a couple in their sixties."

Charles's head snapped up. "He knew we'd track her. Alan slipped her phone into another car." Now the fear swamped him, threatening to suffocate him. "Why didn't she get away from him before now?" he murmured. "Does he have her tied up?" The thought sickened him and he forced himself not to dwell on those kinds of thoughts.

"I've got the airport covered, the major bus lines, the train station. I've got a BOLO out on his Camry." Ryan shook his head. "We'll just have to see what comes in."

"No." Charles refused to accept the wait-and-see attitude. "This guy was in a mental hospital. He's not thinking right— or straight." Charles closed his eyes and pulled on every bit of psychology he'd ever studied. "He'll want to go somewhere familiar, somewhere comfortable. If he's been fixated on Demi, he'll take her to a place that has meaning to him."

"Where? His home?"

Charles nodded. "Yes, that's the first place we need to look."

"But where does he live?"

"He was her next-door neighbor," Charles whispered. "Go to Demi's address in Springfield and we'll find Alan's house."

Ryan shook his head but didn't disagree. He just said, "It's a long shot."

"I know it is. But it's the only shot we've got right now."

Demi squirmed in her seat, desperate for an opening. She had to get away from Alan or she wouldn't live to see nightfall.

Unless she went along with him. Possibly. But it would take all her acting skills and she didn't know if she could do it.

But she had to.

If she wanted to live.

She looked at him. "Where were we going to live after we were married?"

Alan's gaze shot to her. "Keep your eyes on the road."

Demi complied. He continued, "In my house, of course." From the corner of her eye, she saw his jaw tightened. "Pretty soon you'll forget all about that Charles guy and we'll start a family and live like we were meant to live."

Demi swallowed hard. He was delusional. Did he really think it was possible to do that? She looked at him again then quickly back in front of her. "I don't know, Alan. It's pretty hard to just pick up with someone you don't even remember."

His hand reached out to stroke her cheek and she forced herself not to cringe from him. Instead, she swallowed the sudden nausea and concentrated on driving. "Where do I go now?"

She didn't want to let on that she'd regained her memory. There was no telling how that would affect him. Her cheek throbbed a steady beat, a reminder that she was in the company of a vicious man.

"Just keep going on this road. I'll give you plenty of notice where to turn."

"Okay." Her easy agreement seemed to calm him and Demi drew in a steadying breath. As long as she was driving, she was alive.

Where was Charles? She glanced in the rearview mirror as though she expected to see him behind her. Cars passed her on the left and she had a white Chevy behind, but none of them were the red truck she longed to see. Then again, if he realized what had happened to her, he might be riding with someone else.

Her heart-sent prayers to the one she knew could deliver her from this situation. *Please, Lord, let Charles find me. Provide a way for me to escape. I love Charles, Lord, and believe You sent me to him and his family for a reason. Please, please, deliver me from this man.*

She drove and prayed and Alan fell silent. She knew where she was going. He was taking her to her home. Only she knew it wouldn't be to her parents' house.

It would be to his.

But hope swelled. Charles knew where she lived. He would be looking for her. Maybe when Charles arrived, she could signal him somehow. Let him know she was next door. Her mind clicked with everything she could try. Devising plan after plan, she discarded one after the other.

After another forty-five minutes of silence, Alan perked up. "Get off at this exit then make a left at the stop sign."

She did. They were about ten minutes from their destination. She checked the rearview mirror again. Still no sign of Charles—or anyone else—looking for her.

Her knotted stomach twisted into a solid ball of fear.

"Slow down. Turn here."

A helicopter thumped overhead and Demi felt a leap in her

pulse. Could it be searching for her? Alan tensed and stuck his head out the window to stare at the chopper.

The chopper hovered for a brief moment then it banked right and flew off.

Alan relaxed back into the seat and gave a low chuckle.

Tears threatened again.

She'd held her fear in so tight and now that they were almost to Alan's house, she felt like she might explode. And then she was in the driveway. Turning, she begged, "Please, Alan, let me go. Do you really want to be with someone who doesn't want to be with you?"

The fist that cracked against her face seemed to come from nowhere.

Darkness blanketed her.

# TWENTY-ONE

"We've got them," Ryan reported from the backseat. "The helicopter spotted the car. Demi was driving and Alan stuck his head out of the window to stare up at the helicopter so the pilot peeled off. But he circled back to see the vehicle turn into the subdivision. The car is now in the garage."

He'd been right. Charles sat in the passenger seat of Owen's car and felt some of the horrid fear ease somewhat. They knew where she was. Now they just had to get her away from that madman without him killing her.

Charles looked at Owen who was driving. "Can't this thing go any faster?"

"I'm already doing a hundred." The blue lights swirled on the dash and Charles felt the seat belt cut into his shoulder as he leaned forward.

"We're not going to get there any faster by you giving yourself a heart attack. Sit back and try to get your blood pressure under control."

Good advice from his brother, but an impossible feat.

He did lean back, but his fists stayed clenched on his thighs. "I just want thirty seconds alone with him."

Owen nodded. "I know you do, but this guy doesn't fight fair."

Charles snorted. "I didn't exactly have fair in mind."

"Right."

Silence descended.

"Local police are at the scene," Ryan reported. "They're watching and waiting for us to arrive."

"Good," Owen said.

Charles asked, "Have they seen her? Can they get a look through the windows?"

"No, the blinds are pulled and there are heavy curtains over the blinds."

Charles continued his prayers as they pulled off on the exit that would lead them to Demi.


Demi groaned. Her head pounded into a migraine so fierce she thought she might die. Nausea swirled and she rolled to her side.

"Demi? Demi? I know you're awake. I've been watching you."

Memories returned full force. She knew who she was. She knew who Alan Gregor was.

And she knew she was going to die today.

But the way her head felt, dying might be a relief.

Something cool touched her lips.

Water. She took a sip, then another. It tasted bitter and she grimaced. Her stomach rebelled.

Demi let out another pained groan and lay back as gently as possible. "My head," she whispered.

"I know. But that will pass. I put a mild narcotic in there to help with the pain." A cool cloth touched her forehead, covered her eyes and for a moment she panicked, but it felt so good, she decided to leave it there. Alan continued in what he probably thought was his soothing voice. "I didn't want to hit you. But you just made me so mad when you asked me to let you go that I decided you needed some severe discipline in order for you to understand."

Understand? Understand what?

"Because I will never let you go. And if you ask me again, I will punish you again. Are we clear?"

"Yes," she said simply.

The headache receded from migraine to just really bad.

"Good." He sounded satisfied.

"It was you all along," she whispered. "You were the one in the gray hoodie."

"Yes. I tracked you down and was determined to bring you back here. Where you belong. You didn't belong there."

"And that night, in the bookstore. That was you, too?"

"Yes again. Only I wasn't fast enough. I didn't know the layout of the store and you got away from me. Then cops got there so fast..." She could almost picture him shrugging, but didn't want to open her eyes yet. He said, "And yes, that was my message in the church where you were looking all lovey-dovey at Fitzgerald."

The hard tone returned to his voice and she knew she needed to get him talking about something else. "Tell me about my parents."

"I've never met them. One day, once you've accepted your position here with me, I will allow you to introduce us."

The nausea faded a bit and she pulled in a relieved breath.

"You have some color back in your cheeks. Feeling better?" he asked.

"No."

A quiet sigh filtered to her ears. "I'll give you a few more minutes, then we can talk again."

Talking was about the last thing she wanted to do right now.

Unless it was with Charles.

She heard Alan's footsteps recede then the quiet click of the door.

The slamming of the dead bolt jolted her and the cloth

slipped from her eyes onto the bed where she lay. Still she kept her eyes shut.

Her entire face hurt. Her cheek, her jaw. Her head. Everything.

Going by feel, she picked up the cloth and placed it against her throbbing cheek. With every heartbeat, pain pulsed.

But she couldn't lie there. She needed to find a way out of—

Where was she?

Pulling the cloth from her eyes, she squinted, wincing at the shaft of agony caused by the light.

Ignoring the pain, she sat up and did her best to take in her surroundings.

She was in a bedroom. Whose? Alan's? She shuddered. The furniture appealed to her taste, though. Not terribly masculine, but not overly feminine, either. Demi had the awful thought that he'd actually picked it out with her in mind. Another shiver racked her.

She frowned and let her eyes wander from the dresser to the door.

Then back to the window.

She slid gently from the bed, keeping one hand on the edge to keep her balance. Standing, she swayed, caught herself then stayed still until the room stopped spinning and the lightning-sharp pain dulled to a jackhammer throb.

"Please, Lord…" she whispered as she stumbled to the window. "Please let me see Charles again."

She yanked back the curtain—and stared at a cement wall. A sob threatened to break through. She swallowed it and pulled the curtain again into place.

Vaguely, she wondered if Alan could see her. Was he monitoring her with hidden cameras?

She decided she didn't care. She moved to one of the two doors and twisted the knob. The door opened easily and her heart leaped. Then sank to her toes when she stepped into a bathroom. She turned in a circle taking in the perfectly matched towels, little soaps on the sink and the exact brand of facial cleanser that she used.

She stepped away and felt the wall touch her back. Sliding down to the floor, she rested her aching forehead on her bent knees and sobbed.

Charles felt every muscle in his body go rigid when they pulled onto the street where Demi was being held. Still no sighting or any activity had been reported. Charles continued to pray.

They parked and Ryan said, "Stay here."

"Not a chance." Charles didn't wait for permission. He'd been trained to fight, to face his battles. He'd even been involved in rescuing a fellow marine who'd been captured and held hostage by a group of Iraqi refugees.

And he had his weapon.

Ryan didn't argue with him. Instead, his brother approached the command truck that had parked out of sight of the house. Charles followed him.

Once inside the van, Ryan introduced himself to the man in charge, Detective Pierce Sands. Ryan asked him, "Anything?"

Detective Sands shook his head. "I've got a SWAT team on the way. We're getting our equipment in place to get eyes and ears in there. Right now, I have orders to let you be the lead on this since you know the suspect and the victim."

Charles watched the action for a few moments, then turned to study the house. It was an older home, probably thirty to forty years old. From the front, it looked like a single-story house, but he'd overheard Ryan talking about the layout and knew it had a basement. The house next door was Demi's parents' house. The house she'd grown up in. He wondered if it had triggered any memories when she'd seen it.

The small utility shed next to Alan's house looked strange. Out of place. Who put a utility shed *beside* his house? But Alan had proved he wasn't stable and Charles longed to rush the house and pull Demi from that madman's clutches.

Action erupted.

The SWAT team had arrived.

Charles watched as officers swarmed toward the house in silent fashion planting themselves around the perimeter. Alan would not be getting out of that house through any of the doors or windows.

Charles stepped out of the van and watched, praying Demi was all right.

One of the officers with a megaphone yelled, "Alan Gregor, we have you surrounded. Let your hostage go and come out of the house."

Charles waited for a response.

Nothing.

Would he harm Demi when he realized he had nowhere to go?

Gut in a knot, heart beating fast enough to make him light-headed, Charles continued to watch. And wait.

"How did they find me!" Alan screamed as the door to her prison slammed open. Demi held herself rigid. If he hit her again, she wouldn't be able to function. She was barely managing it now.

Passing out would not help the situation. Alan paced, the gun held at his side. He turned on her. "How did they know?" His eyes narrowed and he lifted the gun to point it at her. "You told them."

Demi's heart fluttered. Fear strangled her. "How would I do that, Alan? You threw my cell phone away and I've been with you since we left. I didn't tell them anything, I promise. And remember? The night of the reception? You told me we were neighbors. Charles was sitting there listening." She kept her words calm, praying they were the right words and wouldn't send him off on another tangent.

He stopped. "I did?" Then he gripped his head with both hands, the gun mashed against his skull. "No, I didn't! I wouldn't say that!" He calmed so fast she blinked. He said, "But you're right. You couldn't tell them. And you wouldn't, would you? Because you want to be with me, right?"

"Right." She swallowed hard at the lie and then took a chance. "Do you want me to tell them to go away? That I'm here because I want to be?"

He jerked. "You would do that?"

"If it would help, I would." Help her get out of here.

He walked over and grabbed her upper arm and yanked her toward the door. "Stay in front of me."

She obeyed, climbing the stairs, her heart beating fast as she could almost taste her freedom.

One thing for sure, she wasn't going back down those steps alive.

At the top, they turned left and he steered her with a rough hand toward the front door. "They've got me surrounded," he hissed. "I know how this works. The only way I'm going to get out of this is if you make them believe you want to be here."

She stayed calm, heart racing, knowing that Charles was probably somewhere outside the door. She knew that with all her heart.

The phone rang and Alan jerked. The movement jarred her head and she winced. He either didn't notice or didn't care. "Answer it."

She reached out a shaking hand. "Hello?"

"Is this Demi?"

"Yes, Ryan, hi. It's good to hear your voice."

"Are you all right?"

With a look at Alan's wild eyes, Demi forced a lightness into her voice. "Of course I'm all right."

"Is he listening in?"

Demi flicked a glance at Alan whose eyes roamed the room, never resting, never still. She needed to send a message to Ryan. What could she say? "No, no, I assure you, I'm fine. How are you?"

"He's not listening."

"That's right, we just got here a few minutes ago."

A pause. "My sniper needs a visual. The den blinds are partially open. Can you maneuver Alan in front of them?"

"I don't know. Possibly."

"Tell me where he's standing, can you do that?"

Alan gestured for her to give him the phone.

She hurried to say, "Sure, but um…he wants to talk to you."

Demi held out the phone to her kidnapper and he snatched it from her. "Hello?" He paused and frowned. Then said, "She's here because she wants to be. No, you can't speak to her again. You've already heard that she's fine." Alan listened a few more minutes then rolled his eyes with a huff. "Here, she'll tell you one more time, then you leave. Right?"

Demi took the phone back and pressed it against her ear. "Yes, I want to be here."

Alan motioned with the gun and hissed. "Tell them something useful. Convince them you want to be here."

She nodded and swallowed hard. Holding the handset, she moved toward the den area, the open blinds Ryan had mentioned. Alan stayed right on her, following her, lapping up her words. "I…I mean, why wouldn't I? He's got a beautiful kitchen with granite countertops." Alan's chest puffed a bit and he smiled, nodding his approval. She moved again and so did Alan. "And he's obviously spent time caring for the place." She hitched a breath as Alan moved closer, his smile growing. Demi touched the mantel, praising the craftsmanship. Alan backed up and let her regale them with what a good job he'd done with the house.

"And the…uh…window in the living area is just gorgeous. I know you can't see in because of the drapes, but about two feet to *your* left is Alan's…um, his favorite painting." Would they get it? Couldn't they see him by now? She continued. "And I'm just loving it because from where I'm standing over near the fireplace, I can see…"

The window she'd just described exploded.

Alan screamed and went down.

The front door imploded and Demi launched herself toward it.

"Demi!" Alan's yell of fury propelled her faster.

And then she slipped.

She felt her neck jerk in a whiplash as Alan's hand snagged itself in her hair. Pain like she'd only felt the night Alan had beat her and left her for dead ricocheted through her. The men in the SWAT gear with rifles pointed faded from her vision.

Alan jammed the gun against the side of her head and everyone froze. Without a word to the men yelling at him to put the gun down, he started backing up. A warm wetness soaked into the back of her right shoulder.

Alan had been shot, but not bad enough to slow him down.

His ragged breathing echoed in her ear. He called her a few choice names then told her, "Keep going. Into the kitchen. Should have just done this to begin with, but I was hoping you could convince them…make them go away…leave us alone. Now we're going to be running forever. Stupid. Stupid."

"Alan, please…" She tried to interrupt his senseless mutterings.

The pressure of the barrel increased. "Move. Now." She backed up like he'd ordered.

Into the large walk-in pantry.

Charles held back and watched, weapon ready as the SWAT team flooded the house. He's heard the scream as the shot entered the window, but now he could make no sense of the jumble of yells coming from inside the house.

He itched to be in the middle of it and for the first time since returning from Iraq, he wished he'd joined the police force.

"Come on, come on."

Then he heard, "He's gone!"

Charles froze. No. He was in there. They'd talked to Demi, taken her cue and shot through the window where she had told them to shoot.

Charles looked at the house next door. Demi's house.

And saw movement from the shed.

The door opened and Charles saw Alan push Demi in front of him out into the sunlight.

He raced toward them, weapon pointed, just as two SWAT team members saw them, too. Charles hollered, "Freeze, Alan!"

Alan whirled and yanked Demi in front of him.

Demi saw Charles sprinting for them. Felt the barrel of the gun back against her head.

And had had enough. "No!" she cried as she went limp.

The move pulled Alan off balance. Her hair felt like it was being pulled out by the roots.

More gunshots echoed around her and then silence.

"Demi!"

"Charles," she whispered. Why did he sound so far away?

She felt his arms go around her and pull her away from Alan's dead body.

# TWENTY-TWO

Charles held her against him, his heart racing. "Demi," he whispered against her battered cheek.

She wilted and if he hadn't had his arms around her, she would have hit the ground. Paramedics on standby now rushed to Demi.

"Ma'am? Can we check you out?"

Charles wanted to tell them he'd do it himself, that he never wanted to let her go, but she pulled away and sank onto the gurney one of the paramedics had rolled toward him.

"He just hit me. It'll heal," she said, her voice dull, defeated.

"I'm a doctor. She needs X-rays," Charles insisted.

The man nodded. "I agree. We'll transport her."

"I'm going with you." Charles climbed in the back and let the one paramedic do his job while the other drove. Charles watched Demi, concerned with her silence, the empty look in her eyes.

But the fact that she held his hand with no apparent inclination to let go gave him hope.

Once Demi was settled in at the emergency department, Charles waited outside the curtain. A rather new and unsettling experience for him. In the future he vowed to have a little more compassion for those waiting on this side.

"How is she?"

Owen's voice intruded and Charles turned to find Ryan with him. "Hey, she's all right, I think. Thanks for everything you guys did."

Ryan slapped Charles on the back. "You're the hero. You're the one who spotted them coming out of the shed."

Owen shook his head. "Who would have figured? He had a set of stairs leading from the pantry in the kitchen, down then over and back up into the shed. Very weird dude."

"I thought that shed looked out of place where it was located, but…" Charles glanced toward the curtain that sheltered Demi. "It doesn't matter now. I'm just glad she's all right."

Owen looked at Ryan. "You want to tell him or you want me to?"

Charles lifted a brow. "Tell me what?"

Ryan said, "You've been cleared in Olivia's murder."

At first, Charles couldn't move. Then relief exploded through him as he said, "What? How? When?"

"Today. Dad called while we were headed over here. We filled him in on all the excitement then he said the DNA report came back. There were two different DNA samples on the rock that was found at the murder scene. The one that's been labeled the murder weapon. One of them was a match for Olivia's DNA, the other one is definitely not yours."

Charles wasn't sure what to say, what to think. For so long, the word *murderer* had been an albatross around his neck.

"Thanks, guys."

"Expect to be flooded with apologies by Fitzgerald Bay residents," Ryan said. "By Meghan Henry, too."

Charles felt months of tension leave his shoulders. Before anyone could speak, the doctor stepped from behind the curtain. "You can see her now, Charles."

"Thanks." Charles looked at his brothers. "Excuse me."

Then he was standing by Demi's bed. She had her eyes closed, her head turned away from him.

"Demi?" She rolled her head to look at him and he gave an inward wince at her battered face. He took her hand. "Hi."

She blinked up at him and licked her lips. "Who are you?"

Charles's heart hit his toes—until he saw the twinkle in her green eyes. He groaned. "You got me."

Her lips twitched. "I'm sorry, I couldn't resist."

He leaned over and planted a kiss on her lips. A soft, lingering kiss filled with all the love bursting through his heart.

She gave a small sigh as he pulled away. Then she frowned. "How can you stand to look at me? I resemble some horror-movie monster."

Through the lump in his throat, he said, "You're the most beautiful woman in the world to me."

Demi felt the tears leak from the corners of her eyes. "I love you, Charles," she whispered.

"I love you, Demi." He gave a low chuckle. "I can't believe I'm saying those words, but I mean each one of them."

Brilliant joy erupted within her. "I want to call my parents."

He grinned. "I already did."

"What do you mean?"

He flushed and looked so much like Aaron, she lifted a brow then winced at the move. Still, she asked, "Charles, what did you do?"

"I...um...asked your father for permission to marry you."

Demi felt her breath catch and for a long moment she stared into those gorgeous blue eyes. "Really?"

"Really."

"What did he say?" She couldn't imagine. Her father was her protector, the man she'd looked up to all her life. What would he say about her marrying a man she'd only known for a short time. A man her parents hadn't even met yet?

"He said he'd let me know after he met me. Then I happened to mention I had two-year-old twins and he offered to bring the minister to the house."

Demi burst out laughing then groaned as her head reminded her that wasn't a good move. But it didn't diminish her joy one bit. "They've dreamed of grandchildren for a long time." She blinked at the sudden surge of tears and whispered, "I can't believe this is happening."

Charles gently sat beside her on the bed and leaned over for another sweet kiss. Then he placed his forehead against hers, smiled into her eyes and whispered back, "Believe it."

\* \* \* \* \*

Dear Reader,

Thank you so much for joining me on Demi and Charles's journey to find God and love for one another. This book is part of a continuity series so there was one issue that was left unresolved at the end of the story. I hope you'll find the last book and see how everything works out in the end. :)

As always, it's an honor to write these stories, to create the characters and breathe life into them. To watch them grow and learn as they deal with what life hands them. Truthfully, even though these characters aren't real, they still teach me! They remind me that God is an incredible God and that He loves me unconditionally. I need that reminder often! I pray that if you're going through a tough time right now, that you will cling to God and let Him walk with you through it.

Until next time, God Bless,

Lynette Eason

## Questions for Discussion

1. Demi works for Charles and is warned about him being a suspect in a murder investigation. Do you think she was foolish to take the job without knowing for sure whether he killed his former nanny or not?

2. Charles's wife left him when things got too hard. Instead of sticking around and trying to work things out, she ran. What do you do when things get hard? Who do you turn to?

3. What was your favorite scene in this book? Why?

4. What did you think of Demi's decision not to get involved with Charles while she still didn't know her identity? Did you think it made sense? Why?

5. Demi wasn't sure how she felt about God simply because she couldn't remember whether she believed in Him or not. Yet her first inclination was to pray. Do you find that believable? Why or why not?

6. Demi is overwhelmed by the large Fitzgerald family and yet she wants to belong. Have you ever felt like an outsider looking in? What was your reaction?

7. What do you think about someone who is so obsessed with his own world, his own goals that it doesn't matter who he hurts in his quest to achieve those goals? Do you know anyone like this?

8. Was there a character in the book that you identified with more than the others? If so, who and why?

9. Charles desperately wanted to do the right thing by Demi and not start a relationship with her and yet he couldn't stop himself from falling in love with her. In spite of his feelings, however, he acted honorably. What do you think of his actions? Do you agree he did the right thing?

10. Do you think Demi was a brave, courageous woman? Or just lost?

11. When Alan appeared in the picture, Demi was stunned. Charles wasn't happy, either. He thought he was going to lose Demi and that scared him. Have you ever felt that you were going to lose someone you loved to another person? What did you do about it?

12. Demi was upset with Alan's appearance, but she was excited, too, because Alan knew her, her identity. Do you blame her for wanting to talk with Alan? Spend time with him? What would you have done if you'd been in Demi's shoes?

13. Alan played on Demi's sympathies to get her into his car. Do you think she should have been more careful or would you have done the same thing if you'd been in her place?

14. When Charles realizes that Demi's been kidnapped and that she's in physical danger, he's determined to save her. And yet, he's not the police. He's frustrated because he feels like his hands are tied. Can you think of anything Charles could have done differently?

15. When Charles's wife left him, he turned from God. He wasn't necessarily angry with God, just apathetic. And yet as the story progresses, we see God drawing Charles back to Himself. How is your relationship with God? Are you angry with Him? Apathetic toward Him? What can you do to draw nearer to Him today?

W9-AJT-863

$\mathscr{D}$on't miss a single misadventure
of the marvelous mistress of mystery—
as Miss Seeton...

witnesses a murder at the opera in PICTURE MISS SEE-
TON ... investigates a local witches' coven in WITCH
MISS SEETON ... assists Scotland Yard in MISS SEE-
TON DRAWS THE LINE ... mixes with a gang of Euro-
pean counterfeiters in MISS SEETON SINGS ... dons
diamonds and furs for a game of roulette in ODDS ON
MISS SEETON ... encounters trouble at a tennis match in
ADVANTAGE MISS SEETON ... visits Buckingham Pal-
ace in MISS SEETON BY APPOINTMENT ... takes a
cruise to the Mediterranean in MISS SEETON AT THE
HELM ... foils some roadside bandits in MISS SEETON
CRACKS THE CASE ... helps to solve a series of suspi-
cious fires in MISS SEETON PAINTS THE TOWN ...
stumbles into a nest of crime in HANDS UP, MISS SEE-
TON ... helps to capture an art thief in MISS SEETON
BY MOONLIGHT ... calls on her maternal instincts to
solve a crime in MISS SEETON ROCKS THE CRADLE
... attends a cricket game in MISS SEETON GOES TO
BAT ... tends to her garden—and roots out a killer—in
MISS SEETON PLANTS SUSPICION ... plays a back-
stage role at the Plummergen Christmas pageant in STAR-
RING MISS SEETON ... and helps trap some murderous
antique thieves in MISS SEETON UNDERCOVER.

Available from Berkley Prime Crime Books!

# MORE MYSTERIES FROM THE
# BERKLEY PUBLISHING GROUP . . .

**THE HERON CARVIC MISS SEETON MYSTERIES:** Retired art teacher Miss Seeton steps in where Scotland Yard stumbles. "A most beguiling protagonist!"

—*New York Times*

*by Heron Carvic*
MISS SEETON SINGS
MISS SEETON DRAWS THE LINE
WITCH MISS SEETON
PICTURE MISS SEETON
ODDS ON MISS SEETON

*by Hampton Charles*
ADVANTAGE MISS SEETON
MISS SEETON AT THE HELM
MISS SEETON, BY APPOINTMENT

*by Hamilton Crane*
HANDS UP, MISS SEETON
MISS SEETON CRACKS THE CASE
MISS SEETON PAINTS THE TOWN
MISS SEETON BY MOONLIGHT
MISS SEETON ROCKS THE CRADLE
MISS SEETON GOES TO BAT
MISS SEETON PLANTS SUSPICION
STARRING MISS SEETON
MISS SEETON UNDERCOVER
MISS SEETON RULES
SOLD TO MISS SEETON

**SISTERS IN CRIME:** Criminally entertaining short stories from the top women of mystery and suspense. "Excellent!" —*Newsweek*

*edited by Marilyn Wallace*
SISTERS IN CRIME
SISTERS IN CRIME 2
SISTERS IN CRIME 3

SISTERS IN CRIME 4
SISTERS IN CRIME 5

**KATE SHUGAK MYSTERIES:** A former D.A. solves crimes in the far Alaska north . . .

*by Dana Stabenow*
A COLD DAY FOR MURDER
DEAD IN THE WATER
A FATAL THAW

A COLD-BLOODED BUSINESS
PLAY WITH FIRE

**FORREST EVERS MYSTERIES:** A former race-car driver solves the high-speed crimes of world-class racing . . . "A Dick Francis on wheels!" —*Jackie Stewart*

*by Bob Judd*
BURN
CURVE

SPIN

**INSPECTOR BANKS MYSTERIES:** Award-winning British detective fiction at its finest . . . "Robinson's novels are habit-forming!" —*West Coast Review of Books*

*by Peter Robinson*
THE HANGING VALLEY
WEDNESDAY'S CHILD

PAST REASON HATED
FINAL ACCOUNT

**CASS JAMESON MYSTERIES:** Lawyer Cass Jameson seeks justice in the criminal courts of New York City in this highly acclaimed series . . . "A witty, gritty heroine."

—*New York Post*

*by Carolyn Wheat*
FRESH KILLS

DEAD MAN'S THOUGHTS

HERON CARVIC'S MISS SEETON

# Miss Seeton Rules

## Hamilton Crane

BERKLEY PRIME CRIME, NEW YORK

If you purchased this book without a cover, you should be aware that
this book is stolen property. It was reported as "unsold and destroyed"
to the publisher, and neither the author nor the publisher has received
any payment for this "stripped book."

MISS SEETON RULES

A Berkley Prime Crime Book / published by arrangement with
the author and the Estate of Heron Carvic

PRINTING HISTORY
Berkley Prime Crime hardcover edition / October 1994
Berkley Prime Crime paperback edition / October 1995

All rights reserved.
Copyright © 1994 by Sarah J. Mason.
This book may not be reproduced in whole or in part,
by mimeograph or any other means, without permission.
For information address: The Berkley Publishing Group,
200 Madison Avenue, New York, NY 10016.

ISBN: 0-425-15006-2

Berkley Prime Crime Books are published by
The Berkley Publishing Group,
200 Madison Avenue, New York, NY 10016.
The name BERKLEY PRIME CRIME and the BERKLEY PRIME CRIME
design are trademarks belonging to Berkley Publishing Corporation.

PRINTED IN THE UNITED STATES OF AMERICA

10  9  8  7  6  5  4  3  2  1

Remember, remember the fifth of November—
The Gunpowder Treason and Plot.
I see no reason why Gunpowder Treason
Should ever be forgot.
—*Traditional children's verse, based on historical*
 *events of November 1605*

**Trea•son:**   **1**   the action of betraying; betrayal of the trust undertaken by or reposed in any one; breach of faith, treachery.
**2** law   **a:** High treason or treason proper: Violation by a subject of his allegiance to his sovereign or to the state. Defined 1350–51 by Act 25 Edward III, Statute 5 c.2, as compassing or imagining the king's death, or that of his wife or eldest son, violating the wife of the king or of the heir apparent, or the king's eldest daughter being unmarried . . .
   In 1795 the offence was extended to actual or contemplated use of force to make the king change his counsels, or to intimidate either or both of the Houses of Parliament . . .   **c:** Constructive treason: Action which though not actually or overtly coming under any of the acts specified in the Statute of Treason, was declared by law to be treason and punishable as such.
                                        —*Shorter Oxford English Dictionary*

# CHAPTER 1

"Call me . . . Catesby."

One by one, taking care that nobody should notice their absence and remark on it, they had slipped away from their everyday concerns to the appointed place. The heavy door had creaked open, had whispered shut behind each new arrival; the blinds had been drawn across windows where no light could risk being seen.

The last of the four had taken his seat in safety. The meeting was about to begin.

Catesby, natural leader of the little group, surveyed with a long, careful look the other three around the table. "Catesby—is that clear? Whenever we have . . . important matters to discuss, Catesby is my name—and nothing else."

"Catesby," came the obedient echo, accompanied by nods.

"Real names," Catesby went on, "are dangerous—the very least slip could betray us. You will all remember that."

More obedient nods. Catesby smiled—a lopsided smile which did not soften the desperate purpose gleaming in those haunted, steel-grey eyes.

"You will all," commanded Catesby, "take new names." The lopsided smile widened; the grey eyes for a moment held a glint of mischief as thin fingers drummed on the table. "You will remember them—you will write nothing down. What is written on paper can be too easily read by those with no business to read it."

A thin finger pointed. "Rookwood."

The newly-christened Rookwood blinked, then nodded, with an air of resignation. "Rookwood," he repeated.

"Keyes."

"Keyes," agreed he who had been given that name.

"Winter."

"Er—Thomas, or Robert?"

Mischief faded at once from Catesby's eyes, though its ghost danced still in those of the reluctant Winter.

"This is no time for joking." Catesby frowned. "There is no need for Christian names. Winter by itself will do."

"I'd rather be Digby," suggested Winter. "Or Percy, at a pinch." Then he sniggered. "Well, perhaps not—but not Winter, either. Winter's so—so ambiguous. Boring."

Catesby slapped a sudden, furious hand on the table. It sounded like a gunshot. Everyone jumped.

"Boring? You fool! We aren't doing this for fun! If you can't be serious . . . "

Rookwood and Keyes stared, too startled to protest. Was Winter to be lost to them before the plan had even begun to mature? They were so few in number—they needed him!

"No," said Catesby, slowly, as if answering the unspoken thought. "No, you have to be serious—you have no choice. Because"—the eyes were steel darts, the voice an icicle—"you already know too much, Winter."

There was menace in every syllable, and it held Winter silent. Catesby's smile was bitter in triumph. "No, we certainly can't risk letting you . . . retire. You are in this with the rest of us, Winter. It's too late for you—for anyone—to back out now."

Once more, steel and ice chilled the hearts of the three around the table in the darkened, anonymous room. ''Is that clearly understood?'' enquired Catesby.

And there came uneasy murmurs of acquiescence from the others: from Rookwood, from Keyes, and—without protest—from Winter: whose eyes had lost their sparkle as he realised that for him—for all of them—there could be no escape until their purpose had been finally accomplished.

The village of Plummergen is in Kent. Rye, at five miles distant the closest town, lies across the county border, in Sussex; and yet, despite its closeness, Rye is not the most convenient centre for Plummergen shoppers needing rather more than the well-stocked local establishments can supply. That honour goes to Brettenden, six miles to the north but, like its smaller neighbour, in Kent—though it is not so much parochialism as convenience which prompts Plummergen to shop from time to time in Brettenden. There is no direct bus service to Rye; the bus to Brettenden, although drastically curtailed from its glorious twice-daily run of older, affluent days, is nevertheless still regular, convenient—and cheap. Indeed, the official county service (once a week on market day) is so shamed by the greater efficiency of the additional twice-a-week bus provided by Plummergen's Crabbe family, owners of the local garage, that the trip—on whichever day of the week it is taken—is thought to give some of the best value for money for miles.

Plummergen's shops, it has been said, are well-stocked. There are three main retail outlets in the village: they all carry a remarkably similar range of items, although with sufficient variety to keep everyone happy. Along with the regulation groceries (green and otherwise), sweets, tobacco, wines and spirits, and deep-frozen pre-packaged foods, Mr. Takeley the grocer sells more Reduced goods than his competitors combined, owing to the temperamental nature of his deep freeze.

Mr. Welsted the draper is not given, as is Mr. Takeley, to Liquidation Sales—Mr. Takeley has a sense of humour—but, in addition to the standard stock, provides Plummergen with general haberdashery, knitting wool and patterns, dressmaking fabrics, and—since Plummergen's second place in the Best Kept Village Competition—a wider range of picture postcards than before.

Postmaster Mr. Stillman has a larger floor area than Mr. Takeley and Mr. Welsted on which to display his wares. His shop, moreover, is on much the best-placed site for gossip-loving Plummergen. It stands, its windows shaded by a striped awning, next door to Crabbe's Garage, and opposite the bus stop. Shoppers in the post office miss no coming nor going of any who travel, in whatever direction. With a little judicious craning of necks they may observe those who post letters in the nearby wall-mounted box, and will freely speculate on the purpose and destination of their friends' correspondence. By blatant snooping, they may study the drivers and passengers of passing cars, for every vehicle which either leaves or enters the village must pass the post office in so doing: Mr. Stillman's invaluable premises are situated in Plummergen's main—its only—street: The Street, as it is known.

And from the windows of Mr. Stillman's invaluable premises, one crisp autumn afternoon, busy eyes were keeping their habitual watch even as busy tongues wagged over the most interesting of the various items of news which were currently in circulation.

"Pretty little thing, she is," said Mrs. Spice, in tones of fond approval. "A real picture. Not like some, with great clodhopping feet in them platform shoes, and hair all over her face." She paused, and pondered briefly. "Dainty, that's the very word."

And no voice was raised against her choice.

"Not a bit of side to her, neither, by all accounts," said

Mrs. Henderson. "Her poor mother'd be proud of her if she was still alive, no doubt o' that."

A general chorus sighed that it did not doubt it. Even Mrs. Skinner, who had once quarrelled with Mrs. Henderson over the church flower rota and had barely exchanged two civil words with her since, could not bring herself to disagree.

Indeed, she went further. "Her mother *and* her poor dad, if you ask me. Reckon he's sorry now things happened like they did, him being thrown out o' the country that way, and her left to be brung up respectable—and so popular, too."

"Better for her he *was* thrown out," said someone more realist than romantic. "Stands to reason he'd have done her reputation no good at all, carrying on the way he was afore they got rid of him, and her near grownup now, bless her. She's a sight better off without him . . ."

And again no voice was raised against the remark.

"Georgy Girl," mused Emmy Putts sadly from behind the grocery counter, as someone murmured knowingly of morganatic marriage. "Princess Petite—that's what they call her. Allus in the papers, she is, as good as a film star." She sighed. "Some folk have all the luck."

"Some folk," said Mrs. Stillman sternly, "are born to it, Emmeline, and some aren't. You keep your mind on your work, my girl, and let's have none of your nonsense about being in the papers. Plummergen's good enough for the likes of you, not being royalty, nor even gentry-born. At least," she pointed out, "you'll be free to marry who you want, when the time comes, and no argument. But there'll be checking, and Acts of Parliament, and—and everything o' that sort for young Georgina, so it said in the paper the other day. You count your blessings, Emmy Putts, and be thankful your blood isn't blue like hers—poor lamb," she added.

The Princess Georgina was one of the youngest, and one of the most popular, members of the current royal scene.

No more than five feet tall, and in perfect proportion from her bubbly blonde curls to her tiny feet, she had been dubbed "The Petite Princess" from her first appearance in public. Her immaculate grooming, coupled with her sparkling personality and apparent enthusiasm for whatever task she might be given to perform, made her a role model the battle-weary parents of teenage England would have been only too glad for their offspring to emulate. Never once had Georgina put a finely-shod foot wrong. When, at the launching of a nuclear submarine, the naval brass band had followed the National Anthem with a spirited version of the Seekers' hit from seven years earlier, Georgy Girl's place in the hearts of the nation was assured, as front-page photographs next day showed Her Royal Highness clapping her hands and laughing with genuine delight for the unexpected compliment.

Georgina's name had never been involved with scandal—unlike that of her father, whose lurid behaviour had led, some fifteen years before, to what the racier elements of the media had dubbed *Exile—by Royal Decree!* It was hinted that she was being groomed as a future Princess of Wales: it was rumoured that half the eligible bachelors in the country would go into terminal decline on the announcement of her betrothal, no matter who the lucky man might be—and, whoever he was, even Prince Charles, he couldn't possibly be good enough for Her Royal Highness. Georgina's postbag—so voluminous that Mount Pleasant Sorting Office had allocated an entire room to her incoming mail—was swamped with well-meant advice and delicate embroidery from doting pensioners, with declarations of platonic affection from an age-range of males between fifteen and seventy-five, with cards and presents from schoolchildren, and with heartfelt offers of marriage and lifelong devotion from daydreamers on whom she had once, in passing, allowed her golden glance to fall.

Georgina, bewildered but flattered by the attention, had been wisely reared: her curly blonde head remained reso-

lutely unturned. Her secretary issued statements that Her
Royal Highness had no mind, as yet, to settle down, deem-
ing her public duties fulfilment enough. Such wisdom in
one so young was hailed as a rare and wholly admirable
quality; Mount Pleasant had to allocate another room.
Georgy Girl was England's darling. Not a voice could be
heard to speak against her; she was mobbed and adored
wherever she went . . .

And now she was coming to Kent.

"I still don't know's they oughter risk it, though." Mrs.
Spice returned to her original argument. "Her being so
young, and with nobody knowing what that radiation
mightn't *do,* if you know what I mean." She cast a quick,
suggestive glance at Emmy Putts, unmarried and wide-eyed
behind the bacon slicer. "In the long term," she enlarged
cryptically, nodding in a way which spoke volumes to
every mother in the room, but which left Emmy still staring.

"There's . . . shields and things, they say," said Mrs.
Henderson, hopefully. "Lead. They'll take no chances with
her, you can be sure o' that."

"There's tales," said Mrs. Skinner swiftly, "of some
poor soul Murreystone way, her husband used to work
there—and out it popped with two heads, poor little thing,
and never lived above a day or so, though he'd had all the
lead shields and special clothes you like."

"They'll say anything," countered Mrs. Henderson,
"over to Murreystone. Two heads, indeed! First *I've* heard
of it. Might as well say as it had—had webbed feet, and a
tail—if it had anything at all, that is, which with Murreystone you can be sure it never did, on account of never bin
born in the first place."

The post office now perceived a great conversational dilemma. Should Mrs. Skinner's tempting Radiation Mutant
Monster theme be pursued? It could not be doubted that
the possibilities were virtually endless—but their develop-
ment required, inconveniently, a credence in Murreystone

news it was not in Plummergen's nature to give. Would it be better to follow the traditional lead of Mrs. Henderson, in scorning any claim to veracity or reliability on the part of the rival village? After all, no Plummergenite had been known to trust a Murreystoner in thought, word, or deed for several hundred years. A feud believed to have begun during the fifteenth-century Wars of the Roses was in full swing by the Civil War, two centuries later, and had never been allowed to lapse since that time.

Torn between two so violently opposing points of view, the shoppers turned, as they often did, to Mrs. Flax for the final decision. Mrs. Flax, Plummergen's Wise Woman, was a person of much authority in the village. Were she to cap Mrs. Skinner's story with one of her own—a new-born baby with a full set of teeth, an infant smothered from head to foot in hair—they would joyfully narrate horrors of their own immediate invention. Should she, however, second Mrs. Henderson in dismissing the two-headed child as a figment of Murreystone's (or even of Mrs. Skinner's) imagination, the topic would be abandoned forthwith.

Mrs. Flax, with every eye upon her, drew a deep, portentous breath. She wagged her head in meaningful fashion. "If they'd come to me," said the Wise Woman, never slow to reinforce her reputation, "Murreystone or no, there would've bin herbs to spare them their sorrow—ah, and more besides, being the devil's work . . . which is no more than a body can expect from that heathen band across the marsh, o' course." She made her decision. "Allus bearing in mind," she added, "as there's no cause to believe a word they devils say in the first place. And even if there was"— for, in the manner of oracles, Mrs. Flax was skilled at hedging her bets—"there was babies born hare-shotten and with clubbed feet—ah, and worse—long afore anyone invented atom bombs and nuclear power."

Any lapse in her logic was overlooked in the relief of having a clear conversational lead at last. The Murreystone Mutant was no more than a myth: they could return to less disquieting topics of conversation—yet, on consideration, not so very much less. There could be no doubt that Murreystone would be as interested in the proposed visit of the Princess Georgina as Plummergen, of whatever age, could be; and Murreystone's reaction to local events involving Plummergen—no matter how indirectly—was seldom of a tranquil nature.

"Poor little mites," said Mrs. Skinner, snatching a face-saving cue from the Wise Woman before anyone else—Mrs. Henderson in particular—could speak. "Oh, there was hard times if you was a kiddie, right enough—and not so very long ago, neither."

Her audience brooded on children pushed up chimneys and sent down mines, or driven, barefoot, out into the fields to pick stones, scare rooks, and herd sheep. Some of the older women muttered grimly of the Union, informing their younger friends that nothing today could match the horrors of the—happily defunct—Workhouse . . .

"But things is better nowadays, you can't deny," Mrs. Henderson reminded them, in accents which dared Mrs. Skinner to make such a denial. "I mean, how many Plummergen folk've had the chance to meet any of the Royal Family the way they've got now?"

"Only the kiddies, though," pointed out Mrs. Scillicough. As the mother of Plummergen's infamous triplets, Mrs. Scillicough felt herself better qualified than most to pronounce on matters juvenile. "On account of 'em learning all about it at school, the paper says, which is what none of us did, nuclear power not being in the Eleven Plus nor nothing."

"The school over to Murreystone's not so big as ours," someone said, thoughtfully.

The fact was hardly surprising: Murreystone's inhabitants number around three hundred and fifty, while Plummergen has a population of just over five hundred.

"And nobbut the one teacher," someone else added, more thoughtful still.

"But one or two o' their dads works down in Dungeness," said Mrs. Skinner, reluctant—despite the opinions of Mrs. Flax—to abandon entirely her Radiation Mutant theme. "And there's not a soul from these parts but works on a farm, or in Brettenden or suchlike—nothing to do with nuclear power at all. Seems to me they'll take unfair advantage, if we're not careful."

"Unfair it may well be," came the automatic retort from Mrs. Henderson, "but I'd like to know what's anyone's notion of what anyone can do about it—because there's summat got to be done, there's no denying." She sighed. "Not as if any of us knows the editor of the *Beacon* for putting in a word, is it? Fine chance! Open to all, so the paper said this competition is, and a daft idea it is, too—all the kiddies, anyway," as she saw Mrs. Scillicough draw breath to protest. She closed her eyes in an attempt to recall the exact wording of the notice which had appeared at the end of a thrilling feature in that week's *Brettenden Telegraph and Beacon (est. 1847, incorporating [1893] The Iverhurst Chronicle and Argus)*.

"For the best essay from a child at present in full-time primary education in the county of Kent, on the subject of Nuclear Power, first prize, a ten-pound book token. Plus"—and Mrs. Henderson opened her eyes—"the honour of presenting a—a bucket to Her Royal Highness Princess Georgina on the occasion of the Grand Opening of Dungeness D Nuclear Power Station."

This feat of memory was received with nods and murmurs of appreciation from everyone save, inevitably, Mrs. Skinner.

"And there's the one advantage we've got over Murreystone," she said. "Alice Maynard, that's to say, on account of presenting bookays"—the pronunciation was scornful—"needs 'em to curtsey nice, and Miss Maynard's a-going to teach the kiddies dances and stuff for the Christmas pantomime, remember. So if it's one of ours as wins the competition, whoever it is'll not disgrace the village by falling flat on her face or tripping over her feet when she gets to meet the princess.''

''There's worse things than tripping over people's feet, where Murreystone's concerned,'' said Mrs. Flax sagely. ''It's for no good reason, you mark my words, they'll want one of theirs to—to give her the flowers.'' Mrs. Flax was wise enough to know when, and how, to mask ignorance with adroit turns of phrase. ''They'll be up to summat, make no mistake about that, if they've half the chance . . . ''

Everyone nodded. During the Civil War, Murreystone had been strong for Protector Cromwell: Plummergen had even more strongly backed the Royalist side. Neither village had ever changed its stance on matters political; and if the Princess Georgina wasn't Royalty, Plummergen would like to know who was. There could be no doubt that the selection of a Murreystone candidate for the presentation honour could lead to nothing but embarrassment, at the very least, for everyone concerned. If the editor of the *Beacon* had his wits about him, for all the vaunted freedom of the press he wouldn't even consider any entries which came from the village five miles to the east of Plummergen . . .

And when someone voiced the opinion that Murreystone—for whatever purpose—was bound to play dirty, not a single voice was raised against this view.

# CHAPTER 2

No voice, indeed, was raised for some moments, as everyone grimly contemplated many previous instances of Murreystone's undeniable rascality. Then mother-of-four Mrs. Newport, sister to the triplet-bedevilled Mrs. Scillicough, ventured the opinion that—for all the *Beacon* said the essay was for the youngsters to write—she wouldn't mind betting there'd be a few Murreystone mums and dads'd want to give their kiddies a helping hand, and in a way you couldn't blame them, could you? Because it was only natural. But if Murreystone was going to do it, well, she didn't know but what Plummergen wouldn't have to, too, to stand any chance of winning, when all was said and done. Not (added Mrs. Newport hastily) as she'd any cause to say such things on her own account, of course, being as hers were all under five and even the eldest not due to start school for another year, but you had to look at it from both sides, didn't you?

It was as everyone was attempting this Janus-like mental manoeuvre that the doorbell jangled.

Heads turned at once to see who had come to join their number: they had all been so busy brooding on Perfidious Murreystone, and pondering the uneasy sophistry of Mrs.

Newport, that their attention had drifted from the world outside the post office. What part of that world was now coming in to join them?

"Morning, Mrs. Blaine." The relieved and welcoming chorus came from those who realised that nobody now need commit herself to the merits or otherwise of stooping to Murreystone's anticipated level. "Morning, Miss Nuttel!" And The Nuts, somewhat startled by the intensity of the greeting, responded with appropriate salutations of their own.

"The Nuts" is the collective title by which these two ladies are almost invariably known to impertinent Plummergen. Some say the name derives from their being as nutty as fruitcakes; others hold the (more probable) theory that it is the rampant vegetarianism of the pair which has resulted in their nuxial nomenclature. Whatever the reason, Miss Erica Nuttel and Mrs. Norah Blaine have around the village been referred to as "The Nuts" for nearly as long as the village has been their home: a home which they set up together a dozen or so years ago in Lilikot, a plate-glass-windowed dwelling of modern style situated almost exactly opposite the bus stop, Crabbe's Garage, and the post office.

If shoppers in the post office blatantly observe each coming and going of those who travel or post letters, there is a recognised—and regretted—restriction in such observation. The Nuts, on the other hand, may observe as much, and for as long, as is their pleasure: and their pleasure is very great. Living where they do, Miss Nuttel (who is also known as Nutcrackers) and Mrs. Blaine (the Hot Cross Bun) are not restricted, as are Mr. Stillman's customers, by his hours of business. Mr. Stillman stays open only from eight in the morning to six in the evening: the inhabitants of Lilikot, during the summer at least, can maintain—should they so wish—a constant vigil on outside events from dawn (around four) until dusk (almost ten). And the ladies would be among the first to support the installation of street lighting, so that their vigilance might be increased.

The Nuts, it must be emphasised, are vigilant from no unworthy cause. Their motives are pure, their intentions philanthropic in the extreme. Their only wish is to serve their fellow citizens to the best of their ability: and they pride themselves that serve them they definitely do. Their devotion to this self-appointed task, they feel, cannot be questioned; and the value of that service (to Plummergen, at least) has never been in doubt—although the editor of the *Brettenden Telegraph and Beacon* has been known to hold forth at some length on the topic of sales and circulation figures in the Plummergen area. For with Miss Nuttel and Mrs. Blaine ever ready to pass on gossip, to indulge in scandal, and to monger all manner of rumour on the slightest excuse, why would anyone in the same community even think of paying good money for a newspaper?

Miss Nuttel is tall, thin, and equine of feature. Mrs. Blaine is short, stout, and black-eyed with either malice or mischief, depending on her mood. When thwarted, she is given to flashes of temper, followed by long, brooding sulks or by providential migraines, which last are known to the village as "one of my heads." Their main purpose, Plummergen agrees, is to make Miss Nuttel feel guilty . . .

And it now seemed clear, from the way in which both Nuts had responded to the greetings of their fellow shoppers, that this current excursion was taking place in a post-sulk (or post-migraine) period; and everyone wondered why the Hot Cross Bun should be so cross today with Eric.

Miss Nuttel, having nodded to the assembled company, marched across to the revolving book-stand, where she stood in a grim silence thumbing through the pages of one of the popular *Mastery* series. These slim volumes held out the tantalising promise of near-professional skills or knowledge upon the expenditure of a modest sum of money and a minimum of effort; *Master Banking in Thirty Minutes* had been selling in considerable numbers since the recent appointment of a new manager to one of the most prestigious financial houses in Brettenden.

Norah Blaine's blackcurrant eyes darted around in search of a sympathetic face. They fell upon Mrs. Skinner, still feeling a little peeved at her worsting by Mrs. Flax in the matter of the Murreystone Mutant, yet too nervous of the Wise Woman's likely reaction to say so out loud.

"If you aren't in a hurry, Mrs. Skinner," said Mrs. Blaine in a winning tone, "would you mind too much if I just popped in front of you to make my few purchases? They're really rather *urgent,* you see," with a pointed glare for Miss Nuttel, whose interest in *Master Fancy Needlework* was as deep as it was unexpected.

"You go right ahead, dear."

Mrs. Skinner's was not the only nose to twitch at the scent of scandal when it became clear that Miss Nuttel had no intention of following her friend to the Ironmongery and Kitchenware section of the shop. Mrs. Stillman, frowning in what she knew was a vain attempt to quench the curiosity of her customers, moved across to the other counter.

"Anything in particular you're looking for, Mrs. Blaine?"

Mrs. Blaine made to consult a crumpled envelope. "Well, to begin with, two new sieves, please, the large ones with fine metal mesh. And two buckets, but they must be galvanised. If you've only got plastic, I suppose"—with a sigh suggestive of martyrdom—"it will have to wait until market day . . . although I'm sure I don't see why I should."

"Well, you don't have to." Mrs. Stillman gestured behind her. "Large sieves, you said? We've three different sizes to choose from, and as for galvanised buckets, was it the double sort for floors you wanted, or ordinary?"

Mrs. Blaine opted, loudly, for the ordinary style; Miss Nuttel slammed *Master Fancy Needlework* back on the shelf. Clearly, the thought of even thirty minutes' dedication to drawing threads and weaving fine silks had depressed her.

"I don't suppose," said Mrs. Blaine, absently banging

the buckets one against the other as Mrs. Stillman placed them on the counter before her, "that you stock glass-cloths, do you? I thought not," with another martyred sigh. And her mood remained resolutely glum even when Mrs. Stillman reminded her of the propensity of drapers to stock tea-towels among the rest of their Manchester goods. It seemed that the very idea of having to cross The Street to Mr. Welsted's little shop was too much for Mrs. Blaine to bear, even though it stood no more than a few score yards from Lilikot's front door.

"I'll pay for these." Mrs. Blaine, wilfully oblivious of the approach of Miss Nuttel, took out her purse as Mrs. Stillman spoke the total. "Goodness, so much? Really, I do think—but there," with a third exhalation indicative of martyrdom, "the housekeeping will simply have to stretch this week, that's all. And if people don't like it, they have only themselves to blame."

Beside her, Miss Nuttel cleared her throat in a whinny, and stared haughtily down her nose. "Rubber tubing?" she enquired, as Mrs. Stillman sorted out change. "Couple of yards," she added.

"Some more home-made wine, Mrs. Blaine?" It was too good a chance for Mrs. Skinner to miss. Mrs. Henderson's attempts at Strong and Wholesome Barley Beer had given her neighbours their biggest shock since the council announced the latest rent increase, and the glaziers of Brettenden their most lucrative employment for months. Gleeful rumour had set the decorators' estimates—their vans and ladders had never, in fact, appeared—at astronomical levels. "I know you takes a pride in your dandelion, o' course, but if you don't mind me saying so it's a bit on the late side, isn't it?"

Mrs. Blaine clashed her buckets together as she lifted them from the counter, but made no reply beyond another long-suffering sigh, and a shake of her head as the sieves rattled in their galvanised receptacles. Miss Nuttel, her nose in the air, ignored Mrs. Blaine to watch Mrs. Stillman wrestling, Laocoön-like, with her tape-measure and scissors against black rubber coils; and she was as deaf to Mrs. Skinner's words as ever Mrs. Henderson could be.

"Yes. Six feet," said Miss Nuttel, as Mrs. Stillman put the inevitable query. "Plaster of Paris, too, if you've got it." She paused, and shot a triumphant look in the direction of Mrs. Blaine. "Twenty pounds."

Mrs. Blaine uttered a squeal of fury, turned on her heel, and, with a bucket in either hand, headed—reproachfully clanking—for the door. She needed only apple cheeks and a wooden shoulder-yoke to be everyone's ideal of the country milkmaid—that is, had the apple cheeks been plumped in a winsome smile. But Norah Blaine was far from smiling now.

"I'm sorry, Miss Nuttel. Plaster of Paris is more what you'd get in craft shops, though I believe we've a bag or two of cement round the back that's old stock I could let you have half price, if you'd like it."

Mrs. Blaine's plump frame vibrated on the threshold as, waiting for a volunteer with unencumbered hands to open the door, she waited also for Miss Nuttel's reply. It might have been supposed that the prospect of so tempting a bargain must please Norah Blaine: but the dark, dangerous gleam in her eyes, and the narrow set of her mouth, suggested that such supposition would be wrong.

"No, thanks." At Miss Nuttel's words, Mrs. Blaine seemed to brighten. "Just this. Fine."

And, as Miss Nuttel forced the slim black rubber serpent into the capacious pocket of her coat, Mrs. Blaine, herself serpentlike as she hissed through clenched teeth, dropped her buckets with a discordant clang, snatched open the door, and, to the tinkling accompaniment of the bell, picked them up again and clanked her way crossly out.

Miss Nuttel paid for the rubber tubing and strode after her in triumph, leaving everyone staring. As Mrs. Stillman tidied away her heavy-duty scissors and the reel of tube, Mrs. Henderson spoke.

"Well!"

Nobody could have summed up the general sentiment more exactly.

"Which isn't to say," Mrs. Henderson went on, she having tacitly been granted the floor, "as there han't bin summat strange about that pair over the past few days, because there has."

"I'd call it more than strange," said Mrs. Skinner at once. "What with digging that hole the way she was, deep as a grave if Mrs. Putts is to be believed, and I'm sure I don't see why not, if you ask me it's a wonder they're still both alive to tell the tale. Ain't that right, Emmy?"

Emmy Putts, thus addressed, jumped. She had been lost in a daydream inspired by thoughts of Princess Georgina, and wishing that the crown she herself, for the second time, had crammed over her long blonde wig as this year's Miss Plummergen, had been as real as the gorgeous tiaras and diadems worn by the fortunate Georgy Girl.

She blinked. "Pardon, Mrs. Skinner. What say?"

"Miss Nuttel's hole," prompted Mrs. Skinner. "Remember, your ma said she saw her digging it when she popped along to the admiral to borrow a jar of honey, and happened to look over the fence?"

Everyone crowded close, though this was a tale they had heard told many times in recent days. Indeed, it had been the main topic of village speculation for almost a week, only being relegated to second place once the forthcoming visit of Princess Georgina had been announced.

Rear Admiral Bernard "Buzzard" Leighton, a relative newcomer to Plummergen, had from his arrival occasioned much discussion in the village, not only by sporting a ginger beard, but by keeping bees: neither of which activities anybody was ever known to have pursued within living memory. The bees—or the beard—alone would have been a cause of suspicion: both together gave Plummergen a field day, and, though rumour had it that Major-General Sir George Colveden planned to go into melliferous partnership

with his new friend next spring, these rumours were not
enough to place the seal of respectability on the Buzzard's
hobby (the beard was reluctantly accepted as beyond Plummergen's control) until his honey won a prize in the Pre-
serves section of the recent Produce Show.

People at once began to recall old country remedies and
recipes which, without honey, were sure to fail. Sugar was
denounced as pure, white, and deadly. The admiral, overwhelmed by this sudden interest, regretted that four hives—
especially hives which had not long since been transported
from another part of the country—were unable to supply
the needs of his new neighbours: the odd jar or two, perhaps, as a present, but he'd no intention of setting up in
business at his age. Of course, with winter coming on, if
anyone wanted to sample his recipe for a hot toddy, they'd
be more than welcome to drop in for a few drinks one
evening . . .

Mrs. Putts, in her own words a respectable widow-
woman of several years' standing, had no intention of
joining the Buzzard in one of his by now (undeservedly)
notorious push-the-boat-out parties, when the green-and-
white Gin Pennant flew from the flagpole in his front garden, issuing its unspoken invitation to all former officers
within the vicinity to consider themselves Bernard Leighton's guests. Guest? For her, plain Clarissa Putts, to mix
with the likes of Sir George and Colonel Windup? Not to
mention Major Howett, who being female and a nurse did
ought to have known better than encourage menfolk to
pickle their livers . . . Though far too sensible to voice the
sentiment aloud while asking a favour, Mrs. Putts was re-
solved that she would do no such thing. On the other
hand, if the admiral could spare just *one* jar: not that she
held with beautification on her own account, of course,
but young Emmy had read in one of her magazines that
honey and glycerine, in equal parts, would soften and
beautify the complexion, and, being too shy to ask on her
own account . . .

Which intelligence had come as a surprise to Emmy Putts, a regular and appreciative recipient of much bluff naval gallantry whenever the admiral entered the post office, or encountered her outside it. Emmy had been sworn to secrecy by her mother about this aspect of the story.

The admiral had been delighted to offer Mrs. Putts—he hastily begged her pardon, to offer on her daughter's behalf—not one, but two jars of honey, along with the chance to watch his bees at their work. A quiet time, October, but interesting, he was sure she'd agree, if she cared to accompany him; which Mrs. Putts, prepared to sell her honour dear, was happy to do. Around the side of the admiral's house went Mrs. Putts in the admiral's wake, hearing him talk with eloquence of brood chambers, and queens, and sugar syrup; and hearing also, as the pair neared the far end of the garden where the four hives were set on their brick-and-wood stands, the unmistakable and energetic sound of digging from over the fence.

The admiral heard it, too, and paused. Was not one of the traditional naval toasts "Sweethearts and wives"? The ladies, God bless 'em, shouldn't really be burdened with the heavy work—though he'd always understood his neighbours to have tended their topsoil so well that it as good as looked after itself.

But the rhythmic chink of spade on stone, the thud of falling soil, still floated over the fence separating Ararat Cottage, home of the Buzzard, from the little house next door. It sounded like very hard work indeed; and—with Mrs. Putts by his side—the admiral popped his head over the top of the fence to enquire:

"Need any help there, Miss Nuttel?"

Erica Nuttel, knee-deep in orange subsoil, and breathing hard, shook her head without speaking. The admiral regarded her with kindly interest.

Mrs. Putts stared with blatant curiosity, and proved the weaker of the two. "My goodness, Miss Nuttel, whatever d'you want with such a great big hole? You'll not be planting a tree so deep, all clay and stones as it is.''

"No," agreed Miss Nuttel, and dug on.

Mrs. Putts suffered in silence for a while, then coughed.

"We're on the main drainage, so it can't surely be a new septic tank," she said, in a pleading tone.

"No," said Miss Nuttel, digging yet deeper.

"Another well, maybe?" The Nuts, when they had first arrived in Plummergen, had employed the services of a water-diviner to find them a spring, and had sunk their own well, insisting that tap water was full of who-knew-what unhealthy chemicals.

"No," said Miss Nuttel, by now almost invisible behind an upthrown pile of sticky clay.

"Then what," demanded Mrs. Putts, who could bear this no longer, "*do* you want that hole for, Miss Nuttel?"

And Miss Nuttel's reply had sent—Clarissa Putts reported later to an enthralled Emmy—ice-cold shivers down her spine, as if she knew what dreadful fate had been foretold and yet could do nothing about it. Miss Nuttel had paused at last in her digging, and wiped an earthy hand across her brow, and uttered those three terrible words that had turned the heart of Clarrie Putts to water . . .

"For the body," said Erica Nuttel.

# CHAPTER 3

Although circulation of the *Brettenden Beacon* was not high in the Plummergen area, there were still those who read the newspaper every week in great detail, down to the Notices of Bankruptcy, Auctions, and Planning Applications. One of these was Martin Jessyp, efficient headmaster of the little village school; and, on the afternoon of the day on which the visit of Princess Georgina had been announced, he had gone into lengthy consultation with his deputy, Miss Alice Maynard, on the subject of Nuclear Power.

It was not, of course, that they wished to encourage the spirit of feuding which any mention of Murreystone was sure to inflame. If, on the other hand, there was a competition open to all local children, neither he nor Alice saw any good reason why a Plummergen child should not win it, fair and square, given sufficient encouragement and help. Early on Saturday morning, therefore, he gave Miss Maynard a lift into Brettenden. The two entered the public lending library with enthusiasm and stout canvas bags, and borrowed as many books on Energy as they could find.

They spent an industrious and productive weekend in

their respective cottages, making notes, planning lessons. And on Monday morning, after Assembly, the fifty-odd pupils of Plummergen School gathered, Bigguns and Tiddlers amongst themselves but Junior Mixed Infants to the authorities, in their appointed classrooms for initiation into the mysteries which their forthcoming trip to Dungeness D would reveal in even greater depth.

"*What is Energy?*" chalked Miss Maynard, at the top of the blackboard; and, underneath, wrote as she spoke that it was the ability of matter to move, to change. It was the power of something—anything—to work, to perform. Without the energy they had that breakfast-time consumed in the form of food, none of them would have been able to walk to school afterwards, especially on such a blustery day.

"Pity we had breakfast, then," muttered someone with a sideways elbow-dig into the ribs of his neighbour. "Fancy a day off school, I do."

His neighbour sniggered, and Miss Maynard, whose hearing was acute, smiled in sympathy while she shook her head. She herself, she pointed out, liked Monday mornings no better than anyone else: unfortunately, just as there was little that could be done about the weather, there was little that could be done about Monday mornings.

"Except," she added, "to make them more interesting, perhaps. I thought we would start today's lesson with some experiments to blow away any weekend cobwebs that the wind hasn't already blown away. Now, who's going to volunteer to bring some water from the cloakroom?"

Every hand shot up as Miss Maynard took a white enamel jug from behind the desk, and held it aloft. She studied the twenty eager faces turned towards her. "Thank you, Paul. As full as you can comfortably carry it, please—you aren't to go straining yourself."

Young Paul jumped to his feet, hurried to take the jug from Alice's hands, and trotted away to the cloakroom while Miss Maynard produced three matchboxes, some rubber bands, a stout pair of scissors, and an empty plastic bottle of the squeezy sort which holds dish-washing detergent.

Three children were chosen to wield the scissors turn and turn about. Christopher cut the top off the detergent bottle, Rachel removed the base, and Laura sliced it down the middle. Sally opened it out and tried to flatten it, so that it lay, a curving rectangle, rocking to and fro on Miss Maynard's desk as Paul reappeared, bright-eyed and slightly out of breath, with water splashing over the blue rim of the jug, assuring Alice that it hadn't been a bit too heavy, Miss, honest.

"Thank you. And now," said Miss Maynard, with a quiver in her voice, "I believe that Miss Seeton left a large bowl here after the Conker Contest, didn't she? Gemma, could you fetch it for me, please?"

Tactfully, Alice ignored the ripple of laughter which ran around the twenty Tiddlers, and Lizzie's ritual moaning for the playground loss of her twenty-oncer in the bout with Rachel's seventeener, the memory of which contest made her friends snigger all the more . . .

Unless, reflected Alice Maynard, they were giggling— and who could, in honesty, blame them?—at the memory of cheating Murreystone's defeat in the official inter-village Conker Contest. Even Miss Seeton's patent soaking mixture, disclosed to the village through the courtesy of her friend Miss Wicks, had not been proof against perfidious Murreystone's use of, not honestly-hardened horse chestnuts, but the more devious painted pebble which only the quick eye of Nigel Colveden had observed. The resulting fracas, of which young Plummergen had been an enthusiastic audience, would live long in village legend . . .

"Thank you, Gemma. Paul, would you fill the bowl with water? Thank you. Now, children, you are too young to use matches, and so . . . "

The Tiddlers of Plummergen range in age from Under Five to Over Seven. Miss Maynard was taking no chances,

although she imagined that Mr. Jessyp, teaching the Bigguns (Between Eight and Eleven), would allow his class to
carry out this part of the energy experiment, supervised,
themselves.

Alice emptied out all the matches, then struck six into
flame, and allowed six different children to extinguish them
with hearty puffs. More children, following her instructions,
inserted the dead matches into the ends of the boxes, one
on either side; others ruled and measured on the white
curved plastic for still more to cut three small rectangles,
while rubber bands were fastened between the protruding
matches, followed by the insertion of one white rectangle
and its repeated twisting until each rubber band was taut.

The tiny motors thus primed, Miss Maynard took upon
herself the honour of launching the first paddle-boat on
young Paul's mixing-bowl pond, with Christopher and Rachel next, the envy of their friends: but all, they knew,
would have their fair turn—as they did.

"And that," said Miss Maynard, as Paul's matchbox
craft beat Lizzie's in the final race, "is only one sort of
energy—one sort of power. There are, as you will see, a
great many others even before we come to nuclear power."

From egg-boxes cut into segments, fastened between two
circles of cardboard spinning around a central nail, they
made a tiny water-wheel, suspended on string beneath
Paul's pouring jug, varying its speed with the speed of his
pouring. Wrapping a length of coated flex around a pocket
compass, fixing the ends to steel nails stuck in a potato,
they made a flicker of electricity. Christopher, trying not to
laugh, with much heavy breathing blew up a balloon, then
rubbed it repeatedly against his shirt-front before sticking
it in triumph to the wall, indisputable proof of the power
of static electricity . . .

"And this will be for when we go outside at break
time." Miss Maynard, with a smile, produced from her canvas bag two lengths of balsa wood, a long metal knitting-
needle, another washing-up bottle, a collection of small

stones for weight, and four disposable paper cups.

"Very suitable," said Miss Maynard, "on such a blustery day. We couldn't have asked for anything better. We are going to make a turbine to show how wind power works . . ."

The wind, reflected Miss Seeton, was certainly powerful. It was as well that there was no sign of rain, for the risk of having one's umbrella blown inside out must be very great—so great, indeed, that there had been no question of taking one's best umbrella, in case it should be damaged.

Miss Seeton's best umbrella was one of her proudest possessions. Of fine black silk, it had a sensible crook handle rather than a knob, or a strap: and that handle, with part of the shaft, was indeed—the proud owner would tell the astonished enquirer—made of gold.

"Not *solid* gold, of course," she would add, fearing to be thought ostentatious, and blushing for the very idea that anyone might suppose her to have caused any added expense to the courteous gentleman who had given her so generous and rare a gift all those years ago. Detective Superintendent—as he had then been—Delphick, one assumed, although of course one would never have been so impertinent as to ask the question direct, had at that time surely not been paid the sort of salary which would allow him to distribute gold-handled umbrellas to anyone he chose, even if perhaps, since his most gratifying promotion, he now might be. Not—Miss Seeton would further explain, paying tribute—that the handle was gold *plated,* either. One would not wish to give the impression that dear Mr. Delphick might have been, well, deceitful, or stingy. The handle was of real gold—though admittedly hollow—but it had been hallmarked for proof by the Royal Mint, or by whoever it was who had stamped those tiny official numbers and symbols in an unobtrusive place.

"A—a token, that is to say a reminder, of a—a little adventure we shared," the explanation would continue, if the enquiry was pursued; and Miss Seeton would blush once more. "The superintendent was kind enough to say that I had been of—of some assistance to him, and . . . "

And Miss Seeton's voice would tail modestly away as she smiled, sighed, and gently changed the subject.

Miss Seeton has no call to be so modest. Chief Superintendent Delphick would be the first to admit that, without her help, Scotland Yard could never have solved the vicious Covent Garden knifing of a prostitute by her drug-dealing colleague, the infamous Cesar Lebel. The breaking of even part of a drugs ring by the forces of law and order has to be a cause for some celebration; the capture of a murderer, effected mainly through the innocent offices of a retired schoolteacher, has to be a triumph.

In Miss Seeton's case, the triumph is regarded by everyone else as miraculous, while by Miss Seeton herself—and not entirely through the little spinster's innate humility—it is, to say the least, misunderstood. Gentlewomen, Miss Seeton knows full well, do not have adventures: therefore she, Emily Dorothea Seeton, does not have them. No matter that, by poking one or other of her many brollies into whatever criminal hornets' nest she might encounter as she goes on her unconscious way, she not only stirs the hornets into confusion, leading to their ultimate capture, but somehow also contrives to blunt their stings before such capture is effected, thereby making the job of the police a good deal easier than they would otherwise expect it to be; no matter that the police have in the past found such poking and stirring to be of so incomparable a kind that Miss Seeton has been co-opted as a consultant into the force . . .

Miss Seeton hardly ever realises that she has poked, stirred, and blunted, and certainly never appreciates that her actions have been so productive for good, pleasing though the intelligence would be should anyone ever induce her to accept it. Though she was trained, and for many years practised, as a teacher of art, Miss Seeton cannot—does not allow herself to—see what others see . . .

And yet it is for the peculiar—the unique—character of her Seeing that Miss Seeton is so valued by the police. The very title of her official position—like the lady herself, unique—reveals her true worth and purpose. She is retained, and paid, by the Yard as an Art Consultant, liable to be called on by her constabulary colleagues whenever they encounter a case of an unusual, irregular, or outré nature. As some fight fire with fire, so the police confront the unusual with the unique . . .

Miss Seeton, on the odd occasions when she takes time to consider the matter, thinks of her appointment as that of an IdentiKit artist. She believes that the meticulous, detailed, and—in the eyes of everyone else—dull drawings she makes of witnesses, scenes of the crime, or certain items of evidence, are required only because the IdentiKit system has, for some reason, on that occasion broken down. Perhaps the Kit has been mislaid, or the operating officer—Miss Seeton is hazy as to details—is for some reason absent from work. In such circumstances, why should someone with a little skill in sketching not be called upon to sketch?

And sketch she does, in painstaking line and shade and hatching, doing no more than a camera could do, and doing it far more slowly: which slow sketches are as much use to the police as a broken umbrella would be to Miss Seeton. But when Miss Seeton's eye Sees as no other eye can see—when eye signals brain to set hand swooping across the pristine page in swift and instinctive movement—when the resulting doodle, cartoon, call it what you will, makes Miss Seeton blush for having Seen beyond what is there, for having taken the type of imaginative liberties only permitted to genius, which she sadly knows herself not to possess . . . it is then that those who can interpret her work—which she has always to be coaxed into showing, blushing for what she regards as her frivolity as well as for her lack of talent—it is then that those who interpret her work use their interpretation, reluctant though it at first may be to reveal itself, to clear a welcome path through the perplexing tangle of nefarious branches to the final resolution of the crime.

It was in gratitude for having presented him with Cesar Lebel, and his associates, gift-wrapped on toast that Superintendent Delphick had in turn presented Miss Seeton with her gold-handled, black silk umbrella. It was after the umbrella had been damaged during a contretemps with a member of an unorthodox and sinister cult—who, pursuing its owner up a ladder with homicidal intent, had in innocent retaliation been bombarded to a well-deserved demise by brolly and handbag and borrowed coat together—it was after this that the suggestion was made by Ashford's Superintendent Brinton, friend to Delphick of the Yard, that Miss Seeton should keep her gold umbrella for comparatively safe occasions, such as afternoon tea with friends; which suggestion Miss Seeton, fearing to risk further damage to her treasured trophy, followed as closely as she could.

On such a blustery day, therefore, it was one of her second-best brollies that Miss Seeton took with her as she hurried up The Street to catch the post. The wind seemed to have died down a little as she clicked shut her gate and headed north from her cottage to the red letter-box in Mr. Stillman's wall. Clouds, grey and gust-ripped into shreds, were moving across the sky with rather more decorum than before; when a glimmer of autumn sunlight eventually peeped through, it managed to gleam for several minutes before being smothered again from sight. Stepping out more briskly than the wind was now blowing, Miss Seeton made for the post office, with her letters in the bag over one arm, her brolly over the other . . .

And with both hands, of necessity, in just the wrong position to make an upward grab when a sudden, sneaky gust of wind snatched her black felt hat from her head, and sent it bowling, skipping, curvetting up The Street . . .

With Miss Seeton, after one little cry of startled vexation, in hot pursuit not very far behind.

# CHAPTER 4

Mrs. Blaine forgot that she was barely on speaking terms with Miss Nuttel.

"Oh, Eric, do come quick! Just look," commanded Norah Blaine, "out of the window. It's really too ridiculous, at her age, making a spectacle of herself in front of the whole village."

Miss Nuttel peered out through the white net curtains to the world beyond. "Undignified," she agreed, at the sight of Miss Seeton sprinting, bag and brolly bouncing as she ran, after her errant headpiece. "Sets a bad example."

"You mean the schoolchildren, of course." Miss Maynard and Mr. Jessyp had dismissed their pupils for the day, and a giggling, chattering, shrill-voiced crowd could be heard approaching from the north as it made its way in the direction of one or other of the Plummergen shops selling sweets, crisps, and fizzy drinks.

"I've never understood," continued Mrs. Blaine crossly, "how Mr. Jessyp can possibly believe That Woman is fit to teach such very impressionable youngsters whenever Miss Maynard's away. One would suppose he'd know better by now, with all the *peculiar* things that happen whenever she's around, but he doesn't seem to. It's too strange. Suspicious, even.''

The shrill giggles had turned suddenly to squeals of excitement, accompanied by the thunderous patter of fifty pairs of feet as the children rushed to Miss Seeton's aid. They hurled themselves in gleeful pursuit after the wayward, wind-tossed hat, and ignored her cries of warning lest her young helpers should, in the heat of the moment, forget all about their Kerb Drill and leap out into the road under the wheels of some passing car.

"Lady Colveden," Miss Nuttel reminded her. "Board of governors. Different if any of *them* had children there, of course, but they haven't.''

"Oh, Eric, you're so right. One would have supposed that Lady Colveden—not that Sir George is exactly the *squire,* too old-fashioned and forelock-tugging, but somehow one does still expect them to set a good example, and not to go encouraging people who . . . ''

"Ought to know better," supplied Miss Nuttel, as Norah Blaine drifted to a halt. She had just remembered that she wasn't talking to Eric, and was feeling a little embarrassed about having been the one to initiate the conversation.

She accordingly uttered only the faintest of murmurs in response to Miss Nuttel's remark, and stared even harder through the window at the frenzied scene without. The capricious breeze, which had bowled Miss Seeton's hat in tantalising fits and starts all the way up The Street just a few yards in front of her eager hands, had allowed itself a short breather, sufficient to drop the hat almost to the ground at the feet of the foremost child: but it had then changed its mind again and sent the by now battered bonnet in a high-flying parabola right across The Street to rest, its proud feathers crumpled, its crown covered with dust, on the striped canvas awning over Mr. Stillman's window.

"Oh, dear," breathed Miss Seeton, as the canvas bounced and bulged beneath the unexpected weight. Mr. Stillman, she feared, was not going to be pleased. The awning was new, a replacement for the curved brown-and-orange canopy which had shielded the post office window from the sun since the heady days of the Best Kept Village Competition, in which Plummergen had come second. With thoughts even now turning to next year's contest, Mr. Stillman had recently exchanged autumnal stripes for mock Tudor black and white, with a smartly scalloped border . . .

And nobody could call crumpled feathers and dusty crown—midnight sable, overpowdered by dingy grey—any great improvement on the original intent.

"Oh, dear . . . Children—do take care!" Miss Seeton, still lamenting the unorthodox resting-place of her hat even as she patted her hair automatically back into shape, caught her breath in a sudden gasp at the sight of the fifty Junior Mixed Infants who from time to time came under her pedagogic sway running pell-mell across The Street, crying that they would throw stones or jump up to bring the fugitive feathers down.

"Children—no, please . . . "

But by the time Miss Seeton, looking carefully to right, left, and right again before setting even one foot on the metalled surface of the road, had reached the post office pavement, the area under the awning had become a mass of laughing, leaping figures swinging satchels upwards on their leather straps to bump against the canvas, attempting to jab pointing fingers and optimistic fists into the underside of the hat to slide it over the edge and into their waiting hands . . . And from inside the shop, Mr. Stillman's customers stood and stared, astounded.

Miss Seeton, blushing, raised her voice above the cries of "Out the way, Henry!" and "My turn now!" to request—to insist—that the children, grateful though she was for their assistance, should stop, and allow her to think the problem through. Recognising the voice of command, they duly stopped; but the effort of stopping them, hard upon the exertion of the chase, had left their commander too frazzled even to start thinking what she should do next.

Giggling, shuffling, digging one another in the ribs, Plummergen's youth watched Miss Seeton ponder, her anxious eyes upturned to the dark, circular shadow visible among the stripes. Whispers of "Dare you, Helen!" and "Go on, Katy, you thought of it first" did not reach her worry-deafened ears, and in the depths of her concentration she failed to observe the curious crowd pressing against the glass of the post office window.

At last: "Use yer brolly, Miss!" came the advice from the school's recognised wag, dared by his friends and with his position to maintain. Leader of the Bigguns, he was already as tall as Miss Seeton, though by more than half a century her junior. "Do it for you, shall I?"

"Ooh yes, Miss!"

"Hold yer satchel while you jump?"

"Betcher don't do it first time!"

The clamour seemed to rouse Miss Seeton from her contemplative trance. She blinked, shook her head, and, sighing with relief, smiled kindly on her young gallant.

"I don't think it will be necessary for anyone to jump, thank you. Mr. Stillman, as I now recall, has a set of aluminium steps behind the grocery counter, so that he may more easily reach items on the higher shelves. I am sure that, once I explain, he will let me borrow them—the steps, that is—and then, with my umbrella, as you suggested, it should be an easy enough matter to . . . "

It was a sadly dilapidated headpiece which was at last tumbled from the striped awning by Miss Seeton, standing tip-toe atop the borrowed steps, poking and prodding with her umbrella. She had refused Mr. Stillman's kind offer of assistance, saying that it was her own fault for having forgotten a hatpin; she had poked and prodded, and had at last achieved success. Fifty pairs of grubby young hands reached out to grab as the battered bonnet tumbled to earth; more feathers fell off in the subsequent scrimmage. Miss Seeton, blessing the yoga which, taken up over seven years earlier for the benefit of her knees, had endowed her with remarkable agility and an excellent sense of balance, hopped sadly to the ground to retrieve her handbag from one child, and her hat—after some confusion—from the midst of a scrabbling horde of the child's companions.

"Reckon it's had it, Miss," someone said, as Miss Seeton surveyed the sorry wreckage of her property, and sighed.

"I rather fear you may be right." She sighed again: one could do—one regularly did—one's best with trimming and decoration, but there was a limit beyond which even the most skilful needle—which she acknowledged that hers was not—was unable to renew the old, restore the ruined. "It is," said Miss Seeton again, "nobody's fault but mine, for having neglected, in my hurry to catch the post, to use a pin to secure my hat, in such very windy weather—which," she added, "is a lesson from which we might all learn. More haste, children, means less speed, in the end."

Fifty small, serious faces nodded their understanding, then hid smiles as Miss Seeton, realising what she'd just said, dropped the hat on the ground and opened her bag to begin fumbling inside for her letters. As some bent to retrieve, yet again, the peripatetic headpiece, others cocked their heads on one side, listening. In the distance, an approaching diesel whine . . .

"Miss, hurry up!"

"Here comes Bert!"

And Miss Seeton slipped her letters through the official scarlet slot just ten seconds before red-haired Bert, Plummergen's expatriate Cockney postman, pulled up in his van outside the letter-box, and prepared to unload its contents into his brown hessian sack.

"Well!" was the general opinion within the post office, as Bert in his van rattled at last on his way and Miss Seeton, having once more thanked the children, trotted off on hers, bearing the sad remains of her windblown hat in her hands.

"Well," somebody promptly enlarged, "if that ain't just what you'd expect o' Miss Seeton, egging on the kiddies to mischief—and her supposed to set them a good example!''

''As good as pulled Mr. Stillman's new awning down on top o' their heads with that brolly of hers—the poor little mites,'' chimed in someone else, having checked that none of the children was present to overhear this unusually fond turn of phrase. ''As if any of us'd ever dream o' doing such a thing! I've allus said,'' she added, ''as there's summat *strange* about Miss Seeton.''

''Which ain't to say,'' said Mrs. Flax, ''as she's the only strange one around these parts.'' The Wise Woman, perennially jealous of Miss Seeton's reputation against her own, steered the conversation artfully away from her rival, and back to the topic previously under discussion. ''If there's anyone here,'' said Mrs. Flax, in challenging accents, ''as can tell me what cause Miss Nuttel's got to go buying *cheesewire,* of all things, them Nuts being vegetarian, or so they've allus said, then I'd like to know what it is.''

''*And* a fishing reel,'' said Mrs. Skinner.

''Not to mention snare wire,'' said Mrs. Henderson.

They stared at each other, astonished that their thought processes should be running so plainly in parallel. It was too much, of course, to suppose that parallel lines could ever meet: but both ladies felt a certain frisson as they hastily averted their eyes, and gazed anywhere but at the face opposite.

''And Mrs. Blaine,'' said Mrs. Spice, ''a-barging in here not ten minutes after, for a breadboard—as if anyone needs two breadboards! Not as if you'd wear 'em out, is it? Take a powerful thick crust on a loaf for a knife to cut through to the surface.''

''An *ordinary* knife,'' said Mrs. Flax, and put her finger to her lips, looking over her shoulder and lowering her voice. ''It's not so long since Halloween, remember—as who should know better than me?'' She cleared her throat, preparing for gnomic utterance, and everyone held horrified breath, and waited in gleeful expectation.

Expectation was not in vain.

"There's kitchen steel," Mrs. Flax, in thrilling tones, reminded her audience, "and there's *cold iron* . . ."

And as pent-up breath was released in an ecstatic sigh, a shiver ran down the spine of everyone within earshot.

Next morning's first lesson was History, and Miss Maynard knew that, in the first week of November, there could be no choice as to the historical event covered.

"The Gunpowder Plot," announced Miss Maynard, writing on the blackboard as she spoke. "Which was also known as the Gunpowder Treason. I'm sure you all know the rhyme," she added, as twenty small hands waved in the air, and twenty treble voices begged to recite.

"Remember, remember the fifth of November—
The Gunpowder Treason and Plot.
I see no reason why Gunpowder Treason
Should ever be forgot!"

came the full-throated response, in an excited chorus. Miss Maynard smiled.

"And what is so special about November the fifth?"

"Guy Fawkes Night!" roared the chorus, more excited still. Miss Maynard smiled again, and nodded.

"And who was Guy Fawkes? Doesn't anyone know?" as there was silence. "Come on, think. Try to remember," she coaxed those who had been in her class the previous year.

"Burn 'im on the bonfire," offered someone at last, to the accompaniment of sniggers from everyone else, who knew this very well, and said so.

"Indeed we do, in effigy—that means," said Miss Maynard, "as a model, a representation. But Guy Fawkes was a real person. The bonfire and fireworks we have each year on Guy Fawkes Night commemorate the explosion Guy and

the other conspirators—the Gunpowder Plotters—hoped to
cause when they tried to blow up the Houses of Parliament
when the King was going to be there . . . ''

Miss Maynard proceeded to narrate the thrilling story of
how Robert Catesby, with fellow Roman Catholics Thomas
Percy and Thomas Winter, headed a deadly conspiracy to
murder the Protestant King James I when he came, with
his Lords and the ordinary Members of Parliament, to open
the new session in the House of Lords on the fifth of November, 1605.

Catesby and his friends hoped to seize the king's nine-
year-old daughter, the Princess Elizabeth, and put her on
the throne in his place as a puppet, pro-Catholic queen: Sir
Everard Digby, Ambrose Rookwood, and John Grant were
brought in to oversee her capture from the house where she
was staying at the time, many miles from London.

''Some of them,'' said Miss Maynard, ''would have preferred to take the young Duke of York prisoner instead, but
then they heard that he would probably be accompanying
his father to the State Opening of Parliament, so they had
to choose the princess. The Duke of York,'' she added, ''in
fact was destined to become King Charles the First . . . ''

The plotters found other people to join them. Thomas
Winter recruited his brother Robert; Thomas Percy brought
in his brother-in-law, John Wright. Robert Keyes was given
the job of keeping watch on Catesby's house in London,
where the gunpowder was stored, and to arrange the boat
trip when it was to be ferried across the Thames from Lam-
beth to the Palace of Westminster . . .

''Thirty-six barrels of gunpowder,'' said Miss Maynard,
''would make a tremendous bang, once they blew up. The
man chosen to light the fuse was Guy Fawkes . . . ''

The conspirators, having acquired their gunpowder—and
that, said Miss Maynard, was as difficult then as collecting
thirty-six machine guns would be nowadays—began to dig
a tunnel from the house of a man called John Whynniard.
This man lived—he was the official Keeper of the Ward-

robe—within the precincts of the actual Parliament building, as you could still do, in those far-off days when people were not so security-minded. Whynniard was happy to rent out his house, and the finished tunnel ran from there to a coal-cellar owned by a merchant called Bright—a cellar which was directly under the chamber where King James would attend the State Opening. The plan was to cram the cellar full of gunpowder, and to time the explosion for the exact moment when most of the country's rulers would be above it.

"But they had made a big mistake," said Miss Maynard. "Between them, they completely misjudged the sincerity and commitment of one of the newer conspirators, Francis Tresham. Nobody quite knows why, but Tresham betrayed the Plot to his brother-in-law, Lord Monteagle. Lord Monteagle told the authorities what he had learned, and a small party went to check the cellar.

"And there," said Miss Maynard, "instead of coal as they might have expected, they found piles of wood, ready for burning—and they found a man who called himself Johnson, who was really Guy Fawkes. But he sounded so plausible that they moved on, and left him in peace—only the next day, November the Fifth, another group of men came, and one of them was a magistrate. And when the magistrate told them to search the cellar, they found the barrels of gunpowder, and they arrested Guy Fawkes . . . ''

The lantern-light searching of the Parliament cellars (Miss Maynard told her pupils) still takes place every year in commemoration of the saving of the King, his Lords, and his Commons. A scarlet-and-gold detachment of the Yeomen of the Guard is sent for this purpose from the Tower of London, and not a single square inch of ground is missed. Only when the Yeomen pronounce the vaults and basement empty of any bomb or infernal device is it thought safe for Parliament to be opened: there must be no repetition of the narrow escape of 1605, when Guy Fawkes, tortured, revealed the hideous plot against the throne, and betrayed the names of his fellow conspirators. After his betrayal, some were taken alive, some died in the fighting—these last being, said Miss Maynard, probably better off, in the long run, for those who were taken were tortured, and stood trial, and were found guilty; and were executed in a public and very horrible manner.

"They may have been cowards," said Miss Maynard, "in the cold-blooded way they tried to kill innocent people when they themselves were nowhere nearby—but they showed the courage of their convictions in the brave way they met their deaths. They were drawn on hurdles, head-down, through the streets of London to the scaffold, and people threw things at them, and insulted them. But Ambrose Rookwood asked his captors to tell him when they passed the place where his poor wife was waiting, so that he could smile at her just once more, and ask her to remember him in her prayers. Guy Fawkes was the last to be executed, and because he had been so badly tortured he was too weak to climb the scaffold without help . . . ''

King James and his Parliament, thankful for their escape, ruled that, from then on, the Fifth of November should be celebrated as a holiday, with bells ringing, cannon firing, and special services in church; and (as Miss Maynard said in conclusion) with parties, and with bonfires. The fireworks came later . . .

"But nobody wants to blow up the Queen now, Miss?" asked one youngster, whose imagination had been caught by the tale, and who was of a naturally anxious cast of thought. "And they don't want to—to go around stealing princesses, or putting gunpowder in places, or—or bombs?"

Miss Maynard smiled kindly as Sally's friends sniggered. "You needn't worry, Sally. It was all a long time ago, more than three hundred and fifty years—besides, as I told you, they search the cellars in the Houses of Parliament for bombs very carefully, every year."

"And," ventured someone, "you said it was treason,

Miss. Which ain't treason against the law?''

"Indeed it is," said Miss Maynard. "Treason is a crime, a very serious crime against the government and the Queen—the Sovereign, or the Sovereign's family. And it's so very serious that nobody would ever dream of committing treason, because nobody would want to go to prison . . . ''

But small Sally did not look altogether convinced.

# CHAPTER 5

Inspector Harry Furneux of Rye was not a happy man.

There were, of course, times when the Fiery Furnace could be the most genial of men: but this was not one of them. The telephone wires between Rye (in Sussex) and Ashford (across the border, in Kent) were red-hot proof of his misery. He had spent the previous fifteen minutes moaning without pause to his colleague and county neighbour Superintendent Brinton; and Brinton—who could sympathise only too well—was growing restless. Old Brimstone would have liked an opportunity to let off some of his own head of steam. Even a few words would have done, they'd be better than nothing: but the Furnace was roaring away at full throttle, and all Brinton could do on the other end of the line was nod sympathetically, and suck peppermints, and roll despairing eyes at the ceiling.

"You seriously think *you've* got problems? With just one lousy royal visit?"

The suffering superintendent groaned. Inspector Furneux had now come full circle for the seventh time, but he still didn't seem to realise that Brinton might want to indulge in a spot of moaning on his own account.

"One half-pint princess," snarled Harry Furneux, "that's all *you've* got to worry about—*and* you get help, which is a damned sight more than I do—"

"Only a couple of toughs from MI5," Brinton—to his eternal surprise—managed to chip in. "And the odd bod or two from Special Branch, but—"

Furneux ignored him. "You've got it made, believe me! What've *you* got to worry about? You know as well as I do, the build-up that young woman's had since she smashed her first bottle of fizz against a battleship's backside, if a bloke so much as harmed a hair of her royal head he'd have the whole damned country down on him like twenty tons of brick. It's a waste of public money—my blasted taxes, and yours—sending more than a lady-in-waiting, if you ask me. Our Georgy Girl doesn't need sharpshooters and body armour and sniffer dogs on the hunt for bombs—"

"Glurp!" Brinton was so horrified at this suggestion that a peppermint tried to go down backwards.

Harry Furneux again ignored his friend, though the sounds coming along the wire from Ashford were alarming, to say the least. "Oh, no, she just flutters those blue eyes of hers and flips her curls, and all the chummies go weak at the knees and say, 'Terribly sorry, but we promise to go straight from now on, and Gawd bless yer for being so forgiving, marm,' and the next thing you know the blighters're handing out tracts and free meals to—"

"Mam!" cried Brinton, goaded beyond endurance, spitting the wayward mint into his handkerchief. "Mam, dammit!"

"What?" The interruption had been so loud, and so sudden, that the Furnace applied an automatic damper. "Sorry, sir," simmering down, "I didn't quite catch what you said. Something about jam?"

"Mam," said Brinton, in more measured tones, after he'd cleared his throat once or twice. "We've had the briefing from Buck House, plus HRH's private secretary.

Snowed under with memos, we've been. Reams of bumf—young Foxon's made paper darts out of half of it—but one thing they said was that the first time, you call her 'Your Royal Highness,' then it's 'Ma'am' to rhyme with jam, not smarm, the rest of the time.''

"Ma'am," said Furneux, experimentally.

"That's right."

"Oh." Furneux brooded briefly, and Brinton was about to seize his chance when his colleague added:

"Tell you how to curtsey as well, do they?"

"For the women police officers," said Brinton primly, "yes, they do. Maggie Laver's been practising her one-foot-behind-the-other-and-bob bit for days now."

"D'you have to buy your own Union Jacks for waving, or is there a sort of central store of the things they send ahead and you send back once it's all over?"

"I wish," said Brinton, now the chance had come round again, "it *was* all over." Glumly, he tried with a dampened finger to rub fluff from the peppermint's surface: it didn't look so appetising now. "I'm the old-fashioned type, I am. Give me solid fuel any day—coal, or gas, or even oil, if you can afford it the way the price keeps going up—but the idea of neutrons and electrons and heaven-knows-what bumping about together inside a hunk of uranium gives me a nasty feeling, Harry. Someone drops a match or a fag-end in the wrong place, and you've got something'll make Hiroshima look like the Teddy Bears' Picnic—and not twenty miles from here, so it'd be right on my patch. Yours as well, come to that, except there'd be nothing much of either left once that power station'd gone up in smoke and a helluva lot worse—''

"Young Georgina doesn't smoke," broke in Furneux, so appalled by this grim scenario that he temporarily forgot his own woes. "Never been known to drink, come to that, and you can bet the lady-in-waiting won't if Georgy doesn't. Anyway, I've been on a tour of the place—well, not this new one, but Dungeness A, it's the same design, another Magnox reactor—and they're a pretty careful bunch, these nuclear generating types. Got to be, of course—but there're great No Smoking notices up almost before you're through the first lot of gates, and—''

"Gates!" groaned Brinton. "What use'd gates be if some terrorist or other got the idea of planting a bomb and lighting a fuse and skedaddling before the place went up? Or turned suicidal and thought he'd chuck a grenade into the reactor, or whatever it's called—and don't tell me,'' hearing Furneux clear his throat, suspecting a lecture was about to begin. "I don't want to know. Chain reaction? Nuclear pile? I've seen *Dr No* like everyone else—*and,*'' grimly, "*Dr Strangelove,* so you needn't think I don't know what I'm worried about, because I damned well do.''

"If you say so.'' Furneux sounded almost cheerful now: he knew very well that his friend's misery was not so much caused by fear of some maniac-begotten cataclysm as by anticipation of the horrendous traffic problems likely to attend so public an event as the official opening of a new centre of local employment by a young, pretty, and popular princess.

"And another thing," growled Brinton, making the most of it now the younger man seemed to have given up for a while, "why D, I'd like to know?''

"Wye Dee?'' echoed Furneux, puzzled. "The rivers, you mean? Or is there some sinister oriental element in all this you haven't told me about before?''

"Why,'' enlarged Brinton, through gritted teeth, "is this one D, if the other bally thing's called A? I thought your average egghead types were meant to be logical! There's precious little logic if you go missing out B—or even C, dammit. Why's it D?''

"Haven't the faintest idea, I'm afraid. You could try,'' suggested Furneux, with a quiver in his voice, "ringing the Central Electricity Generating Board to ask them—or maybe if you unfold some of young Foxon's paper planes you'll find the stuff from Buckingham Palace tells you.

They brief their stars pretty thoroughly, I gather.''

"Ha! We'll be seeing stars, all right, if anyone puts a match to that damned Dungeness construction. Talk about Guy Fawkes Night—it'd be the whole blasted three hundred and seventy years rolled into one, and that's just for starters, because—''

"It'll be more the end of everything, rather than the start,'' interposed Furneux swiftly. "At least it'd stop you worrying, because there'd be nothing left to worry *about*. But when it comes to Guy Fawkes Night, well, you should have *my* worries for a bit and then you'd know what worry really means . . . ''

And Harry Furneux was off on the old, old story for— to Brinton's irritation—the eighth time, which had to be a record. Most years, he'd managed to shut him up around the fifth or sixth run-through. By now, he could recite it from memory, though he still couldn't see how the Bonfire Boys of Rye—dragging their boat through the streets of the little town, tearing down official notices of prohibition as they went, escorted by a selection of Guys in every shape and size, assembling for a gigantic bonfire on the Town Salts with the products of their riotous journey—could compare in the anxiety stakes with a royal visit. Traffic congestion? Furneux didn't know the meaning of the word. A few bob more on the rates to pay for replacing the No Parking signs? Peanuts. A handful of drunks in the cells, the odd window smashed? Worse had happened when the local football team went on the rampage after a win.

" . . . dead from the blast, then it'd be the radiation, and if that or the fallout didn't get you then the nuclear winter pretty soon would,'' Furneux was saying, as Brinton reluctantly tuned back into the miserable monologue. "Now, if you were to tell me anyone'd been monkeying around with shrapnel, I might just think you'd got a point. An ounce or two of big-bang mixture in a metal box—weedkiller, sugar, easy enough to find—pack a few nuts and bolts round it and light a fuse—yes, that's nasty. Or clockwork,'' he added, as Brinton, grinding his teeth on peppermint, bit his tongue and was rendered speechless. "Yes, if anyone tries a trick like *that* anywhere around young Georgina, I agree you've got problems—but they won't," said Furneux, firmly. "She's everyone's favourite girl, and they'd be lynched if they so much as hinted at hurting her. You've got nothing to worry about, sir, believe me. Everything," said Harry Furneux, "will be fine . . . "

The Brettenden bus had left Plummergen with Miss Nuttel, but with no Mrs. Blaine, on board.

This unwonted nuxial schism thrilled the entire village, both on the bus and off it. Those who stayed behind felt in duty bound to maintain surveillance on Bunny; those who went with Eric to Brettenden knew they faced a harder task, but, in the true Plummergen spirit, faced that task undaunted. It might be thought difficult, if not impossible, to remain unobtrusive when following someone into an ironmonger's: yet a small and determined detachment managed somehow to achieve this laudable end, thereby encouraging others to emulate their achievement in the hardware shop and, shortly after, in the electrician's.

The three groups found it more than frustrating that they were unable to discuss the matter with their friends on the return journey. Miss Nuttel, brown-paper-parcelled to the eyebrows, was, inevitably, their fellow traveller; for which reason, on their arrival in Plummergen, they repaired at once to the sanctuary of the post office. Having seen Miss Nuttel stalk up Lilikot's garden path and enter the house through a grudgingly-opened (and viciously-closed) door, everyone heaved heartfelt sighs of relief. Only now could they present their report to the Home Front, demanding in exchange the full details of Mrs. Blaine's activities during the absence of Miss Nuttel . . .

"Not seen hide nor hair of her all day," said young Mrs. Newport, with a sigh.

"Popped out once for a new washing-up bowl," young

Mrs. Scillicough volunteered, then flushed at the look of scorn on her sister's face. "Well, at least I *saw* her—not to speak to, though. Regular Hot Cross Bun today, she was, and no mistake—you ask Emmy," turning to Miss Putts on Groceries. "Hardly a civil word did she say, and nothing else did she buy beyond the bowl—eh, Em?"

"That's right." Emmy Putts was pink with pleasure at being the centre of attention, even though, with little to tell, she knew it couldn't last long. "Not even a tin o' them mock meatballs they're so fond of—and very brisk about it she was, too."

In fact, Norah Blaine had almost bitten Emmy's head off when the shop assistant had in all innocence expressed the view that Mrs. Blaine might risk breaking her glass and fine china washing up, and wouldn't a plastic bowl be better than enamel. "Told me," said Emmy, "as I oughter be ashamed of meself encouraging folk to—to deplete the world's natural resources, plastic bein' made of petrol or summat, she said. And off she went in a huff, and not seen since beyond shaking a duster out of the landing window," concluded Emmy, who had been fortunate enough to witness this exciting episode when popping home for her midday meal.

Public opinion did not take long to decide that washing-up bowls, whether plastic or enamel, lacked the glamour and intrigue of what Miss Nuttel had bought in the ironmonger's, the electrician's, and the hardware shop. Plummergen understood the necessity to clean crockery, cutlery, and glass, to wash dirtied dishes and kitchen utensils . . .

But it had—even after much racking of its collective brain—absolutely no idea why Miss Nuttel should wish to purchase (among other items) three yards of triple five-amp cable, three feet of bare copper earth wire, a conduit box, a sewing-machine belt (when everyone knew it was Mrs. Blaine as did all the needlework in that house!), ten sheets of asbestos board, a length of asbestos rope, eight steel angle joints, eight Jubilee clips, and a large selection of nuts, bolts, nails, screws, and metal washers.

After considerable discussion, it fell to Mrs. Flax to summarise the general opinion.

"Well," said the Wise Woman, "if you ask me, she's Up To Summat . . . "

And there, for the present, the matter had to rest.

Miss Seeton was busy in her kitchen with a fork, a bowl, and a waiting slab of rich, golden butter. Scrambled eggs, she had decided, were on the menu for tonight's supper. After all, since one had one's own chickens, and thanks to dear Stan these always laid so well . . .

When Cousin Flora had left her house and all her worldly goods to her grateful god-daughter Emily, she left also the perhaps more valuable bequest of Stan and Martha Bloomer; or rather (lest it be supposed that the old lady had approved the unwholesome practice of slavery) the bequest of their skilled horticultural and domestic services. Farmhand Stan had for some years past tended the gardens, both front and back—flowers, fruit, vegetables—of Sweetbriars, Old Mrs. Bannet's, now Miss Seeton's, cottage at the southernmost end of The Street, on the corner where it divides sharply in a right-angled bend to form Marsh Road, running west towards Rye, and narrowing to run between high brick walls down to the bridge over the Royal Military Canal.

One of these bridge-bound brick walls belongs to Sweetbriars, for the garden is of considerable length. As Flora Bannet, long widowed, increasingly deaf, and depressingly arthritic, was beginning to feel overwhelmed by the size of her responsibilities, Stan Bloomer, who lived in a cottage in the shadow of the Sweetbriars wall, made the providential suggestion that he should take over caring for the entire outside area of the property, Mrs. Bannet to select the pick of such crops as it produced, himself to sell the remainder at a profit, such profit to be in lieu of wages.

As for the inside as worrited her so much, well, there was his wife, London born and sharp as a needle, more than willing to come twice a week to cook and clean and do aught else the old lady might require, not just for the money but because they were neighbours, good as family living so close—and Miss Emily, popping down from Town to visit every now and then, like family as well, and no denying. Martha and him, they'd take a pleasure and more in looking after the place and the folk as belonged to it . . .

The folk belonging being in turn Mrs. Bannet and, for the past seven years, Miss Emily Dorothea Seeton.

Miss Seeton, blissfully contemplating, as she so often did, her great good fortune, sighed with mingled pleasure and regret as she prepared her supper. Pleasure as she pondered the sweet, smooth curves of the speckled shells; regret, as she destroyed their mellow brown perfection by cracking them, one at a time, into the glass bowl. She set the empty shells aside to be crushed for the compost heap, then whisked with an energetic fork until yolks and whites had combined in a froth of late summer sunshine. Pepper, a sprinkle: but no salt until later, for salt before scrambling made eggs sadly tough.

A dab of butter in the heavy metal pan; an aromatic sizzling. Miss Seeton's nose twitched. She picked up the bowl, preparing to tip its contents into the skillet—

"Bother." She set the bowl down again. Could one ignore the doorbell? Even at supper-time it would be, she supposed, discourteous. Whoever it was must know, from the kitchen light reflected on the wall at the side of the house, that one was at home. Besides, the matter might be one of some importance, even if one's friends, on these darker evenings, were given more to telephoning first than to turning up on the doorstep . . .

The bell pealed a second time. Miss Seeton clicked her tongue for her tardiness, pulled off her apron, dropped it neatly over a chair, hurried down the hall; heard strange scuffling sounds outside as she turned the handle, and the door swung slowly open.

"Evening, Miss."

" 'Lo, Miss."

A clustering giggle of children stood on the mat, nudging one another as they piped their youthful courtesies before falling into an awkward silence.

Miss Seeton, smiling, greeted her visitors in reply, her eye drifting momentarily over their heads as it was caught by further scuffling and giggling at the end of the garden, where more children hovered by the gate.

Miss Seeton was normally the most prompt of hostesses to invite her guests into her home. Her guests, however, were seldom so many in number, or so young, or in so obviously mischievous a mood—which one recognised, of course, from one's years in teaching. Children—mused Miss Seeton—as this particular group continued to giggle without utterance, did so enjoy laughter, which was, of course, so good for them. For anyone, indeed, especially after practical jokes, which—always provided they were not of a malicious or unpleasant nature—could often amuse even the adult mind, and certainly helped them to let off steam. The children, that was to say, not the adults, although dear Sir George and Lady Colveden had sometimes spoken in most, well, eloquent terms of the antics of dear Nigel and his cronies from the Young Farmers . . .

Miss Seeton's kindly smile grew wider as she thought of the aristocratic owners of Rytham Hall, for they were among her closest friends. She smiled; and the leader of the little giggling group on her doorstep was emboldened, with nudging elbows his support and prompt, to clear his throat.

"Er—Miss . . . "

Miss Seeton smiled on him as he fell silent again, and nodded encouragement. Evidently it had been proposed that she, as one sympathetic to the needs of the young—and, without being immodest, perhaps in some ways better qualified than others in the village to be their recipient—should, well, receive them. Or it. The joke, or jokes, not the children, or their needs. As guests, because although one tried to be hospitable, one's cottage was hardly . . .

"Er, Miss," came the second attempt, forced out of the speaker by a nimble prod in the small of his back. "Miss, the other day, when it was so windy . . . "

Miss Seeton nodded again. "I remember, yes."

"We was wondering . . . with it bin a rare old mess on account o' dust, and tumbling about, and us having to catch it afore it blew away again . . . "

Miss Seeton blinked.

"Please, Miss, could we have your hat?"

# CHAPTER 6

Miss Seeton blinked again.

"With it bin," went on the small petitioner, warming to his explanation, "not so long to go now, Miss—an' us've collected the sacks, an' the straw—"

"An' made the notice, too," chimed in someone else, with obvious proprietorial pride in this achievement.

"An' made the notice." The first speaker scowled at his companion. "An' got most of the clothes, Miss, as folks was happy to throw out—all of 'em save the hat, Miss, acksherly. So—well, we was wondering ..."

Miss Seeton looked a little startled: but then, after a pause, as realisation dawned, smiled once more. Waste not, want not. Of course. An admirable precept—and with so many applications, although it was remarkable how many of these were not necessarily convenient to one's immediate purpose. Remarkable, for instance, how frequently what would at first glance appear to be the exact article required could not be used for that purpose because there was still good wear in it: which surely explained why—having asked, one assumed, their parents—they had come to her. Naturally—one's small part to play in village life—one was pleased to be able to help; flattered, in some ways, to have been asked, to have so won their confidence and trust that they had turned next to one who was, on occasion, their teacher. One could not—indeed should not—suppress their creative urges, though one had certainly never expected that one might be so—one could hardly call it *complimented* . . . yet the opposite—which would be, if deliberate, an insult—was far from their minds, as was any spirit of mockery, she was sure . . .

Miss Seeton twinkled down at the eager faces raised in anxious anticipation to her own. "I believe," she said slowly, "that I may well be able to help you. I had, you know, intended to try a few repairs—but really, when I come to consider the matter, I have had several years' wear out of it. And though one is not, I trust, a slave to current fashion, the wind was, as you rightly point out, very strong the other day. And it would perhaps be a trifle selfish of me to refuse when I do, after all, have others." She uttered a small sigh. "Indeed, I suspect that even if I had remembered my hat-pin it would have been unable to hold it on, or at least not without being rather uncomfortable. If you would wait there for just one moment . . . "

Miss Seeton—blessing her yoga-nimble knees—trod lightly up the stairs and into her bedroom, where she quickly retrieved from her mending basket the battered black felt with its woebegone feather trimmings. Clicking her tongue, she shook her head one last time for the loss of a Monica Mary creation. The celebrated Brettenden milliner would not, she hoped, be offended at such an unusual fate, should she hear of it, for the child of her imagination . . .

Miss Seeton blushed at herself in the glass for so very fanciful a notion, then hurried out of the room and back down the stairs to her front door. Here, she found that the original daring few had been joined by their less courageous companions from the gate.

Miss Seeton smiled on them all. The young: so full of

energy, and such a sense of fun, if only one could channel it correctly. Their undoubted energy. *Constructive play* she believed was the term she'd heard mentioned . . .

"But remember," warned Miss Seeton, as her offering was received with squeals and grateful giggles into the grubby, eager hands, "I expect to see something—something special, when the time comes. Something more than a little out of the ordinary, you know. This is, after all, a Monica Mary hat." Her twinkle was disarming, her tone amused, and the youngsters found themselves twinkling back as she went on:

"If you come back tomorrow after school, I might have found some more feathers to replace these—but not now," as further squeals suggested that tomorrow was a long way away. "The chickens, you know, have been put inside for the night, and I've no wish to disturb them by taking a torch down to the hen-house in the dark. Tomorrow, after school, and we will see what can be done."

"Ooooh, Miss," came the obedient chorus. "Thank you very much, Miss!"

"Um—pins, Miss," said the leader, made even more bold now the trophy was safe in his hands. "Allus have 'em on hats, do they?"

Warily, Miss Seeton confirmed that many persons did, but added the swift rider that many others did not. Pinning (or an absence of pins) was partly a matter of personal preference, and partly dependant on the style of hat; no, she wouldn't say there was any hard and fast rule about it, and certainly not *always*. And, of course, on the availability of the right sort of pin. No, she wouldn't call them *rare*, exactly, though she would certainly agree that there weren't as many around as there had been some years ago . . .

Miss Seeton's wariness increased. Service to one's community was all very well: one was only too happy—indeed, proud—to play one's modest part: but surely one was not expected to play it to such an extent that one was required to sacrifice one's prized personal possessions? Dear Cousin

Flora, old-fashioned though some might call her—not that her god-daughter would ever dream of such a thing—had left many charming and unusual items of jewellery—though not valuable, of course—to her heir; and Miss Seeton took a pride in wearing them on suitable occasions, enjoying the memories which the wearing brought to mind as well as the aesthetic pleasure it gave. A hat-pin, of course, could not be considered in the same class as the quaint glass necklace with its yellow beads, or the tiny silver brooch in the shape of a flying swallow, but . . .

"If there *was* a lot of 'em around, Miss, then you could wear more'n one at once," suggested he of the hat. "Couldn't you? A bit prickly, but more—more prongs, Miss, to hold it on. Like a fork."

"Or just one big one, Miss," ventured somebody else, when it was clear Miss didn't mind folk saying things. "Bigger 'n' thicker, I mean, like a—like a skewer, 'cept you'd have to take care of hurting yer head, but it'd be stronger by far nor any old fork in a wind like that . . . "

"Let us hope," said Miss Seeton, hiding a smile for the curious—and gratifying; one's teaching was perhaps bearing a little fruit—imaginative powers of her pupils— "that it will not be so windy again for a very long while. Fresh air is like so many things, acceptable in moderation but—"

She broke off. Fresh air? She sniffed. Sniffed again, nose twitching. "The scrambled eggs!" she cried; and, with a hurried farewell, closed the door on her young visitors before turning to trot, as fast as she could, down the hall to the kitchen, from which ominous curls of smoke were starting to drift.

Miss Seeton gasped, snatched her apron from the chair, wrapped it around her hand, and dragged the pan from the heat to rest on the coolness of the tiled kitchen table. Seized tea towels from the rack and threw them with a smothering motion over the sizzling skillet, then wrenched the red-and-white striped hand towel from its wall-mounted roller and added it to the rest. She darted to the cooker and switched off the ring; she turned back to the table, holding her breath. With a spitting, spattering, hissing sound, a vicious, roaring sigh, the danger seemed at last to be over.

Miss Seeton released her breath, inhaled too deeply with relief; coughed. She moved on trembling legs to the window, and threw it open. She breathed again, feeling the welcome draught. Her next cough was less hacking. Perhaps, thought Miss Seeton, she could now relax.

Except that one could hardly relax when, thanks to one's carelessness, the house had very nearly burned down about one's ears. It could be no excuse that the children at the door had been a distraction: perhaps one was, for all one's high hopes of the yoga, starting to feel—and, worse, to act—one's age. One's memory, concentration, clarity of judgement seemed to have been woefully at fault . . .

Or maybe—Miss Seeton brightened at the thought—one was just a little tired; though memory added that the day had, in all conscience, hardly been exhausting. A little gardening—deadheading, some light pruning, half-an-hour's gentle hoeing between rows of over-wintering vegetables . . . And one could not deny that one was not—well, not quite as young as before. Perhaps, before starting a second attempt at supper, a few of one's favourite postures—it was always best, as the book said and as Miss Seeton had learned by experience, to perform these on an empty stomach—for the alleviation of fatigue would improve matters . . .

The Headstand or *Sirsasana* was the most beneficial, she knew, to the brain and thought-processes, to the pineal and pituitary glands which, the author of *Yoga and Younger Every Day* explained to his readers at some length, controlled the growth and mental health of one's body. Seven years ago, one would never have dreamed of attempting such control: but seven years had made an amazing difference to far more than one's knees. Starting from the *Salamba Sarvangasana,* or Shoulder Stand, one could move up smoothly to the Headstand, to hold it for as long as comfortable before tipping slowly over into the *Halasana,* or Plough Posture, all the while doing one's deep breathing. Ten or fifteen minutes' practice, Miss Seeton hoped, would work wonders. She would slip upstairs now, and see how she felt after a brief workout followed by five minutes in the restful *Savasana,* or Dead Pose.

She had to admit that she felt better: refreshed, one could almost say. Miss Seeton opened her eyes, stretched, and rolled over on the travelling rug to arch her spine before rising nimbly to her feet. Refreshed, indeed: but she had somehow lost her appetite for scrambled eggs, normally one of her favourite dishes. The very idea of whisking eggs in a bowl with a fork made her fingers tingle, made them twitch and fidget in a most peculiar way . . .

Or maybe not so peculiar, after all. As if on automatic pilot, Miss Seeton adjusted her clothing, folded away the fringed tartan blanket, and made her way back downstairs. She found herself ignoring the kitchen, heading for the sitting room, for her bureau; for the drawer in which she kept her sketching implements . . .

With a swift pencil, Miss Seeton sketched a hat: but no ordinary hat. This was a black, broad-brimmed hat, high in the crown, almost as if the traditional witch's headgear had been lopped off halfway. A wide band decorated the crown, an enormous buckle decorated the band, and a tall, curling feather stood proudly at one side . . .

Miss Seeton blinked. This was not her hat, the hat she had given the children: this was—good gracious . . .

Smiling to herself, Miss Seeton drew a face beneath the hat: a man's face, dark, saturnine, intense of gaze, with some suggestion of the Spaniard; more than a suggestion of the fanatic in the set, the stare of the eyes. A short, trim beard on the determined chin. The hint of a collar about the neck: then more than a hint, as Miss Seeton grew inspired with her creation, enlarging it to show strong, cloth-clad shoulders . . . from which, to her surprise, sprang arms, not of flesh and blood under fabric, but arms of cold, cruel metal—straight, firm, gleaming; and ending not in fingers, but in sharp, curved, predatory prongs. A muscled body invisible within a belted tunic, close buckled on wide leather; legs, like arms, not of flesh and blood and bone, but of pronged metal, fourfold. Four limbs, four prongs on each: not fingers and toes, but tines.

Not arms and legs, but forks.

Guy Fawkes.

Miss Seeton, recognising the face if not the remainder of the personage, the suggestion of seventeenth-century costume, nodded. The woodcut of Guy, otherwise Guido, Fawkes was well known to those with any interest in history, and even to those who had little or none. Every November found that face reproduced on countless boxes of fireworks, on advertisements for Grand Public Displays, on posters warning children to take care when playing with matches and—even in this small way—with gunpowder. Guy Fawkes. Forks. Her cast-off hat—the children—her promise of feathers for tomorrow . . .

And the coils of smoke which wreathed about his head were, of course, only because of her carelessness with the skillet of hot fat. One must be thankful one had not gone so far as to add the eggs. A little longer for the air to clear, and maybe one might venture a second attempt. Just long enough, perhaps, to try a more, well, serious approach to a portrait of the nation's most famous, although one ought really to say infamous, terrorist . . .

The hat, the face, the beard and costume were much as Miss Seeton had drawn them in her first sketch. And surely it could not be so very unrealistic to have shown him with a dark lantern in one hand? There had been no pocket flashlights, no electricity, in the time of King James the First— as one was hardly able to forget, when the annual basement searching of the Houses of Parliament by the Yeoman of the Guard, in their renowned—although, one believed, misnamed—Beefeater uniforms, was always carried out using candle lanterns. Guy Fawkes: with coils of smoke again around his head . . . but that was no egg, dark-shelled, in his other hand. It was much darker, rounder; spherical. That was no string of albumen trailing from one side, but . . .

"Oh, dear."

A fuse.

A bomb.

And the fuse already alight . . .

"Melodramatic self-indulgence," Miss Seeton scolded herself, even as she sketched sparks and flames spurting from the fuse to the distant piles of . . . of what, she wasn't to decide, since the explosion which had destroyed it—them—had enveloped the entire background in smoke, and in further flame: which was foolish. Guy Fawkes had *not* (she knew very well) succeeded in his wicked intention of blowing up the Houses of Parliament, of murdering King James and his ministers. Why should she suppose that she, Emily Dorothea Seeton, had the power—even on best-quality cartridge paper—to re-write, or rather re-draw, history? The King and Parliament had all been saved, and nobody could have wished it otherwise—not even those who, for one reason or another, had little faith in politicians: which one could in some ways understand, even if one knew one's knowledge of the finer points of politics to be, well, limited. One voted, of course, but . . .

But so few of them appeared to talk sense, at least not for very long; though it certainly could not be denied that they *talked*. Indeed, most of the politicians one saw on the television, or heard on the wireless, seemed to be so fond of the sound of their own voices it was the only thing they ever did—talk—which meant they were so desperate to keep talking they often ran out of good ideas, and didn't. Talk sense. Or if they did it was far too wrapped up in rhetoric and—and "Flapdoodle," said Miss Seeton, out loud.

She smiled, sighed; frowned. One had to have politicians,

of course, to pass laws and govern the country and—she sighed again—to put up taxes—one couldn't remember the last time they'd come down—but, though one could not wish to return to the bad old days of King John, before the Magna Carta, or of Henry the Seventh and his Star Chamber, there had been, she supposed, something to be said for the system whereby the monarch—always provided that he or she had courage and kindness and wisdom, mercy and common sense—did not merely reign, but ruled. Exercising a benevolent, not a despotic, power . . .

"Off with his head," murmured Miss Seeton, doodling a tiny playing-card in one corner of her second sketch, thinking of *Alice* and the Queen of Hearts. Queen of Hearts. Did not Queen Elizabeth the Second, so dear to the hearts of her people with her obvious common sense, her great love of her country, with her family about her to help and support—the Queen Mother in London throughout the Blitz; Prince Philip with his Royal Navy training—make an excellent ruler? Nobody would ever wish to harm Her Majesty, Miss Seeton felt sure: she would never do anything foolish enough to deserve such harm. Neither (she felt equally sure) would anybody distress Her Majesty by harming those close to her. The Prince of Wales, an admirable heir—though not to inherit, one most fervently hoped, for many years. The Queen must be so proud of the way her young relatives had grown up to take their places in the public eye. Good training, firm principles. No wonder they were so popular. There was no chance of a modern Guy Fawkes with a Royal Family like this. Violence, revolution, anarchy . . .

"Not nowadays, thank goodness," said Miss Seeton. "Not in England."

And, tunelessly humming "God Save the Queen" to herself, she packed away her sketch-block and pencils with fingers that no longer twitched or tingled; and headed happily back to the kitchen, and her supper, having dismissed all thought of violence completely from her mind.

# CHAPTER 7

"Hedging and ditching," said Nigel Colveden, receiving the loaded plate from his mother with a nod of acknowledgement. "And jolly tiring it can be, too. Hundreds of calories, I should think I've used up today."

With a gentle sliding motion, he insinuated the plate underneath the pages of *British Beekeeping,* which rustled at the table's top end in the hands of one the knowledgeable onlooker must have assumed to be Major-General Sir George Colveden, KCB, DSO, JP. "And me still a growing lad," went on the baronet's only son, a mere—albeit lusty—infant in his middle twenties. "Could I have another couple of spuds on that, please?"

"I do think it's unfair." Lady Colveden spooned two more potatoes from the dish to her son's plate, handed it across, and enviously watched him pour gravy in a thick, rich, fattening flood. "How you manage to eat so much without putting on weight, I really don't know. You certainly didn't inherit it from my side of the family. Even in summer, with salads and things . . . "

She sighed. Nigel grinned. "Mayonnaise," he murmured, just loud enough for her to hear. "Come out with us," he invited, more loudly, "tomorrow, and work some of it off. I'm sure we could find you a set of overalls and a spare hedge-trimmer. Heaving one of those around for an hour or so must be easily as good as a keep-fit class—if not better. And a great deal more productive."

Her ladyship wrinkled her nose. "I hope I'm not one of those silly squeamish females, but I have to admit I don't care too much for the smell of petrol. Besides, I thought our hedges were all billhooks, and saws, and things like that, bent over and woven."

"Rather sharp and prickly," suggested Nigel, "though undoubtedly good for training the muscles . . . Cut and bend and weave first," he hastily agreed, as his mother frowned at him for such frivolity. "Trim the line afterwards—it encourages thicker growth. Or you could drive an excavator, if you'd prefer."

"No, thank you." In response to her son's gesturing fork, Lady Colveden passed the potato dish, and watched him cheerfully spear the largest. "Potatoes—that reminds me, George." She raised her voice. *British Beekeeping* rustled again as her husband turned a page. "George? George!"

"Plenty, thanks," came an absent voice from the head of the family. "Let Nigel finish them." He coughed. "Growing lad, remember."

"There," said his wife, as his son spluttered, "I knew you were listening all the time. I wasn't asking whether you wanted any more to eat, because there wouldn't be much point. Nigel's scoffed the lot. I was talking about next week's bonfire."

This blatant distortion of the truth made Nigel drop his knife. He bent at once to retrieve it, and was a long time coming up for air. *British Beekeeping* scrunched down on the table to reveal the glittering eyes and shaking shoulders of a pink-faced Sir George.

"There's no need," said her ladyship loftily, "for the pair of you to be so silly. You know very well that what I meant was that potatoes reminded me of Guy Fawkes.''

''Naturally,'' said Nigel, ''they would.'' His shoulders, as he sat upright once more, were—like those of his father—shaking, and his face was red where Sir George had been pink: though this could have been due to his lengthy bending in search of the elusive cutlery.

Lady Colveden cut a thick slice of treacle sponge, and kept it defiantly for herself. Two smaller portions were passed to her grinning menfolk, and the custard was slow to follow. ''Because,'' said Lady Colveden, ''of having them for supper afterwards. In their jackets. Honestly—you two! Roasting them,'' as grins turned to outright laughter, ''in the ashes, as I'm sure you knew as well as I did. Know, I mean. And do.''

''Sorry, m'dear.'' Sir George's toothbrush moustache quivered with apparent remorse.

His son's remorse was less immediate. Nigel had been all too enchanted by a sudden vision of newly-dug potatoes, their eyes bright, dressed in dinner jackets and—a loud guffaw erupted, hands shook, inundating sponge with custard—frilled shirts, complete with cummerbunds, cufflinks, and black bow ties.

''I simply feel,'' said Lady Colveden, on her dignity, ''that it wouldn't be such a terribly good idea for us—for the village—to build our bonfire too soon in advance. And that anybody who has . . . well, any influence over them ought to say something before they do. Or ought to do something about it if they've done it already—not that I noticed anything when I drove past this afternoon,'' as her husband and son stared at her in some bewilderment, ''but you know how Murreystone are sure to try to spoil things if they can. After the Best Kept Village Competition, and the Conker Contest and everything—not,'' came the voice of the temptress, ''that I'm suggesting for one moment anyone should revive the Night Watch Men . . .''

''Oh no,'' said her son at once, in decisive tones. ''No! Not just to keep watch over a heap of woodworm-riddled

chairs''—his father stifled a groan—''and the odd tree-
trunk worth about fourpence ha'penny the lot, including
tax. You'd never dream of suggesting any such thing,
would you, Mother darling?''

His darling mother hid a smile as his father, forgetting
to groan, began to huff gently through his moustache.
Young Mr. Colveden, however, paid no attention to either
parent as he pressed on with his excuses.

''Oh, I'll admit that in theory things are reasonably quiet
at this time of year, but there's *always* something to do on
a farm—which is where pretty well everyone in the Village
Watch works. And we like our beauty sleep,'' he added,
with great firmness. ''Especially when the nights are so
long—and so cold.'' He shuddered, elaborately. ''My vote
goes for fluffy blankets and my eiderdown every time,
when I have to be up at the crack of dawn next day, every
blessed day of the week—and you can bet everyone else
you ask is going to say the same.''

''Week?'' echoed his mother, wide-eyed and innocent.
''But Guy Fawkes Night's only four days away, for goodness' sake. And Murreystone,'' she pointed out, ''are *five
miles* away at the most . . . ''

Nigel sighed. ''I had no idea, Mother darling, that you
had so great a thirst for violence.'' Gently, he fingered the
eye which had been blackened during the most recent inter-
village fracas, on the occasion of the Conker Contest; then
he found himself automatically clenching his fists at the
memory, and frowned. ''On the other hand . . . ''

Sir George cleared his throat. ''Shouldn't think they'd
risk another punch-up quite so soon. Taught 'em a thing or
two, I'd say. Need to get in training before they tackle us
again.'' His use of the first person plural was instinctive,
even though his part in the proceedings had been limited
to that of umpire, referee, and—on the stage of the village
hall, with PC Potter and the admiral beside him—overseer.
''Still, your mother could be right, m'boy. About *some*
things, that is.''

Lady Colveden wasn't going to argue one point when she seemed on the verge of winning another. "I do wish you didn't sound quite so—so grudging about it, George. You know very well I'm right—and I'm not"—unable to resist the temptation—"talking about your armchair now, though you know I'm right about that, too. But Murreystone are always . . . unreliable."

Despite himself, Sir George emitted a bark of laughter. "Can think of better words, m'dear—but, well, after that business in the spring—the arson—putting ideas in their blasted heads . . ."

"Please, Dad." Nigel stopped laughing, and looked pained. "Vandalism is one thing—anyone half decent'd want to put a stop to people digging up cricket squares or pinching garden ornaments—but when it's just a bonfire—"

"Burn it down," said Sir George, as Nigel broke off in despair, "and there'd be nothing left, dammit." The potential loss of his favourite armchair was as nothing to the idea of Murreystone victorious. "Can hardly waste decent coal to build another, or go using green wood—don't want the place riddled with sparks when it's alight, setting fire to people's clothes. And as for the smoke . . ."

"Got it!" Nigel's eyes were bright. "Don't let's build the bonfire at all! Not yet, I mean," as his parents looked startled. "I quite agree we shouldn't let Murreystone get away with anything, whatever it might be, but I fail to see why my nights should be permanently disrupted just so somebody can keep an eye on the blighters when they're in"—he grinned at his mother, winked at his father—"an unreliable mood. And they're bound to be unreliable after the Conker business, of course. Give 'em half a chance, and they'll be sneaking down here in the middle of the night to use up our entire stock of dry fuel in one fell swoop . . . but they'll only be able to sneak *if they know where it is.*"

"But how," enquired his mother, "could they *not* know?

The bonfire isn't exactly small—at least, it hasn't been in previous years, and I don't see why this year should be any different. And then, if it *is* built small, on purpose, wouldn't that be—be giving in to Murreystone?'' Her ladyship shook her head. "That isn't how we won the War, Nigel. I really can't see that sort of—of spineless behaviour being very popular with anyone in the village, not even Constable Potter, just for the sake of peace and quiet.''

"The Colvedens,'' protested her ladyship's husband at once, "aren't cowards, Meg.'' Sir George seldom spoke of the events which had led to the winning of his Distinguished Service Order, but the citation had left no doubt as to the baronet's courage in battle. "Boy has a plan, if you ask me—right, Nigel?''

"Right.'' Nigel nodded vigorously. "Thanks for the vote of confidence, Dad. I'm wounded beyond belief that my own mother should think her son would propose anything so—so dashed cowardly. Cunning, not cowardice, is the strategy applied by the Colvedens in moments of crisis—I say, that was rather good, wasn't it?''

"A cunning plan. Good show. Thought as much,'' said his father, as his mother begged her son's pardon, and pressed him for further details.

Nigel shrugged. "Easy, really. Each person stores his or her own hunks of wood or bits of rickety furniture''—he shot a sympathetic look in the direction of his father—"or tatty old tea-chests *in their own garden shed*—and we don't bring them out until the afternoon of November the fourth. Then we go hell-for-leather building the bonfire, and set a round-the-clock guard until the Fifth, and all the fun. We can do without sleep for a few hours for one night, heaven knows, if we work the rota right. It's just the—the constant patrolling I object to. I mean, Plummergen's our own village, yet if you stop to think about it we're practically under siege half the time from those Murreystone blighters across the marsh.''

"Not a bad idea,'' said Sir George. "Well done, Nigel.''

The old war-horse paid compliment. "Should have thought of it m'self—still, near enough. Keep it in the family. Fox those beggars thoroughly, I should think. Er—want me to give Jessyp a ring, or will you?"

Headmaster Martin Jessyp was renowned as Plummergen's finest paper-shuffler. The school timetable, the cricket team batting order, and the Christmas pantomime rehearsal schedule were no mystery to his methodical mind, even if Sir George, with his army experience, could not be faulted on overall organisational ability.

"Me? Good Lord, no. The cricket reshuffle when poor old Bert was stung by that bee was bad enough, thanks very much." Nigel turned pale at the memory, though the events to which he referred had taken place all of two months before, when postman Bert had tried, with unfortunate results, to deliver a parcel at the house of Admiral Leighton. Had the guilty admiral, a last-minute stand-in, not proved to be a master of the googly—the sneaky sideways-curving ball which caught batsmen on the hop—the result of the Murreystone needle match would have been very different . . .

"Ring him m'self, if you like. Ahem! Later, though." Sir George, like his son, had been put in mind of Admiral Bernard "Buzzard" Leighton, not only a brilliant bowler, but also Plummergen's resident apiarist. Pushing away his empty pudding-plate with a contented sigh, the baronet returned to the irresistible pages of *British Beekeeping*'s most recent issue. He and the Buzzard, who had lent him this invaluable periodical, planned to go into partnership next spring; Sir George was dreaming now of dessert sponges sweetened, not with treacle, but with the finest honey . . .

"And there's the hedgehogs, too," said her ladyship, as she and Nigel began to clear the table. "Only think how much better for them, poor things. I'm sure you didn't mean it that way at the time, Nigel, but it was rather clever of you. Maybe we should do the same thing every year."

With the gravy-boat in one hand, the jug of cold custard

in the other, her son gazed in bewilderment at his innocent parent, piling plate upon plate to slide them through the hatch, beaming at him with approval. He shot a wary look in the direction of *British Beekeeping,* but could see only the top of his father's head. Unable, with his hands full, to scratch his own pate in a parody of perplexity, he ambled across to the hatch, divested himself of his burden, mimed his confusion with an expressive shrug, and said:

"For the cricket? Alice in Wonderland played croquet, as I recall, with hedgehogs—but she used flamingoes, which are a bit thin on the ground around here. Would, um, herons be an admissible substitute? Hedgehog and Heron Cricket." He grinned. "Unusual, I grant you. Perhaps a little uncomfortable for the animals involved, but—"

"Nigel, don't be tiresome. Come and do the pans while I load the washer—you know perfectly well it was hibernation I was talking about. They creep," said her ladyship, kneeling before the open, rubber-sealed door, "into corners, and cover themselves with leaves, and sleep right through until the spring . . ."

"Sometimes wish I could, slaving away as hard as I do." Nigel scraped absently at a burned patch. "You wouldn't see me for six months—then, the first warm day and there I'd be, sitting in the sun doing nothing at all, just resting."

His mother rose, slamming the dishwasher door. "You'd be bored in a minute, you know you would. Just as you know," switching on, "that hedgehogs hibernate, and sleep so deeply they don't notice they've crawled into the middle of a bonfire, and when it's time to light it . . . Such a horrid idea, and I think you've been very clever, Nigel. We should have thought of it ages ago. They're so good for the garden—eating slugs and things, and you don't have to give them bread-and-milk to encourage them. They're rather fond of tinned catfood, apparently."

"Apparently," echoed Nigel, rinsing his final saucepan under the tap, "you've had a talk on hedgehogs at one of your meetings. What, as a matter of interest, did they say about fleas?''

''Not the same sort as dogs and cats,'' returned his mother at once. ''So Mrs. Ongar said, anyway—you know, Miss Seeton's friend from the bird sanctuary in Rye—oh, yes. That reminds me, I didn't want to say anything to them until I'd asked her, but . . . ''

''Wounded Wings,'' murmured Nigel, giving the sanctuary its full title. ''It only shows how you learn something new every day. I, er, never realised hedgehogs could fly.''

His mother ignored him. ''I do hope she won't be offended, although I'm sure they didn't mean it that way— they'd never dare,'' with a little giggle. ''They're much too—not scared, exactly—but wary, perhaps. You know how some of their parents are silly enough to say she's a witch. That's why they always behave themselves whenever she teaches them, of course. I would have said she had far too much common sense to take it as an insult, because they really have made rather a good job of it—one can't say *him,* in the circumstances, though I suppose one should, logically, or at least *historically.* And I know I said they didn't mean it that way, but it still feels a bit uncomfortable saying *she,* even if she *did* give them one of her old hats, or something that looks remarkably like one, anyway. And if she did, she must have known what it was for, or at least guessed—and Miss Seeton,'' concluded her ladyship, ''surely would have refused, if she thought it was meant as an insult. But I'd feel so much happier having heard her say so herself . . . ''

# CHAPTER 8

"Penny for the guy, Miss?"

Miss Seeton, emerging from the draper's, found her attention being addressed by a huddle of her sometime pupils outside the post office, diagonally opposite. With a nod and a smile, she responded to their waving hands and shrill cries; she raised her umbrella in acknowledgement of their further salute, then carefully, looking first to the right, then to the left, then to the right once more—one should never assume that children, even in so quiet a place as Plummergen, would remember their Kerb Drill on all occasions without a good example having been set by responsible adults—crossed from one side of The Street to the other.

In the light from Mr. Stillman's window, the vociferous huddle was more plainly to be seen amid the gloom of a late autumn afternoon. Giggling, shuffling, nudging one another, the children moved aside to display their handiwork to best advantage.

Miss Seeton looked; smiled, politely; looked again; seemed, though she tried to hide it, disappointed. Offended? Possibly. On the paved footpath at her feet, gigantic arms and legs akimbo, sporting a shapeless smock, denim pan-

taloons, and a black felt hat with a once-proud feather
cockscomb, sprawled a sacking form that was larger than
life, or at least larger than any member of the enthusiastic
bodyguard who now begged Miss Seeton again for the
modest sum required by the tradition of almost four hundred years.

"Penny for the guy, Miss?" Eager hands pointed to the
straggle-lettered sign, to the sprinkling of coins in the cardboard box beneath.

One should, of course, encourage them; but . . .

"The hat, naturally, I recognise." Miss Seeton's eyes
twinkled. "And I must commend the effort which has gone
into the body, and the limbs, though I do hope that none
of your parents will prove to have been especially attached
to any particular item of clothing . . . "

As she hesitated—honesty was the best policy, yet one
did not wish to discourage them—someone said:

"Funny face though, ain't it, Miss?"

Miss Seeton's sigh of relief drowned out the furious re-
torts of those who had struggled with the features of the
straw-stuffed figure on the pavement. One did not, after all,
have to prevaricate. "Well," began Miss Seeton; then
stopped. The tip of her umbrella touched in turn the blank
button eyes, the smudged nose, the lipstick gash of mouth.
"I'm sure you must have worked very hard," said Miss
Seeton, gently. "But . . . the difficulties of working on such
coarse material, of course . . . perhaps a paper mask, when
you are all children who can, as I know very well, produce
such splendid work in class . . . "

"Dunno what he looked like, Miss."

The admission was echoed by the rest of the little band.
Miss Seeton frowned.

"But surely—on the boxes of fireworks . . . "

"Not allowed to buy 'em."

Of course: only parents, or those organising displays. So
very wise of Mr. Stillman and the rest, though it was now,
she believed, also a matter of law that children below a

certain age should not be permitted to buy fireworks. There were, regrettably, some who could not be trusted to behave in a sensible manner with squibs and jumping-jacks . . . Yet this was no excuse.

"There are boxes in shop windows," said Miss Seeton, "if you only take the trouble to look. And to see," she added, sounding by turns stern and regretful. It was Miss Seeton's firm opinion that everyone should learn—should be taught—to see as clearly as possible. Her evident lack of success in this respect . . .

Sighing for her failure, with her umbrella she indicated Mr. Stillman's window display.

"Can't draw beards," she was promptly informed by an excited, and hopeful, chorus as it turned severally to look over its shoulder. "Nor hats, neither—nor make 'em. Nor—nor lend, like trousers . . . "

"Lend? You mean borrow?" The teacher's attempt at enlightenment faltered. Had tradition, then, changed so much? "You mean you aren't going to burn this guy on the bonfire after all? You intend to give everything back?"

Misinterpreting the guilty grins on the faces before her— the children's concept of borrowing differed considerably from that of most of the adults of their acquaintance—Miss Seeton smiled in sympathy. "Oh, I assure you the hat and feathers are of no further use to me. On the other hand," she added, "if your parents . . . "

With the tip of her brolly, she prodded doubtfully at the straw-stuffed hessian Gargantua, at its assortment of strange attire. One could hardly, of course, say anything against the tastes of others; but these were not, in Miss Seeton's eyes, clothes she could imagine anyone lamenting unduly if they were not, after all, given back once the business of collecting money to buy fireworks—or to hand to an adult to buy fireworks on one's behalf—had been accomplished. Besides, the children had clearly worked hard, even on that apology for a face. While the sacking might bulge, it had not burst: it did not leak. "Someone," said Miss Seeton

with approval, "has spent a great deal of time stitching this
together—and very neatly, too. How much money have you
collected so far?"

The chorus, much gratified, told her. People in cars, it
said, had stopped to look: not but what they couldn't do
with more, to buy an even bigger box, like. Anxious feet
nudged the cardboard collecting-tray still closer. "Get a
whole heap more bangers," ventured one brave soul, "iffen
we was just t'have a proper face on it . . . "

Miss Seeton hid a smile. No doubt this was what they
had intended all along, but had been too shy to ask. Would
it be churlish to refuse if one felt, as in fact one did, that
they could perhaps have made a little more of an effort for
themselves? Although . . . A slight twinge of disappointment, of guilt, made Miss Seeton sigh again. Her failure,
her fault . . . Yet a guy—even one which was not, or so it
seemed, to be burned—ought surely to be the work of the
children to whom it belonged. Not that one would be so
foolish as to call it cheating: there was no pressure to pass
an examination, no spirit of competition . . . there was, instead, or ought to be, an element of fun, the pleasure of
creation. And they had, one assumed, chosen to make the
guy in their free, not their school, time, which they must
have regarded as fun, because children didn't do things out
of school unless they wanted to do them. And their failure
to see the face under their very noses was of course far
more the fault of their teacher than of her pupils . . .

Miss Seeton stared at the display in Mr. Stillman's window, memorising the bearded face and fanatical gaze of the
figure on the firework boxes. "I can promise nothing," she
said, "but I will see what can be done—if you, too, will
promise to try again. We will exchange notes," she said,
with another twinkle. "And, in the meantime, you may
have not one, but ten, pennies for the guy . . . "

Amid a grateful hubbub, she opened her handbag, took
out her purse, and popped two small silvery coins into the
waiting cardboard box. "I suppose," she added, "that you

can all tell me who Guy Fawkes was, and what he did, or rather tried to do?''

And the hubbub erupted once more as the children, in unison, told her.


Four times the heavy door had creaked open; had whispered shut behind each of the conspirators in turn. The blinds were drawn, the one central light casting a dull, yellow gleam on the faces round the table in the darkened room.

Breaking the pregnant silence came the sudden sounds of a clearing throat, the tapping of expectant fingers on age-hardened wood. There was no real need for Catesby to call the meeting to order: already subdued, the conspirators had long since conceded their leader's authority. But it could do no harm to reinforce that authority whenever the chance should present itself . . .

"We are all here."

Even Winter, the light-hearted, did not smile at the self-evidence of this remark. Matters were too serious now for laughter. Three heads nodded gravely; voices murmured low acknowledgement of the universal presence.

"To business, then." Catesby, already sitting upright, seemed at once even taller. Cold grey eyes surveyed others which, uneasy, could not meet that steely gaze, and fell to the table-top, to their clasped and anxious hands.

"She is coming," said Catesby. "There has been no last-minute cancellation: there has been no substitution of one who would be less . . . less useful to us."

Again, this was something they already knew: but nobody cared to point this out.

"The *Beacon*," volunteered Keyes, "has just announced the winner of the competition."

Catesby looked a question. Keyes shook his head. "As you know, we tried . . . a little pressure, but we couldn't risk being too . . . obvious, in this particular instance. We had, in the end, no influence over the eventual choice."

"A pity, in some ways—but not an insuperable problem,'' said Catesby, frowning. ''We have at least managed to exert our influence in . . . other areas.''

The others nodded. Keyes said, slowly:

''Everyone has their price—or almost everyone,'' as Winter stirred on his chair. ''There are always secrets to discover—pressures to be applied. If only everything goes according to plan . . . ''

''But we didn't plan for a child from Plummergen, of all places.'' Rookwood, trying not to sound anxious, sounded instead almost too calm. ''There will, however, be a large local presence as . . . compensation.''

''As large as possible, I trust,'' Catesby said. ''The larger the crowd, the greater the confusion. The greater the confusion, the better for our purpose.''

Winter looked up. ''Plummergen. Isn't that where that old girl with the umbrella comes from? The one the papers call the Battling Brolly—you know, Scotland Yard's tame art consultant they never mention by name any more.''

Catesby frowned again: it was Rookwood who replied, as Keyes sighed softly, a look of concern in his eyes.

''Yes.'' His voice was as calm as ever. ''Yes, it is.''

Winter nodded. ''Thought so. They used to write her up rather a lot a few years ago, didn't they? But she's obviously someone with clout—or else she's got friends who can lean on the editors—that's why I wasn't sure.'' He shrugged. ''I can't remember her name. Sort of dropped out of the public eye a bit now, hasn't she? Unless you live near her, I suppose,'' he added, venturing a sideways look in the direction of Catesby.

He did not need to enlarge the point. Catesby, still frowning, clasped white-knuckled hands on the table. ''There is no need to worry about this woman, whoever she is. It is simply a coincidence that it is a child from her village who has won: I see no reason why this . . . ''

''Beeton,'' supplied Rookwood, as the grey eyes searched for inspiration. ''Something like that, anyway.''

''I see no reason why this Mrs. Beeton,'' continued

Catesby, "should hinder us in our plans. She might, indeed, be of use, if even half of what the papers have said about her is true. As I said, the greater the confusion, the better for our purpose."

"And according to the papers," said Winter, "this Brolly woman—I think it may have been Beeston—doesn't half let everyone in for confusion once she gets going."

"Beecham?" ventured Keyes. Winter, despite the gravity of the situation, grinned.

"Sargent," he suggested. "Boult? Or maybe even von Karajan?"

Catesby's eyes narrowed. "Winter, this is no time for your infantile jokes! Nor is this the place to flaunt your knowledge of orchestral music, or its conductors. The only interest you, or any of us, should have in music at present is knowing exactly what will happen from the instant the National Anthem has been played . . . ."

"Sorry." Winter's apology sounded forced: at the bleak look in Catesby's eyes, he tried again. "I'm sorry. Though I'm not sure what the anthem's got to do with anything. Surely it—it all starts happening . . . some time after the girl's cut the ribbon and made her speech? After the Plummergen brat has handed over the flowers?"

Catesby, through gritted teeth, spoke in a tone so controlled that Winter quailed. "From the instant the anthem has been played, I said—and that is what I meant. Everything depends on accurate timing, on knowing her movements and those of . . . others. On knowing where everyone will be . . . and when. Among 'everyone,' of course, I include our . . . agents. Willing," came the grim qualification, "or . . . less so. There is no room for mistakes. Is that clear?"

And, as on every previous occasion, there came murmurs of uneasy, but resigned, acquiescence as the other three bowed to the will of the conspirator called Catesby.

\*    \*    \*

Plummergen seethed with excitement. The teaching of Miss Maynard, of Mr. Jessyp, had paid off: a local child—a girl, fortunately, because of having a best frock already, while a boy'd mean a new suit and trying to get away with a borrowed tie, not to mention no Plummergen boy but secretly thought bowing over the hand of a lady a sissy notion—had beaten all competition to win the glory of presenting the bouquet to Her Royal Highness Princess Georgina. Young Sally was the envy of her friends, while her mother was the object of much behind-the-back remarks in the post office and other village emporia.

"It's not so much to say as three of 'em," announced Mrs. Scillicough, "wouldn't've looked a treat together, because the paper did say *school age*—only I can't help but think, even if it did keep 'em out in the normal run o' things, an exception might've bin made on account of three together being so out o' the ordinary. When there's that Sally just the one—and her mum'll've helped her write it, I don't doubt," she added. "Which, if it was accepted as fair, I'm sure I don't know as other mums couldn't've done just as well, if they'd've bin given the chance."

Mrs. Newport nodded vigorously at her sister's side. Mrs. Newport's quartet of under-fives was far better behaved than their triplet cousins, and Mrs. Newport herself—in her own opinion, at any rate, she having passed *O* Level English (Grade 6) while her sister only managed CSE—was far better able to write an essay on Nuclear (or any other type of) Power than anyone else in the family. Why couldn't Alice Maynard (demanded Mrs. Newport) have given lessons to any as asked? Open to everyone, such a competition did by rights ought to have bin, with everyone wanting the chance to meet a real live princess, and Georgy Girl so popular and pretty, though with no kids to look after and no real worries t'weren't no surprise . . .

"She'll be wed and worrited soon enough, poor lamb," said Mrs. Spice. "*And* brought to bed within the year, knowing her duty as the whole family's raised to do. Let her have her fun while she's able, the pretty dear, that's what I say. She'll be stuck with him for life, whoever he turns out to be, them not holding with divorce, and the kiddies when she's had 'em hardly her own, with bin so close in line to the throne, and—and national treasures,'' she concluded, quoting a recent article in that much-read (and occasionally accurate) periodical, *Anyone's*.

Heads were nodded gravely as Mrs. Spice, sighing, reached her rather wistful conclusion. Even Emmy Putts, on whose imagination the royal lifestyle had inflicted daydreams more bizarrely optimistic than her wont, had to admit, with some regret, that the life of a princess wasn't everything it was cracked up to be. Fun, did Mrs. Spice say? For all that she wore beautiful clothes, and jewels, and was for ever having her photograph took, well, it wasn't what anyone'd call private, was it? Not ever. And being dragged off—or sent, which came to the same thing—visiting all manner o' places you could be sure she'd never really wanted to see—that was hard on her, and no mistake. Never any freedom for the poor girl; never the chance to choose. And if anyone thought Emmeline Putts could be talked into traipsing over Nuclear Power Stations day after day, well, they'd got another think coming, on account of you could never be sure what it mightn't do if someone was to drop a match, and blow the place to smithereens . . .

"They won't,'' said Mrs. Stillman, sternly. "Neither ask you, nor blow the place up—so you just stop your nonsense, young Emmy.''

Emmy tossed her head, and sniffed. Mrs. Skinner was even more outspoken than the postmaster's wife. "The very idea of you being curtseyed to—it's downright blasphemous, Emmy Putts!''

"Treacherous, you mean.'' Mrs. Henderson, gleeful, was quick to correct her rival. "Pretending to be royalty, why, that's treason. Torture you in the Tower o' London if you don't watch your tongue, they will!''

Emmy sniffed again. ''What's wrong with a curtsey? They say Maggie Laver over t'Ashford's had 'em a-curtseying to her all around the station, and not in the Tower yet. And young Sal's bin practising to Alice May-nard, I heard tell, ready to meet the princess . . . ''

''Which she'd better get right,'' someone said, ''or else we know what'll happen if she doesn't. Don't we?''

A long, penetrating stare raked the horrified assembly, which let out its breath in a shuddering sigh. There was no doubt of what would happen if young Sally let them down: the local paper had printed the name and address of the runner-up, winner of the second prize.

The runner-up who hailed from Murreystone . . .

# CHAPTER 9

The road between Plummergen and Dungeness is almost level over the entire distance. On normal occasions there are those with a bent for natural history who often bicycle in a south-easterly direction across the marsh to go fishing, or to study the many varieties of bird-life—gulls, terns, grebes, shelduck, mallard, and many more—which frequent the flint-grey, pebbly peninsula.

On this particularly momentous occasion, however, it was considered neither practical nor dignified for even the most devoted cyclists to travel from the village to the Official Opening under their own power. Car owners with unoccupied seats offered lifts to their pedalling—and pedestrian—friends; Crabbe's Garage laid on both the regular bus, and the spare.

Crabbes have been mechanics for four generations. Old Crabbe (whose son, Young Crabbe, died in the last War) is well advanced in years, and has been forbidden by his family to drive either of the buses, much as he would relish the challenge. A distant connection of Daniel Eggleden, most recent in the line of village blacksmiths, Old Crabbe moved to Plummergen at the request of a previous Cousin

Eggleden around the turn of the century, when the coming of the internal combustion engine could no longer be ignored. Though trained as a smith, Old Crabbe (as he soon became) felt more at home with the petrol-driven beast than he ever had with any number of hay-eating horses.

Old Eggleden, Dan's grandfather, accordingly agreed with his Cousin Crabbe to divide responsibility for local transport between the two establishments; and thus it remains to this day. The bus, taxi, and hire car services are run from the garage on the eastern side of The Street; the farrier's and smithy stands where it always did, its double doors freshly painted in a rich grass-green, farther down on the western side, near Miss Wicks's little cottage with the wrought-iron balustrade which is one of Dan Eggleden's finest creations.

Very Young Crabbe, Young Crabbe's son, drove what might be termed the civilian bus: pensioners (including his grandfather, grumbling loudly), car-owners unwilling to lay out good money on petrol, and non-car-owners unable to obtain a lift. His son Jack had the arguably more important task of driving the bus which carried Plummergen's fifty-odd Junior Mixed Infants (including young Sally and—a concession which irritated every other parent in the village—her mother) with their three teachers: Mr. Martin C. Jessyp, Miss Alice Maynard, and Miss Emily Dorothea Seeton.

"I think it's very sensible of Mr. Jessyp to invite Miss Seeton to go with them on the bus," said Lady Colveden, as she tidied her wavy brown hair beneath her hat, a beautiful and costly Monica Mary original from the renowned Brettenden milliner. "Goodness, how one feels constricted, dressed like this—but it's only for an afternoon, thank heavens, and rather fun, once in a while. Naturally, I'd planned that we should offer her a lift, but he'd already spoken to her, as she's really very good at keeping them on their best behaviour. Only think how awful it would be if HRH saw them the way they can sometimes be. She rang earlier, you know, to ask me what to wear," she added, tucking a final mischievous curl in place.

"Georgy Girl?" enquired Nigel. "I should've thought she had enough advisers at Buck House, without having to phone all the way to Plummergen for help." He loomed over the top of his mother's head, checking the knot of his tie in the hall mirror. "Perhaps I'd better do it again—what do you think?"

"I think you're trying to annoy me. You know very well I meant Miss Seeton. She's a teacher, after all, even if it is only part time—and it would be like a lady-in-waiting, wouldn't it? So HRH will understand. Poor Sally—she's as jumpy as anything, even though Miss Maynard's rehearsed her for simply ages. And so's she—and her mother is, too."

"I would've thought," said Nigel, "that if Mrs. Maynard's been curtseying all over the place she'd be more than jumpy, she'd be crippled. The number of times that poor woman's been stuck in bed with her back, with her daughter rushing off to look after her . . . Hence Miss Seeton's part-timing, of course, which saves us taking another car, as Dad's not coming and the two of us can easily fit in the MG."

Lady Colveden sighed. "Such a shame he had a sitting today, of all days—but justice has to be done, and someone has to do it." She frowned. "Dispense it? Anyway, you'll never make a magistrate, Nigel, while you have such a dreadful sense of humour. I meant that Miss Maynard is jumpy, and so is Sally's mother. Miss Seeton is always so wonderfully calm, she'll do them a tremendous amount of good, especially now she doesn't have to worry about her clothes."

Nigel, thoughtfully knotting his tie, spluttered. "Life classes are one thing, Mother, but surely even Miss Seeton can't propose to attend an Official Opening in the nude. The imagination boggles—sorry."

But his grin did not suggest undue repentance, and

his mother shook her head at her undutiful son, and sighed.

Miss Seeton shook her head, and sighed. The mirror—not always, she felt, an entirely reliable guide. Lady Colveden had said that the sort of clothes one had worn to the Royal Garden Party at Buckingham Palace would do very well— but, as one would have expected her ladyship to recall, that had been in the middle of summer: this was November. At least the forecast was neither for fog, nor for rain—which meant that a warm suit should suffice, being mostly, as one understood, indoors, rather than standing about in the open air. Lady Colveden—intending, no doubt, to be helpful— had added *but warmer, of course.* Perhaps one should, after all, wear over one's suit the Parisian coat which, when reversed, was so sensible a shade of gaberdine, but which was an undoubtedly smart, if a trifle flamboyant, red-and-black check on the other side. It did not exactly match the suit, but that would hardly matter, since it was unlikely to require unbuttoning in so short a time . . .

The suit: a discreet and reassuring tweed, with a sensible blouse. One's yellow beads—dear Cousin Flora! A hat? Naturally. Even on normal occasions, it was seldom that one cared to venture forth with one's head uncovered: but with what to cover it now? The red felt with its cheerful cockscomb would be an exact colour match, but perhaps somewhat too . . . spritely, for a teacher there in her official capacity. On the other hand, to reverse the coat to gaberdine would mean a hat in fawn or grey, which by itself, as a contrast, would do, but which with an entire coat would be—for royalty always wore such gay colours—imperial purple, royal blue—not only a little dull, but also, perhaps, disrespectful.

Miss Seeton bobbed a hurried curtsey at the very idea, and continued planning her wardrobe. Gloves, of course. Not white, which was a summer colour, as one's neat straw had been a summer hat: but leather, black and soft, with those three neat lines along the back. Court shoes, despite the suitability of the name, were perhaps a trifle lightweight for a royal occasion in November: luckily, one had a pair of walking shoes in grey which, at a pinch—except that they in fact fitted very well—would do. A new handbag; and, naturally, no other umbrella but the black silk, with the gold handle. Dear Mr. Delphick! What, wondered Miss Seeton idly as she began to button and zip herself at last into her chosen attire, was he doing now?

In Scotland Yard, Chief Superintendent Delphick had turned from his mid-morning perusal of the *Daily Negative* to gaze with some amusement at his long-time sidekick, the enormous Detective Sergeant Ranger.

"*What* did you say?"

Bob coughed. "Sorry, sir, I'd forgotten all about it. You know how busy we've been recently with . . . Sorry, sir." He coughed again. "We heard a day or so ago, when Anne's mother rang." Bob's wife, the former Miss Knight, had before her marriage lived in Plummergen, where her parents still ran the local nursing home. "It was only when you mentioned Dungeness just now that I remembered."

"Remembered," prompted Delphick, "what?"

"That one of the, er, Plummergen kids has won some newspaper competition for the job of handing a bunch of flowers to Princess Georgina, sir, when she goes to open the blessed thing." It had been Delphick's heartfelt comments on the probable traffic and security problems attendant upon the princess's visit, and his gratitude that the Yard, for once, was spared such problems, which had jogged Bob's memory. "Mrs. Knight says most of the village seems to be going to watch the fun, sir, even poor old Miss Wicks, with her arthritis: and half the, er, ambulatory patients"—Bob shot a look at his superior: jargon didn't always impress the Oracle—"are cadging lifts on one of the buses."

"And who, might one ask, goes on the other?"

"The, er, school, sir. All fifty of the kids, with the, er, teachers." Bob shot another, more wary look in Delphick's direction. "All three of them, sir."

There was a long, thoughtful pause.

Delphick ended it. "Wherever Royalty goes, police officers and members of the security forces—MI5, MI6, and, for all I know, MI one-hundred-and-thirty-seven—go with it: before, behind, between, above, below. Done, as one might say"—he permitted himself a brief smirk, though the joke was lost on Bob—"to a turn. There will—or at least there should—be a copper on every corner, directing errant cars and buses to their appointed place; there should be plainclothes men and women mingling with the crowds, their eyes watchful for the least hint of trouble. Given the, ah, combustible nature of this particular occasion . . .

"I wonder," he murmured, "how many of them have been deputed to keep an eye on Miss Seeton?"

Miss Seeton, with Miss Maynard and Mr. Jessyp, was too busy keeping an eye on her fifty small charges to notice whether anyone else might be keeping an eye upon herself. It would have interested Chief Superintendent Delphick to know that there was, in fact, no such curious, overseeing eye. Moreover, had there been, and had Miss Seeton noticed it, she would have considered this attention on the part of the security forces to be quite unnecessary on her own account. Miss Seeton, as has already been mentioned, does not—cannot—accept that she leads on occasion a life of incident, of drama, of criminal connection deserving of official concern: her involvement in such occasions, she believes, has ever been a matter of mere passing chance, and is in no circumstances anything over which she—or anyone else—need feel the slightest concern.

As Crabbe's coach pulled into the car park at Dungeness D, Miss Seeton's immediate concern was for the health and safety of those who had been entrusted to her particular care. The journey from Plummergen may have been short—no more than a dozen miles, along level marshland roads—but it had been crowded with incident. Children, wildly waving Union Flags, had prodded other children in various soft portions of the anatomy. Umbrage had been taken, insults hurled, challenges issued. A fully-fledged fencing duel had been fought up and down the central aisle before anyone could prevent it. The juvenile jousters had been forcibly parted by Mr. Jessyp just as they closed, their broken weapons discarded, in hand-to-hand combat on the floor; their supporters, leaping and squealing on either side, had contrived to sit on their packed lunches, to the detriment of the sandwich fillings, the seat covers, and the children's nether garments.

Several infants had succumbed to the first stages of motion sickness, and now drooped, pale and glassy-eyed, across the armrests overlooking the aisle, their heads bumped by other children, more robust, rushing (despite every stricture from Mr. Jessyp and—striving valiantly against her own nausea—Miss Maynard) to and fro as they sought the best view of the tall, brooding shape of the power station which loomed at them out of the distance.

Amid all the chaos, Miss Seeton's seat was a haven of calm. No riot or upheaval, no duelling or fisticuffs dared approach the place where she sat with young Sally and her mother, chatting brightly, reminiscing about her attendance at the Buckingham Palace Garden Party and the graciousness of Her Majesty the Queen, assuring her charge that curtseys would come easily, especially after so much coaching, since she herself—the yoga, of course, but Sally was so very much younger—had managed without any coaching at all . . .

Sally and her mother held out until Jack Crabbe pulled on the brake and switched off the engine. Forty-nine shrill voices were raised in a clamour to be first off the bus; one sad pipe addressed itself to Miss Seeton's ear.

"Please Miss, Mum—I don't feel well."

"It's only natural you should be a little excited," said

Miss Seeton, after a quick look at the girl's mother had shown that such comfort as the child required must be offered by herself alone. "A short walk, you know, in the fresh air will work wonders."

Miss Seeton hopped nimbly up from her seat, and twitched her umbrella down from the overhead rack. Holding it like a baton, she brandished the brolly before the startled noses of the other forty-nine children, and made it plain that the first to leave the bus should be herself, young Sally, and—as pale, now, as her daughter—Sally's mother.

Jack Crabbe caught her eye, and pressed a lever to open the door with a hiss, and a rubbery thud.

The little procession descended the steps into the cool, windswept landscape of the shingle flatlands which comprise the unique promontory of Dungeness, the headland at the tip of Denge Marsh. Overhead, seagulls swooped and wheeled, screaming; higher still, clouds scudded across a slate-grey sky. The air felt damp against the skin, and there was a sudden taste of sea-salt on the lips.

Sally shivered. "Miss, I really don't feel—"

"A short walk," said Miss Seeton firmly, deciding with regret that the girl's mother, quaking and speechless at her side, must fend for herself. The second coach had pulled in next-but-one to their own, decanting older friends who could administer rather more brisk assistance than Miss Seeton—the child's teacher, but to the mother merely an acquaintance—felt would be acceptable.

"Come with me," Miss Seeton instructed the junior star of the forthcoming ceremony. Sally trotted meekly in the little figure's wake, taking deep breaths as Miss told her, counting the red-and-black squares on her coat, and maybe not feeling quite so queer as she'd thought she felt, five minutes ago . . .

"Look at the lighthouse, Sally." The umbrella pointed to the solitary structure, tall and weatherbeaten, almost at the water's edge. "Try to guess how far away it is. Could you draw it, do you think? What colours would you use?"

"Oh, Miss, everything's cold, and grey, and horrid!"
The complaint came loud and clear. Miss Seeton smiled to
herself: her prescription had worked. "Can't we go back
now, where it's warm? Mum 'n' the rest'll be wondering
where we've gone."

The roses had returned to the child's cheeks; and there
was sure to be one last rehearsal for her to attend. Miss
Seeton nodded, turned, and headed back towards the power
station entrance. There would, no doubt, be some official
at the gate who could advise her where she should deliver
her young charge for the final run-through . . .

Peak-capped security guards issued directions; smiled at
Sally, patting her on the head; paid compliment to her appearance as they checked lists, then stamped and handed
out those cardboard oblongs which granted access to the
less public parts of the building. An escort would, of
course, be provided for such a pretty young lady. She and
Princess Georgina together would be a sight for sore eyes.
Just wait for the pictures in the papers, on the television!

The hum of voices echoed down the third—or was it the
fourth?—corridor: they must be nearly there. Sally, however, was starting to turn pale again. Nothing more (Miss
Seeton hoped) than the contrast between the fresh autumn
breezes and the surprisingly—one had always understood
such places to be air conditioned, for the sake of the
delicate machinery—the surprisingly stuffy atmosphere
indoors. The oppressively—one might almost say
aggressively—fresh paint, she supposed, silently wondering
how Royalty survived such atmospheres day after day, visit
upon visit. Noblesse oblige, no doubt, as well as habit: their
escort, a tall and very upright, broad-shouldered young
man, did not appear to be affected, while she herself, of
course, was long accustomed to paint, and its smell. But
one had to admit that in such large quantities, and in these
windowless passages . . .

"Miss," came small Sally's even smaller voice, as the
trio rounded the last corner to confront the waiting crowd,

to see the anxious faces; to hear the hurried footsteps of an unknown dignitary as their arrival was greeted with sighs of relief. "Miss, I think I feel—I don't feel well, Miss, please." A tug on Miss Seeton's sleeve, the voice, still small, rising to a pitiful wail.

"Miss, please—I got to go!"

# CHAPTER *10*

In such moments of juvenile crisis, the experienced teacher well understands that there is no time at all to be lost. As the young man with the shoulders, audibly gulping, could only gaze at Sally in mute alarm and begin to edge away, Miss Seeton glanced rapidly about her. Observing nearby a female figure in a discreet check overall, she recognised with relief the uniform worn by the waitresses in Bretten-den's Cosie Tea Rooms.

It did not occur to Miss Seeton that aprons and caps of this design were so convenient for catering personnel that they were popular among many other establishments besides that run by Miss Enden. Miss Enden's staff were renowned for their courtesy, promptness, and willingness to help: and, at that particular moment, courteous promptitude was precisely what was needed.

"Excuse me." Miss Seeton, standing on tiptoe, waved her umbrella to catch the discreetly-checked young woman's full attention. "Excuse me!"

Drawn by the compelling force of a practised pedagogic eye, the young woman hurried over. The problem was quickly explained: the remedy less quickly found, although she spoke as quickly as anyone Miss Seeton had ever met.

The little girl wanted the toilet? Oh dear, well, she really couldn't say, having only just popped in to see the fun, with being busy over t'other side setting out the buffy for later: what the boss'd called a collation—not that it mattered, she reckoned, what fancy name they gave it for the likes of Princess Georgina, living on caviare all day long the way she did, never nothing so dull as fish and chips or beans on toast or scrambled eggs. Only the best for Georgy Girl—a brand-new toilet brought in special—no (as Miss Seeton managed to squeeze in a word), not the Portaloo lot, but local, KarriKlozzet, that was them, and with a mink-lined seat, she wouldn't wonder, and a regular crying shame she couldn't let the little girl use it first, but there it was, more than her job was worth, though if it'd bin up to her she'd have said use it, and welcome—

"Please, Miss!" Sally's face was pale with the agony of tension. The gulping young man gulped again, realising he would soon be called upon to act; then he allowed stiffened shoulders to relax as the unknown dignitary finally succeeded in making his way through the throng.

"The lavatory?" Dignity's relief, on at last seeing the missing flower-girl within a few yards of where she was supposed to have been ten minutes ago, soon changed to shocked dismay as his words boomed and echoed around the room. "The lavatory—at a time like this?"

Immediately, every head within earshot turned towards the little group. Dignity flushed purple, Shoulders scarlet, Miss Seeton demurely pink: but she did not forget her duty to young Sally, and explained, quietly but firmly, that she could not possibly allow her pupil to present the princess with her bouquet until she had first been permitted to refresh herself.

"Her Royal Highness," Dignity informed Miss Seeton in an irritated whisper, "is already drawing close to Dungeness D, I am informed. Within five minutes, I must be at the main gate to welcome her." The whisper grew more important. "And she will be making her speech, and cutting the ceremonial ribbon, within a quarter of an hour from now!"

"In which case," said Miss Seeton, in her best school-mistress tone, "there should be ample time for Sally to pay a visit to the nearest cloakroom. Moreover . . . " Really, one did not wish to sound rude, but if there was no other way of putting one's message across . . . "Moreover, if you will excuse my saying so, the longer we stand about discussing the matter, the more time is likely to be lost."

Despite clear evidence to the contrary, Dignity was so powerfully reminded by Miss Seeton's manner of his prep school headmaster's refusal to accept any excuses for the cricket ball's breaking of the gymnasium window that, within seconds, the still-blushing Shoulders had been deputed to whisk Sally and her chaperone down yet another passageway to a suitably discreet door, and to comfort.

Nigel Colveden, in company with every other male present, fell instantly in love with Her Royal Highness. Georgina's eyes were sparkling orbs of sapphire blue; her hair was a riot of rich, burnished gold, her smile a radiant ruby curve about pearl-white, regular teeth. Her photographs, Nigel decided, didn't do her justice: he doubted if anything but the reality could.

"Gosh," breathed Nigel, a devout worshipper, from that moment on, at the shrine of Royalty's youngest star. "Oh, gosh, I wish I was Miss Seeton!"

Lady Colveden had never before known her son—heir to a baronetcy, in the prime of life, tall, muscular, and (even to a mother's partial gaze) good-looking—express the desire to be metamorphosed into a small, thin, grey-haired spinster of a certain age: but her ladyship was, on this particular occasion, unsurprised at his expressing such a desire. Indeed, she had a strong suspicion that the sentiment was shared by almost everyone else, male or female, present: for Miss Seeton was nearly as close to the princess as her lady-in-waiting, and looked set to continue this closeness for the remainder of the royal Power Station Tour.

Returning young Sally, under escort, from her visit to the cloakroom, Miss Seeton had been asked by those responsible for the Presentation of the Bouquet to stay, in the regrettable absence of her pupil's parent, as moral support for that parent's child. Though the Plummergen presence was strong, it was, sadly, by one presence less strong than it had originally been. Sally's mother, overcome with emotion, had succumbed to stage fright in a bout of mild hysteria. She was being cared for (out of sight) by a posse of first aiders armed with smelling salts, burnt feathers, and sips of cool water: but the Show Must Go On, Regardless. Should anxiety about her mother prevent the child from carrying out her ceremonial duty, there was always—the sly official remarked—the competition runner-up in reserve . . .

Sally was a true daughter of her village, and resolute that nobody from Murreystone should even attempt to steal the thunder of a Plummergenite. When the time came to make her floral offering, the curtsey she swept would have turned Margot Fonteyn green with envy. She threw a beaming look of triumphant relief towards Miss Seeton, who had been so very kind; and she gasped with audible delight when Georgina, beaming back, exclaimed:

"Oh, thank you. What beautiful flowers—and such a lovely ribbon! Do you know, it almost exactly matches your frock?" So tiny was she that she hardly had to bend at all to hold the wide satin streamer against the skirt of Sally's best dress. "It does!" She laughed with sheer pleasure. "Don't you think it would make an absolutely perfect sash?" And those sparkling sapphire orbs made their appeal to the nearest person. To Miss Emily Dorothea Seeton.

Teachers of art have, of necessity, an excellent eye for colour; Miss Seeton is one of the most truthful persons in England, if not the world. This combination of circumstance made it inevitable that, thus appealed to, Miss Seeton should bob a curtsey, smile a modest smile, and agree.

"Wonderful!" Georgina straightened, plucked a single flower from the bouquet, and handed the rest, with a grateful nod, to her lady-in-waiting. "This is just for now," she said, presenting the flower to young Sally with a little bob and smile of her own. "You mustn't go too far away," she told the blushing infant, "while we all walk round, or I'll lose you in the crowd, and I shouldn't like that. And then, once we've seen everything, I'm going to let you have the ribbon to keep for your very own, if you'd like it. Would you?"

"Oh!" Sally almost dropped the flower in her excitement, and forgot all the etiquette she had ever known. "Oooh, Miss—I mean Mam—Princess—oh, yes, I would!"

"Then you mustn't let me forget. Promise?" And Georgy Girl's wink thrilled the hearts of many more than Sally.

Having been issued with regulation hard hats, the tour party moved off. Her Royal Highness, escorted by Dignity, was followed by Shoulders escorting the lady-in-waiting, who carried the bouquet—and Georgina's set of earmuffs, until these should be required. A small huddle of lesser beings from both parties, the Power Station and the Palace, walked in the rear, their helmets on their heads, their muffs in their hands; and, caught up by Royal Command in that same huddle, ahead of everyone else—Press and Plummergen and Murreystone included—walked Sally and Miss Seeton.

As they walked, hearing Dignity's running commentary in the near distance, Miss Seeton felt an overwhelming sense of power, harnessed but ready—should chance decree otherwise—to be unleashed upon an unsuspecting world. Inevitable, of course, in such a place. The air hummed, the very walls seemed alive with some huge, invisible animal presence that whined, muted, muzzled, restrained: a wild animal, capable of terrible force, of horrific destruction if

once—a fanciful notion—the beast broke its fetters, and ran
free. To one of Miss Seeton's generation, the names of
Hiroshima and Nagasaki spoke only too clearly of just what
terror and horror there could be . . .

And yet here, now, it seemed that terror and horror had—
by a miracle of science she knew she could never hope to
understand—given way to good. Electricity: light and heat
and transport, power for industrial use, warmth and safety
for people in their homes . . .

Miss Seeton looked with bewildered approval on pipes
and wires and metal tanks, on dials and switches, on rows
of knobs and buttons, on ranks of television screens. She
blinked at wall-mounted cabinets containing, so Dignity's
boom informed all within earshot, potassium iodate tablets;
she smiled with the rest as Princess Georgina made fun of
herself in huge earmuffs, and led the way, laughing, up
narrow concrete stairs and through the huge Steam Turbine
Hall, where the ever-present whine of the beast was
drowned out by the roar of its even more monstrous parent,
water-driven.

Dignity, earmuffs now removed, spoke in learned tones
of boron steel and concrete shielding, of refuelling gantries
and access pits. The princess heard that a tenth of London's
entire electricity supply would come from here. Red
lights—the eyes of the beast—glowed as the party passed
by; its warm breath blew from ducts and internal vents on
the exposed faces of the intruders as they passed changing-
rooms filled with white overalls, free from dust and con-
tamination.

Tiled floors, ceilings, walls. Desks covered in paperwork;
swivel chairs, the seats of power in more ways than one.
From staircase windows, a glimpse of the cooling ponds
outside; talk of band-screen-filtered salt water siphonically
discharged, of local fishermen happy to eat, or to sell, what
they had caught. Georgina made a little joke about sea-trout
and salmon; with chuckles her words were repeated, ripples
spreading across the whole company.

Before leaving the controlled area for the next part of the tour came the Radiation Check. "Do you think I'll light up in the dark?" enquired Georgina, thrusting her hands happily into the spring-rubber slots of the cream enamelled metal box, huge and floor-standing, with its winking eyes of dull red, clear green. Smiling, she twirled in a slow pirouette, arms outstretched, as Dignity took it upon himself to run the scanning beam of the monitor, microphone-shaped, from head to dainty foot over her royal person, and pronounced her radiation-free.

The others followed in turn: Dignity, ministered to by Shoulders; the lady-in-waiting, scanned by—at her own regal request—Her Royal Highness Princess Georgina, after instruction from a proudly blushing Shoulders. Not a man in the party but would willingly have changed places with him as Georgina, allowing Lady Vaudine to pass on a steady green light, blew him a quick kiss of gratitude for having let her share the fun.

The second rankers came next, watched with much interest by Her Royal Highness, reluctant to rejoin Dignity and her bouquet as the queue snaked slowly on its way. She would love, she said, to try again. A brief, silent consultation, and she was permitted to operate the scanner upon the portly form of the Chief Physicist, the slender shape of the Electrical Engineer. "What would happen," asked Her Royal Highness, "if there *had* been a leak?"

The crush, the chaos in the monitoring lobby grew greater as the rest of the tour—lesser beings, slower walkers—gradually arrived. Those waiting to be let pass outside milled about, crowding; those already outside pressed closer for their first glimpse of the princess. Sally and Miss Seeton, mindful of royal command, tried not to be swept aside: there were many taller, heavier, more self-important than they to make their importance known, and Sally uttered a little cry of vexation as the crowd surged past them.

Miss Seeton—indignant not for her own sake, but for

Sally's disappointment—took the child's hand in hers, used her brolly as a pathfinder, and edged her way to the monitoring station, where a white-coated figure demonstrated the rubber slots, the cream-and-silver microphone.

"Hold my rose, please, Miss?"

Small Sally, on tiptoe, felt rubber clamp gently about her hands, saw green lights gleam. The microphone wafted up and down her infant frame, and she danced aside.

Miss Seeton handed back the rose, slipped her umbrella up her arm, and imitated Sally and the rest with the placing of her hands. Green, silent permission was granted.

The silver microphone sniffed the soles of the shoes one by one, trailed in a swooping zigzag up the stockinged legs, the tweed checks of the coat; swerved around the buckled belt, the neatly-buttoned breast—

And came screaming, whooping, clanging to a sudden halt just as it reached Miss Seeton's face.

Everyone leaped as lights flashed, bells pealed, gongs deafened the ears. Every head turned to Miss Seeton where she stood, wide-eyed with dismay, trembling for the clamour she had wrought. With a clatter inaudible above the sound of the alarm, her umbrella slipped to the tiled floor and lay there, its golden handle seeming to blink as the redness above flickered on and off, on and off, on and off.

Dignity rushed to the rescue. "Switch it off at once!" Without waiting for the white coat to obey, he pressed levers down with shaking hands. The clamour was stilled, the red eyes dulled. "You—you must have done it wrong." Dignity mopped his brow: he did not dare—nobody dared—to glance in the direction of Georgina. "Let's hope it isn't . . . you haven't broken it. Try again. And carefully, this time!"

All eyes watched the monitor once more weave its upward, swooping path; all ears prepared for the clamour to begin again, though none believed that it would . . .

It did.

"Oh, no," breathed Miss Seeton: but nobody heard her.

Dignity, now deathly pale instead of purple, kicked aside the umbrella, snatched the silver microphone from the white-sleeved hand, and turned it upon himself, first clicking the switches off, then on again.

Nothing.

Nothing, until it was held again to the collar of Miss Seeton's red-and-black checked coat. Some, with less self-control than others, already had their fingers in their ears against the racket which ensued.

"Take your coat off, woman!" Dignity, overwrought, had no time to spare for the social niceties. Obediently, Miss Seeton began with trembling fingers to undo her buttons.

Dignity pressed the switch for silence, then beckoned to another minion. "The Geiger counter," he commanded; and it was brought. Dignity gestured towards Miss Seeton as she stood revealed in her light tweed suit and discreet blouse, with her favourite yellow beads about her neck, her neat felt hat—even the proud cockscomb looked embarrassed—on her head, her leather gloves and bag invisible under sleeves which had slipped down her arms as the coat swung open.

Tick. Tick. Tick. Tick, tick, tick, tick tick tick tick tickticktickticktick . . .

"The necklace!" Dignity pushed aside the second white-coated assistant to spin Miss Seeton bodily round on the spot, fumbling with the catch of her necklace as the Geiger counter rattled out its warning. "The necklace . . . "

With Cousin Flora's beads well out of range, the Geiger counter was held once again to Miss Seeton's neck.

Nothing.

"I've—I've never heard of such a thing in my life." Indignant Dignity tossed the beads to one of the minions with instructions to measure their output properly.

"Great heavens!" He ordered a second measuring. He—everyone within sight—gaped.

"Great heavens—madam," recalling his manners with

an effort. "Do you realise that you have been walking about with two and a half thousand becquerels of radioactivity around your neck?"

"Good gracious," was Miss Seeton's weak, bewildered, and utterly helpless reply. "I'm—I'm really very sorry. Is it serious?"

Dignity rolled his eyes in speechless despair. It was one of the white-coated minions who replied. "Let's say you shouldn't wear those beads of yours for too long at any one time, Miss. The glass they're made of is coloured with uranium salts—those yellow streaks, you see. There was quite a vogue for that sort of thing back in the Twenties, when folk didn't realise how dangerous the stuff could be. You gave us quite a shock, I must say."

"Good gracious," gasped Miss Seeton again. "Oh, dear, I really must . . . " And she began to explain that Cousin Flora had left her, as well as her dear cottage and a modest sum of money, the contents of that cottage, these including her personal possessions and, of course, her jewellery, which she only kept for best, and, naturally, in honour of the princess's visit—

"Great heavens!" Dignity again went white. Never mind the confusion caused by this untoward occurrence; one could not with impunity ignore one's guest of honour—especially one whose blood was of the bluest, and whose influence on those responsible for compiling the Honours List could be considerable.

"I must humbly beg your pardon, Your Royal Highness, for the interruption." He thrust Miss Seeton and her apologies aside as he began to make his way back to where Georgina waited.

"But everything is now under control, Ma'am, and . . . "

To where she was not waiting.

"Ma'am?"

Attention snapped away from Miss Seeton, darted about the room. The lady-in-waiting uttered a little squeak, then began to turn pale.

"Ma'am?"

Heads turned, searching back and forth. Was Georgina playing—the nation's darling was surely not so foolish—a practical joke?

Surely not!

"Ma'am . . . "

Dignity was pleading now. Lady Vaudine's white lips parted in a whisper. Other voices, low at first, then louder, took up the cry.

There came, no matter how loud the crying, no reply.

No reply at all.

Her Royal Highness Princess Georgina had completely disappeared.

# CHAPTER 11

"She—she can't have disappeared!" Dignity cast a frantic look at the lady-in-waiting. "She—she must be playing some—some trick on us . . ."

For all the tension of the moment, Lady Vaudine Elliot visibly winced. "Her Royal Highness," she said, with icy scorn, "does not"—her lip curled—"play tricks." After her first white, stunned silence, Vaudine's aristocratic training had come swiftly to her aid. Her voice did not shake as she echoed Dignity's desperate words; and her head was high, her spine was straight as she went on: "Nor, let me assure you, is she given to—to *disappearing* whilst engaged on her official duties."

Lady Vaudine's voice did not shake—but her hands did. Dignity's gaze was irresistibly drawn to them as, despite her ladyship's air of studied calm, they writhed beneath their burden of Georgina's earmuffs and bouquet . . .

The bouquet! The child . . . and the old woman with the child—the old woman who had caused so much commotion even before the princess's arrival, and who had caused even more just before she—surely there could be no other possible word—disappeared . . .

Dignity whirled to face Miss Seeton, who, though quite as puzzled as the rest by Georgina's strange behaviour, had recovered herself sufficiently to begin the instinctive retrieval of her fallen brolly. "You!"

As he pointed a challenging finger, and uttered his one bitter syllable of blame, Miss Seeton, bending, jumped. She blinked. The umbrella clattered again from her grasp . . .

"Leave that alone!" Dignity was now in full command of himself and, he hoped, of the situation. He glanced round for the security people, and found, to his relief, that they had forestalled his next instruction. They were closing in on Miss Seeton—not one of them under six feet tall, all of them broad-shouldered, narrow-eyed, menacing—and Miss Seeton, startled by their menace, was taking a few nervous steps backwards.

She had left, as ordered, her umbrella alone. One of the security team muttered sideways to his companions and left them to continue their closing action while he veered from his course to begin a cautious approach to the sinister gold-and-black shape on the floor. Miss Seeton, surrounded, uttered one muffled squeak, then was frozen into silence by the force of the multiple slit-eyed stare directed at her from high above her head . . .

The security man neared the umbrella—held his breath—bent, warily, low . . . peered at the handle. His scrutiny passed slowly, intently, from the handle to the spike; he leaned over and squinted, frowning, at the ferrule, then seemed to have reassured himself that the rubber did not conceal the muzzle of some custom-built weapon; and moved back to the handle once more. Taking a deep breath, he thrust one hand behind him, motioning everyone away . . . while, with the other, he reached out for the exact centre of the umbrella, and picked it up. Smoothly, he rose to his feet . . .

He rotated the umbrella three times before deciding that it might be safe to examine it in yet more detail. He held it to one eye—squinted down its length; he held it in the middle and twisted the handle to and fro, aiming the fer-rule—for safety's sake—at the floor.

Nothing happened. No explosion—no bullet—no swift steel blade. It seemed there was no bomb, no gun, no sword-stick concealed in the umbrella's hollow steel shaft . . .

It seemed: but seeming was not believing. Expert knowledge of the ways of villains warned that the apparently harmless could even yet be something else. There was one check still to be made before the brolly's innocence could truly be believed. As there came a long, thrilling sigh from the watching crowd, the security man signalled again for continued caution, then fumbled with the fastening strap and, with a resigned grunt, slid the steel ring slowly up the shaft to its connecting notch. The spokes sprang wide apart . . . And the umbrella, in all its silken glory, was safely open.

Another sigh; murmurs of relief. It was no more than an umbrella, after all . . .

But was the old woman who had dropped it no more than an old woman?

All heads turned, as they had turned before, towards Miss Seeton. Dwarfed among her captors, she was gradually coming to the realisation that, somehow, everyone thought everything that had happened was all her fault—as, indeed, one had to confess that much of it was. Dear Cousin Flora's beads . . .

Miss Seeton saw the turning heads, the accusing eyes—and blushed.

"Oh, dear," said Miss Seeton. "I'm—I'm really very, very sorry . . . "

"I'm really very sorry, sir." Detective Constable Foxon was on his knees in front of Superintendent Brinton's desk. "If you hang on a sec, I'll just . . . "

With a further hitch of his well-pressed trousers up and over his knees to spare the crease, he flopped back on his heels, leaned forwards, and began to pick up the bright white bullets which Brinton, in an unusually exasperated moment, had hurled at him. Since cellophane bags of sweets are aerodynamically unsound, the bullets had not gone far in their flight before falling to the floor; and Foxon, who realised that he had, perhaps, himself gone rather too far on this occasion, had come rushing from his chair to the rescue. The rasp of Brinton's frenzied respiration was accompanied by a counterpoint of sharp plops as the peppermints were dropped, one by one, into the envelope Foxon held in his spare hand—the envelope which, as he saw his chief's empurpled face fade slowly to reassuring red, he moved a little farther away with each dropping. As the plops grew louder, Brinton's breathing grew calmer—or at any rate, by contrast, less noisy. Foxon, with an elaborately courteous cough, ventured to speak again.

"I'm afraid the packet's gone for a burton, sir. Burst its sides and fit for nothing—I'll bin it, shall I? But a bit of a dust-off and the mints should be okay."

"Throw away the lot," growled Brinton. "Then throw your own damfool self after 'em! It's time I traded you in for something easier on the eye, laddie—high time," as Foxon, risking a discreet grin, rose to his feet. "Why I've put up with you all these years, I'll never know . . . "

Foxon carefully readjusted the knees of his trousers to their former knife-edged elegance before folding down the flap of the envelope, crumpling the torn packet, and heading for the waste-paper basket. Its grey metal mouth yawned greedily as he held his booty directly above. "Could be the the contrast, sir," he ventured. The basket clanged. "Opposites attract, and all that. Me with my dress-sense, and you . . . well, yours is very different, sir, you've said so yourself. And there's you with all your experience of police work, sir, compared to me hardly off the bottom rung of the ladder—"

"If that's a reminder you've had thoughts about putting in for sergeant, you've picked a bad time for it." Brinton sighed, then absently pulled open the drawer of his desk to grope within. Somewhere, he knew, was his emergency packet: not that triple strength was anything like strong enough, though. Nowhere near it, when a man with his worries had worries like his . . .

"Oh, sit down and stop hovering!" His fingers had found cellophane at last, and he relaxed as he drew the packet out and tore the top open. "It's bad enough waiting for news, without having you prance about the place like some blasted grasshopper in that godawful outfit . . ."

Foxon's choice of shirt that day had been a rich emerald paisley, adorned by a burnt-orange tie striped with gold. His trousers were not only flared, but pale green; and there had been a Gala Dinner the previous night which the hapless superintendent had been obliged, in the course of his professional duties, to attend. The early-morning combination of a hangover and Foxon's spritely sense of colour had been altogether too much for the choleric Chris Brinton, though he had managed to suppress the full majesty of his wrath until the young constable had dared to tempt fate by speaking the unmentionable name . . .

But now, with peppermint soothing his savage breast, it was Brinton himself who mentioned Miss Seeton. "I should think," he said, replying to Foxon's not-so-innocent remark of ten minutes earlier, "she's having a whale of a time, if I know women. Hobnobbing with the bluest blood, best bib and tucker . . ." Then he grimaced. "With a swanky titfer to top the lot, of course. I've no idea why females *will* have a new hat whenever there's anything special going on, but they always do—and it doesn't come cheap, Foxon, believe me." Mrs Brinton, like many of the local ladies, was a frequent—their loving husbands would say far too frequent—customer of Monica Mary Brown, Brettenden's renowned, and expensive, milliner. "Thank heavens Maggie Laver's gone in uniform. I shudder to think what the bill'd've been for her to do the plainclothes bit . . ."

The words reminded him of his first sight of Detective Constable Foxon's *plain clothes*. For the second time he closed his eyes, groaned softly, and shuddered.

Foxon grinned. "Fetch you some coffee, sir, if you like." His voice was that of one wise in the ways of alcohol and its after-effects. "Black with two sugars'd do you best. Tone up your system for you nicely, that would. Give you, um, pep, sir—"

He broke off, looked at Brinton, and grinned even more broadly. "Well, it'd keep you going for an hour or so, anyway. Want some?"

"I don't want toning." Brinton's eyes were still shut. "I don't want pepping. The only *going* I want to do is home to bed, and the only *want* I have apart from that is for a nice, peaceful existence—"

The telephone's sudden jangle drowned out the rest of his wants as it woke him from his daydream. He opened his eyes, uttered a curse, and grabbed for the receiver with one hand while his other reached automatically for a pencil.

"Brinton." The telephone squawked in his ear. After no more than half-a-dozen words, the superintendent went rigid. "Dungeness? What's wrong? Don't tell me the blasted roads are snarled up and her precious Royal Highness is stuck in a jam somewhere, because—" Further, frantic squawking.

"Worse? You mean the girl's been in an accident?" His eyes darted to the large-scale map on the opposite wall, then narrowed with irritation. "Either it is, or it isn't. For heaven's sake stop babbling, girl, and answer a straight question. Is the princess all right?"

The telephone was slow to respond, then squawked in a manner that was almost hesitant. Brinton let out an exasperated snort. "What the hell d'you mean, you don't know? Call yourself a police officer when you can't make a proper statement? Once and for all, what the blue blistering blazes has happened?"

The telephone seemed to take a very deep breath. Then it told him.

"Princess?" Brinton blinked. "Disappeared?" He glared at Foxon, who had been a fascinated eavesdropper of the one-sided conversation, and clapped a furious hand to his forehead. His fury was so great that he forgot to wince. "This is no time for jokes, Laver. How the hell can the princess have *disappeared*?"

In his ear, Woman Police Constable Maggie Laver's voice rose to a wail. "I'm sorry, sir, I just don't know. But—but she has, sir. Gone, I mean. She just . . . vanished. Sir, she's c-completely disappeared . . ."

Now that Brinton had heard the worst for the second time, he was prepared to believe it. He became the epitome of professional calm to anyone who could not see him, though Foxon observed, with some alarm, that his face had already begun to turn purple. "Stop keening like that, Constable, and take a deep breath, and start again from the beginning. How long ago did this—this disappearance take place? And how"—the calm was starting to fray around the edges—"the hell did it happen?"

As Maggie Laver told him, Foxon—who'd been frozen into immobility at his chief's first words—shook himself out of his stupor and headed for the extension on his own desk. He had just reached for the receiver when he dropped it back on the cradle at Brinton's startled bellow.

*"What?"* roared the superintendent. The walls of the office thrummed. The central light began dancing on its flex. *"Miss Seeton?"*

And then, through gritted teeth, he added grimly:

"I might have known . . ."

"I don't care where he's gone, or who he's with, or how big the blasted building is." Brinton's tone left no room for argument. "Find him—and find him fast. Tell him if he's ever had an emergency to deal with, this is an emergency with bells on—and no,'' as the switchboard at Scotland Yard tried a little discreet pumping, ''I'm *not* telling you what this is all about. Just you get me Chief Superintendent Delphick on the line, pronto—and you needn't bother,'' bitterly, ''listening in, my lad. You'll find out soon enough, believe me.''

The switchboard recognised the voice of a superior under considerable stress, and permitted itself only the briefest mutter of wounded feelings before asking Brinton if he'd mind hanging on again while various extensions were tried—

''Can't you put out something over the public address system? You must have one, for heaven's sake. Or send out a search party—a dozen search parties!'' Brinton knew how many floors there were in New Scotland Yard. He could guess how many offices there must be, hidden behind so many windows; and he hadn't realised, until he'd been put through and had to suffer the long, hollow ring of an unanswered telephone, just how much he'd counted on Delphick's being there when needed. ''Take a look in the canteen, for a start. Ask if anybody's ceiling's buckling under the weight of young Ranger on the floor above—the lad's with the Oracle more often than not. At a pinch, he'll do instead of Delphick—but it's Delphick I really want. Now!''

''I'll do the best I can, sir, but it may take some time. Would you like to give me your station number, and I'll get him to call you back when we've found him?''

Brinton spoke through gritted teeth. ''No, I wouldn't.'' Even in this moment of crisis, he had sense enough to know that the very mention of the word *Ashford* would prompt the question ''Middlesex, Derbyshire, Devon, or Kent?'' And the ''Kent'' reply, coupled with the urgency of his request to speak with Delphick, would immediately alert the most dull-witted detective—and those were pretty thin on the ground at the Yard—that the crisis had something to do with the Oracle's personal discovery, Miss Emily Dorothea Seeton . . .

"Chris?" It seemed an eternity later that the welcome voice appeared on the other end of the line. Brinton was moved to groan aloud in sheer relief. "Delphick here, as if you didn't know. You've been hunting for me high and low, after all: but why such heartfelt thanks to almighty powers? What's up?"

Brinton groaned again, but even now did not fully abandon caution. "Anyone with you?"

"Detective Sergeant Ranger, of course; and the assistant commissioner. We're in his office. Sir Hubert had summoned not a few of us to a meeting on the subject of terrorism, but everyone else"—did the oracular voice here quiver with faint amusement?—"has, ah, made his excuses, and run for cover. They—we—guessed that your cry for help was not unconnected with a certain, ah, lady of our acquaintance—and it seems," as for the third time Brinton groaned, "that our guess was correct. It must be pretty serious, for you to have browbeaten the switchboard into interrupting a top-flight terrorism briefing—so tell me, Chris. What's Miss Seeton done to upset you?"

In Ashford, Brinton could only gulp. He groaned; he gasped. He ran a hand around the collar of his shirt, took a deep breath—and gave up. He cast a pleading eye in the direction of Detective Constable Foxon, listening—at his chief's command—on the extension; and even the normally ebullient Foxon could only respond in the most hesitant of tones.

"It—she—it's not so much what MissEss has done to upset us, sir—well, I suppose she started it, so you could say she *has*—but it's got to be some mistake, sir," said Foxon, warming to his role as Miss Seeton's champion. He'd had a soft spot for MissEss ever since the night (as she herself was wont to say, with a twinkle in her eye) they had spent together, in a disused church, looking for atmosphere and ending up in the middle of a full-blown Black Mass, with a witches' coven thrown in for good (though he supposed he ought to say bad) measure. "It's got to be! I mean, she's not the sort to complain, never has been, but it's bound to have upset her, being arrested like that—not that they had any choice, because—"

"Arrested? Miss Seeton?"

There came a series of clicks on the line as Sir Hubert Everleigh, Assistant Commissioner (Crime), followed at once—permission be damned—by Detective Sergeant Bob Ranger, snatched up telephone extensions and began to fire a volley of questions which deafened Delphick quite as much as those listening at the Ashford end.

The babble seemed to bring Brinton to his senses. "For the dear Lord's sake, *shut up!*" In his wildest dreams he'd never imagined himself telling an ass. comm. from the Yard to shut up, but what'd happened now was one hell of a lot wilder than that, and if his pension suffered it was just too bad. "All right, Foxon, thanks," as everyone subsided. "Yes, Oracle, *arrested.* Miss Seeton. And Foxon's right, there was nothing else they could do, in the circumstances, but I agree with the lad, there's got to be some mistake. That's why I want you to come and sort it out, because I'm only a humble copper, and in a. case like this—when I'm damned if I can understand the way she works, though she might even be of some use, because God only knows what other leads we've got to go on—"

"Chris!" Delphick's desperate cry broke into Brinton's torrent of explanation. "Take a deep breath," he instructed, in an unconscious echo of Brinton's earlier instructions to Woman Police Constable Laver. "Let's start right at the beginning. You say Miss Seeton's been arrested, and that the arresting officers had no choice. Why not? What's the charge?"

"You aren't going to believe this, Oracle. I can still hardly believe it myself." Brinton drew in one of the deepest breaths of his life. "The charge . . . the charge is . . . treason."

# CHAPTER 12

The distance between Scotland Yard, in London, and Ashford, in Kent, is—as the crow flies—about fifty miles. The distance between Ashford and Dungeness is just under twenty: but the roads are not as good. In such circumstances, it should have come as no great surprise to Superintendent Brinton that the vehicle bearing Chief Superintendent Delphick and his sergeant should arrive in the Ashford police station car park at almost exactly the same time as that bearing the bewildered, and unhappily handcuffed, form of Miss Emily Dorothea Seeton.

The cars might have parked around the back, but—since this was November—their passengers had to come in through the front door. The rear entrance only stood open during very hot weather, when even Desk Sergeant Mutford, a staunch member of Brettenden's Holdfast Brethren, was prepared to yield Security to Comfort: open doors, although technically a potential risk, gave a through-draught which no number of electric fans could supply. Although Mutford was but seldom known to smile, a chilly day always gave him a slightly more cheerful aspect than one of scorching heat.

As the first arrivals pushed open the double doors, the sergeant looked up from the Occurrence Book, which he had been studying with the glum thoroughness of a man who always suspects the worst of his fellows, and has never yet been proved wrong.

"Ugh." Mutford nodded his recognition of the newcomers, and raised a hand in slow salute. "A good day to you, Chief Superintendent." Mere sergeants, being of equal rank with himself, did not deserve the honour of the greeting direct. Mutford simply nodded again as Bob passed by in Delphick's wake, then turned back to the Occurrence Book and resumed his pessimistic perusal of its pages.

Within fifteen seconds, the double doors clanked open again. Mutford, the gleam in his eye announcing to the initiated that he was enjoying himself as much as a Holdfast Brother would ever admit to such a thing, glared across at the noise: and froze.

"Constable Laver! What may be the meaning of this, if I might enquire?" He frowned awfully at the wrists of the hapless Miss Seeton, handcuffed in front of her. Maggie Laver had hated having to use them, but without her promise that they would remain fastened until her charge had been handed over to a higher authority, the security forces would have insisted on whisking Miss Seeton away in an armoured van to a destination unknown.

"All wickedness," said Mutford, in reproving tones, "is but little, Constable, to the wickedness of a woman. Ecclesiasticus Twenty-five, verse nineteen."

"Oh, dear," breathed Miss Seeton. "Oh, dear . . . "

WPc Laver, with a toss of her head and a muttered "Take no notice of him, dear," hurried Miss Seeton—she couldn't think of her as the prisoner—past the desk and down the corridor in the direction of Superintendent Brinton's room. Having favoured her charge with a sheepish grin, she knocked on the door, hearing at once Brinton's bellow for her to come in, and quickly, if she was Maggie Laver—and, if she wasn't, she could—

Constable Laver flung open the door before Brinton could say anything to fluster Miss Seeton any more than she'd already been flustered. "Miss Seeton, sir!" she announced, and ushered her charge gently inside.

Four pairs of masculine eyes fastened upon Miss Seeton and her uniformed escort.

"Oh, dear." Miss Seeton would have wrung her hands, but the short chain of the cuffs wouldn't let her. She lowered her gaze, her cheeks unusually pink, her brow furrowed in a look of helpless confusion. Delphick, Brinton, Foxon, and Bob couldn't think when they'd last seen her look so lost: it must, they each independently decided, be because she was, for once, without her umbrella.

"Miss Seeton." Delphick was the first to recover his wits; the first to rise from his seat to welcome her. "From what we've heard," he said, as Bob leaped to his feet to fetch a chair, and Brinton muttered to WPc Laver to take those blasted things off the poor woman's wrists before the weight of them dragged her arms out of their sockets, "you have been"—he saw her anguished expression, and smoothly changed tack—"well, you have been . . . somewhat in the thick of things today, haven't you?"

Miss Seeton was the only person in the room not to marvel at the enormity of this masterly meiosis. Still blushing, she glanced up at the chief superintendent's tone of—despite the undeniable gravity of the situation—faint amusement, and found herself relaxing, just a little, as she was coaxed towards the chair. As she sat down, Bob patted her on the shoulder, and gave her a reassuring wink out of the eye Brinton couldn't see.

Miss Seeton took heart from the encouragement of her adopted nephew, and spoke in tones less trembling than might otherwise have been the case. "I'm—I'm rather afraid I have, Mr. Delphick, and I'm really very sorry, because I'm sure I never meant to. Poor Cousin Flora!" Miss Seeton sighed. "She would have been profoundly shocked, for they were some of her favourite beads and I only wear them for best, which in the circumstances—the princess, you know—I naturally considered . . . oh, dear.'' She gulped, and looked hastily away, her cheeks reddening, her hands, now free of their fetters, writhing on her lap.

''Oh, dear, indeed.'' Yet Delphick—with some effort, admittedly—still contrived that his tone should be one of faint amusement, though from the frantic messages they'd been getting every five minutes from Buckingham Palace via the Yard and the security forces, he didn't in all honesty see how anyone could find the present circumstances in the least degree amusing.

But seven years' knowledge of Miss Seeton stood him, he believed, in excellent stead. Fluster her—browbeat and bully the poor woman, as he'd no doubt the MI5 people had done—handcuffs, indeed! If those hadn't been Security's daft idea, he'd happily surrender five years of his pension . . . worry, confuse, upset her, and goodbye to any chance he or anyone else might have of harnessing her unique abilities to assist in solving this undoubtedly unique case. While the combined constabularies of Kent and neighbouring Sussex searched for clues; while squads of handpicked detectives and Intelligence men rushed down from London to interview known anarchists, communists, and similar subversives, he, the Oracle of Scotland Yard, watched the hands of the chief suspect dancing on her lap, and knew beyond any doubt that those hands held the key to the mystery. A key which could only be turned with great care . . .

''I do see, of course, that one cannot blame them.'' Miss Seeton's voice was almost steady, though it sounded little above a whisper. ''The—the unexpectedness, you see, of the noise, and Her Royal Highness . . . '' She faltered, blinking rapidly several times. ''They hardly do her justice, you know, when one sees her in real life. Such a—a joyful young woman, and bringing so much pleasure to so many . . . The police, that is, although Miss Laver was most kind, but one has, naturally, one's duty to perform, and I can quite understand . . . '' She sniffed, very discreetly, and her hands ceased in their aimless dancing to search for something more definite. ''My bag,'' she murmured, sniffing again, her eyes downcast. ''Oh, dear . . . ''

''Here, Miss Seeton.'' WPc Laver had argued loud and long with Security before they'd let her take the bag in the same car as its owner: nor had they let it go without giving it a very thorough check. It was emptied out on a table in front of Miss Seeton's startled, but obedient, gaze; a list was made of its contents; the power station staff were asked where there might be a convenient X-ray machine, to save ripping out the shot-silk lining. At this last, even Miss Seeton made a faint protest: but there had, fortunately, been no need to pursue the threat. While a detachment of MI5 operatives scrutinised for hidden horrors Miss Seeton's little purse, the modest sum it contained, the comb, lace-edged handkerchief, and mirror, her diary, address book, and sketchpad, the pencils, pens, and similar useful items, another group bore the bag itself away for the most rigorous of radiographic examinations. Neither party, despite the most detailed investigation, could find anything amiss. The contents were duly restored to the handbag, and the whole committed—albeit with reluctance—to Maggie Laver's care.

''I'm sorry,'' she said, ''not to have remembered before, Miss Seeton. And I'm even sorrier about—well, I'm sorry, but I did the best I could . . . '' She mimed helplessness, and Miss Seeton forced an understanding smile, though it was very shaky. Despite every argument Maggie Laver could put forward, Security had insisted on retaining, as hostages for Miss Seeton's subsequent good behaviour, her necklace of yellow glass beads . . . and her gold-handled umbrella.

''Thank you.'' Miss Seeton's whisper was barely audible, and to Delphick's keen ear it sounded as if there was more than a hint of emotion in her voice. When she took out her handkerchief and blew her nose, he was sure of it:

he didn't know when he'd ever seen her so upset.

"Miss Seeton, perhaps you'd like a cup of tea before we talk about what's happened? Chris, I think we could all do with some, to be honest."

Miss Seeton's slender frame quivered. "That would be most kind, Mr. Brinton, but please don't go to any trouble. I feel quite dreadfully to blame for—for everything . . . "

With the fingers of one hand, she crumpled her handkerchief into a damp, nervous ball, while with the other she opened and closed the metal clasp of her bag with quick, repeated snaps. Miss Seeton, it was only too obvious, was more than a little disturbed.

"I'm really sorry to press you, Miss Seeton," Delphick began, as Foxon slipped out with WPc Laver to organise tea and biscuits. "But I'm sure you appreciate the gravity of the situation. Everyone is doing all they can to help find the princess, and you, with your special talents, are bound to be of more help than most. You were, after all, an eyewitness—I'm sorry," as she flinched, and blushed again, and murmured of dear Cousin Flora, and how very dreadful it must seem, but she'd had no idea . . .

"Of course you hadn't." Delphick's mouth twisted in a wry smile. "As far as I can gather, your necklace is something rather out of the ordinary. You couldn't be expected to know that it had such . . . remarkable properties."

"No," said Miss Seeton, mouse-quiet. "I—I suppose not—except," she added, more firmly, "that dear Cousin Flora—that I had always noticed the beads, even as a child, and ought perhaps to have realised—the eye of an artist, you see . . . and she would sometimes allow me to wear them for—for fun, because they had so distinctive an appearance . . . " Reminiscence was helping her to relax. "Unique, indeed," she added, even more firmly. "Or at least, so I imagine."

"Indeed, yes, as far as we can tell. As, Miss Seeton, are you." Delphick smiled again. "Not merely as an eyewitness of—of recent events; not merely as an eyewitness who has been trained to use her eyes more than most. But as a trained eyewitness who has been retained by Scotland Yard as a consultant . . . ''

Miss Seeton winced, nodded, and slowly sat up straight. Any appeal to her sense of professional duty was bound—as Delphick didn't need to be an oracle to know—to urge her out of any mood she might be in; though he couldn't honestly blame her, on this particular occasion, for not being her normal happy, innocent, untroubled self.

"I will," said Miss Seeton, "do the very best I can, of course, Chief Superintendent, but . . . '' Her fingers danced and writhed again, fiddling with the clasp of her handbag, pleating her handkerchief, stroking the light tweed of her skirt in a quick, repetitive motion.

"But I can't—" said Miss Seeton—"I'm so sorry, but I simply can't seem to *see* anything, Mr. Delphick . . . ''

"And she couldn't." Delphick sighed at Miss Seeton's would-be rescuers, who had arrived half an hour after her departure. "She did her best, as she always does, but she'd been too upset by everything to see clearly, I think."

"Well, for heaven's sake, that's hardly surprising." Nigel Colveden was giving his best-ever performance as Sir Galahad. "The way everyone jumped on her—those Intelligence brutes with their beastly bullet heads and revolting slitty eyes—"

"Of course it isn't." Lady Colveden was every whit as indignant as her son, but was old enough to know how to temper indignation with guile; she also had no wish to be sued for slander by the security forces. "Poor Miss Seeton!" She brandished the gold-handled umbrella under Delphick's nose. "Without this, naturally she was . . . disorientated." The word pleased her, if the circumstances did not. "She wasn't just worried about the princess—though, goodness knows, nobody in their right minds would dream of harming Georgina because they'd never live to tell the tale—but *you* gave her this, Chief Superintendent, and she was worried it might be . . . well, damaged—or lost—or something—''

''Whereas,'' supplied Delphick, as she drew breath for a further protest, ''it was Miss Seeton herself, as you so rightly point out, who was, ah, lost. Without her umbrella—any umbrella . . . '' He fixed her ladyship with a curious eye. ''Incidentally, the last Superintendent Brinton and I heard from Woman Police Constable Laver, the MI contingent had—had received that into protective custody, and seemed highly unlikely to let it out again. How did you manage to effect its release?''

''We didn't post bail for the blessed thing, if that's what you're thinking.'' It was Nigel who answered: Lady Colveden was still being discreetly indignant. ''We called in the cavalry. Brought in the heavy guns, as it were.''

''Sir George,'' said Delphick at once, observing the look on her ladyship's face. ''I'm not surprised—or rather, I am. That the major-general allowed things to go as far as they did before he, ah, responded, I mean—''

''George wasn't there.'' Indignation forgot courtesy, and interrupted briskly. ''As soon as he heard, of course, he came across at once. Oh, there were interviews and things going on all over the place, and people giving statements, but he said he knew the moment he saw the umbrella that Miss Seeton must be in it somewhere—''

''And he was pretty peeved,'' Nigel broke in, ''to find out she wasn't, any more. In it, I mean—the power station, with all the rest of us, because she'd already gone. It was only when he heard she'd be coming here, and guessed it'd be Mr. Brinton, at least, and most likely you as well, who'd be dealing with her, that he calmed down enough to start organising everyone Martin Jessyp hadn't already organised.'' Nigel grinned. ''The village back on the bus, the schoolkids on *their* bus, the Crabbes keeping an eye on both lots, and Miss Maynard keeping an eye on young Sally and her mother . . . you can't say we didn't leave Plummergen in good hands, with Dad and Martin C. in charge.''

"I would never dream of such a thing. But," Delphick enquired, "why did you? Leave, I mean. One hesitates, of course, to suggest that it was desertion in the face of the enemy. May I assume that it was more in the nature of obedience to command?"

"Got it in one." Nigel chuckled. "Dad said she'd be completely lost without her brolly, and to bring it along pronto, so we did, once he'd had a quiet word or two with the MI blokes." Nigel had no more idea than his mother what Sir George had said to influence the fate of the umbrella: but "MI" stood for Military Intelligence, and Sir George's wartime career had not been without distinction. "We'd no idea you'd, um, got rid of her quite so quickly."

"Miss Seeton," Delphick informed him, "was sent— was driven home in an unmarked police car, with the recommendation that she should make herself a strong cup of tea, and stand on her head for half an hour or so, to relax. After which—"

"After which," said Lady Colveden, "you'll expect her to start drawing, poor thing, and goodness knows what you'll see if she does, if she's been silly enough to follow your advice, which normally she wouldn't, because Miss Seeton has a great deal of common sense, in normal circumstances. Only she's so upset today she probably already has, so it's too late. With her insides swimming in tea, and then turned upside-down—she'll have nightmares, at the very least, and I can't see that they'll help you at all." She regarded the chief superintendent shrewdly. "You'll have been meaning to pop in to see her later on, of course, once you've checked into the George."

Meekly, hiding a smile, Delphick confessed that such had been his intention.

"Well, it's not very practical." Lady Colveden patted the umbrella on its gleaming handle, and sighed. "Really, although George has his good points, I sometimes think men, on the whole, are . . . still, never mind. There are enough of the Security people around to keep everyone happy for tonight, aren't there? And the sooner we give this back to Miss Seeton, the better she'll feel about things in general. Just give her time to calm down, and don't arrive on her doorstep until after you've both had breakfast tomorrow. And then,'' said Lady Colveden, ''you just see if she doesn't draw exactly the sort of drawing you want.''

# CHAPTER 13

It was not Miss Seeton, but Martha Bloomer, who opened the door next morning to the pair from Scotland Yard. Her face, on seeing them, expressed a strong conflict of emotions. In the normal way, Mrs. Bloomer would be more than short in her manner towards anyone who had upset her dear Miss Emily—and there was no denying Miss Emily was still upset, even after a chance to sleep on it, with the wireless news and the papers full of nothing else but the Disappearance from Dungeness; but Martha—as did Miss Seeton herself—felt much admiration for Princess Georgina, and if Delphick and Bob were really going to find that blessed girl, they couldn't, she supposed, be blamed for coming to badger the poor soul so soon after breakfast . . .

"But you're not to go getting her in a state," came the sternly-whispered warning from the loyal domestic dragon. "In any more of a state, I mean, the way she's been already. Hardly touched a bite, then sits with her pencils and paper as miserable as if it really was her fault—which anyone with any sense knows it wasn't, no matter what she might've said yesterday, with the shock of it all being only too easy to take advantage of if it hadn't been for Sir George, bless him, and her ladyship seeing her right.''

Martha pointed to the umbrella-rack on the wall. Clipped firmly in its usual place was the gold-handled brolly of which its owner was so proud. "Brought that back yesterday evening, and you'd've thought it'd cheer her up—which I dare say it did, a bit, but she's really not herself this morning, and no mistake.''

"We're very sorry to hear that, Martha." There was no doubting the sincerity in Delphick's voice, or the look of compassion in his eye. "But you understand that we do need to see her, even though I imagine she's had more than her fill of questions from police and security people—they're off in pursuit of their own theories, and good luck to them. If they find Her Royal Highness before we do, then we'll be delighted; but something tells me things aren't going to go as smoothly as that.''

"That blessed lamb!" Martha shook her head. "How anyone could even think of such a thing I can't imagine, her being one of the sweetest girls you could hope to meet, they say. If only I'd been near enough to—but you want a word with Miss Emily, don't you? If there's anyone," said Mrs. Bloomer proudly, "can help you, then it's her, and never you mind MI5 and Scotland Yard—begging your pardon, Mr. Delphick.'' She didn't bother apologising to Bob. Since his marriage to a daughter of the village he counted more or less as an intimate, among whom apologies for the obvious were rarely deemed necessary in Plummergen etiquette.

"Come on through," said Martha briskly; and led the way to the sitting-room.

They found Miss Seeton, as Mrs. Bloomer had predicted, seated at the table, with her drawing equipment spread out in front of her. On hearing the click of the opening door she started, and hastily flipped shut the cover of her sketchpad before turning to greet her visitors.

When she recognised them, she blushed.

"Chief Superintendent," she murmured, rising from her chair to shake hands. For Bob, she forced a smile: the sergeant and his wife had long ago adopted Miss Seeton as an honorary aunt. This relationship she was more than happy to acknowledge, except that when he was in the presence of his superiors it made choosing the correct form of address a trifle awkward. A smile, Miss Seeton generally felt, was the safest solution; but she didn't feel much like smiling just now . . .

"I hope you're feeling none the worse for yesterday's little adventure," said Delphick, as they took their seats. "I'm pleased to see that you've already started work," with a nod for the sketchpad, pencils, and eraser arranged on the table. He tactfully ignored the even pinker blush which now tinged Miss Seeton's cheeks: she was always embarrassed at the creation of one of her special Drawings, and her embarrassment no longer caused him any great surprise. One had to coax her, perhaps remind her of her professional obligations if she seemed particularly bothered: he was used to it. "We know," he said, "that we can rely on you to fulfil your contract, and more than fulfil it: you've never let us down, Miss Seeton. May I see the drawing, please?"

As he smiled, and held out his hand, Miss Seeton's face flamed. Her eyes dropped to the closed cover of her sketchpad, on which her fingers twisted in a tormented knot, as if protecting—withholding—the sketch from Delphick's sight. She murmured something the chief superintendent didn't quite catch, and her hands moved suddenly apart as if to wrench and tear the sketchpad in two.

"Miss Seeton!" Delphick glanced at Bob, who shook his head, bewildered. "This isn't like you, Miss Seeton. You mustn't even think of destroying your picture, no matter what you think of its—its artistic merits. Scotland Yard owns the copyright, you know." And once more he held out his hand.

"Oh . . . " Miss Seeton, still pink-cheeked, raised her eyes to meet Delphick's firm but kindly gaze. "So—so very . . . disloyal . . . '' she gulped. ''T-treas-treason . . . ''

''Not,'' said Delphick, ''if you give it to me now, without further delay. I'm a servant of the Crown, remember, and my duty, quite as much as yours, will be called into question if I fail to follow up every possible clue in this case. No matter how obscure or,'' and he smiled, ''unusual. Please?''

He reached again for the sketchpad. Reluctantly—as reluctant as they'd ever seen her—Miss Seeton allowed him to take it; then she pushed back her chair and jumped up from the table before he could inspect her work. ''I'll—I'll just see if Martha is making a cup of tea,'' she said; and fled.

Delphick looked again at Bob. ''Entirely natural, of course, that she should be less than her normal happy self, but I can't help wondering whether the shocks of yesterday haven't, after all, been too much for her. We've grown so used to her bouncing back from her numerous trials and tribulations that we tend to forget she is, alas, not as young as—great heavens!''

As he spoke, Delphick had opened the stiff paper cover of the sketchpad. The exclamation had come the moment his brain had advised him that what his eyes had seen really was what Miss Seeton had drawn. ''Great heaven and earth . . . ''

There was a long, fraught silence. Bob, who had craned his head across to look at the sketch, had frozen in mid-look, too startled even to whistle.

''No wonder,'' said Delphick at last, ''that she spoke of treason . . . ''

Miss Seeton had drawn a woodland glade in high summer, surrounded by leafy trees, carpeted with luxuriant grasses. In the middle of the glade, taking their ease on the grass, were three figures: one man, one woman, and one of indeterminate gender, who sprawled, leaning on one elbow, to the right of the little group with the other arm outstretched, the hand holding a bottle. The figure's face was shaded; the hand and bottle were sharply defined. The middle figure—like the first, decorously clad in jacket and trousers, but with a tie rather than (as the first) a frilled cravat—leaned rather than sprawled away from his companion, as if conversing privately with the third member of the trio.

This was a young woman, petite but shapely, her hair a mass of bright curls, crowned with a jewelled tiara. The young woman's face was instantly recogniseable as that of Her Royal Highness Princess Georgina; her body—with one knee bent up, one arm resting to conceal her bosom—was discreetly, but completely, nude.

Bob stared, blinked, and gulped. He was speechless. He stared again: there could be no doubt. The naked young woman was indeed Georgy Girl, the darling of the nation.

"Tastefully done," said Delphick at last. "No artful wisps of gauze or similar abominations—not that she needs them, of course. The pose, in itself, is quite unexceptionable—if somewhat surprising, given the subject."

"I'll say," muttered Bob. "I know she's used to nudity—Aunt Em, I mean—life classes and all that—but . . . ''

As words seemed to fail his subordinate, Delphick said: "But you appear to have paid rather less attention to the foreground of the picture. The hamper, the tablecloth, the food waiting to be eaten—the wine . . . ''

The hamper, tablecloth, and food were more impressions than definite shapes. The bottle of wine, however, elegant and slim, was so sharply drawn that Bob almost felt he could read the letters on the label; and the glasses beside the bottle were diamond-bright crystal, not feeble flickers of light and shade. The wine . . .

Bob looked at Delphick. "That's twice she's made a—a feature of the booze, sir, with this, er, chap here holding the other bottle—but surely she can't be trying to tell us young Georgy's an alcoholic!''

"I think not." Delphick smiled. "I think not, indeed—though she is, of course, trying to tell us *something*—and

I will hazard a guess as to what that something might be. Tell me, do you recognise this picture?''

"You mean it's a copy of a—a real picture, sir? Then I can't say I do. Sorry."

"The, ah, real picture is itself, in a way, a copy—of an engraving by Raimondi, after Raphael. *The Judgement of Paris*—in the Metropolitan in New York, I believe. But the copy, as it were, is, unless I'm very much mistaken, Edouard Manet's *Dejeuner sur l'Herbe*."

"Oh," said Bob, who felt he ought to say something, even if he'd forgotten most of the French he ever knew. "Er—breakfast?" he hazarded and Delphick did not smile.

"That's *petit dejeuner*, Bob: literally, 'small luncheon.' A good guess, though, since some people have large breakfasts, others have small luncheons: people's appetites, as you should know more than most, vary enormously."

He smiled as he said this, and Bob had to grin. Anne often teased him that she cooked for three and ate for half, while he—more than twice her size—had the rest.

"The original title would translate as *Luncheon on the Grass*," said Delphick kindly. "Not that I imagine it's so much the sylvan setting as the more casual nature of the meal which has caught Miss Seeton's interest." He sat up, his eyes bright. "The buffet, Bob—the dining arrangements laid on for the aftermath of Georgina's visit. That's where we must start our investigations, I fancy . . . "

Bob frowned. He couldn't exactly see it himself—but then he wasn't the Yard's Seeton expert the way the chief super was. Even the assistant commissioner, who kept trying to sneak Aunt Em's originals out of the files to add to his private collection, could never make much sense of them while a case was still going on. But once the Oracle had—had . . . Bob frowned again, groping for the right word; then thought of breakfast and luncheon, and had to grin. Once the Oracle had translated the Drawings . . .

"You find my theory, I gather, attractive." Delphick was observing his subordinate in some amusement. "I'm glad it meets with your approval, Sergeant. It now remains for me to obtain Miss Seeton's approval, or perhaps I should say permission, for the use of her telephone. As a member of the family, do you think you could slip along to the kitchen and ask her?''

Two minutes later, he was standing, with a curious Bob at his side, in the hall, holding the telephone receiver in one hand while the fingers of the other beat an impatient tattoo on the table. ''Come on, Chris—Foxon—anyone, just answer this damned phone!''

The station switchboard broke in. ''Sorry, sir, there's no answer from Superintendent Brinton.'' Delphick resisted, with a considerable effort, the impulse to retort that he knew this very well. ''Would anyone else do instead?''

''No, thank you.'' The idea of explaining to a stranger how a doodled bottle or two of wine had inspired a Scotland Yard ace to demand a detailed investigation of the catering firm hired by the Central Electricity Generating Board did not appeal. ''Couldn't someone run a spot-check around the station? Today, of all days, I can't credit that he isn't on the premises—and my call has some bearing on the matter of Her Royal Highness's disappearance, which means it's more than urgent.''

''I'll put you through to the front desk, sir. Sergeant Mutford's more likely than most to know where Mr. Brinton's gone—if he's gone anywhere, that is.''

Delphick acknowledged the worth of this suggestion; he knew Mutford of old. The Holdfast Brethren maintained the most strict adherence to rules, regulations, and biblical law of any sect he knew: for a Brother to allow a telephone to go unanswered when his job was to answer it would be a serious lapse in observance.

It came, therefore, as some surprise when the telephone, yet again, went unanswered, though the switchboard let it ring for over a minute before breaking in to enquire whether the chief superintendent wanted to hang on, or whether he was quite sure nobody else would do.

"Try Mr. Brinton's office again, please. Even if he's not back, perhaps young Foxon could take a message—and I can't," he said, aside to Bob, as the connection was made, "stand much more of this. We're wasting valuable time here while—hello? Hello!"

"Hello," came the cautious response on the other end of the line.

"Chris, is that you?"

"Who wants to know?"

"Chris, stop playing games. You have a serious case on your hands, and there isn't time to—"

"Oracle!" The relief in Brinton's voice was obvious. "Thank the Lord for that. I've only just escaped with my life from a crowd of reporters out the front—Mutford and his gang are doing the Horatius-at-the-Bridge bit while Foxon and I made a run for it—and I was afraid you were another of the blighters who didn't believe that No Comment was honestly all I had to say right now."

"Reporters," said Delphick, momentarily sidetracked by memories of his own suffering at journalistic hands. "Yes, I can well imagine the sort of thing you've had to put up with. It's a great pity that Mel Forby and Thrudd Banner are still, as far as I know, out of the country—they tend to have a civilising influence, of sorts, on their more importunate colleagues."

The pair to whom he referred—Amelita Forby of the *Daily Negative,* and her close friend Thrudd Banner of World Wide Press—were acquaintances of long standing. They had severally entered the Oracle's ken by becoming involved in one or other of Miss Seeton's many adventures, and—being as fond of Miss Seeton as they were of headline exclusives—had succeeded in persuading Fleet Street and the news broadcasters that it was in everyone's interests to keep Miss Seeton's name, if not her adventures, out of the public eye. Nobody quite knew how they had managed to achieve this, but achieve it, on the whole, they had: for which Delphick and the rest of Miss Seeton's friends were more than grateful to them . . . and for which Miss Seeton was not in the least grateful, since in the first place she remained unable to conceive that her adventures were adventures at all—and, even if they were, she would suppose them to be the business of nobody but herself and (because they paid the retainer for her sketches) the police.

If anyone could make life at a press conference easier for Superintendent Brinton, it would have been Mel and Thrudd: but they were both, as Delphick had thought, out of the country. Thrudd had recently achieved a spectacular Drugs Scandal scoop, involving high-ranking officers in the Swiss Navy and an eminent pharmaceutical conglomerate. The supplying of substandard seasickness pills to Helvetian matelots had been only the first step on the downward path of corruption which Thrudd, with his usual brilliance, had excavated. His World Wide employers had given him worldwide coverage—and a bonus, which he had summoned Mel to the fleshpots of Geneva to assist him in spending.

"Importunate," spluttered Brinton, "be damned! All they *said* they wanted was a statement, to begin with—and then once they'd got me there the blighters were firing questions at me left, right, and centre. How many times does a bloke have to say he doesn't know before Fleet Street starts to believe the poor devil?"

"I sympathise," said Delphick, who certainly did, "but I have a notion that I may be able to increase your knowledge somewhat. You may have gathered that I am speaking from a—a village not a million miles from Ashford—"

A weary groan interrupted this circumlocution, followed by a thud as—or so Delphick deduced—the superintendent dropped heavily into his chair. "Don't tell me," begged Brinton. "You-know-who's been sketching again!"

"She has." The time for circumlocution was past. "And something she's sketched suggests to me that it might well be worth your while investigating the firm of caterers who supplied the food and drink—especially the drink—for yesterday's beanfeast. In depth," he added, as there came a long silence from the other end of the wire.

"Bragbury's," said Brinton at last. "Bragbury's Banquet and Buffet Service: they did the lot. They're a family firm—the electricity people like to support local industry as far as possible—and how the hell," he cried, "did Miss Seeton know? Though I ought to be over letting her surprise me, after all these years . . ."

"Know what?" Delphick tried to suppress his excitement. "You mean she's on to something—confirmed something—you already knew?"

"In a roundabout way I suppose you could say that, but there's a good few checks I'm going to arrange right now before I'll say she's hit the nail exactly on the head—"

"For heaven's sake, Chris!"

"Sorry. It's just that it isn't my case, as such, with Georgina on my plate enough for any man—not that I'd be likely to handle an ordinary RTA anyway, at my rank—"

"A road traffic accident?" Delphick's response was swift. "And one of the Bragbury crowd was involved?"

"The father," said Brinton. "He and one daughter were both there yesterday, mum and sister stayed home to cook for other orders and do the washing up. Daughter and another girl were waitressing—silver service to impress the nobs with how well they could dish out the smoked salmon patties; dad drove the van, helped set the stuff out, hung around in a bow tie and swish jacket looking lofty. Quite a performance. They've done one or two of our police bashes, and they know—knew—their stuff, all right."

"Past tense," said Delphick, thoughtfully. "I see."

"For the father, yes. Car came off the road last night, went into a tree, and bingo. Dammit, Oracle, it seemed like a straightforward accident! The chap was known to be a fast driver, except in the van—Traffic've given him more tickets than he's given them hot dinners. Nobody was surprised to hear he'd finally written himself off. But now . . ."

"Now," advised the Oracle, "you'd better have what's left of that car checked and doubled-checked, Chris. There is the distinct possibility that it was a third party who did the writing, in this particular instance—and, if so, it would be of the greatest help in recovering Georgina if we could only find out who that party might be."

# CHAPTER 14

Delphick and Bob thanked Miss Seeton for the use of her telephone, caught Martha's eye, and drank a hasty cup of tea. Then, making their excuses, they were gone.

By the time they had driven to Ashford, a distance of fifteen miles at most, official inspection of the Bragbury car was well under way.

"Good, you've made it in time." They might have expected rather more by way of salutation, but Superintendent Brinton was never one for the niceties when there was work to be done. Before either Bob or Delphick could blink, he had whisked them along to the garage where a team of experts was subjecting to rigorous examination the wreckage of the vehicle in which Donald Bragbury, founding father of the catering firm, had died the previous night.

They watched, and waited. Mechanics in oil-stained overalls crawled underneath the ruined car, and peered knowledgeably inside it. People wandered about with spanners and wrenches, looking important. Notes were jotted on pads of paper clipped to boards, measurements were taken; and taken again, as photographs were consulted.

"Then she was right—as if we couldn't have guessed."

Brinton's tone was resigned as he read the report rushed to him by the leader of the expert team, and discussed over a brief, private huddle. "Driving that route, he'd never have stood a chance, the way he always used to motor on the first clear stretch of road . . . "

"May I?" Delphick, unable to bear the suspense, took the clipboard from his colleague's hands, and studied it as if the mysteries of the internal combustion engine and its working were to him no mystery at all. "Ah, yes."

Without a word, he handed the clipboard to Bob, who received it with a faint grin. Brainy though the Oracle undoubtedly was, that brain had its limitations. Understanding what went on under the bonnet of a car was one of them—especially if what went on was anything at all out of the ordinary. Come to that, Bob didn't go much for custom motoring, either . . .

"Track rod ends," he said, having reached the relevant passage. This, at least, Sergeant Ranger understood, even if he had his suspicions that the Oracle didn't. As a loyal subordinate, he'd better help the old man out. "You mean somebody mucked about with the poor devil's steering?"

"Looks like it." Brinton, like Bob ignoring Delphick's little sigh of relief, jerked a head in the direction of the wrecked car. "From what you said on the phone about wine bottles, I might've wondered if he wasn't drunk, or'd had somebody slip him a Mickey Finn—and I suppose the autopsy could well show something-or-other on top of the rest—but it was the steering. Lucky it didn't catch fire in the crash, because it was easy enough to find the evidence, once MissEss'd put us on the right track—and that's a laugh." He wasn't laughing. "Talk about tracks, that's what chummie did—loosened the lock-nut on the track rod end, then knew he only had to wait for Bragbury to try taking a sharp bend. *Try* being the operative word, of course. Go in a straight line, and he was perfectly safe. Take one corner, and . . . "

"And the tree he hit," said Delphick, "is, I assume, on

the first corner he would reach after leaving home?''

Brinton rolled his eyes. "Give you three guesses."

"Top marks to Miss Seeton, then." Delphick nodded to Bob, who passed the clipboard back to his superior without a word. "There seems little doubt," murmured the chief superintendent, "that someone wished to take advantage of Donald Bragbury's known propensity for speed . . . Do we know yet why he was on that particular route at that particular time?"

"Have a heart." Brinton sounded hurt. "We've only this minute found out he was murdered, never mind a blow-by-blow timetable of his movements for the past twenty-four hours—but if you'd like to bring your young giant along to take notes, I think we should be able to remedy the situation before very much longer."

There were no obvious signs of mourning at the Bragbury home: no curtained windows, no black-ribboned hatchment on the gatepost, no procession of callers to the front door bearing condolences and flowers—food, of course, in such a circumstance would have seemed, perhaps, tactless.

When Brinton rang the bell, it clanged, unmuffled, in the hall. Hurrying feet soon came to answer it.

"Yes?" Mavis Bragbury, a massive white apron around her ample form, frowned at the three tall men on her doorstep. They gazed at her with some interest: here were no swollen eyes, no tear-stained cheeks, no haggard look of a sleepless night. "Yes? You looking for me?"

"Er," said Brinton, recovering himself, and producing his identity card. "Mrs. Bragbury, we're police officers. We're extremely sorry to have to disturb you again at a time like this, but—"

"Whatever it is you're about, it'd better not take too long." Mavis took the offered card and peered at it, then sighed as she handed it back. "I suppose you'd best come in—but we're very busy today, you know."

"I can imagine," said Brinton, in his most sympathetic

tones, as Mavis led the way into a chilly parlour, papered in muted tones of beige, grey, and a peculiar green which matched the ugly pattern of the carpet. The only sign of frivolity in the entire room was the flock of plaster ducks winging their mournful way across the wall opposite the net-curtained window—the window through which, since it faced north, no sun could ever shine to lighten the gloom.

"Can you, indeed?" Mavis sniffed. "I very much doubt it—not unless *you've* ever been expected to cater a sit-down meal for sixty people forty miles off with nobody to drive the van. Have to pay someone, I will, even if I can find 'em at such short notice, which'll mean double wages, in any case. Can you *imagine* a way round that?"

Brinton goggled. "Well, er . . . "

"You are a courageous woman, Mrs. Bragbury." Delphick came promptly to the rescue of his floundering colleague. "To be able to sublimate your grief in your work—your late husband would, I am sure, have been very proud of you."

Mavis favoured the chief superintendent with a sour look. "Satan's never found *mine* a pair of idle hands, nor any in this house, believe me—and I've no patience with them as'd rather be passengers than crew. We've our living to earn, whether Donald's here or not, and never a minute to waste in earning it." She looked pointedly in the direction of the sad-faced clock on the marble shelf above the empty grate, and sniffed again.

"Then we'll try to waste no more of your time before we let you get back to work," said Delphick, as Brinton, at his side, still gaped in stunned amazement. "We have reason to suspect, Mrs. Bragbury, that your husband's accident was not, in fact, an accident. We think that someone tampered with the steering of his car, and—"

"Not an accident?" Mavis went pale. Her voice rose to a squeal. "The car's bin tampered with? Oh, that's wicked lies! I won't—I don't believe you!"

"Please try not to distress yourself too much, Mrs. Bragbury. This must be hard for you, I know, but there is the strongest evidence—''

''Evidence?'' Her eyes widened in horrified dismay. ''You mean it's true—it weren't an accident?'' She saw his nod, and turned white. She gulped. ''But—but that means the insurance mightn't cover it!''

It was Delphick's turn to goggle, though he recovered himself more speedily than had Brinton. ''I really couldn't say about that, I'm afraid. Perhaps your financial adviser will be able to—''

''Financial adviser? There's another thing!'' Mavis was growing red-faced now, and her eyes were angry. ''Donald it was kept the books for the business, with me not seeing why we should pay good money for someone outside the family to do what anyone with a bit o' gumption could be doing for us for free—and now that'll mean more money down the drain, neither me nor the girls being much inclined to sums, and busy with the cooking, what's more. And now here you come telling me the insurance won't pay out on the car—and nothing to get on his life, most like, if what you say about tampering's true . . . ''

As even her indignant breath had at last to give out, Delphick leaped into the breach. ''It appears so, Mrs. Bragbury—which is why we've come to you. We've no reason to suppose this tampering was a—an episode of random spite, or casual vandalism. Did your husband, do you know, have any enemies?''

''That's libel,'' snapped Mavis, inaccurately. ''And I'll thank you not to go spreading tales o' that sort around the neighbourhood—this is a respectable family, let me tell you, and we've kept ourselves to ourselves right from the start. We don't go in for no nonsense, and that's a fact.''

''A business rival, maybe?'' Delphick wasn't going to give up easily. ''Bragbury's has an excellent reputation in these parts—and justifiably so, I'm told. It could well be in someone's interests to, ah, curtail your activities by—by reducing your workforce: especially if, as you suggest, your husband was the only one capable of handling the larger vehicles such as the delivery van.''

"Handling? Yes, and,'' said Mavis, as the grim realisation dawned, "servicing, which is summat else we're going to have to pay for now, me and the girls not being inclined to oil and grease, never mind the taste it'd give the food, and the customers not paying to eat in the inspection pit. Oh, it's a black day for Bragbury's, and no mistake!''

Delphick, for all his training and experience, was at something of a loss over the correct response to her remark. Fortunately for his composure, however, Mavis continued to enlarge on her theme for some minutes to come, and he was able to collect his scattered wits and jump into the next conversational breach as soon as it presented itself.

"It would be the greatest possible help in our investigations if we knew why your husband was out so late last night, and where he was going. After all the excitement and upset of the princess's disappearance, I would have thought that he and your daughter, as witnesses of the event, would prefer to spend a quiet evening at home.'' And he hoped he'd be forgiven the lie: he couldn't remember when he'd last seen so unrestful a house. It didn't seem probable that any of the other rooms were more welcoming; he dreaded to think what the Bragbury daughters were like if, as so often happened, they took after their mother. Since Donald had been responsible for the service and maintenance of his car, if it was learned later that he'd tampered with the steering himself, and committed suicide, the Oracle wouldn't be in the least surprised.

"Evening at home?'' Mavis looked astounded at the very idea. "When there's business to be done? The girls were washing up—all that good food gone to waste, none o' the Dungeness lot bothering to eat it, and never thinking to put it in the cool until too late—and then helping me get ready for today, which is no more'n you'd expect, us with a business to run.'' And once again she sniffed, and stared at the clock on the overmantel; and she sighed, and wiped restless hands down the front of her apron.

"So your husband went out on a—a business matter?" The deduction, thought Delphick, wasn't unreasonable; he was pleased to observe Mavis's brisk nod of confirmation. "Was this a long-standing appointment? Would an outsider have known—could he or she have expected—him to leave the house and drive in that particular direction at that particular hour?"

For the first time, Mrs. Bragbury's look was neither hostile nor disbelieving. Her dark eyes narrowed, and her forehead creased in a frown. "You wait there," she said; and, wheeling, marched out of the room without another word.

As she failed to close the door behind her (saving time, each of the three policemen independently guessed), nobody dared say anything in case, on her return, she overheard it. Their expressions, however, were more than eloquent as they looked at one another in a strained, thoughtful silence.

"Here," said Mavis, marching back into the room with an appointments diary in her hand. She slapped the book on the table in front of Delphick, and opened it. "Read that!"

Whatever the female Bragburys' ability with sums, nobody could fault their handwriting skills. The booking was plain for all to see, and Delphick—after a startled gulp—duly read it aloud.

"Eight-thirty, Mr. Mountfitchet. About his daughter's wedding." Above the gasps of Brinton and Bob, he addressed Mavis Bragbury with a note of more than urgency in his tone.

"Mountfitchet? Do you mean *Charley* Mountfitchet—from Plummergen?"

"That's who he said he was."

Something in her voice told Delphick what his next question should be. "You didn't believe him?"

She shrugged. "No reason why not."

"But Charley Mountfitchet's a bachelor, for heaven's

sake. He hasn't got a daughter!''

Mavis gave him an old-fashioned look. ''Not as we've heard of so far, no, but they're a funny lot over to Plummergen. No telling what he got up to in his young days a-coming home to roost now, is there?''

The landlord of the George and Dragon was a cheery, open-natured soul who delighted in helping the police with their enquiries on the least excuse. The most unlikely persons, Delphick knew, had the darkest of secrets hidden in their pasts; but Charley Mountfitchet seemed even more unlikely than most.

''So this . . . Mr. Mountfitchet telephoned to ask for some help in catering for his daughter's wedding. Did he ask for Mr. Bragbury by name?''

'' 'Twas allus Donald as did the driving and the bookings, me and the girls being busy with the preparation and the cooking. Everyone knows that.''

''Do they, indeed.'' Delphick frowned. Mavis pounced.

''They do, and if you're trying to name me a liar, I'll thank you to keep a civil tongue in your head! Me a poor lone widow-woman as I am—you oughter be downright ashamed o' yourself, and that's a fact.''

Once more, Delphick gulped. The idea of Mavis Bragbury as a grieving widow had long since passed from his memory. ''I—I apologise, Mrs. Bragbury. I'm just . . . confused, you see. Didn't it occur to you that the call from Mr. Mountfitchet might not—might not be entirely aboveboard?''

She shrugged again. ''Thought it weren't so likely he'd a daughter being wed, that's true . . . ''

''Then why did you allow your husband to go rushing off on what might well have proved to be a wild goose chase?'' Delphick restrained himself nobly from reminding her of what Donald Bragbury's errand had finally proved to be.

Mavis sighed. She answered in the voice of an exasperated adult addressing a very stupid child. ''Just acos he'd no wedding for the catering didn't mean as there weren't no cause for Charley Mountfitchet to do business with us. The George and Dragon's good enough eating, but nothing fancy—and for all I knew he was a-planning to bring in our stuff by the back door and try for a rosette in one o' they hotel guides—ah, and I'd've made sure he'd paid handsome for the privilege, and all!''

Delphick glanced at Bob, who was making a note to check with Charley the instant they returned to Plummergen. There was, he supposed, always the outside chance that the landlord hoped to go up-market: ever since the Best Kept Village Competition, and Plummergen's second prize, there were more visitors than ever before. But such a hole-and-corner way of improving the George's *cuisine*, which was good plain fare rather than particularly *haute*, was very unlike the Charley Mountfitchet they'd known for so many years . . .

"Then it never occurred to you, Mrs. Bragbury, that the message might be a hoax? You thought that Mr. Mountfitchet was about to propose to your husband some . . . some slightly dubious—ethically, if not commercially—deal?''

For the last time, Mavis shrugged. She looked at the clock with impatience; she looked at Delphick with scorn. ''And why not?'' she demanded. ''Why not? 'Twould have bin a good bit o' business coming our way, wouldn't it?''

# CHAPTER 15

Catesby gazed slowly around the darkened room. The other two at the table gazed back, without speaking. Winter moved restlessly on his chair; Keyes sighed, and licked his lips. His feet shuffled on the floor; his fingers pattered on the tabletop in a nervous dance of which he seemed unaware.

Catesby frowned. "Where is Rookwood?"

"Checking on . . . on our visitor," said Keyes, stilling his fingers for no more than a moment.

"That one," volunteered Winter, now the silence had been broken, "is a bit of a handful, and then some." He winced as he rubbed his shin. "Call her the spitfire type, and I won't argue. She doesn't come across like that in public, though, does she? Quite a surprise. None of your blue-blooded stand-on-your-dignity-at-all-times nonsense about *her*. She's not going to give in easily, believe me— if she keeps on like this much longer, I vote we think about doping her rations." He ventured a grin. "Or d'you reckon that would be, um, treason?"

"Treason?" Catesby's echo was an icy hiss. "It would be closer to the truth to call it stupidity—and dangerous stupidity, at that, when not one of us would have the least idea of what we were doing. What use would she be to us . . . damaged—or dead?''

''We could ask someone,'' said Winter. ''Or look it up in the library—just a few sleeping pills, tranquillisers, something like that. Just to keep her quiet.''

''She's hardly,'' said Keyes, ''a noisy guest.''

''Noblesse oblige.'' Winter grinned. ''Anyway, wouldn't do her much good if she *was*. Noisy, I mean, stuck out in the middle of nowhere like she is . . . ''

''Nowhere, as you call it,'' Catesby reminded him, ''has its advantages.''

Winter tried hard to give his answering shrug an air of bravado. He almost succeeded. ''Did I say it hasn't? Nobody's going to complain about the—the planning of this operation. None of *us,* anyway.''

Catesby's shrewd glance made him fidget again, and lower his gaze. Beside him, there was an empty chair: in the next chair to it, Keyes continued to patter his fingers on the tabletop. Suddenly, he cleared his throat.

''I—I don't know about complaining,'' he began. ''But—well, there's been talk—''

He broke off. From outside, there had come a rattling sound, followed by a soft thud as someone opened the door. Every head turned.

''Rookwood!''

''You are late,'' Catesby informed him.

Rookwood, breathing hard, slipped, limping, into his seat. With a tender hand, he massaged the top of his head. ''From now on,'' he said, ''we go in twos.''

''We have already agreed it is too dangerous—''

But Catesby, for once, was not allowed to finish. ''In twos,'' insisted Rookwood, ''and to hell with whether anyone notices we aren't there!'' He himself did not notice that Keyes stopped his relentless finger-pattering, and winced; neither, for once, did the all-observant Catesby. ''Do you know''—Rookwood sounded incredulous—

"she kicked me on the kneecap, and hit me on the head with the tray when I dropped it?" He ignored the sudden snort which burst from the listening Winter. "She'll have to go hungry tonight, and serve her right—though of course we don't want her to starve," he concluded, catching Catesby's eye, and calming down a little. "I mean, a kid like that . . . "

"A spitfire," corrected Winter, with feeling. "Sleeping pills, that's what she needs—"

"No!" Catesby slammed a forceful hand on the tabletop. "No, we might do more harm than good. If . . . if things should, by some horrible mischance, go wrong . . . if we are discovered—it will look better for us if we have treated her with . . . with the respect due to her position. As far as possible, that is. In the circumstances."

There was a long silence.

"Well, naturally, after all the trouble you—we've gone to, we don't want to be discovered," said Winter.

Keyes clasped his hands together, tightly clenching his fingers. He coughed, and blushed. "It—it wouldn't do any harm to—to think about Stage Two . . . "

Rookwood glanced at him: at the white-knuckled hands. He said nothing, but his look was eloquent.

Catesby's loss of command had lasted but a moment. A cleared throat; a darkling frown. A finger, tapping on the tabletop . . .

"Stage Two," said Catesby. Keyes looked up, silently pleading. "The day after tomorrow," Catesby went on, "not before. There must be a—a discreet distance from the Bragbury episode."

"Still a lot of cops sniffing around," said Winter, the irreverent.

"Sniffing in the wrong places," the loyal Rookwood reminded him. The rebellion had been brief, and, now that Catesby had appeared to yield, would not be repeated. "Just the way—Catesby—predicted . . . "

Keyes, once again, shifted on his chair. Catesby looked

at him, and raised an enquiring eyebrow. Keyes dropped
his gaze to his clasped hands.

"There's . . . talk," he mumbled, at last, when the look
of enquiry had become overwhelming. "I couldn't help
hearing . . . they've brought a man in from Scotland Yard."

"In a case like this," Catesby reminded him, "you
would expect nothing less."

"But—but he's not an ordinary Yarder." Keyes blushed
again. "I mean, he's not one of the Big Four, or anything,
but he's big, all right, and—"

"Once again," Catesby broke in, "we would have expected nothing less."

"Yes, I know, but . . . " Keyes, hot-cheeked, thanked the
shadows in the room for hiding so much of his embarrassment. "But it's that man Delphick—the one they call the
Oracle."

"And?" prompted Catesby, as Keyes began to cough
again.

"And . . . and—he's the one who's always hanging
around with the Battling Brolly," brought out Keyes, at
last. "And you know how she—she helps him with his
cases—it's in the papers all the time . . . "

"And they know," said Winter, "about that business
with the Bragbury car, and the Mountfitchet phone call. So
I've heard," he added, as everyone stared at him. "You
know how people gossip—and there's bound to be at least
some truth in what they say . . . "

"There is, indeed." Catesby's lips were thin, white; as
white as the knuckles on the clasped hands of Keyes. "Has
anyone," demanded Catesby, "heard . . . anything else?"

Winter, for once reluctant to stir up trouble, favoured
Rookwood and Keyes—especially Keyes—with a meaningful, sideways stare. Rookwood looked unhappily at
Catesby, and tried to speak, but failed. It was Keyes who
made the great effort, and finally brought out:

"There really is . . . talk—questions. Curious looks," he
gabbled, "and gossip—nothing definite," as Catesby gave

him a particularly curious look of his own, "but I can't help thinking—thinking that Stage Two oughtn't to wait for the day after tomorrow," he finished, bravely. "Once people start to suspect . . ."

Catesby stared at him, in silence—a silence neither Rookwood nor even Winter dared to break. The leadership of a natural leader is not readily challenged a second time in any encounter if it has already once prevailed.

"Any one questioner above another?" enquired Catesby.

Keyes licked dry lips. "Well . . ."

With the silent encouragement of Rookwood and Winter, he enlarged, stumbling, on his remark; and Catesby's frown was awful. This time, the unbroken silence stretched into what seemed an eternity.

"Stage Two tomorrow, then," decreed Catesby, at last. An audible sigh of relief filled the room—to be drowned out by the final, ominous rider:

"And if gossip and suspicion are correct . . . we may have to consider amending our plans somewhat. After Stage Three, we may have to devise a Stage Four . . ."

"Posted," said Brinton, going over the evidence yet again, "in Maidstone. First class stamp, and for once it only took a day to arrive . . . not that it helps us much. If we'd only known in advance to put a twenty-four-hour watch on the busiest post office in the area, we might have spotted the blighter who popped it into the box. As it is . . ."

"As it is," said Delphick, "he, or she, could have come from anywhere—and probably did. Maidstone, unfortunately, is hardly off the beaten track—only thirty-six miles from London, around thirty from any of the Channel ports—"

"Oh, God!" Brinton was too despondent even to tear his hair. "If they've taken her abroad—"

"I don't think they have." Delphick was studying, for the umpteenth time, photocopies of the envelope and letter received that morning at Kensington Palace by the private secretary to Her Royal Highness, Princess Georgina. While copies of the documents had been rushed to all investigators concerned in the case, the originals remained in the care of the security forces, being subjected to the most detailed scrutiny. "These, Chris, unless I'm much mistaken, are not foreign typefaces." He coughed. "It was Sherlock Holmes, of course, who could instantly recognise the differences between the leaded bourgeois type of a *Times* article and the slovenly print of an evening newspaper—but I trust that our own experts do not, nowadays, lag so very far behind Holmes in their expertise. If, just by looking, a humble Yard chief super can see that these cut-out capitals are from headlines in the British tabloid press, the experts should surely be able to tell us which tabloids they are, and which their days of issue—maybe even which edition, and in which region of the country it was sold. After all, Holmes would have done no less almost a century ago."

"And he'd have done it a damned sight faster!" Brinton sighed. "How long does it take to read one of those yarns? He makes it all look so easy . . . "

Delphick had to smile. "Conan Doyle played with loaded dice, my dear Chris—as is the case with all writers of mystery fiction. They have, remember, the distinctly unfair advantage of knowing in advance how much significance is to be attached to the fact that the letter was posted in Gravesend by a man with a dirty thumb—"

"Gravesend?" Brinton gaped at him, horrified. "Are you trying to tell me they're dragging the poor girl from one side of Kent to the other just to keep us off the track?"

"Nothing," Delphick assured him, "could be further from my thoughts . . . " But then he frowned. "Unless . . . perhaps a true word, spoken in jest . . . Might there be at least an element of disguise? I don't for one moment suggest a tangled red wig or a repulsive scar, but Georgina certainly has been much photographed. Her appearance is more than well-known—her face, her hair . . . "

"Princess Petite," said Brinton, with a snort he would

never have dared to emit in the presence of his wife, for Mrs. Brinton was a devoted fan of Georgy Girl. "Five foot nothing and curls like Shirley Temp—oh. I see what you mean. If they've got her anywhere people might spot her, they'll've had to—to camouflage her, if that's the word I want . . . No, it'd be too risky. Wouldn't it?"

Delphick did not reply. Foxon and Bob, hitherto silent participants in this discussion, looked at each other; and it was Bob who cleared his throat and ventured to speak.

"Surely they wouldn't force . . . wouldn't risk hurting her, sir? I mean—assaulting a member of the Royal Family—that'd be treason, wouldn't it? She's always seemed such a—a nice kid. It—it doesn't seem right, sir."

"I doubt," said Delphick drily, "the folk who have taken HRH are sticklers for the conventions, Sergeant Ranger. One can hardly be considered obedient to the strictest rules of etiquette when one kidnaps a princess of the Blood, takes photographs of her blindfolded, and sends them with a demand for half a million in used notes to be delivered as and when later instructions shall be received. These are not *nice,*" crisply, "people, Sergeant Ranger."

Bob went red, and gazed at his boots. "Sorry, sir . . . "

Delphick was already shaking his head. "No, I'm the one who should apologise, Bob. Blame it on sheer frustration, if you will. There ought to have been a multitude of clues, but whatever we've tried has come to nothing . . . "

"Nothing." Brinton's echoing groan was heartfelt as he began to enumerate the dead-end leads which they had, at one time or another, pursued: which they were still, for want of anything more hopeful, still pursuing. "The girl's *probably* not left the country—might not even have left Kent—but that's a hell of a lot of places to start looking, without a nudge or two in the right direction. Every nark in the land's been asked to keep his ears open—but nobody's heard a thing, though the blighters all worship the ground she walks on. That snap's no real help. There isn't a house in England doesn't have white sheets, and apart

from young Georgina in the foreground that's all anyone
can make out, no matter how they take their magnifying
glasses to the thing. Every blasted chemist and photo-
graphic processor in the country's been told to sing out if
he's handled snaps of a blindfold girl—and there hasn't
been a murmur . . . '' He looked up, frowning. ''Wonder
why they didn't use an instant camera? The amount of
money we're talking about, you'd've thought they could
afford a Polaroid—except, I suppose, they can't afford it
till they've got the cash . . . ''

''Perhaps,'' said Delphick, very slowly, ''they wished to
occasion no remark by a sudden, out-of-character purchase.
Perhaps they are not, as has been suspected, the anonymous
international gang beloved of mystery writers around the
world, but a—a more home-grown enterprise, whose every
action would run the grave risk of being observed by their
friends and neighbours . . . ''

It was not, of course, to be supposed that the presence of
a large portion of the Plummergen populace at the kidnapping of a princess would not occupy the greater part of local
gossip for many days after the event. It occupied, in fact,
the entire part of village conversation for at least twenty-
four hours, fuelled and fermented by a large Press presence:
in response to which presence Mr. Jessyp made it firmly
known that all classes would be held, for the duration, behind shuttered windows, in case illicit close-ups of young
Sally should be snatched against his (if not the child's
mother's) wish. The headmaster further decreed that the
additional expense incurred by the use of artificial lighting
during the day should be charged, on receipt of the electricity bill, to the Press Complaints Council; and he added
that anyone venturing to enter school property did so at his
or her own risk. It would be nothing to do with Mr. Jessyp
if, in the course of regular autumnal care for the school
playing-fields, trespassers were inadvertently sprayed by
tractor-driving farmers with high-octane liquid manure.

The journalists—not one of them born with mud on his boots, and all (thanks to their editors' monumental lack of foresight) without waterproof clothing—duly took the hint, and decamped to besiege the palaces of Buckingham and Kensington, with small detachments on the steps of New Scotland Yard and the headquarters of MI5.

And so Plummergen was left in peace—in relative peace, that is. Discussion of the events at Dungeness was not, naturally, abandoned: it formed, as has been explained, the greater part of local gossip: but there was room, now, for fresh subjects to be introduced, for older subjects to be revived . . .

"I still say it's summat *queer* they're about, the pair of 'em." This from Mrs. Skinner, in the post office, and at full volume, the pair in question having safely—and severally—departed.

Her words were accompanied by nods, and a general murmur of agreement from everyone—including, to her chagrin, Mrs. Henderson: but there was no denying the truth of her rival's observation. *Summat queer* was, if anything, an understatement of the position which had now been maintained by the parties under discussion for some weeks past.

"Not a word," said Mrs. Spice, "has there bin from either of 'em, save good morning and such, since long afore that business at the power station—"

"Sulking on the bus there and back," chimed in young Mrs. Newport. "Regular old misery-guts, the pair of 'em . . . "

"And what cause Miss Nuttel's got, of all people," said Mrs. Scillicough, "to go buying *an icing set* beats me, on account of it's the Hot Cross Bun does all the cooking in that house, which we've heard tell many a time."

"The Bun," Mrs. Henderson pointed out, "bought three new spatulas and a scale-pan, didn't she? You'd'a thought she'd enough o' such things already, and to spare."

"Not forgetting," added Mrs. Spice at once, "the pal-

ette-knife—which ain't to say as she couldn't sharpen that
up and do someone, mentioning no names, a fair bit o'
damage if she'd the inclination, which from the way the-
y've bin a-snapping and snarling at each other'd never
come as much of a surprise, would it?''

Even Mrs. Spice had to agree it would not, although the
gleam in the eyes of Mrs. Henderson as she spoke of knives
made her frown. But Mrs. Flax, to whom all heads turned
for the definitive opinion, defused the burgeoning squabble
by approving this general agreement with a ponderous nod:
following which she decided that the time was ripe for adding her own scandalous—and generous—pinch to the brew
of speculation and surmise now that (thanks to the hard
work of everyone else) it was coming close to the boil.

Mrs. Flax drew a deep breath. She gazed slowly round
upon the assembled company, and lowered her voice.
Everyone flinched in horrified delight: some awful revela-
tion, it was clear, was about to be made. Hadn't the Wise
Woman's son as worked for Farmer Mulcker bin to Brettenden that very morning, for tractor spares? And hadn't
Miss Nuttel nipped into town on the same bus, so quick
there'd bin no time for any to follow her?

''Aah,'' said Mrs. Flax, ominously exhaling. ''Ah, and
when Miss Nuttel was fixing to buy *angle irons,* of all
things,'' gloated Mrs. Flax, in doom-laden tones—''did she
tell anyone what for she wanted 'em? She did not!''

The response to this sinister statement was all the Wise
Woman could have hoped. Angle irons? Those who knew
the purpose of these small metal fastening-plates paraded
their knowledge with glee: those who didn't clamoured to
be told more, and Mrs. Flax looked on in a smug silence
as they were told. Angle irons? Why should Miss Nuttel
want such contraptions? And screws, to fasten 'em?
There'd bin no talk of her taking up carpentry, had there?
Putting up shelves? Making boxes?

''Oh!'' Mrs. Skinner's scream of realisation curdled the
blood in everyone's veins, and froze their tongues in mid-

wag. "Oh . . . it was *boxes* made me remember . . . when
Mrs. Putts was at the admiral's asking for honey, and—
and Miss Nuttel was a-digging that—that hole . . . ''

She could not continue.

She did not need to.

"For a coffin," gasped the post office, with glee . . .

And then gasps turned to echoes of Mrs. Skinner's
scream as there came, from outside, an explosion.

# CHAPTER *16*

"They pesky brats!"

Mrs. Skinner was not the only one of Mr. Stillman's customers to feel justifiably indignant. People's nerves, already frayed by intimations of Miss Nuttel's apparently sepulchral intentions, had now been stretched to their limit by the high-spirited detonation, right outside the post office, of a large firework by a small group of children begging pennies for the guy from passing motorists. The noise had not so much been loud as startling in its suddenness: and as sudden was Plummergen's response. Once everyone realised what had happened, mothers indoors rushed outside to clip their offspring (if present) about the ear, while others looked smug, and spoke loudly of the manners of the younger generation.

The latter speakers included the childless, those whose children had long since reached years of discretion, and those whose children had made a different guy, and set it up on a different pitch—these last having spent the previous few days lamenting the unfairness of life when, just because others'd got Miss Seeton to give 'em her bashed-up hat and had made the biggest guy, they'd been mean enough to stake their claim to the pavement outside the shop with the best-lit windows in the village, so that everyone driving by, strangers and all—who'd even slow their cars for a proper look, which was unfairer still—threw money in the hat, leaving nothing for t'other kids farther down The Street . . . who would never (their mothers now insisted, at virtuous full volume) dream of doing such a dreadful thing as to set off a firework just to attract the attention of a car as didn't look as if it was going to give 'em any money, their kids not being as mercenary-minded as Some They Could Mention . . .

As the outside mothers came back in, they caught the tail end of these remarks, and waxed even more indignant than they'd been before they went out. Who was being called mercenary? They'd thank Some People not to use words they most likely couldn't even spell, and even if they could were slander, in any case. Everyone knew it was the luck o' the draw each year when it came to getting a pitch for Guy Fawkes, and if Some People's kids were bad losers, well, they'd had to have learned it from somewhere, and where else but home? A pity to set kids a Bad Example, they thought, but then there were Some People as just didn't know no better, and you had to make excuses for 'em, poor souls. Besides, what else could you expect, Guy Fawkes Week and kiddies with fireworks? One or two let off early once in a while couldn't hurt . . .

And in all the flurry of insult and counterblast, the matter of Miss Nuttel's conjectural coffin-building was quite forgotten.

"Guy Fawkes Week, you expect one or two fireworks let off ahead of time," said Brinton, slowly. "Just a bit of fun, that's what anyone'd say—and mostly they'd be right, because there's no real harm done. But sometimes things go wrong . . ."

He was addressing Sid Noakes, leading fireman of the first appliance to reach the scene. The rest of Sid's crew were busy packing away their equipment; the crews from the other engines, having played their part, had already packed up, and gone. There was no sense in staying where they were no longer needed: and, indeed, there was some element of risk if they did. As Brinton had said, the week of Bonfire Night was invariably crowded with emergency calls: at any time, the fire brigade might be summoned to tackle some conflagration or other, large or small, which they could hardly do with their tenders dry, their hoses improperly coiled, their turntable ladders sticky with soot. There were all too few tenders to spare once a fire was definitely out; moreover, those there were, were manned by crews with their own lives to live.

In rural areas of England, the fire service is Retained, rather than full-time. The firemen come from every walk of life, from every town or village or hamlet within bleeper-range; a retained fireman, when on duty, is never without his radio pager, and it is not so very long ago that the old air raid sirens from World War II were finally phased out with the arrival, in most homes, of the telephone. The bleeper, a more modern invention yet, is better even than the telephone: it can be worn, and its summons heard, in the middle of a field, or the middle of the street . . .

Sid Noakes, indeed, had been in the middle of his supper when the alarm was raised: but he had, in the circumstances, small hope of being back in time to enjoy his lamb chop and peas, whether his wife left them warming in the oven or not.

"How long," Sid now enquired, glumly, "d'you reckon they lads'll be, Mr. Brinton?"

The lads to whom he referred, whose every movement he and Brinton were watching with deep concentration, did not belong to any fire crew. Though they wore uniforms, it was of a constabulary rather than conflagrationary nature, for they were under the command not of Leading Fireman Sid Noakes, but of Superintendent Chris Brinton . . .

"Sorry, Sid." Brinton shook his head. "As long as it

takes—afraid I can't say better than that. There's your
statement to get as well, of course. We can't afford to cut
corners when it's a question of a body . . . ''

Sid sighed. First appliance on the scene, first man among
the crew: it was his responsibility to check, and his luck—
whether bad or otherwise he wouldn't care to say—to have
been the one who discovered the dead man in the burned-
out building. At least, he'd supposed the body was that of
a man: it had been much more badly burned than the building, not to mention damaged by part of the roof collapsing
on top—but the bits that were still visible had looked like
a trousered leg, a heavily-shod foot. Still, you couldn't go
jumping to conclusions in this job, any more'n you could
if you were police . . .

"Know their stuff," said Sid, paying compliment as the
uniformed figures searched through the rubble, warily
moved beams, shifted timbers, took photographs and measurements, all in an efficient silence.

"So do you." Brinton returned the compliment. As soon
as he found the body, Sid had banished everyone else from
the immediate neighbourhood, and taken up his position as
guard. He detailed one man to call the police, and sent
another to fetch Dr. Wyddial from her sister's house: everyone for miles around knew the doctor's car, and by a lucky
chance he'd just happened to spot it as they were hurrying
to answer the nine-nine-nine call to the KarriKlozzet site.

Dr. Wyddial was not given to sloth. By the time the
police arrived, she had examined what she could see of the
body, pronounced it—as required by law—dead, and said
she'd be only too happy to do an autopsy on the poor chap
once he'd been retrieved, which she expected would take a
couple of hours, at least. She'd get back to her family
knees-up for now, if they didn't mind; she would apologise
to her sister and leave for the mortuary in an hour or so—
all right?

"Er—all right, Doc—and, er, thanks." Brinton was long
accustomed to the brisk efficiency of Dr. Wyddial, but it

always unnerved him slightly. "Er—sorry about the party," he added: but she'd already been out of earshot.

As Sid, still brooding on his lost supper, sighed again, there came the purposeful sound of footsteps crunching over rubble and ash and fallen timbers. Delphick, with Bob and Foxon close behind, arrived to join his colleagues as they contemplated the steady searching of the KarriKlozzet ruins by the ranks of uniformed police.

He raised an enquiring eyebrow in the direction of the leading fireman. "What do you think, Mr. Noakes?"

"Well, now . . . " And Sid frowned. He was not unduly awed by having his opinion sought by a man from Scotland Yard: it was no more than you'd expect, him being as much of an expert on fires as this Oracle was an expert on crime. Each to his own: it made good sense if you wanted to know the why and wherefore of anything. But Sid Noakes wasn't to be rushed into an opinion without first giving the matter careful thought. He rubbed the tip of his nose, and frowned again. "Well, now . . .

"Bonfire Night, o' course," he said at last, "and days not so distant either side o' the Fifth, we do tend to have a fair number o' what you might call accidents o' the high-spirited sort . . . "

"But?"

Brinton closed his eyes, and groaned softly. It wasn't as if he hadn't had his own suspicions. He prided himself he was as good a detective as anyone from the Yard, and he'd only been waiting for the preliminary report to back up what his good copper's instincts had already told him, loud and clear, before he launched into a full-scale murder investigation. Trust Delphick, though, to be the one to put it into words when they weren't absolutely sure just yet . . .

"But," said Sid, with a nod of approval. With all the fuss the papers, which everyone knew were allus out to make a story, 'd given this Oracle for being the great detective, seemed they might for once be right. "But—well, there's not just the matter of the dead'un, whoever he is, though I've my own ideas about him—but this looks to be more'n kids lobbing a cracker or a jumping-jack careless-like, if you ask me.'' He waved an expressive hand towards the wreckage, and sniffed once or twice. ''There's a queer sort o' smell t'all this—and I don't just mean they chemicals for the toilets as spilled when the drums bursted with the heat—which is what you'd expect, and dissolving stuff and disinfectant, so far as I can make out with talking to young Mr. Cuthbert—he's off home now,'' as Delphick's look made it plain he sought further information. ''Reporting to his ma, most like, if I know him.''

''Cuthbert?'' Delphick glanced about him at the ruins. ''Ah, yes, the owner of KarriKlozzet, of course.''

''Not exactly.'' Even at such a moment, Brinton couldn't help a rumble of laughter. ''Cuthbert Kelshall, that's who was here earlier—we only had a few words, with him not staying long once he'd seen what'd happened and how we were dealing with it. Sid's right, he'll have hopped off home to report to his mother. She's a tartar, that one.'' He rolled his eyes, and grinned. ''Mrs. Caroline Kelshall, she is, and don't you forget it in a hurry. Never even thought of retiring when her old man died, no idea of handing over to the younger ones—keeps as close an eye on the business as she ever did, and when she says jump, they jump. Cuthbert and Claud, of all the daft names.''

''And Cleopatra,'' put in Sid Noakes, also grinning.

''Good heavens.'' Delphick shook his head, wondering at the peculiarities of human nature. ''Some people, I fear, have far too restricted a sense of responsibility when naming their offspring.''

''Young Cleo married one of the Therfields—Peter,'' said Brinton, ''the youngest boy. They're a farming family, but he'd no taste for it. Went in with his wife's lot instead. He and Cleo have a pair of twins called Oswald and Osbert—not quite as bad as Cuthbert and Claud, but near enough. The poor little devils have been having a tough time of it at school, so I've heard.''

"I'm not surprised." Delphick shook his head again. "Irresponsibility clearly runs in the family—as does the business," he added, returning to his original muttons. "A family concern—a large, presumably influential, family. Are they," he enquired, "popular?"

Sid Noakes shifted on one large foot. He glanced at the superintendent beside him; Brinton nodded.

"Go on, Sid. Give the man the local colour."

Mr. Noakes cleared his throat, and took a deep breath. "Since you insist, Mr. Brinton—well, no, Mr. Delphick, right now I have to say they ain't. They've laid a good few folk off this past couple o' months, which jobs lost don't make them as caused 'em losing none too popular, and open to all manner of mockery, though in part 'tis the kiddies' daft names, I won't deny—and then, with talk o' yet more jobs going afore too long, I can't help but wonder . . . well, if you was to tell me there was petrol or summat o' the sort in among the chemicals, I'd not call you a liar."

Everyone sniffed. The air was heavy with the acrid tang of burned ash, moist and lingering. The firemen's hoses had spouted thousands of gallons of water to extinguish the fury of the flames, and the spillage from the burst drums of chemicals had only added to the black, muddy, reeking mess. It was hard, of course, to be sure whether the reek was simply that of cinders mixed with disinfectant: they did not all have the long experience of Leading Fireman Noakes in the aftermath of conflagration. Cuthbert Kelshall, when the matter had first been raised, remarked that a heavy smoker like himself had an impaired sense of smell, but that he could not, in any case, seriously credit that anybody would wish to harm one of the largest employers in the district, if that was what Sid and Mr. Brinton had been hinting, let alone risk harming any of the employees. It was nothing more or less than a shocking accident—some honest worker working late, whose honesty had been cruelly rewarded . . . still, if they wanted to stir up a mystery, they were welcome to go wherever they chose to look for it.

They had his permission, just as he was sure his mother
would give it, if she'd been there—and, talking of his
mother . . .

Cuthbert had beaten a hasty retreat, to present—as Sid
Noakes (who'd voiced the first hint of mystery with his
discovery of the body) and Brinton guessed—his report to
Mrs. Caroline Kelshall, relict of Caradoc, and currently
head of KarriKlozzet Limited, the nation's third largest supplier of portable cloakrooms for all occasions. As the slogan
had it, KarriKlozzet Cared for the Convenience of the Public in Private, and with Discretion.

"So Cuthbert," said Delphick, once Sid and Brinton had
brought him up to date, "doesn't believe, or shall we at
least say doesn't want to believe, in a—a vendetta of any
sort, recent sackings notwithstanding. Would his view, do
you know, be that of the other family members? The re-
doubtable Caroline, in particular."

"Carrie likes to keep her finger firmly on the pulse."
Brinton grinned. "That's just with one hand, of course.
With the other, she holds the whip that gets cracked over
the heads of the rest of the family—the rest of the firm,
come to that—if they set one toe across the line she's
drawn. If Cuthbert says he doesn't believe in a vendetta,
then he's saying what Caroline'll say, and the rest, once we
get around to asking them—he'd never dare be different.
*She* probably thinks it's a downright liberty of the natives
even to think of such a thing—always very lord-and-
peasant style, KarriKlozzet, even while old Caradoc was
alive. Hire and fire—not, mind you, that they did so much
firing until recently. Noted for looking after their people,
in some ways—so, well, in some ways I could almost believe our Cuthbert when he said there was nothing—nothing vindictive about what's happened. You don't turn round
all of a sudden and bite the hand that's fed you for so long,
do you?"

"You might," said Delphick, "if the shock of being fed
no longer had sent you slightly round the bend."

Sid Noakes reminded everyone of the petrol he'd felt sure he'd smelled, and pointed out that the fire—wherever it had started, which was hard to tell, and if that weren't a suspicious circumstance then he didn't rightly know what was—did seem to have spread awful quickly, considering. Portable toilets being by nature not exactly tinder-dry, that was to say, and back to what he'd said earlier about crackers and jumping-jacks on their own not liable to cause such an inferno . . .

Delphick was frowning. "A strong suspicion of arson," he murmured. "A firm with a paternalistic style of management suddenly starting to let its dependants down . . . Chris, this *could* be a simple grudge matter. And that poor chap, whoever he turns out to be, could be dead by a dreadful mischance . . . yet it seems more than strange for someone, no matter how great the grudge for having lost his job, to ruin the chance of employment for others in the community . . . "

"Round the bend," Brinton reminded him. "You said so yourself—and you could be right. Could be the grudge got to him faster than thinking about the effect on everybody else—on everybody he worked with, I mean. He'll have been only too aware of what the effect'd be on the Kelshalls—on KarriKlozzet as a whole. They'll lose a fair bit of trade by all this, never mind whatever insurance cover they've got—there's goodwill, lost orders, that sort of thing. Could take 'em years to get back on their feet again . . . "

"If," said Delphick, "such was the intention. An ordinary, sordid business motive makes it all too easy . . . "

Brinton looked at him; at the eager, interested faces of Bob and Foxon; at the puzzled frown of honest Sid Noakes. "I'm a humble country copper," he said, slowly. "I'm not up to your big-city complications—I like my crimes nice and easy and straightforward. But I've got a very nasty feeling you're going to complicate this one for me, with bells on. Am I right?"

"I don't know." Delphick shook his head. "Maybe I'm imagining it—but the coincidence cannot, surely, have escaped your attention. We have not one, but two deaths to be investigated here. The first, of the caterer who was in attendance at Dungeness when the princess disappeared. The second—"

"Don't tell me!" Brinton almost howled the words. "Why can't it be a common-or-garden coincidence, for once? Just for once, an ordinary crime? With Guy Fawkes Night three days away, and fireworks all over the place, and if it's not yobs being careless it's their dads angry for losing their jobs . . . "

Delphick regarded his friend with some sympathy. "Maybe I'm imagining it," he said again. "Maybe. I hope, in some ways, that I am, although in others it would be helpful if I'm not—the more complex the coincidences and connections, the easier a crime can be to solve. It's always the run-of-the-mill affairs, the ones with nothing to distinguish them from a hundred other cases, which are the most difficult to bring to a satisfactory conclusion. Don't we always look for the pattern, where we can? The more bizarre the crime, the easier the pattern is to establish; and, once a pattern has been established, the solution is so much closer. It's a question of looking at the facts in the right way . . . "

He chose to ignore Brinton's horrified wince, his groan of despairing resignation. "And," he went on, "in order to look at things in the right way, it helps more than a little if one consults someone who is fortunate enough to possess the eye of the trained observer . . .

"I rather think, you know," concluded Chief Superintendent Delphick, "that I could do a great deal worse in this case than consult Miss Seeton."

# CHAPTER 17

By the time they had driven back to Plummergen, it was past supper-time—yet not (Delphick decided) too far past to pay an evening call, if the callers first took the precaution of telephoning to enquire whether or not their visit would be inconvenient. Besides (as he reminded Bob) while Charley Mountfitchet would be only too happy to rustle up a snack and a drink for his guests at whatever hour they requested them—even happier than usual on this particular occasion, since the thrill of being a suspect, however obliquely, in a murder case had delighted the landlord's enthusiastic soul—Miss Seeton might well have some of her adopted nephew's favourite gingerbread in the larder.

But Miss Seeton, it seemed, was not at home. The chief superintendent let the rhythmic "unanswered" tone ring for a count of twenty, then broke the connection.

"She might," said Bob—who'd had no thoughts of gingerbread until Delphick raised them, and who was now feeling hungrier by the minute—"be standing on her head or something, sir. You know she doesn't really like to stop in the middle of her exercises unless it's urgent. How about, er, trying again a bit later?"

"While we," murmured Delphick, "force ourselves down to the bar—there to indulge in some of Charley's excellent sandwiches, no doubt." He pondered this proposal for a few moments, then slowly nodded, as if resigned to the sacrifice of entering the saloon bar of the George, and partaking of its excellent supper menu. "It is, of course, Sergeant Ranger, in the very best interests of the investigation that the investigators should remain at all times in full possession of their health and strength. An inefficient sidekick is"—he permitted himself a quiet smile—"something up with which no superior should have to put." He smiled once more, in a Churchillian manner, then frowned.

"I can't recall whether or not there were any lights showing in Sweetbriars as we pulled on to the forecourt of the pub. If Miss Seeton is not, in fact, standing on her head, but has gone out somewhere for the evening, it will be wasting valuable nourishment time to telephone again before we—you—eat."

Bob ignored the slur on his gourmandising. When a bloke stood six-foot-seven in his socks, he needed to keep up his strength. (Keep his strength up? Good old Churchill!) If he'd been the size of Miss Seeton, say, or young Georgina, the pair of 'em not an inch above five foot high and eating no more, he'd bet, than sparrows—well, that'd be different: but he wasn't. What he was—and he weighed seventeen stone, which he'd guess was about ten stone more than either MissEss or Georgy Girl—was *hungry*.

"Come to think of it, sir, I didn't notice any lights, either. But you know what this place is like for minding everybody else's business. If we ask downstairs where she's gone while we're having a bite to eat, fifty-to-one there'll be at least six people who can tell us."

Delphick was no more immune to the summons of the fleshpots than other men who have worked hard all day with little time, or thought, for food. He sighed. "Since you appear, Sergeant Ranger, to be growing weaker even as I look at you, it would seem that I have no alternative than to agree. We will therefore," he decreed, "take cheese-and-pickle sandwiches and a helping of gossip before another five minutes are out . . ."

Yet for once the Plummergen grapevine was unequal to the task required of it. Both the saloon and the public bars were almost empty, and the few drinkers therein did not, when asked, seem to know anything of Miss Seeton's probable whereabouts. They were rather more informative on the probable whereabouts of their (possibly) more knowledgeable friends. The Christmas Pantomime committee meeting, and the planning of the imminent Grand Firework Display, not to mention the proposed revival of the Night Watch Men in view of Murreystone's suspected sabotage of the Village Bonfire, had all taken their toll of the George's regular customers. Iffen Mr. Delphick was to come back t'ask the same question in a week or so, they didn't doubt but what they'd be able to tell him a bit more, but as for now . . .

"As for now," said Delphick, "we will address ourselves to these drinks, and this menu, and to asking Charley for an alarm call after, for once, a relatively early night. We want to be ringing Miss Seeton's doorbell before she's had time to slip off for the day."

But when they rang her bell at half-past nine next morning, it was not Miss Seeton who answered the door.

"Oh, Mr. Delphick, it's only you!" Martha Bloomer stood before them on the threshold of Sweetbriars, her eyes dark with anxiety. "Oh, dear, I made sure you must be Miss Emily come back from shopping and forgot her key and having to ring, with it being one of my days and knowing I'd be here to let her in . . . " She peered over his shoulder, past the looming form of Sergeant Ranger, northwards up The Street in the direction of the shops. "She's not usually out this early, you see, not unless she's teaching, which I know for a fact Mr. Jessyp said she needn't, with

Miss Maynard there in any case, until she'd got over all the—well, the upset, poor soul, from the other day—but I can't think what's happened to her. It's only half an hour, I know, not such a time as I'd worry about normally, but *with* all the upset, and no note left, and her always so careful to let me know what she's doing, even if it's just pop out for biscuits or a jar of coffee, specially when she thinks she mightn't be back in time to give me my wages, her not liking to get in a muddle about money, though dear knows I'd trust Miss Emily to pay up sooner than I'd trust most of 'em—and of course I know if you've come straight from the George you'll not have had much of a chance, but—but have you seen her anywhere at all?''

Delphick glanced at his sergeant in some concern. Bob returned the look without speaking, though in any case he didn't need to. The same sudden presentiment had gripped them both at exactly the same time during Martha's agitated monologue. They remembered last night's silent telephone calls; they knew, almost as well as Mrs. Bloomer knew it, Miss Seeton's daily routine . . .

"I'm afraid we haven't," said Delphick, trying to sound matter-of-fact about this negative response. Nothing would be achieved by letting Martha worry herself into hysteria if Miss Seeton should, indeed, be missing. With anyone else, of course, there could always be the rational explanation: pausing for a chat (but Miss Seeton didn't gossip), stopping off to visit a friend (but Miss Seeton would never call on anyone so early in the morning). When Miss Seeton, however, was concerned, years of experience had taught them that it was the irrational explanation—the bizarre, the outlandish, the recherché—the unnerving—which was, more often than not, correct.

"There's her shopping basket still here," said Martha, opening the door wide in an unspoken request for Delphick and Bob to enter. "And she's not in the garden, because that was the first place I looked when she wasn't in the house—and wherever she is, for all it's a chilly morning she's not took her warm coat, see?''

She showed them the heavy tweed, hanging on its hook. A vision from the past flashed across Delphick's inward eye: Miss Seeton, newly returned from Switzerland via Paris, arriving at London Airport in a stylish hat and a woollen coat patterned loudly in red and black. She would keep it, she'd told him, for best. It reversed to a fawn-grey gaberdine for wet weather: might she now have decided that it looked like rain (which indeed it did) and gone out duly prepared for whatever the November clouds might send down?

The next thought was inevitable. ''Which umbrella,'' he demanded, ''did she take?''

Although this had been one of the first things Martha had seen fit to check, at Delphick's enquiry she did so again, running an experienced eye along the rack, a row of neat clips fastened to one wall with a rail underneath, holding their points above the drip-tray. ''Her best gold,'' she said, ''but it's not Lady Colveden, because I took the liberty of phoning to ask, and there's nobody there. Busy about the farm, I shouldn't wonder, and market day in Brettenden, which her ladyship always likes to pop in when she can to look at the stalls and things . . . ''

''But Miss Seeton can't have popped yet,'' Delphick said, ''because the bus''—he checked his watch—''won't be leaving for another quarter of an hour, will it? And if she'd been offered a lift by Lady Colveden, I agree with you that she would have left a message.''

Mrs. Bloomer's eyes fixed themselves on his. ''You *don't* think I'm fussed about nothing, then! Oh, dear, whatever's happened to her? Poor Miss Emily—''

''Have you looked,'' broke in Delphick, ''upstairs? What's missing from her wardrobe?''

''Perhaps,'' suggested Bob, in a warning tone, ''it would be better, sir, if—''

But he got no further. Martha had already darted off on her errand. Only as Bob groaned softly did it occur to Delphick that there could be a less sinister, though even more unfortunate, reason for Miss Seeton's apparent absence. She might well be—indeed she was—one of the fittest and most healthy old ladies of their acquaintance, but such things as strokes and heart attacks were no respecters of pers—

"Oh!" Martha's cry startled the listeners below. They did not stop to think. They headed together for the stairs, collided at the bottom, and as they tried to sort themselves out to hurry upwards, met Mrs. Bloomer hurrying down.

"I never," she gasped, "thought to look before, with her always up before I come—I just took a quick peek, and only natural I should think she'd made the bed after breakfast same as she always does, but she—she hasn't, Mr. Delphick. That bed's made, all right—but it was made yesterday, and never been slept in—you just come and see!"

"How do you know?" He didn't waste time asking if she was sure. Martha Bloomer wouldn't—couldn't—make a mistake about something like Miss Seeton's failure to sleep in her own bed: but hard evidence was always best in the case of a missing—for whatever reason—person. Even to himself, he hardly liked to use the word *abducted*—but he had a strong suspicion it would not be very long before he was forced to say it out loud . . .

"Clean sheets," said Martha. "Look!" With a flourish, she showed them her proof. She had already turned back the counterpane: now she whisked the top bedding—sheet, blankets, eiderdown—in one quick open movement halfway down the bed, revealing to their startled gaze Miss Seeton's neatly-folded nightdress resting beside a smooth white pillow on another sheet, just as smooth. Impossibly smooth . . .

"They were late," she explained, "with the deliveries this week, the laundry I mean, on account of one of the drivers catching flu and having to double up on the rounds, so the minute I heard the engine, a nasty diesel thing makes a terrible racket, I nipped across before she could do herself an injury, yoga or not, trying to turn the mattress on her own, which is what we like to do once a week, even when it wasn't one of my usual days—and this is how we left it, the two of us, yesterday afternoon. And if that sheet's been slept on I'll—I'll . . . ''

Her face began to work. She let the bedding fall from her hands. ''Oh, dear, poor Miss Seeton—you know how she is, Mr. Delphick, the way things will *happen* to her, and her not noticing until it's too late. You can't help worrying about her, can you? Where on earth can she have gone?''

Delphick briefly considered, then ruled out, any idea that Miss Seeton might have suffered a brainstorm after what Martha had so tactfully referred to as *all the upset*. Miss Seeton was far too level-headed and unimaginative to allow any such a thing to happen to her.

Whatever else might happen, of course, was entirely out of her hands.

Her hands . . .

''Martha, I'd like to examine Miss Seeton's sketchbook, if I may—and I think I'd better look at the contents of her portfolio, as well. First, though, if you wouldn't mind checking in the wardrobe . . . ''

''Her Paris coat,'' said Mrs. Bloomer, after a careful search. ''And her hat, the red one with the ribbon—and her leather bag she's only had a week or two, bought special for the Opening—all her smartest clothes, gone. But she's not,'' she said again, ''gone off with Lady Colveden, I know she hasn't. And in any case, why would she dress up smart just for Brettenden market?''

Delphick shook his head, without speaking. Bob, patting the faithful retainer gently on the shoulder, said that Miss Seeton, she must remember, always came bouncing back in the end, didn't she? To which bromide Mrs. Bloomer, with one of her more expressive sniffs, retorted that she wished he'd sound a bit more sure of it himself, and not try to fool her he wasn't as worried as everybody else. And if Mr. Delphick thought looking at Miss Emily's pictures would help, then the sooner they stopped talking and he looked, the better it would be!

Delphick and his sergeant clattered down the stairs in Martha's wake, automatically registering their surroundings as they passed. No sign of any struggle: but that meant nothing. Wherever Miss Seeton had gone—no, be honest, wherever she'd *been taken*—she'd been tricked into going: the last thing she'd want would be to worry Martha by going off without leaving a message—and she hadn't left one, so they'd obviously hustled her away with some excuse for the hurry, and she'd swallowed it. Trickery, then, not violence—yet they weren't so confident in their tricks they'd risk letting her leave a message: another pointer to the amateurs he'd hypothesised, rather than the professionals the MI boys suspected? They wouldn't need to be professionals to trick Miss Seeton. Absolutely—almost, sometimes, painfully—truthful and law-abiding herself, MissEss must be a confidence man's dream. How she'd survived this long unscathed, he'd never know. She found it hard to believe that anyone would deliberately tell lies with intent to harm her: she would always suppose there must have been some mistake. He only hoped she'd survive this latest *mistake* as well as she'd come through all the others . . .

"Guy Forks," said Delphick, smiling despite himself at Miss Seeton's sketch of the bearded man in the broad-brimmed hat with his cutlery arms and legs. Odd: he'd never really thought of Miss Seeton as having a sense of humour—though there was, of course, that sketch she'd drawn in Paris of a lady of dubious virtue, nude, flaunting herself on top of a pile of suitcases. *Abandoned Baggage,* she'd called it—and with good reason, if his recollection was correct. They'd found the lady in question, very much deceased, inside an assortment of trunks and cases deposited at left-luggage offices all around the French capital . . .

"Oh." He stopped smiling; he stiffened. He had pulled the next sketch out of the cardboard folder: and there was Guy Fawkes, with a lantern in his hand—with a bomb in the other. In the background, smoking ruins; in the top corner, a tiny playing-card. He peered. A picture card—a female, crowned . . .

"We must advise Chris Brinton," said Delphick, "that the KarriKlozzet fire was definitely arson—probably caused by some sort of bomb. And that it's more than probably tied in with the Bragbury murder, just as we suspected—and that both are almost certainly connected with Georgina's disappearance, as witness the queen, or in Miss Seeton's version the princess, of hearts . . ."

He put the two sketches aside, and turned to the third, for which Miss Seeton had brought out her coloured pencils. "And here she is in person, bless her curly royal head—on this occasion, almost respectably attired, one might say. Although . . ." For an instant, he paused in thought; then he nodded, and smiled. "Of course—Manet, again. His version of Zola's *Nana* at her toilette . . ."

The setting was intimate: the corner of a room carpeted in red, furnished with heavy curtains, an ornate table, a velvet-covered sofa on which satin cushions were heaped. In the foreground stood the celebrated courtesan, in her underdress of cream frilled petticoat and blue satin basque, and wearing dainty black high-heeled shoes. Her body was turned towards an oval looking-glass, mounted on a slim wooden pedestal between two candles in gilded sticks; her head, the rich curls tied up with ribbon, was turned to face the onlooker—and the face was unmistakeably that of Princess Georgina. One hand sported a glittering ring, the wrist a golden bangle; the other—

"To my recollection," Delphick muttered, "that's rather different from the original. I wonder . . ."

Nana-Georgina's right hand held a powder-puff of phenomenal size, fluffy and of dazzling whiteness, the focal point of the picture.

"Yes," said Delphick, slowly. "I wonder—and there's another difference. In the original, as I recall, it's the figure of a top-hatted man in evening dress, but now . . . "

On one end of the sofa, close together, sat a little girl in frills and laces, carrying a bouquet—and, beside the girl, a small, elderly female figure in a suit, wearing a fancy hat and a necklace. And carrying an umbrella . . .

"Catharsis, perhaps." Delphick frowned, stared again at Nana, then turned to the next drawing, and sighed. "Yes, I thought as much. She's been trying to work it out of her system—and, though drawing her problems is far more in character with Miss Seeton than a course of professional psychoanalysis would be, I fear it doesn't help us as much as I hope it helped her . . . "

The scene was full of movement, of energy and urgency expressed once more in stark black and white. Two police cars, their lights flashing—you could almost hear their sirens—raced across the paper, with a fire engine, its bell being furiously rung by a burly man in oilskins and a helmet, close behind, and hotly pursued by an ambulance, its beacon ablaze. Keeping watch over the scene, its rotors awhirl, hovered a helicopter; in the background, seeming to float on a low bank of cloud, or mist, was a moated building with a drawbridge and portcullis, with turrets and towers. From the highest window in the tallest tower, a tiny Rapunzel leaned out, her tumbling locks crowned with the daintiest of tiaras . . .

"HRH in danger," said Delphick, "as if we didn't already know. And this," he went on, leafing quickly through the other sketches, "is the last of the recent batch. Not as much help as I'd hoped, I'm afraid." He looked up. "I'm sorry, Martha. We're going to have to find Miss Seeton by good old-fashioned detection—and that, unfortunately, will take time . . . "

# CHAPTER 18

Miss Seeton had just finished putting away her portfolio and the rest of her sketching equipment when the doorbell rang. She glanced at the clock. It was most unlikely to be dear Martha again, since it was almost supper-time: the Bloomers, like all country-dwellers, preferred to keep regular hours. Martha would have telephoned, surely, if there had been anything of particular importance—yet she had mentioned, when she'd been so kindly helping to turn the mattress, that Stan was off to a meeting later at Rytham Hall, about the Village Watch, and the bonfire. Perhaps her visitor was dear Stan, on his way to the Hall—although if he intended asking for her advice on the matter of Murreystone, she very much feared that he would be disappointed. How could a mere teacher of art, no more than seven years a resident of the village, possibly be expected to know how to end a feud which had endured for hundreds of years?

Miss Seeton, musing sadly on the many machinations of Murreystone, clicked her tongue as the bell rang out again and she hurried down the hall, unable to stop a slight pucker of disapproval creasing her forehead as she finally opened the door.

Oh, dear. She banished the frown. A stranger: one must not appear unwelcoming. He had, she supposed, lost his way, and was seeking directions. Her eyes drifted down the front path to the car parked just outside. Although Plummergen is not furnished with street lighting, the moon was almost full that night, the sky was unusually clear for November, and there were glimmers from carelessly-curtained windows in nearby houses—and more than glimmers from the George and Dragon, diagonally opposite across the road. A dark, sleek, official-looking car . . .

"Er—Miss Seeton?"

Miss Seeton admitted her identity. The tall man fumbled in the breast pocket of his jacket, and produced a wallet, which he flipped open and held out to her. "I'm with the security services, Miss Seeton." He snapped the wallet shut before she'd had time to do more than blink at it. "You can call me Rookwood, if you will." He lowered his voice. "We need your help rather urgently. May I come in?"

He seemed to be taking her agreement for granted, Miss Seeton couldn't help but think as he almost pushed his way past her into the hall. Well, perhaps not pushed—as she trotted behind him after closing the door—but he certainly was in a hurry. But then he had, of course, said that the matter was urgent: another IdentiKit, no doubt, which dear Mr. Delphick or his colleagues—hers, too, she supposed, and blushed—wished her to supply. Urgently.

"My sketching things," said Miss Seeton, conscious of the need to save every second, "are in the bureau in the sitting-room. If you would care to follow me—that is," realising that in order to lead him down the hall to the room she had just left she would have to squeeze past him, which would be—well, embarrassing, as the gentleman was a complete stranger, "if you would care to walk through—"

"Sketching things?" Mr. Rookwood didn't move: he stood with his mouth open, staring. Miss Seeton, who had taken his movement for granted, stopped in mid-step, and blessed the muscular control which years of yoga had given her. She was able to recover her original position with only the slightest of wobbles, and with no loss of dignity.

"Sketching things?" Mr. Rookwood came out of his trance, and shook his head. "Er—no, thank you, Miss Seeton, that won't be necessary. Her Royal Highness doesn't so much need her portrait painted as a—as a chaperone," he concluded, in a rush.

Now it was Miss Seeton's turn to stare. Her Royal Highness? Chaperone? "But—but surely," she enquired, with a flustered look, "her lady-in-waiting . . ."

"Is at Kensington Palace," Mr. Rookwood told her, "while you, Miss Seeton, are here. There's been no time, you see, to fetch . . . er, her ladyship from London—we've only just discovered where the princess has been kept prisoner. She—that is, her lady-in-waiting—will be informed, of course, as soon as possible—a helicopter of the Queen's Flight and she'll be here in half an hour—but for now we want someone else Her Royal Highness can . . . well, can trust, while she . . . while she's being debriefed. Someone she can relax with after her, um, ordeal—someone to reassure her, now it's over. Another woman—you know the sort of thing—so, if you wouldn't mind coming with me now . . ."

It almost seemed that he would take her by the arm: but no, she must have been mistaken. Or was she? As she looked at him, puzzled, Mr. Rookwood thrust his hands in his trouser pockets, and took a deep breath. "As quickly as possible, please," he said, in a voice which shook, just a little—from worry, no doubt. Such a grave responsibility; and here she was with her foolish objections, delaying the poor man when he'd said it was urgent—but . . .

"But surely a—a more official person than I would be the best choice to—to accompany Her Royal Highness? A policewoman, for example, since she would be trained, as I am not, even if so many years with children—not that one would consider Her Royal Highness a child, naturally,'' with a blush, ''although she is still very young, of course—but I would have thought—the uniform, so reassuring, besides being closer in age—''

''No!'' Mr. Rookwood saw the startled expression in her eyes, and laughed. It sounded, to Miss Seeton's ears, somewhat forced: but he was, she reminded herself, a young man with much on his mind. ''No, I'm sorry, Miss Seeton, but—but she has asked for you in particular. An older woman—not exactly a mother figure—'' Miss Seeton, even more startled, blushed a deep red. Mr. Rookwood coughed. ''I'm sorry, Miss Seeton, I'm expressing myself very badly, but—but, well, if you'd just like to look on this as—as being by Royal Command . . . ''

Miss Seeton paled. Would it be treason to refuse? When the poor young princess had been, one imagined, having so unpleasant a time—although surely they, whoever they were, would not have harmed her—Mr. Rookwood hadn't mentioned anything of the sort, though perhaps he was trying to spare one's feelings—but there had, of course, been one's First Aid training, even if girls fainting at school had been the limit of one's experience—and yet . . .

''Asked for me in particular?'' Even now, she couldn't quite take it all in. ''I'm sure I don't see why—''

''You met,'' broke in Mr. Rookwood—he sounded close to exasperation: the anxiety, of course—''at the Power Station Opening, remember?''

And Miss Seeton, who remembered only too well and had hoped that nobody else did, blushed again, and sighed, and murmured that if Her Royal Highness had indeed expressed a wish for Emily Dorothea Seeton, then Emily Dorothea Seeton would be only too happy to do her loyal duty.

Waiting in the hall—for one moment, she'd half expected him to insist on accompanying her upstairs—Mr. Rookwood tapped his foot with impatience at her saying she must wear, not her everyday coat, but her smart check from that very expensive—such a generous present of kind Mr. Stemkos!—shop in Paris, with her best hat, and that she would take the new handbag, which meant transferring her purse and keys and handkerchief from the one she used the rest of the time. And, of course, what other umbrella but her best, with the gold handle? When one was meeting Royalty . . .

Miss Seeton did not—could not—explain to Mr. Rookwood (she still blushed at the memory) that her sketch of Princess Georgina clothed in—well, in so informal a fashion had made her more than usually conscious of the sartorial respect due to a member of the Royal Family. *Treason . . .*

"Please hurry, Miss Seeton!" Mr. Rookwood was looking at his watch even as she trotted down the stairs, buttoning her coat. Miss Seeton, still preoccupied with thoughts of treason, trotted even faster. She did not stop at the hall stand to check her hat in the mirror; the notepad by the telephone was ignored as she snatched her umbrella from the stand, slipped the handle over her arm, and announced that she was ready.

Mr. Rookwood, who'd thought she meant it, continued to fret while Miss Seeton locked her front door, then whisked her down the path before she'd properly closed her bag on the keys, and had her buckled into the passenger seat and the car door locked—for safety, he told her— while she was still trying to recall whether there was anything she had forgotten . . .

And then, as the engine turned over and the car moved off, she realised there was nothing she could do about it, in any case.

Mr. Rookwood hadn't told her, when they set out, how far they had to go, or even where they were going, except that it was to the princess: but, although in all the hurry one hadn't thought to check the sitting-room clock, it would come as no great surprise to learn that they had already been driving around the winding, shadowed—for the moon had gone behind clouds long ago—lanes of Kent (or per-

haps by now they were in Sussex) for half an hour, at least.
Which naturally made one wonder—though of course they
were the experts, and must understand such matters far better than a humble teacher of art—why Mr. Rookwood and
his colleagues couldn't have arranged, in the time it had so
far taken, for the lady-in-waiting—Lady Vaudine Elliot, as
she recalled—to fly down from Kensington Palace in the
helicopter. But as Mr. Rookwood was driving so fast, and
seemed so very preoccupied—which must be why he had
appeared to forget Lady Vaudine's name—one hardly cared
to put the question to him. Or to ask why he had been
driving with only his sidelights for the past few miles and
not with his—Miss Seeton smiled—main beam. Dear Nigel! He was always so courteous when telling her things;
it was a pleasure to ask for explanations, except that she
could not, she felt, ask Mr. Rookwood in the same friendly
way, in case it should appear to him not only impertinent,
from a stranger, but a distraction. One knew that unless
they themselves chose to open the conversation, one should
never directly address the men at the wheel . . .

"Nearly there." Mr. Rookwood sighed, slowed the car,
and switched off even his sidelights. Only the faint glimmer
from stars and moon in a patchy sky showed where they
were going. Security, Miss Seeton supposed, pleased with
herself for having worked it out at last, although she hoped
they would meet no other darkened cars coming in the opposite direction; and it was perhaps a little odd that one
could see—except, of course, that it was dark, so that it
would be more accurate to say that one could make out—
no other signs of a—a security presence, as one understood
from films that it should be called. Should she ask Mr.
Rookwood to confirm her guess? But he seemed increasingly reluctant to talk, and in the greater dark it would be,
of course, still more of a distraction if he did.

Mr. Rookwood flicked the indicator, then flicked it off
again with a muttered exclamation Miss Seeton found
somewhat surprising, in a man of his type. The worry, no

doubt, of so grave a responsibility as the princess's safety. The car slowed almost to a halt, then turned through an open gateway flanked, as far as Miss Seeton could tell, by tall pillars; but the road ahead, which one supposed should with greater accuracy now be called a driveway, was rutted, and bumpy. One was too busy holding oneself steady on the seat, despite the belt, to bother trying to see more closely; it almost appeared that Mr. Rookwood was deliberately trying to shake his passenger from one side of the car to the other—which was, Miss Seeton told herself firmly, ridiculous, and showed how one's imagination—on which one had all too seldom been able to pride oneself— had been stimulated by the excitement of the occasion; by the darkened, mysterious speed of this unusual journey. Miss Seeton felt a little thrill run down her spine, and her fingers, when not clutching at the seat for support, tingled in the old, familiar way . . .

The car rumbled and jolted along for several hundred yards, then stopped. Mr. Rookwood switched off the engine, and climbed out; he did not at once come round to open Miss Seeton's door, but seemed more interested in checking that nobody had followed them up the drive, or was hiding behind the bushes near the house: security, of course. Miss Seeton unbuckled herself, tried the door handle, remembered, and waited for Mr. Rookwood to release her.

It was a pity that, in her haste, she had not had time to transfer the torch she always carried from her everyday bag to her best: except, of course, that one had somehow received the impression that the princess would be . . . well, somewhere rather less isolated than this. More—more civilised. Somewhere with proper lighting; somewhere much busier, with more people. But one had to assume that Mr. Rookwood and the others, wherever they were, knew what they were doing . . .

Mr. Rookwood unlocked the car door, warned of the need for caution, and helped her out. "This way," he said, in a voice hushed but firm—and this time he did, very definitely, take her by the arm. One might almost have said that he gripped her, hurrying her away from the car almost before she'd had time to pick up her umbrella or adjust her hat. And as for the chance to practise her curtsey, he'd given her none at all . . .

He guided—not *pushed,* surely? Not *thrust,* no matter what it felt like—Miss Seeton across to the house, up some steps, and through a darkened doorway into a shadowed hall. He seemed to know, even in the dark, exactly where he was going. "We go upstairs," he said quietly, edging her towards the steep rectangular greyness of the light from a tall window, and urging her to mount. "Careful, now . . . "

Silently lamenting the absence of her torch, Miss Seeton did her best to be careful, feeling her way with the point of the umbrella she held in her free hand. Mr. Rookwood was very like a cat, one might say, able to see in the dark, and treading so very softly and with such a sure step . . .

"Down here," he said, and led Miss Seeton towards a door at the far end of the landing: a door around the edge of which shone a narrow, golden, electric gleam, a most welcome sight in the grey, glimmering shadows . . .

"In here." He fumbled with the handle, bent, opened the door, and as he did so thrust a hand inside and switched off the light. Miss Seeton heard a rustle of movement, a little cry—and herself cried out, as she felt something—someone—push her sharply in the back, so that she lost her footing and staggered into the room . . .

And heard, to her amazement, the door slammed shut behind her, and the key turned sharply in the lock.

# CHAPTER 19

"Who's that? Whoever you are, keep still!"

The voice which now addressed Miss Seeton out of the anonymous dark was young, cultured, and female, and . . . not frightened, thought Miss Seeton, her hands gripping her bag and brolly for reassurance: but wary. And—judging by the accent—clearly accustomed, from birth, to command . . .

"Stay just where you are," commanded the voice, with a hint of breathlessness. "I'll put the light back on. Don't move an inch!"

The soft patter of feet sounded in Miss Seeton's ear as, despite those breathless commands, she found herself turning to track the sound around what instinct, and the accompanying echoes, told her was probably the perimeter of the room. There came a gentle, muffled scraping, and a click.

In the sudden light, Miss Seeton blinked.

And blinked again, though this time from astonishment rather than glare: for, beside the switch—with a pillow in her upraised hand and a furious gleam in her eye—stood, in a martial attitude, Her Royal Highness, Princess Georgina.

The gleam mellowed almost at once to a look of recognition—those born in the purple are raised according to the strictest principles of etiquette—and, at the same time as Miss Seeton recovered her startled wits and sank in a curtsey, the pillow, likewise, was lowered to the floor.

"We've met before," said Georgina, above Miss Seeton's murmured salutation. "At Dungeness." Miss Seeton, rising from her curtsey, blushed, and fumbled with the strap of her handbag to avoid meeting the princess's eye. Georgina nodded. "The little girl with the flowers . . ."

"My—my pupil, Your Royal Highness." Miss Seeton began to breathe a little more easily. Perhaps, after all, there would be no need to mention . . .

She relaxed too soon. Georgina had a thoughtful pucker between her brows. In normal circumstances, Royalty does not willingly cause embarrassment to its loyal subjects: in normal circumstances, the princess would never have dreamed of mentioning Miss Seeton's unfortunate encounter with the radiation alarm. But these circumstances were very far removed indeed from being normal.

"And the alarm, of course," said Her Royal Highness, fixing Miss Seeton with a brilliant blue eye. "It went off when they scanned you, and the next thing I knew I'd been grabbed—but it wasn't your fault," hastily, as Miss Seeton blushed still more, and bobbed another curtsey as she tried to frame a suitable apology.

Her mind, however, had gone blank with dismay. It was Georgina's voice which now said: "Whoever they are, they haven't said much I've been able to hear, but at least I've managed to work out that they'd planned to snatch me anyway, later in the day. Your, um, little misfortune just allowed them to bring their plans forward a bit."

"Oh, dear . . ." Miss Seeton, looking incredibly guilty, didn't know where to begin apologising. "Oh, Your Royal Highness, I do most humbly beg your pardon. My poor Cousin Flora would be so very mortified to think—"

"Don't worry about it!" Georgina ran across to give her

companion a quick hug. "I told you, it wasn't your fault—
but I thought the little girl was called Sally?"

Miss Seeton was so overwhelmed by such kindliness
from a member of the Royal House of Windsor that, in her
confusion, she dropped her umbrella. In ducking to retrieve
it, she narrowly missed bumping heads with Georgina, who
seemed to share the same automatic instinct for tidiness:
and, too startled even to blush, Miss Seeton cried:

"Oh, do be careful! Ma'am," she added, recollecting
herself hastily, and reverting to the traditional formula. "I
do most humbly beg your pardon . . . " And she essayed
yet another curtsey.

It was not, however, third time lucky. Even the agility
imparted to the knees by years of yoga cannot be equal to
a curtsey from a crouching start. Miss Seeton, wobbling,
gave a little cry, and fell over, dropping her umbrella again
as she did so. Georgina, caught unawares partly by the
wobble, partly by the handle of the brolly, likewise gasped,
and fell. The two ladies ended up side by side on the floor,
rubbing their posteriors and—after a few moments—trying,
for some reason neither could understand, not to giggle.

They tried: but failed. Miss Seeton, on the point of apologising for the umpteenth time, but too breathless with dismay for her unintentional—treasonable?—discourtesy to
do so, caught the eye of Princess Georgina. The well-
known sapphire orbs were sparkling: the ruby lips were
curving in a grin. "There—there aren't," said Georgina,
choking, "any—any bells this time, are there?"

Her laughter was infectious. Miss Seeton, relieved that
the princess didn't appear to be badly damaged, laughed
with her—chuckled, rather, and smiled; and then, quite
without thinking, reached over to pat her on the shoulder.
The poor young creature. A note, perhaps, of hysteria in
her laughter. Miss Seeton, experienced in the ways of teenage girls, patted the royal shoulder again: it was no wonder
that she seemed just a touch . . . overwrought. Anyone else,
with a less rigorous upbringing to strengthen her character,

would doubtless have given way to hysteria long ago . . .

"Come now, my dear." Miss Seeton, the years of teaching overriding all other considerations, administered one last, bracing pat, then gathered up her bag and brolly and rose gracefully to her feet. "It would be better for both of us, you know, if we were to sit comfortably on chairs, rather than on the floor."

As she dusted herself down, for the first time she did more than glance at her surroundings. She was in a bedroom of reasonable size, carpeted, and furnished with a single bed, an easy chair, a small, low table, and a bookcase with a selection of paperback volumes on its shelves. Above the bookcase was a window, thickly curtained. There was a wardrobe against one wall, and what looked like a communicating door directly opposite.

"The bathroom," said Georgina, who had recovered herself almost completely, and was contemplating her visitor with as much interest as her visitor contemplated the room. "All mod cons, I believe the saying goes. For a prison, in fact, it's rather comfortable—that's where they spilled my food the other day," she added, as Miss Seeton shuddered on noticing a large, red-brown stain on the carpet, just inside the door. Her Royal Highness giggled. "It looks awfully like a bloodstain, doesn't it? Quite horrid, but harmless, really. Tomato ketchup"—she made a face— "and gravy, I think. You see I kicked one of them on the shin, and tried to hit him over the head with the tray—but he was too quick for me, more's the pity."

Miss Seeton looked discreetly scandalized. One did not somehow expect that a princess of the Blood would be so . . . so vehement in expressing her—understandable, admittedly—indignation at—one could not, it seemed, mince one's words—at being—Miss Seeton gulped—being held captive. Not, perhaps, entirely ladylike—something rather more subtle might be more appropriate . . . except, of course, that one found it hard to envisage exactly what, in the circumstances, would—or indeed could—be considered appropriate . . .

Georgina observed Miss Seeton's expression, and was reminded of her old governess. Her giggle was apprehensive, her tone slightly aggrieved as she said:

"Oh, I suppose that sort of behaviour would send the Buck House crowd into vapours, if they knew about it—but they don't." There was a little quiver in her voice as she spoke the final words. "And—and what else could I do? The dignity of one's position is all very well in—in normal life, but you can't call . . . being kidnapped *normal,* can you?" Her voice shook again; and again she rallied. "Believe me, I've no intention of sitting about meekly waiting for a knight in shining armour to come galloping to the rescue. The Lord—and I don't mean Sir Shining Armour—helps those who help themselves, doesn't He?"

And then her face crumpled, and her eyes sparkled with something more than bravado, as Miss Seeton—whose thoughts had turned automatically to Nigel Colveden, the nearest to Sir Galahad she'd ever met—sighed, and without thinking patted her on the shoulder yet again. "Oh, dear!" gasped Georgina, and for the first time since her capture she permitted herself a few snuffles of self-pity.

Miss Seeton said gently, "There, there. You must not distress yourself, my dear—Ma'am," she added, remembering. She blushed. Should she, perhaps, curtsey? In the circumstances, it might, perhaps, be regarded as . . .

Georgina straightened, and fumbled in her pocket for a handkerchief. "Oh, please don't! You're the first friendly face I've seen since I've been here—the first face, if it comes to that, because they always wear masks—and we're in this together, aren't we?" Blowing her dainty nose, she favoured Miss Seeton with a sudden, intense look from those sparkling sapphire eyes. "Aren't we?"

Miss Seeton, her conscience—apart from the curtsey—clear, looked steadily back at her. "If it is not an impertinence on my part to say so, I suspect—indeed I fear, Ma'am, that we may be.''

Georgina sighed as she emerged from her handkerchief. ''Then I didn't imagine it? We can't—can't escape, because they . . . they have locked the door again?''

''I believe,'' said Miss Seeton, slowly—one had no wish to distress the child—the princess—further—''they did, Ma'am. That is to say, he did. Mr. Rookwood. Which came as a considerable surprise, because—''

''You know him?'' The sapphire sparkle was all interest now as Georgina—who despite her earlier words had crossed to the door to try it, just in case—glanced back over her shoulder. ''You know who they are?'' And she rattled the handle with brisk emphasis as she spoke.

Miss Seeton's brow creased with the effort of memory. ''He told me that he was a member of the—of the security forces, and from my extremely limited knowledge I have to say that he''—thoughts of the imminent Christmas Pantomime came unbidden—''he certainly looked the part, except that now I am forced to the conclusion that this could well have been a—an untruth, as he has locked the door, and there can surely be no need for such behaviour now that Your Royal Highness has been rescued. If that is in fact what has happened. And since he has locked us in, it would seem somewhat unnecessary—if a rescue has been effected, I mean, even though I explained to him that I was hardly the most suitable . . . ''

She sighed. ''He told me, you see, that''—she blushed— ''Your Royal Highness had—had particularly requested my presence—which I confess I found most surprising, when they are so much better trained than I—women police officers, I mean, the full-time sort, when my—my attachment to the police, or rather my connection with them . . . ''

She blushed again, and drifted to a halt. One ought to have remembered sooner that etiquette required Royalty, not Royalty's companions, always to initiate, and thereafter to direct, any topics of conversation. Her Royal Highness had wished only to know the identity of Mr. Rookwood: should she wish to know the identity of Miss Emily Dorothea Seeton, she would, naturally, ask.

"Then who," asked Georgina, "are you? You said you were a teacher. How can you be a policewoman as well?"

"But I'm not," said Miss Seeton, forgetting etiquette in her desire for accuracy. "At least—I was, but I have been retired for some seven years now, Ma'am, although sometimes, when Miss Maynard is away . . . That is—I never have been, I assure you, Your Royal Highness."

She drew a deep breath. Had she made herself, she wondered, entirely clear? There was a puzzled furrow between Georgina's delicate brows, and a dancing light in her eyes. Miss Seeton tried again. "A teacher—of art. In Hampstead—Mrs. Benn's school, and evening classes at the Polytechnic, though I have from time to time helped out when Miss Maynard has been unable . . . But certainly not a police officer. In Plummergen, that is, not Hampstead. A retaining fee, no more—which, although in my opinion most generous, Your Royal Highness would doubtless regard as—"

"Oh, do stop!" Georgina clapped her hands to her ears, and shook her head. The golden curls bounced, the blue eyes danced still more. "As long as you're not on their side, I'm honestly not bothered—it's so lovely to see a friendly face, after all this time. Just tell me your name, and forget about the rest. It's too confusing."

"Er—Seeton, Ma'am. Emily Seeton—from Plummergen." And Miss Seeton bobbed her best curtsey yet.

Georgina glanced at Miss Seeton's left hand as it rested on the crook of her umbrella. "Miss Seeton, how do you do? And it would be too silly for me to suppose you don't know who I am—but please, you must call me Georgy, the way my family does. You've no idea how lonely . . . " The quiver was back; was gone as she continued:

"And we can't afford to be too formal, can we? When—when we could be shut in here for days—though I do hope," she added, blinking away a hint of further tears, "we won't be—and then, perhaps we won't. Two heads are heaps better than one, after all. Don't you think?"

Miss Seeton smiled. The child—the princess—seemed so much more cheerful and relaxed than at the start of this rather unorthodox conversation. It was up to an older, if not necessarily a wiser, head to encourage her in her new-found optimism . . .

Besides, she did. "Indeed yes, Ma'am, I do," said Miss Seeton firmly. "Er—that is," as Georgina twinkled at her, and waved a warning finger, "that is—er, yes . . . Georgy," in her most respectful tones.

Georgina beamed. "That's better! That's the first kind word anyone's said to me since . . . But never mind. If we just keep going over and over it, we'll never get any-where—and we want to, don't we?" She pulled Miss Seeton across to the bed, and made her sit beside her. "What we want is to get out of here. Have you any ideas?"

Miss Seeton, still bemused at the turn taken by recent events, blinked. One had seen such situations many times, of course, on the television—Miss Seeton was an Old Movie fan of considerable devotion—but in real, as op-posed to black-and-white, life, it was difficult to know ex-actly how—or, indeed, where—to begin.

"Begin with what you know about where we are," Geor-gina promptly suggested. "I never saw a thing while they were bringing me here, and all the windows are shuttered somehow from the outside, so that I still can't, any more than I can hear anything, either. And it's not for want of trying, either, believe me!"

Miss Seeton sighed. One disliked being the bearer of bad news, but . . . "It was, I fear, well after dark when Mr. Rookwood came to fetch me—and he had only the side-lights on, which meant that I could see, unfortunately, very little of where we were going, since it is a cloudy night—which is a pity, as the moon is almost full at the moment. And just before we turned into the drive, he switched them off altogether—the lights, I mean.''

Georgina muttered about planning. Miss Seeton sighed again. ''Although, of course, I have ridden my bicycle on many occasions around my own neighbourhood, I have seldom ventured farther afield—if, indeed, we are. Far afield, I mean—to know now where we are, or to attempt a guess. For all I could tell to the contrary, even though we must have driven for half an hour or more, we might have been travelling in circles, and have ended up no more than a few hundred yards from my home—except, of course, that one would have expected Your Royal—er,'' as Georgina shook her head in gentle reproof, ''that one would have expected, er, you to have recognised some sounds of village life, which you say you have not. Which means that we probably aren't. There are, you see, no street lamps in Plummergen, so that sounds would be almost the only way of telling one was not in the very depths of the countryside instead.''

Georgina sighed. ''Which could mean that we really are—in the depths, I mean, miles from anywhere. So even if we managed to escape, we'd have miles to walk afterwards—not that I mind walking, of course. Grouse moors and so on . . . It's just a pity I wasn't wearing something a bit more suitable for a cross-country hike when they kidnapped me.''

The mattress lurched as she jumped off the bed to reach beneath it for her shoes—smart, dainty, thin-soled leather shoes which perfectly matched her outfit, but which could not be as comfortable as the slippers she now wore. ''Just right,'' she said cheerfully, ''for opening a power station, but not much use for the great trek, are they?''

Miss Seeton, surveying her own tiny feet in their best patent leather instead of her usual stout walking shoes, had to agree, sadly, that they were not. If only she had known what Mr. Rookwood really had in mind . . .

''Then you probably wouldn't have come,'' said Georgina. ''At least, I hope you'd have rung your friends in the police before you did—you didn't, did you?'' with a wild flash of hope in her eyes—a flash which soon faded as Miss Seeton, sadly, shook her head. Why (she pointed out) should she be supposed to think of telephoning the police when she had been given to understand that they already knew? That was to say Mr. Rookwood had not exactly said as much in so many words; but it was not, she thought, unreasonable of her to have taken him for a colleague of dear Chief Superintendent Delphick, who did from time to time, if Her Royal—if Georgy would not think it immodest of her to say so, choose to—to consult her on certain matters; or even Superintendent Brinton, except that he was from Ashford and Mr. Delphick—being from Scotland Yard, when matters of security were always dealt with in London, as far as she knew—might be more reasonably thought of as being a colleague . . .

"Stop!" cried Georgina again, quite lost in the maze of explanation and counter-confusion. "I'm sorry, but—but it's all so muddling—I need to sort things out before we even start to plan our escape. First you're a teacher, then you've retired, then you're on friendly terms with Scotland Yard, and superintendents from Ashford . . . ''

She shook her curly head. "Miss Seeton—who exactly *are* you?"

# CHAPTER 20

"A—a teacher." Miss Seeton was somewhat perplexed. "Of art—or rather—that is . . . " She thought she had explained this once before: but it would be a shocking breach of etiquette to contradict Royalty. The princess was, no doubt, a little confused, in the circumstances: circumstances which one understood rather better, perhaps, than Her Royal—than Georgy realised . . .

Miss Seeton was herself no stranger to abduction. There had, in the past, been a red-haired young man who had popped a sack over her head—ruining, to her annoyance, a perfectly good hat—and carried her off in the back of a battered van, causing her to roll around most uncomfortably with boxes of soap flakes and bottles of ginger beer which (and one had to agree that it served him right, even if—as Mr. Delphick and the others afterwards explained—it had done the engine no good at all) she had poured into the petrol tank to stop him.

"Seven years," murmured Miss Seeton, remembering. "And then, of course, I retired . . . "

"Apart from helping out," supplied Georgina, "when Miss Maynard can't—not to mention being paid a retainer

by the police, as well.'' Royalty's training is more thorough, its intellect more lively, than many outsiders ever
know. ''But do please tell me—what is the retainer paid
*for*? Are you some kind of chaperone for—for kidnapped
girls? I can't imagine they keep you terribly busy, somehow.''

Her blue-eyed twinkle met Miss Seeton's own look of
calm amusement at the very idea. Miss Seeton twinkled
back, and chuckled. ''Oh no, my dear—or rather they do,
from time to time, but not with chaperoning anyone. Keep
me busy, that is. Really, I'm not entirely sure I would be
at all the right person for such a task, despite having taught
for so long, and the yoga keeping me fitter, I believe, for
my age than—that is,'' for a lady did not discuss her age,
even by mistake, ''with IdentiKit drawings. I am often kept
very busy with those. Only the other day, indeed . . . ''

Her hands began moving to and fro along the gold umbrella on her knees: the gold umbrella which had been
given to her by dear Mr. Delphick, who had so very recently asked her for another IdentiKit sketch, and she had
shown him—oh, dear. Blushing, she remembered her most
unusual version of *Le Dejeuner sur l'Herbe;* and she
clutched in some dismay at the umbrella, then blushed all
the more as Georgina looked at her with wide-eyed interest.

''My hat,'' murmured Miss Seeton, desperately trying to
turn her thoughts back to less—less embarrassing matters,
when the subject of her sketch was sitting right beside her
quite oblivious of the dreadful—

''Guy Forks,'' said Miss Seeton, firmly. ''So very foolish,'' as Georgina's look of interest grew even more intense. Well, better appear foolish than treacherous. ''My
hat,'' she enlarged hastily. ''Not the one in the sack with
the soap flakes, but the other, which was blown off by
the wind when I forgot to put in a hat-pin, and rolled
all the way up The Street in the dust. It was quite un-
wearable by the time they had fetched it down from the
awning. And when they came as I was scrambling eggs, I

naturally said they could have it for the guy, as it was of
no particular use to me any longer—not without a great
deal of work, when there are several others which match
quite as many of my outfits—the children, I mean. Which
was where the forks came in, when I was thinking about
the hat-pin. So very foolish,'' she said once more. ''The
play on words, although with it being so close to November
the Fifth it is hardly surprising—the bonfire, that is. And
the fireworks . . .''

But then Miss Seeton hesitated. *Did* Royalty indulge in
such rituals? Would they really wish to commemorate the
remarkably narrow escape of their Jacobean forebear from
the Gunpowder Plotters? Was she being—not rude, for
such had certainly not been her intention—but perhaps tactless? Miss Seeton blushed again. Her fingers fluttered the
full length of the furled umbrella on her knees, and came
back restlessly to the handle, and, catching at it, missed.
With a clatter, it tumbled again to the floor.

This time, Georgina did not bend to pick it up. A light
of gleeful excitement gleamed in her eyes. ''*I* know who
you are!'' she cried, as Miss Seeton, pink from stooping,
once more retrieved her property and sat upright again.
''You're the one the papers call the Battling Brolly!''

One should not, Miss Seeton reminded herself, contradict
Royalty, much as one would wish to; and, of course, if
there was anyone who would know how the newspapers
tended to—to distort, to exaggerate, then it must surely be
a member of the Royal Family. Miss Seeton, still pink—
though now for a different reason than stooping—sighed,
and lowered her eyes to the handle of her gold umbrella,
and sighed again.

''I'm sorry,'' said Georgina, giving her an impulsive
hug. ''You must be so tired of people treating you as a
celebrity, but I promise I won't ask for your autograph,
or anything.'' She smiled. ''It's so lovely, though, to
meet someone for once who knows what it's like!''

Miss Seeton looked up, and smiled faintly. ''It was,

of course, a long time ago," she murmured. "My poor hat . . . "

Georgina, who had not been talking so much about the shared experience of abduction as the similarly shared experience of being the darling of the newspapers, glanced at Miss Seeton's hat, and smiled; then did more than glance, as she recalled what Miss Seeton had said before.

"A hat-pin!" she cried, her eyes bright. "Are you wearing one today?"

It was not the first time since she'd met Georgina that Miss Seeton had been startled by an almost abrupt change of subject: but one had, of course, to follow wherever Royalty—even in the more informal relationship into which it had been proposed one should enter—might lead. Miss Seeton nodded. "It was, as I understood it, a special occasion," she said. "By Royal command, Mr. Rookwood told me—his idea of a joke, no doubt, since Your Royal—since you, that is, did not know I was coming, and therefore could not possibly have asked for me. Which is why I brought my very best umbrella, of course, as I had no reason to suppose that he was—was guilty of as many untruths as it now appears probable he was . . . "

Georgina seemed not to mind that Miss Seeton had let her explanation run away with her a little. She neither interrupted her, nor fidgeted with boredom: she was frowning in thought, her blue eyes moving repeatedly from Miss Seeton's hat to the door, and back again. Miss Seeton, suddenly conscious that she must be wearying her royal audience with her chatter, fell silent. Georgina still did not speak. Miss Seeton went pink; her hands plucked at the fastening of the gold umbrella. If only she had her sketching equipment . . .

She did not know she had spoken the wish aloud: but even to this unexpected remark Georgina made no reply. She was still thinking. Miss Seeton, sighing for her absent pencils and paper, continued to sit in silence, waiting.

"Yes!" Georgina came out of her trance, and clapped

her hands. "Two of us—we'll manage this time, you see if we don't! I'm not staying here a minute more than I must, and nor are you—and you haven't had anything to eat this evening, have you, Miss Seeton?"

Yet another change of subject; but Miss Seeton, at once forgetting her missing sketchpad and fearful of boring her lively young friend, confirmed quickly that she had not; and said nothing more.

"Goody—then they'll be back, because they aren't going to let you starve, any more than they've let me." Georgina grinned. "As I said before, considering they're kidnappers they're really rather, um, considerate—gosh, that sounds silly, but you know what I mean. Proper plumbing, and meals three times a day, except for that once . . . " She giggled, then sobered. "But then there was only me. With two of us now . . . " She seemed sublimely able to ignore the fact that neither she nor Miss Seeton was more than five feet tall, whereas each of the kidnappers she had encountered was a good head taller than they, and far more solidly built.

"We must be ready the minute they arrive," she went on, as Miss Seeton listened in a dutiful silence. "We'll hear the car arrive—at least, I always did before, though he must have left it farther from the house when he brought you." With a nod, Miss Seeton confirmed that he had.

With some satisfaction, Georgina nodded back. "That's how he managed to catch me by surprise, then. They don't usually bother, not since they've taken to coming in pairs—there's safety in numbers." She giggled. "Since that kicking business with the tray—but never mind. Safety in numbers: two of them—and two of us. We must use our wits, Miss Seeton . . . "

For the first time, a note of uncertainty entered the confident young voice. The myriad remarkable exploits of the celebrated Battling Brolly, even as reported in the less sensational newspapers read by royal households, had led Georgina to suppose vaguely that the lady in question—

seldom, if ever, referred to by name—must be a termagant of far more than Amazonian proportions. The sober reality—inch for inch and ounce for ounce no bigger than Georgina herself, surprisingly smartly dressed (though far more surprisingly hatted)—gave her pause for thought.

But not for long. One had, after all, to do *something*. "Use our wits," repeated Georgina, firmly. "Miss Seeton, do you think you can?"

Miss Seeton, who hated to dampen enthusiasm in anyone, young or old—and who could not help but feel they should not remain incarcerated here for a moment longer than necessary—nodded again.

"One carries the tray; the other keeps watch and guards the door," said Georgina, warming to her theme. "When they come in, you must be ready to jab your hat-pin into—oh, some convenient piece of the one by the door—you've taught art, so I bet you'll think of somewhere absolutely splendid for jabbing. Anatomy, and that sort of thing—and it will make him yell, if you jab hard enough. The one with the tray won't drop it right away—I think there's a sort of instinct not to, I had to positively tug and tug before he'd let go, even though he was hopping on one leg and using the sort of language umpty-great-grandma Victoria would *not* have found amusing—but he'll be startled, which is what we want, because I'm going to kick him again, and trip him up, then you can grab the tray and hit the other one with it, and they'll both be knocked off-balance while we throw blankets over their heads and tie them up with sheets and things, and make a run for it—and can you drive a car?"

Miss Seeton, whose vicarious black-and-white experience of battle had never evoked in her any wish to indulge, found herself nodding yet again at this further non sequitur, then shaking her head. One should not, after all, forget that there was once an occasion when a hat-pin applied to a gunman's hand had saved the daughter of an earl from kidnap, or—Miss Seeton blushed—worse; and if one could justify such action for an Honourable, how much more justified must it be in the case of a princess? If—she gulped—hitting people with trays and tying them up was what patriotism required of Emily Dorothea Seeton, then—she drew a deep breath—hit them and tie them she would. But as for the car . . .

"I can," said Georgina, interpreting Miss Seeton's mute signals to her own satisfaction. "Not awfully well, though, when I don't know the car—still, if it messes up their horrid gearbox, then it will just have to serve the beasts right, won't it?"

She sounded so fierce about the prospect of messed-up gears that Miss Seeton would have nodded even if she'd disagreed with her. Since, however, she was coming to feel that the kidnappers deserved every possible punishment for their act of treason—and since behind all the bravado it was not hard to see that poor (mentally, Miss Seeton braced herself) that poor Georgy had been having a bad time of it . . . she duly nodded with as much fervour as she could, and added a quiet *Yes, it will* for good measure.

Georgina did not hear her. "All we have to do is take the keys from whoever's pocket they're in, and that will be that. Freedom!" And the princess cast a most expressive look about the chamber which had been her prison for the past few days.

Miss Seeton said gently, "Both sets, of course—if you will excuse me, my dear. Keys," she enlarged, as Georgina blinked at her. "One set for the car," said Miss Seeton, "because girls are so much more practical nowadays with mechanical matters, but—though yours is an excellent plan, if we can only carry it out successfully—but should we not lock the—the gentlemen in question into this room as they have locked us? One reads so often in books, or sees on the television, or films, that it is comparatively easy to free oneself from bonds of—of an unorthodox nature, and particularly so when they have been fastened in—in something of a hurry, as these, of course, will be."

"I do know my knots," Georgina informed her, with some pride. "I was a Girl Guide—family tradition, you know—but yes, I see what you mean. You can't really tie people up so well in sheets as you could if you had proper rope, and of course there's no rope anywhere in here. They've taken care of that." She forced a laugh. "We can't have our hostage climbing out of windows and sliding down ropes, now can we? And the beastly sheets are nylon or polyester or something. You can't tear them into strips—and don't think I haven't tried—but then, there are heavy shutters across the windows, so it wouldn't have been much use even if I'd managed it."

A fleeting vision of Douglas Fairbanks flashed before Miss Seeton's inward eye, followed by a much more vivid impression of the blonde Georgina as Rapunzel: but neither sight was reassuring. Short curls, she knew, might well lengthen into gracefully-waving locks, but that would take far too long, even if—

Miss Seeton shook herself. The strain of her (or rather of Georgina's) situation was obviously affecting her common sense. How foolish even to imagine escaping down a rope of someone's hair, whether from the turret of a castle or from the bedroom—perhaps bathroom—window of a house. Far more foolish, indeed, than . . .

"Guy Forks," murmured Miss Seeton. She sighed. It seemed that—regrettable though such a step must appear to all right-thinking persons—there was no alternative for her but to obey the royal command . . .

"That's wonderful, Miss Seeton." Georgina, thinking it wise to ignore the cryptic reference to Guy Fawkes as she'd previously ignored the repeated motif of Miss Seeton's hat, chose to hear just as much of Miss Seeton's current murmuring as best suited her purpose. "You agree? I knew you would!" And the young princess threw her arms about the older woman in a heartfelt embrace. "The minute we hear the car arrive," she went on, "we'll take our places. You stand by the door—try to look helpless, won't you?—

and I'll be over here, looking miserable, but really ready to kick the tray beast just as soon as you've hat-pinned the other.''

With another sigh, Miss Seeton signalled her willingness to adopt this—unpleasant, but necessary—tactic. If only one could be sure it would succeed . . .

Georgina dismissed Miss Seeton's doubts with a wave of her hand. Her sparkling eyes hinted at further refinements to the plan. ''Let's turn the tables on them—give them a taste of their own horrid medicine! Just before you pink the one by the door, Miss Seeton, switch off the light. And they won't be expecting it any more than I— we—did, which will give us a bigger advantage. After all, people our size need to wangle every advantage they possibly can . . . ''

A sentiment with which Miss Seeton could not, in the circumstance, honestly disagree.

The Night Watch Men were at the other end of the village. Just one solitary passer-by was in The Street to witness the sudden extinction of the Lilikot lights, to hear the great outcry which arose immediately afterwards . . .

But by next morning almost all of Plummergen was speculating on the affair.

# CHAPTER *21*

Miss Seeton, forcing herself—in the circumstances, *forcing* was no exaggeration—to remember that a gentlewoman should, on every occasion, strive to maintain her composure, closed her eyes, and made an attempt at her most beneficial deep breathing exercises.

It was not easy.

It was, in fact, almost impossible. Such an *undignified* way to move from one place to another. And so very . . . Miss Seeton smothered a cough . . . dusty. Or rather, to be moved. Not active, but passive. Except that neither she nor Her—nor Georgy (as far as she'd been able to tell, with so much . . . excitement, one must in all honesty term it) . . . neither of them had been especially passive in their action, or rather their reaction, to the reprisals which their captors had wrought upon them after the hat-pin-kick-and-tray assault (as she'd feared from the start that it might) had— softly, she sighed—failed. The superiority of numbers . . . no, because there had been two of them, and two of *them.* But superiority, one must admit, of size. Miss Seeton sighed again, with caution. And weight. She coughed, quietly. And

then perhaps—she felt a guilty flush creep up her cheeks—
her heart, and as a consequence her energy and effort, had
never been entirely in the enterprise from the very first.
Which was understandable, since she found violence of any
kind more than distasteful, but which (she reproached herself) must also be regarded as disobedience to a Royal command—in respect of which, if Emily Dorothea Seeton,
admittedly a gentlewoman but without pretensions to noble
birth, felt so very undignified in the current situation, how
much more undignified for Her Royal Highness, Georgina
Elizabeth Mary Alexandra Edwina Victoria, Princess of the
Realm? Always assuming—and here Miss Seeton's heart
gave a horrified thump—that—

She suppressed the awful thought with a sigh of relief
as the car—or was it a van? (In the hurried darkness, they'd
had no proper chance to find out)—juddered over a bump
in the road, and a muffled squeak of indignation advised
Miss Seeton that Her Royal Highness was, like Miss Seeton
herself, in full possession of her faculties. And in a position
reassuringly near to Miss Seeton.

And in—again like Miss Seeton—a sack.

Much cheered by this information, Miss Seeton breathed
too deeply the wrong way, and inhaled fibres from woven
jute. She spluttered, and coughed out loud.

Georgina at once called, "Are you all right, Miss Seeton?" And herself began to cough.

Above the stereo soprano clamour of their dust-induced
fusillade, Georgina and Miss Seeton could just make out
the frantic muttering of male voices somewhere close by:
in the confusion of the hessian dark, it was hard to tell
exactly where, but it was not—Miss Seeton was startled by
a sudden sideways thud, and was even more startled to hear
Georgina say something extremely unregal—not within
kicking range.

"Please remain calm, Your Royal Highness," said a
voice Miss Seeton recognised as belonging to Mr. Rook-

wood. "You'll do yourself no good with these heroics—
and there's no need for them, in any case. We mean you
no harm."

"You've a funny way of showing it," said Georgina,
once her coughing fit had subsided.

"Idiosyncratic," said Mr. Rookwood, in tones of the
deepest deference. "If, that is, I may venture to correct
Your Royal Highness. Eccentric, if you prefer—but never
*funny*. We regard this whole business in a very serious light,
Ma'am—deadly serious, indeed."

"Deadly?" Georgina wasn't going to show this kidnapper that she was in the least scared. "You use words like
that, and then try to tell me you don't plan to harm me?"

"I do," said Mr. Rookwood, above the sound of chang-
ing gears, "and we don't. You'll have to take my word for
it, I know—but it happens to be true. Please believe me,
Ma'am. We have no intention of harming a hair of your
head."

The car lurched, turning off the smooth asphalt road
along what felt like a rough track. The engine laboured in
bottom gear, the wheels rumbled and bounced; stones
clanged upwards against the vehicle's metal underside. Mr.
Rookwood, unable to compete, perforce fell silent.

Miss Seeton, rolled sideways by the sudden turn, was too
busy wondering at the identity of the objects—one hard
and thin and spiky, one more square and yielding—bearing
her company inside the sack to wonder why Mr. Rookwood
had been so very careful to assure Georgina, and only Georgina, that the kidnappers meant her no harm . . .

But Miss Seeton, through all her myriad adventures, had
never been able to accept that anyone, anywhere, could ever
wish harm to herself. Should harm occur, she would always
feel that it must have been a mistake: and—though on
many occasions it had been far from a mistake—her luck,
so far, had held. The harm had never been lasting . . .

But was her luck, for the first time, about to run out?

\*     \*     \*

Delphick said, "We still haven't a clue where she's gone. We've no real idea whether she's with the princess—or even, indeed, whether she's been taken by the same people who took Georgina. If taken, of course, she has been," he added, trying as ever to keep an open mind.

"Young Georgina," growled Brinton, "there's no doubt, she has. As for MissEss, you've shown me those sketches, and I've got to say I agree with your original translation— though I can't see there's any doubt of a connection even without translating the things. Miss Seeton isn't one to be out on the tiles all night, never mind not leaving a message for Martha Bloomer—and if that doesn't mean something's happened to her, I don't know what does. If you're asking me to go along with the hunch you're not quite sure you want to put into words, I'll come right out and agree she's been snatched because she knows—if that's a term anyone can use about Miss Seeton—something in that crazy way of hers, and the snatchers—though don't ask me how— know she knows it. I'll bet my pension she's with HRH— find one, you find 'em both. And you don't need to be an Oracle to predict that when we get 'em back, MissEss'll be waving her brolly same as usual, tut-tutting and wondering why on earth we've all been so worried . . . "

Delphick said, "You're trying to reassure me, Chris, and I appreciate the attempt—but reassurance is hardly enough, is it? We need facts, and as yet we've really none to go on. We need inspira—oh." His tone changed. "What was that you just said?"

"I said MissEss is bound to turn up safe and sound as usual, waving her brolly in the air and—"

"No, before that—let me think. You said she'd been snatched because she knew something, but you didn't know how the snatchers knew she knew anything worth snatching her for . . . Chris, you could just be on to something here. Miss Seeton's identity as the setter-off of the radiation alarm has been kept out of the papers, hasn't it? The British ones, at least."

Brinton grunted. Although over the years he'd come, grudgingly, to accept that Thrudd Banner of World Wide Press and the *Daily Negative*'s Amelita Forby could be relied on to play as fair as could be expected of any scoop-hunting newshound—and though the pair had more or less persuaded their Fleet Street colleagues to mention Miss Seeton's name as seldom as possible when chronicling her adventures ... he just didn't—couldn't—feel quite as happy about such a very informal arrangement as the Oracle evidently did. And Banner's influence on the World Wide crowd was mostly limited to the home market: Miss Seeton still hit the headlines in the foreign press ...

"I know, Chris, I know, but I refuse to posit a sinister foreign abductor unless I absolutely must. Everyone inside that power station—everyone with access to Georgina, at any rate—was Security cleared. The nearest anyone came to having what might be called exotic connections is the head of the cleaning staff, whose husband is Welsh. And there has, I would remind you most emphatically, been not the slightest hint that the kidnapping of Her Royal Highness was carried out by Plaid Cymru."

"It's a long way to Wales," Brinton conceded. And even if the Principality had been just around the corner instead of a good couple of hundred miles away, he couldn't honestly hold the Welsh National Party responsible for the abductions of a princess and an elderly spinster: considering they were political animals—and Brinton's view of politicians was as jaundiced as any—Plaid Cymru, he thought, had far too much sense for that.

"I couldn't agree more." Delphick was inspired. "Which means that if the kidnappers are sure Miss Seeton's a threat to them, they must be local. The grapevine in these parts is more efficient than MI5 at its very best—which, Chris, means we must take another close look at Miss Seeton's sketches, for clues with a purely local emphasis. If," said the Oracle thoughtfully, "we can only work it all out, that is."

"I don't know," said Brinton grimly, "about working it
out—but it's running out, all right, if you ask me. Time, I
mean. Do you realise it's Guy Fawkes Night tomorrow?
And if they're planning anything—anything spectacular, on
top of snatching young Georgina, then fifty-to-one tomorrow's the day they'll let everyone know about it, if you ask
me."

But Delphick did not ask him. Instinct had already told
him that the superintendent spoke nothing but the truth.

The Night Watch Men were organised according to a highly
sophisticated rota drawn up by Martin Jessyp, paper-
shuffler extraordinary to the village of Plummergen. While
to Sir George Colveden were due the honours of the original idea, it was Martin Jessyp who had thrashed out the
finer points of a schedule which never, except around the
hours of dusk and dawn, saw fewer than six men patrolling
the area at any one time. These men—nearly all of them
hardy sons of the soil—were as fit and muscular a band as
any in Kent. Even those who were not farm workers had
been selected for their ability to toss an opponent into a
ditch with as little effort as their agricultural colleagues
could toss a bale of hay to the top of a stack.

In the afternoon and evening of the fourth of November,
most of Plummergen had turned out to assist in building
the bonfire for which various logs, broken pieces of furniture, and bundles of straw had been stored, according to
Nigel's suggestion, in various outhouses around the village.
There is a considerable art in the construction of a bonfire.
You may pile it as high and as wide as you please, but it
must have a strong foundation and a supportive spine—or
rather ribcage, since it is the inside which is the least strong
part. As the fire burns, so it will collapse from the outside
to the in, by this means sparing onlookers the risk of injury,
or worse.

Everyone entered into the spirit of the occasion with as
much enthusiasm as Plummergen regularly applies to any

cooperative endeavour. Jack Crabbe directed traffic into the playing-field in a one-way stream, while his father ensured that departing vehicles did not collide with those bringing further bootloads of burnables to add to the collection. After school, before it grew too dark, Mr. Jessyp and Miss Maynard formed their pupils—each bearing a bundle of twigs or a small branch brought from home—into a neat queue, and sternly warned those who giggled to excess that they must behave themselves. Nigel Colveden and Daniel Eggleden—the latter, skilled in the science of the smithy, putting to good use his specialised knowledge of combustion—supervised the stacking of the heavier items, the placing of the lighter ones.

Sir George, bowing sadly to the commands of his wife, watched as his favourite armchair—its spring and horsehair stuffing gone finally to that great upholsterer's in the sky—was hoisted by brawny arms to the very top of the celebratory edifice, and Guy Fawkes, his monstrous sacking body stuffed with equal amounts of fireworks and straw, was settled in state on his throne, crowned with Miss Seeton's hat above the lopsided mask. Nobody had thought to remove the battered felt until too late, and the sight made people uneasy, though nobody quite knew why; and Mrs. Flax did not help their mood by hovering in the background, dredging up folk-memories of Napoleon, against fear of whose invasion the Royal Military Canal—not a quarter of a mile from the recreation ground—was dug, and beacons were prepared to be lit at a moment's notice.

"And never mind warnings for Boney," said Mrs. Flax, enjoying herself hugely as the more susceptible within earshot shuddered at her awful tones. "Nor fires for Guy Fawkes, neither—ah, further back we go, and further yet. Roasted in sulphur—steeped in gulfs of liquid fire—there's wend-fire, and bale-fire, the flames of Samhain and the Beltane revels, the—"

"Excuse me," broke in Nigel, who'd had quite enough of the Wise Woman's posturing. "If you wouldn't mind moving out of the way, Mrs. Flax, we can let this carload through. The ground's all churned up everywhere else. Thank you,'' as—grumbling, but not daring to speak out against one she couldn't help but regard as the squire's son—Mrs. Flax stepped aside.

It was not thought necessary to post a guard on the bonfire during daylight hours. Not only do two rows of council houses overlook the recreation ground, but the residence of Constable Potter and his family stands almost opposite the entrance. Even if Potter himself were out in his car on one or other of his various patrols, Mabel Potter and (after school hours) young Amelia—not to mention tabby Tibs, a cat credited by many with powers every bit as awful as those of Mrs. Flax—would be sure, for the sake of village honour, to remain vigilant as long as the sun was above the horizon.

But the sun sets, in England in early November, no later than half-past four; and people went home to their suppers, conscious of a job well done. Now it was up to the Village Watch . . .

"Been one or two cars slowing down to take a look, Jack tells me," said Sir George to Mr. Jessyp, as they checked the final arrangements for the night's vigil. "Cars he didn't recognise, that is. Wouldn't have mentioned them if he had, of course. No need. Could be perfectly harmless, mind you: idle curiosity—lost their way . . . "

"It *could*," echoed Mr. Jessyp. The echo did not ring with much conviction.

"Maybe even a few tips for their own fire," said Sir George, duty bound to give people the benefit of the doubt. A magistrate should at all times remember that people were innocent until proved guilty. "Left it a little late, though, I'd've said. Unless . . . "

"Unless," supplied Mr. Jessyp quickly—and concisely. Nothing more needed to be said. The schoolmaster and the baronet looked at each other in an understanding silence.

"Murreystone," said Sir George at last, with a nod. "It's

possible. Potter told me this morning they hadn't begun to build just yet." Murreystone was one of several villages on PC Potter's motorised beat, and his choosing to live in Plummergen was yet another source of annoyance to the rivals across the marsh.

Mr. Jessyp gave a short, barking laugh. "I imagine they must be as worried about us as we are about them—but with far less reason, of course," he added hastily. "Perhaps they'll be so busy guarding their own fire tonight they'll have no time even to think of tampering with ours . . . "

"Perhaps," replied Sir George. Once again, the echo did not ring with much conviction; there was more on his mind than just the likely machinations of Murreystone. Still no word about the little woman—either of them. Mayhem up and down The Street tomorrow night would be the final straw . . .

"Straw," he muttered, gazing at Guy Fawkes on the summit of the bonfire, his giant arms and legs akimbo, his sacking belly bulging. Well away from the pavilion, of course; safe enough for the houses, the hedge, the fence. Unlikely to be a serious accident even if—

"About tonight," said Sir George, bringing himself back to the present with a start. "How many men, d'you think?"

And the conversation thereafter became technical in the extreme.

Although the bonfire was, in the nature of things, the likely focus of any attack, the Night Watch Men were instructed to patrol the whole village. Should Murreystone employ even half the cunning attributed to them by their ancient foes they could well—while attention was focused at one end of the village—try something sneaky at the other. There was the church: never, by tradition, locked, for the healing power of prayer was not to be denied to any man, at any hour of the day or night. There were the bells, which could be stolen; there was the clock, on which sabotage could be wrought. There were, outside the church, hedges and gardens and topiary trees, garden gnomes and gatepost statuettes . . .

But it was around the bonfire that the keenest eyes and the fastest reflexes were set on guard.

The keenest eyes—and the sharpest ears. At midnight on the dot, Nigel Colveden sat up. He nudged Jack Crabbe, the best mechanic in the village. A car was approaching: a car whose engine-note Nigel didn't think he recognised . . .

And Jack Crabbe, flexing his muscles, confirmed that to him, likewise, the approaching engine was unknown.

# CHAPTER 22

The engine rumbled closer. No hint of headlamps could be seen in the moonless dark: whoever was inside the car was clearly up to no good.

With a judder, the engine died. By the faint, flickering light of the stars, Jack and Nigel exchanged urgent looks with Len Hosigg, the third man sharing their bonfire vigil.

"Don't like the thound o' that," muttered Jack, lisping with slow deliberation. Youthful acquaintance with poachers had long since taught him that sibilance carries farther, by night or day, than almost anything else.

"Came from the north," murmured Nigel. Murreystone lies to the east of Plummergen; the most likely road across the marsh enters the rival village from the south, between the high brick walls which bound Miss Seeton's garden and that of the vicarage opposite. "Could be a trick, though."

"Th'right," chimed in Len, a quick learner. The three young men, united in suspicion, strained their ears to hear, their eyes to see . . .

"Over by the gate." Jack Crabbe was pointing; staring. The other two followed his gaze. Something was moving near the hedge: something dark, swift, bulky—too bulky for a fox, a badger, any other creature of the night. Any other creature save a human . . .

"Blimey!"

"Barmy!"

Definitely human. Foxes and badgers do not, as a rule, carry torches. Nor do they emit eldritch cackles as they leap up and down in full view of an audience . . .

"After him!" Jack was ready to roar off in pursuit, but Nigel grabbed him by the arm.

"No, wait! While he's over there, he can't be *here,* can he? Maybe he's not so barmy, after all."

"S'right!" At once, Len spun round to survey the bonfire behind the three whose attention had been so cunningly diverted. Beside him, Jack and Nigel did the same.

Nothing. No movement, no sound—save for the eldritch cackling on the far side of the field. Warily, they glanced back over their shoulders. The torch was still leaping—

Was extinguished.

Silence.

"Could be the Nuts," suggested Nigel, as they peered into the starlit gloom for further signs of movement. "Gone off their heads at last, I mean. You know how oddly they've been carrying on these past few weeks. The way they blew a fuse, or whatever it was, last night—maybe this is some kind of crazy light-bringing ceremony . . ."

"Could've bin a woman," conceded Jack, rubbing his chin and frowning. "A racket like that's hard to tell one way or t'other. What you reckon, Len?"

Young Hosigg was seldom given to speech when a gesture would do. He nodded, his eyes never leaving the distant hedge; then shrugged. Nigel—for whose father Len worked as farm foreman—was used to his idiosyncratic methods of communication. "Len agrees—but where does that leave us? It hardly helps, whichever it turns out to be. If it's a Murreystone male, we either jump him or let him go—and if it's a Lilikot female we've got no choice, have we? We have to let her go—imagine the fuss . . ."

Len and Jack, shuddering, imagined it. Jack said:

"But we don't have to let 'em go if they're Murreystone. Capering about like madmen—one man, anyhow—they're up to summat, and t'wouldn't hurt to find out what—"

"And why," said Nigel. "If it isn't just a Nutty fire-festival, I mean. Whoever it is—"

He broke off. The cackling had begun again, the torch was being waved—but in the opposite corner of the field this time.

"Heading our way, or making a dash for it?" demanded Jack, not seriously expecting a reply. The whole proceeding made so little sense that any reply he received could only confuse things even more.

"Could be either," said Nigel, slowly. "Suppose we—"

He never finished. With a yelp and a muffled oath, Len Hosigg was sprinting back to the bonfire, fists flailing as he ran. With a whoop and a yell, Jack and Nigel charged in his wake—charged towards the three dark figures around the base of the bonfire, who appeared to be struggling with a fourth . . .

"The guy!" As Len waded wordlessly into the mêlée, Jack emitted a roar of rage. "Steal our guy, would you? Damned if we let you, you buggers!"

And then, with Nigel, he joined the fray.

Three against three were reasonable odds, on paper: and the six were reasonably matched. Len, though the slightest of the combatants in build, was stronger than his appearance would suggest. Years of farm work had toughened him: he was no longer the town-bred boy who had needed a stout stave in his hand before he could face the enemy. He was everywhere now: leaping, dodging, punching, parrying.

Nigel and Jack were not to be outdone. They likewise leaped, dodged, punched, and parried; they were themselves punched, and even kicked: but no weapons were used by either side, and slowly it became clear that the Plummergen trio was beginning to prevail. The Murreystoners gasped, and wheezed, and faltered as they were wrestled farther and farther from the bonfire; it seemed that the rival village had not, on this occasion, sent a hand-picked team of the fittest men to do its dirty work—whatever that work might have been. The attempt to kidnap the guy had, after all, been thwarted—

*Or had it?* The same thought occurred to each of the Plummergenites at the same time. The odds hadn't been three against three, but three against four: the fourth being that mysterious torch-waving cackler whose purpose in drawing so much attention to himself—

They did not stop to think. Their punches flew thick and fast as they realised they hadn't so much buffeted their opponents away from the bonfire as been led by them out of range of whatever mischief had been planned—

*Was probably being done right now!* "Let 'em run, lads!" commanded Jack, as the vanquished foe took suddenly to its heels and began making for the gate, nearer now than the bonfire and guy which had been the target of its attentions. "We'll see what they've been up to, the varmints!"

Seeing was easier said than done. While combat seethed below, the stars above had been covered in cloud: only the faintest prickle of light now shone through the few wispy patches which, even as Jack led the rush to the rescue, grew ever more faint until, with a final flicker, it vanished. The whole world now was wide and dark and shadowed grey, a world where shapes were illusion and senses confused . . .

But at last they found the guy. It lay some yards farther from the fire than when they'd seen it in the hands of the invaders; and it was almost unharmed, though its mask was a little more lopsided, its hat jammed even lower over its painted eyes. Apart from such minor damage, the kidnap attempt had failed. Tomorrow's celebration was safe.

With groans of relief as their sore hands and aching muscles came into play, the Plummergen three hoisted the straw-stuffed figure—still heavy with its internal burden of squibs and crackers—back into the old armchair on top of the bonfire. They rubbed their stiffening shoulders, and let their arms fall to their sides, and permitted themselves the luxury of a few minutes' ritual grumbling and comparing notes about how much damage each had sustained.

"Could a-bin worse," said Jack, whose left eye was, like Mr. Weller's turkey, swelling visibly. Nor was Mr. Crabbe's the only black eye; Len's right was rapidly closing, and it was doubtful whether Mr. Colveden would be as handsome next morning as he'd been the night before.

"But no serious hurt, thanks be," said Jack, a sentiment echoed by the other two. "So long's them varmints don't think of coming back, or sending their friends, that is, for I'm not so sure we could chastise 'em as well a second time, are you, boys?"

Nigel, on whom delayed reaction was starting to work, shivered as he shook his head. "We should be getting a few reinforcements before much longer, though." Tenderly, he massaged his knuckles. "I wonder why nobody heard all the kerfuffle while it was going on?"

"Why we never heard the car drive away, neither," Jack was quick to point out. "Though that's what it must have done, surely, the way they took off—and it's not as if we can've bin skirmishing for so very long, if the truth be told. Time's a queer, misleading thing, on occasion—and so're the senses, most of all at night. You'd've thought they'd light up their houses, wouldn't you?" with a jerk of his thumb in the direction of the black squares against the steel-grey sky. "Yet I disremember there was that much shouting, after the first, and all over in minutes, if you stop and consider the matter careful-like."

"You can't," said Nigel, grimly, "be too careful, where Murreystone's concerned . . . "

And the other two agreed with him at once.

\*      \*      \*

It was not until day had well and truly dawned that the Bonfire Watch was at last suspended. Even Murreystone would never dare to invade enemy territory when witnesses by the several hundred might observe the invasion: coming from the south, they must pass the post office; from the north, the council houses. The final group of Night Watch Men returned to their homes conscious of a job well done, for the bonfire—and the guy, untroubled on its armchair high above them—remained, as it had done since that one thwarted attack, unassailed.

It was breakfast-time when the Night Watch Men finally went home; it was almost lunch-time when a small female figure, limping on weary feet, leaning for support on a gold-handled umbrella, found its way to an isolated house, and rapped with the brolly on the knockerless door.

Nobody answered. After a pause, during which she looked over her shoulder more than once, the small female rapped again, more loudly.

There came an irritated clattering from above, and a gaunt, red-haired man in his forties peered out of an upstairs window. "I'm busy," he informed the small one, waving at her to go away. "No tradesmen, no hawkers, no pedlars. Good morning!"

He was about to slam the window shut when a crisp voice enquired from below:

"No princesses?"

John Douglas stayed his hand. He leaned at an acute angle out of the window, and gazed thoughtfully down at the dainty young woman beneath—and blinked as she gazed quite as thoughtfully up at him.

"I think," she said, "you look friendly—I do hope you are. I must have walked miles, and these shoes just weren't designed for hiking—but I simply couldn't risk going to any of the nearer houses, in case they were in league. You wouldn't want to live too far from where you were holding someone hostage, would you?"

"I suppose I wouldn't." Her tone was so reasonable that Mr. Douglas found himself giving serious consideration to the possibility that a harmless bookseller such as himself might at some time hold someone hostage. Then he came to his senses. "*Princesses?*" He leaned at an even more acute angle out of the window. Once more he gazed down at his pint-sized visitor: at the pale, heart-shaped face—the aristocratic features and the tip-tilted nose—the sapphire eyes—the bouncing blonde curls . . .

"Hostage?" said John Douglas, with a gulp.

"Captive, if you prefer," said the pint-sized blonde. "Or prisoner—I don't really mind, now I've stopped being one. But I do rather feel it would be a good idea to let someone in authority *know* that I have—stopped, I mean. They're bound to be interested, I would have said. And yours is the nicest-looking house for miles—and I'm sure you wouldn't mind if I used your telephone, would you?"

"Your Royal Highness!" Mr. Douglas slammed the window shut, pelted down the stairs, paused in front of the hall mirror to smooth his ruddy locks, and, breathing heavily, rushed to the door to open it, and to usher Georgina inside.

"It was all," explained Georgina, to an enthralled audience of officials, "thanks to Miss Seeton's umbrella, you know." She patted the gold handle as she spoke, and smiled. "When they took her away, poor thing—I don't know when, but it was after they'd taken us out of the sacks and given us both some perfectly frightful tea or something, which they *said* was only herbs, though I have my doubts—anyway," as at the mention of *herbs* Delphick and Brinton exchanged glances—"whatever it was, we both fell asleep. We were pretty tired anyway, with the disappointment and everything of having tried to get away and—and not managing it."

For a moment, the sapphire eyes lost their sparkle, and the perfect mouth quivered as Georgina recalled the fright and disappointment of her recent escape attempt. But royal nerves are among the strongest, royal emotions under better control than most; the princess was very soon able to go on with her recital.

"We were so hot and dusty in those beastly sacks, being dragged halfway across Kent in the back of that horrible car or van or whatever it was, and we were frightfully thirsty, of course, so we drank the tea because they told us that was all there was . . . And when I woke up, I was . . . alone. Miss Seeton had gone. And so had one of the sacks—they'd put the other one over me as a sort of counterpane, because this new house wasn't anything like as well equipped as the first place they'd—they'd kept me locked up."

Her eyes filled with tears. "I thought that was why they'd moved us, you see—because there weren't the facilities for two people. Just one bed, and one chair—and if they meant to keep us both for any length of time . . ."

She wrinkled her dainty nose. "At least we had decent loos in both places, thank goodness. I mean, I dare say I could have coped, but Miss Seeton—so undignified, at her age. Or it would have been, except that it wasn't, either time—but in the end it didn't matter, because—oh, I do hope you find her soon! I'm so worried—I thought she was positively the dearest old duck, and if it hadn't been for her umbrella I'd never have got away . . ."

"The umbrella, you said, Ma'am?" prompted Delphick, as Her Royal Highness sniffled discreetly, and weakened just enough to reach into her pocket for a handkerchief.

Georgina blinked once or twice, then smiled. "Gosh, yes—such luck for me they left it behind, even if they took her bag. She might," she said, contemplating her aching feet with a whimsical grin, "have had enough in her purse for me to ring for a taxi, or something, once I'd found a phone—but they didn't leave it, so I never had the chance to try." She looked up. Her eyes were twinkling. "Which is probably just as well, because I expect I'd have made a mess of it." Now the grin was the old, high-powered

Georgy Girl beam. "You know how Royalty's, um, not used to handling money . . . "

Her audience laughed along with her. Members of the Royal Family have attendants who habitually carry all cash for day-to-day transactions, while expenses of a more exotic nature are dealt with on account, settled by the Comptroller of the Household at the end of each calendar month.

Georgina soon sobered. "Anyway, once I'd woken up and seen Miss Seeton wasn't there, I started to feel a little—a little twitchy. I wanted to know she was all right—but the horrid man who brought my breakfast wouldn't answer any of my questions. He was in a frightful temper. There was only one man this time—if I'd only known before, I could have worked out some scheme for hooking the beast off his feet and hitting him again, but I didn't . . . " She sighed. "I'd hidden the umbrella under the mattress, you see. Miss Seeton had told me it was her very best, and I knew she was so proud of—oh!"

The blue eyes widened. "Mr. Delphick! You're the one who gave it to her! Miss Seeton told me all about it—how absolutely thrilling to meet you!"

"Er—thank you, Ma'am." Delphick inclined his head. "Most kind of you to say so." He made up his mind. The rest of Georgina's narrative could be—must be—postponed to a later date. Now that she seemed to have talked the worst of the experience out of her system, it was high time to ask her what else Miss Seeton might have told her: what else she might have said that could be a clue, no matter how unlikely, to rescuing her from wherever the kidnappers had chosen to confine her . . .

As he drew in his breath to ask the first question, he realised he'd left it too late.

"I told you this place wasn't as—as civilised as the first one," said Georgina, who was still young enough to relish the notion of being the heroine of a real adventure, even a kidnap. Hadn't she, after all, contrived her own escape, as in the very best fiction? "Not as efficient, for a prison. Bars

across the windows instead of shutters, for one thing, not
that I could loosen them—and they'd put the bars on after
they boarded up the windows, because it was too awkward
for me to wiggle more than the odd nail out of the frame,
no matter how I tried.'' She looked sadly at the umbrella.
''I do hope Miss Seeton won't mind: I'll have it repaired,
of course. It's the very least I can do, because without it
I'd never have got away, I think.''

She sat up, her eyes bright. ''The door, you see, didn't
fit as well as the other one—and it didn't have a proper
lock, just bolts, top and bottom. I'd heard him draw them,
so I knew there were only two. And at first I thought I'd
see if he came back alone at lunch-time, and catch him
bending from the lower bolt, and hit him—and then I
thought he might have the sense to leave the top one for
last, which would be no help to me at all. Besides, there
might be two of them again by lunch-time. And then''—
her eyes brightened still more—''I realised there was a gap
between the door and the frame, and I poked the umbrella
through to make it wider—and I jiggled the point, and wob-
bled it about—and I don't know what sort of bolts they
were, or why he hadn't twiddled the handle bit up and
round to lock it, but he was in a strange mood, I told you—
and the more I jiggled the brolly, the looser the bolts
seemed to come. And in the end . . . '' She smiled a dazzling smile of triumph. ''They came. And I went. And,
well, here I am . . .

''Here I am,'' she repeated, her eyes clouding. ''Safe and
sound—but oh, please,'' she begged, leaning forward with
clasped hands, ''*where* is poor Miss Seeton?''

# CHAPTER 23

"Well, there goes one worry the fewer—thank the Lord."
Delphick wasn't prepared to stand watching the helicopters
out of sight. The instant the second—the important—one
had risen, rotors clattering, safely into the air, he began to
make his way back indoors.

Superintendent Brinton, with an obscure feeling that you
couldn't just let Royalty vanish into the blue without some
sort of ceremony, stood with his hand upraised in a vague
gesture of farewell, and watched the choppers of the
Queen's Flight (they'd sent three, one for Georgina and two
for her escort) revolve slowly into position—Georgina's in
the middle, the blue-blooded meat in the base metal sandwich—before heading off to London from Ashford Police
Station's hastily-cleared car park. Although it had been explained to them that it was all for Georgy Girl's benefit,
those officers who'd had to move their vehicles out to the
road were not happy about the moving: the war which was
permanently waged between the town's motorists and traffic wardens did not admit of a truce, even in these excep-
tional circumstances. There could well be blood in the

streets before long—good red peasant blood, of course, not blue.

Brinton wondered what sort of welcome young Georgy would get from her loving relatives. Orders had been she was to go straight to Buckingham, not to Kensington, Palace: top-notch doctors and counsellors to check her over, he'd bet. Plenty of fuss and cossetting from Cousin Lilibet (or whatever she called the Queen), and from the Queen Mum, everyone's favourite granny. And—

"Chris! What are you waiting for?" Delphick had halted in mid-stride once he'd realised that his friend wasn't with him. "She's not our responsibility any longer—for which relief, much thanks: I thought the wretched girl would never leave. Now at last we may direct all our energies towards the finding of Miss Seeton—and the sooner, I would remind you, the better."

"Sorry." Brinton, red-faced from a combination of haste and embarrassment, joined his colleague by the door. "It sort of slipped my mind for the moment—not that I take MissEss for granted, you know I don't, but when you think of the number of scrapes she's been in over the years, and how she always seems to survive them—"

"So far," Delphick broke in grimly. "Remember the old saw about a first time for everything? And, talking of *old,* Miss Seeton is growing no younger, Chris. For heaven's sake let's find out what's been happening while we've had to dance attendance on HRH half the day and pander to the whims of the security boys with their damned debriefing."

He strode off in the direction of the communications room, with Brinton puffing in his wake as he tried to walk and talk at the same time. "Be fair to the girl, Oracle. She gave us enough info to locate the house—the second house, at any rate, and I call that pretty good going, when you think what she's been through." He was trying to cheer his friend as much as himself. "It's not just that she's a complete stranger to the district—but for a kid like her this sort of thing's hardly the—the run-of-the-mill affair it is for Miss Seeton, now is it?''

As he caught up with his colleague, he saw the faint smile of acknowledgement in the cool grey eyes, and nodded. ''You know what she's like, Oracle. Being gassed or coshed or chucked in the canal's all in a day's work for MissEss, more or less. Why, she hardly notices it's happened and even if she does she's always sure it must have been a mistake to begin with—she's never had half the nightmares she gives the rest of us, I'll wager my pension she hasn't. If that's what yoga does for you, I'm all in favour of it. Happy as a sand-boy she'll be when she finally turns up, you mark my words.''

He was almost starting to convince himself. ''And it can't be that long—we're sure to find her soon, with the start young Georgy's given us. She'll be back at the first house, I imagine—the logical place to take her, keep her out of the way while they collect the ransom or whatever— and they'll know by now the girl's escaped. Why, they've probably let MissEss go already, and it's just a question of picking her up from wherever she is once she gets to a phone the way young Georgy did. Nobody's going to pay a king's ransom for the poor old biddy, and they know it. I tell you, we're sure to find her soon . . . ''

''If only we knew why they'd snatched her in the first place, it would help.'' Delphick frowned as he followed the superintendent—whose headquarters, after all, these were—into the operations room. ''If only we had more to go on than Georgina's garbled memories of what Miss Seeton said—if only she'd been able to *draw* something . . . and then maybe she did, and the princess was too preoccupied to notice—or perhaps it was while she was asleep . . . if only they'd forgotten to take her bag, as well as her umbrella . . . ''

He was left to lament alone. Brinton's hurried arrival had set heads turning. Anyone not speaking on the telephone, or making notes, or sticking coloured pins into the large-scale map on the wall, began to gravitate nervously towards the two senior officers as they looked from one face to another, inviting someone to present a more up-to-date report than those they'd been hearing on and off throughout the morning.

But nobody, it seemed, could update any of the reports in more than a negative manner.

"*Nothing?*" Superintendent Brinton's bark was widely supposed to be far worse than his bite; everyone prayed now that the truth of this supposition would never be put to the test. They couldn't remember when they'd last seen Old Brimstone in such a state. "Nothing at all?"

Heads were shaken in dumb regret; guilty boots shuffled on the floor. "Call yourselves detectives?" bellowed Brinton. "The whole boiling shower of you couldn't detect a— oh, God! What's the use? Never mind bleating you're under strength with two suspicious deaths to investigate. Never mind telling us *again* it's a derelict property that's been on the market so long the blasted estate agent's collected his pension and retired to heaven-knows-where—we know that already! Somebody, somewhere, must know something else! Just keep looking—keep asking questions—ring round every damned estate agent in the country, if you have to—and report to me in my office the instant you hear anything. Anything at all!"

He would have slammed the door on his way out, but Delphick was too close behind him. Brinton groaned, clutched at his hair, and gritted his teeth as he strode off down the corridor in the direction of his office.

"I was so sure they'd have found her by now," he threw over his shoulder to Delphick, hard on his heels. "So—so damned sure, I couldn't believe—" He flung open the door with a crash that had the walls juddering. "You—Foxon! Here, lad—and make it snappy!"

Detective Constable Foxon, his ears ringing, dropped the box of pins he held, and leaped in three urgent strides across the room to his superior. As Sergeant Ranger rose hurriedly from his borrowed desk, Foxon drew himself as close to attention as anyone can who sports the informality of a flowered shirt and a salmon-pink paisley tie. "Sir!"

"Never mind *sir*," snarled Brinton. "How about *sir, something to report* instead?"

Foxon—who was quite as anxious about Miss Seeton as anyone else, and whose blood pressure was in far better shape than Brinton's—ventured a quick look at Chief Superintendent Delphick. The Oracle's left eye flickered in the merest suspicion of a wink; and Foxon, reassured, allowed himself the luxury of a faint grin before turning quickly back to Brinton.

"Funny you should say that now, sir, because not two minutes ago—of course, it might not be anything to do with all this, but—your, er, standing orders, sir—"

Brinton broke in with a groan. From being red in the face, he turned pale. He clapped a hand to his anguished brow, staggered to a convenient chair, and sat down.

Foxon stared; Bob smothered a grin; Delphick sighed as he observed his sergeant's expression. "Break it to us gently, please, Foxon. What news on the Rialto?"

Foxon looked puzzled. They'd done *Macbeth* at school: he didn't recognise the quotation from *The Merchant of Venice*. "You mean what's the word on The Street, sir? But how did you guess?"

Delphick sighed again. "It hardly strains my oracular powers, Detective Constable Foxon. Your mention of standing orders would have warned someone far less astute than I that there have been happenings in Plummergen of which Constable Potter feels his superior should be apprised . . ."

A forceful and heartfelt blasphemy burst from Brinton's lips, and he shuddered. From his first encounter with Miss Seeton, the superintendent had realised her remarkable, not to say unique, qualities; accordingly, he had issued detailed instructions that PC Potter should advise him—in office hours or out, at home or (heaven forfend) on holiday—of any, repeat any, untoward occurrence in the immediate neighbourhood of Miss Seeton's cottage, or in the general neighbourhood of the village in which that cottage was situated.

Police Constable Potter was a man with much insight into local affairs, with an enthusiasm for his work which meant that, had he so wished, he could long ago have put in for promotion and been moved to a larger beat. Potter, however, was possessed of more than insight and enthusiasm. He had a strong preference for a nice, peaceful life, with which was coupled a certain native cunning. Admittedly, his life had been rather less nicely peaceful since Miss Seeton's arrival in Plummergen seven years earlier: but Potter—whose nerves were stronger than Brinton's— approved of the little art teacher. He considered her an asset to the community, and was gratified whenever her innocent gyrations contrived (as they so often did) to sweep him into their ultimate toils.

This sentiment, he knew, was not shared by his Ashford superior. While Brinton was known to like—even to admire—Miss Seeton, she made him uneasy. She set his blood pressure leaping to heights previously unscaled on medical charts, or so he claimed: and who was Potter, a mere uniformed constable, to argue with a superintendent? He would never dare do anything to invoke the wrath of one set in authority above him; nor did he care to cause anxiety to one whose health was apparently in so precarious a state . . .

Which was Potter's planned defence should Brinton ever discover that an officer under his nominal command had exercised considerable insight and judgement on various occasions in the past, withholding more than one Untoward Occurrence in the neighbourhood of Sweetbriars until it had become absolutely necessary that a report must be made.

As made, just now, it had been.

"A punch-up with Murreystone last night," said Foxon, in succinct response to Brinton's growled instructions to spill the blasted beans without smothering 'em in a load of sauce. ''By the bonfire, at the playing-field—seems they had some notion of pinching the guy, then thought better of it when Nigel Colveden and his pals—er, showed 'em it mightn't be such a good idea. Sir.''

Some judicious probing on the part of Delphick—Brinton having been rendered once more speechless by the enormity of his subordinate's intelligence—extracted the full story of the Last-Minute Bonfire-Building Scheme. Further probing—Foxon was never quite sure how the Oracle had managed it, but decided that a Yard training could overcome any number of scruples about betraying one's friends—elicited the retribution proposed to be visited by the Village Watch upon their rivals should Murreystone attempt further skulduggery at tonight's Grand Firework Display and Jacket Potato Roast.

''No doubt,'' Delphick said, ''they were inspired to their attempted guynapping by the abduction of Princess Georgina—though it must be said that Murreystone, even in my limited experience of them, have seldom seemed in need of inspiration to the darker shade of deed. There would appear to be an innate strand of wickedness in Plummergen's near neighbours—but has this current outbreak, do you suppose, anything to do with Miss Seeton?''

Brinton rolled his eyes, but said nothing. Bob ventured the opinion that it might have. Foxon, grinning faintly, said that he had no idea, but that as occurrences went it was certainly untoward (with a flick of the eyes towards his silent superior). And, with MissEss undoubtedly still missing, perhaps it was a coincidence they ought not to ignore. After all, they hadn't had much luck so far going along, well, the normal lines of enquiry; and there were, so Potter had said, quite a few empty properties in the Murreystone area—and if the kidnappers were local, as everyone seemed to be starting to think—and with search parties from Plummergen not exactly official, and wanting as little trouble with the authorities as possible . . .

"So Potter says," supplied Delphick, as Potter's mouth-piece fell silent, blushing. "I'm inclined to agree with you—with him, that is." He glanced at Brinton, brooding on his chair. "One village constable, even in a panda, can-not aspire to a thorough search of a wide-ranging area by himself, no matter how large his band of unofficial volun-teers. By the way, are we to assume that such extended and multiple searching explains Potter's . . . slowness to report the bonfire incident?"

"Of course," said Foxon at once, rushing to the defence of his friend. "Er—sir." He saw Delphick's look, and rushed on: "The Colvedens knew last night she was miss-ing, sir, but it was dark, not to mention the bonfire busi-ness'd already been set up and they knew they'd be, well, asking for trouble if they left it. So Sir George got them organised for first thing this morning, and off they went as soon as it was light. Potter says the general said they'd set a limit on how long they'd search before giving up, because even if they just checked the places they could get into it would cut it down for the ones that were locked they'd need warrants and stuff for, sir. So, well, that's what the-y've done, and we've got the list right here. Sir."

Bob passed him a sheet of paper, which he took, then hesitated, and handed to Delphick as Brinton, brushing it aside, lumbered to his feet and stumped across to the large-scale map on the office wall. He stared at it, and grunted.

"Pinned 'em already, have you?"

"Er—some of them, yes, sir, but . . . "

"But our arrival," said Delphick, whose brief reference to the list of locations had told him almost nothing, "pre-vented your completing the task." The eye with which he gazed upon Detective Constable Foxon was now almost warm in its regard. "Pin on, Foxon—unless, that is, your local knowledge is such that you could guide us to each in turn."

"Between us, sir, I reckon we could," replied Foxon after a moment, as Brinton grunted again, and Bob, adopted local, nodded at his friend's side. "They're none of 'em close to any of the others, unfortunately, so it wouldn't be a quick job to check 'em all out—"

Brinton groaned. Foxon glanced at him, and continued: "But they're in the general area, sir, so it wouldn't be all that difficult to check 'em. If that's what you wanted to do, sir."

Brinton turned from his study of the map to glare at his colleagues. His manor: his responsibility: his word of command, to go or to stay. He let out an exasperated snort at the expectant look on the three faces.

"*Want?* Good grief, there's nothing I fancy more than go wandering around Kent in the dark in winter checking a blasted telephone directory of empty houses on the off chance there's a little old lady tied up in a sack in one of 'em—but it sure as blazes beats sitting on our backsides waiting for news, which is what we'd be doing otherwise, the way things are right now. Dammit, you should be halfway to the car by now, laddie—and you Yard types with him!"

"Right, sir!" Foxon bounded joyously to his desk, took out a set of keys, then leaped to the peg on which hung his leather jacket. "On my way . . . "

Bob Ranger, for all his size, wasn't far behind him; and not far behind Bob came Brinton and Delphick, the former detouring via the operations room to bellow the advice that he was going out on patrol, and was to be informed by radio if there should be the slightest breakthrough in any of the three cases under investigation. Then he thundered in Foxon's wake to the car park, where the engine was already revving for the off. He wrenched open the door, flung himself inside, and buckled the seat-belt as Foxon jammed his foot on the accelerator.

With a roar and a rush, Delphick's car, with Bob at the wheel, caught up with them and sat on their tail. The hunt for Miss Seeton was, with a vengeance, on . . .

For—as Delphick reminded his sergeant, who was too

busy concentrating to reply—find Miss Seeton, and they would more than likely find—with her interpretation of those puzzling sketches—the solution not only to the kidnap of Princess Georgina, but to the murders, as well.

# CHAPTER 24

Although many of its citizens, with Miss Seeton's contin-
uing absence, were troubled in spirit, Plummergen contrived to rise above itself for the sake (as some of the more
vocal put it) of the kiddies. The Grand Firework Display
and Potato Roast had been planned for weeks; the search
parties had done all that could reasonably be expected of
them, anyone would admit; the police were known to be
doing their best—and there was no sense now in spoiling
things for everybody else. Besides, wasn't Miss Seeton herself so fond of the youngsters she sometimes taught? She'd
hate to have them disappointed. What's more, if they can-
celled the festivities as one or two had suggested, wouldn't
Murreystone (said those as cunning as they were vocal)
choose to see it as Giving In?

It was the final point which clinched the argument. Never
mind the truth of the matter: the village knew, only too
well, that opportunist Murreystone, gloating, would forever
publish it abroad how Plummergen had refused to run the
risk of being outdone by a bigger guy, a brighter fire, a
more spectacular display from its smaller rival. And no
amount of explanation (not that Plummergen would stoop

to explain itself to Murreystone, but there were other villages on the marsh who might get the wrong idea) would banish from local legend the Murreystone-inspired accusation of cowardice. Nothing short of a cloudburst, Plummergen realised, could be accepted as an excuse for failing to commemorate the Gunpowder Treason with all due ceremony and celebration; and the committee duly announced that the Plummergen bonfire would be lit, as had originally been planned, at six, sharp.

By five o'clock, the sun had long since set, although in London the sky was never truly dark. There were too many street lamps to cast an upward golden glow against low-lying clouds, too many public buildings with floodlights and with high, uncurtained windows.

From behind the red velvet hangings of her room in Buckingham Palace, Georgina, curled up among cushions on the window-seat, a fleecy blanket draped around her shoulders, gazed without seeing to the shadowed gardens below. There was no question (her cousins had insisted) of her returning to Kensington that night; after all the shocks and disturbance of the past few days, she must have peace, and quiet, and nothing more to worry her. The private wing of Buck House was as peaceful and quiet as anywhere in Town; now that she had done her duty by the security forces, she must retire for a well-earned rest, and have her supper brought to her on a tray just as soon as she felt like it.

Georgina didn't feel like it just yet. She'd managed, with coaxing, to swallow half a cup of tea on landing, but the helicopter flight had been rather bumpier than she would have wished. Her insides still had some way to go to catch up with the rest of her before she could believe herself safe on terra firma again. The aftermath of the trip from Ashford, coupled with the strain of having dutifully repeated, for the benefit of yet another group of detectives, her story for what must have been the umpteenth time, had left her wanting to do no more than sit in silence for a while, thinking.

Princess Georgina might be young and pretty and golden-haired, but she was no dumb blonde. She took her responsibilities as seriously as any member of the Royal Family; and she couldn't help but think of Miss Seeton—whom she'd been so pleased to see in her captivity, who had been so kind and encouraging when she'd most needed it—as the greatest responsibility of her life. She wouldn't, she knew, be able to rest until she'd heard that the old lady had been found . . .

Old lady? Georgina found herself smiling at the very idea. One hardly thought of Miss Seeton as old, for all her grey hair and quiet demeanour. She had been so cheerful, so spry, so—so indomitable in the face of what common sense said had been danger: some old ladies might have threatened the vapours at the prospect of who-knew-how-long in durance vile, but not the Battling Brolly. Not, of course, that the battle had been successful, on this particular occasion, but one had to admit that Miss Seeton's support for the escape attempt had been marvellous, even if at first she'd looked a bit embarrassed about it all. And the brolly! She must be sure to check that the chief superintendent had—as he'd promised—arranged for it to be repaired where her poking and prodding at the bolts of her prison door had damaged it.

Mr. Delphick had given that gold umbrella to Miss Seeton in memory of her earliest adventure—but what other adventures she'd had since then! Not, of course, that she'd seen them as adventures. Georgina smiled again at the memory of how hard it had been to urge her new friend to speak of herself. She guessed that it had only been Miss Seeton's wish to take her mind off their present situation which had persuaded her to say anything at all . . .

And, indeed, even now Georgina's knowledge of Miss Emily Seeton was based less on what Miss Seeton had said than on what the papers had told her of the Battling Brolly, and on what Chief Superintendent Delphick had tried to explain at the earlier debriefing, in Ashford. It had been so confusing, she feared she hadn't really taken it in as well as she ought—but now there was something niggling at the back of her mind. Something about *when Miss Seeton talks about her drawings, you know she's on the right track . . .*

Drawings! Suddenly, Georgina thought of family gossip: of the kidnap of distant cousin Artemis MacSporran, of some crazy plot to overthrow the Crown in Scotland, and of how both had been thwarted through the good offices of—

"The Battling Brolly," breathed Georgina, sitting up, the blanket slipping from her shoulders. "Drawings . . . when she talks about drawings, she's on the right track . . . "

Just what was it that Miss Seeton had said?

"Last on the list," said Brinton, glaring back through the night at the shuttered windows of the empty farmhouse. "And nobody home here, either." Glumly, he watched Foxon score a pencil across the final address on his clipboard sheets, and winced as a distant flurry of crackling bangs signalled the ignition at some festive bonfire of yet another string of jumping-jacks. It was, in his present humour, far too violent a sound for the superintendent's liking.

He scowled at his companions, who were as disappointed as himself by the outcome to their search. "So what do we do now—anyone any ideas?"

In the distance, the silver-sparkling trail of a rocket flashed across the Guy Fawkes sky, and exploded against the clouds in a riot of rainbow stars.

"Ask for an update when you check in," suggested Delphick. "Something may just have come up since we arrived—"

"All of ten minutes ago," snapped Brinton, then swallowed his intended remarks about watched pots never boiling as Foxon reached into the car for the radio handset, and switched it on. The other three crowded close in an uneasy silence, broken only by the rainbow rocket's series of explosions, faint but clear across the quiet, level marshland. After a few frantic moments, Ashford Control crackled into life, and gave reluctant tongue in response to Foxon's quick enquiry . . .

"So *now* what?" Brinton had gone through despair, and beyond. He turned to Delphick, and gestured helplessly. "You're the Oracle, for heaven's sake. Say something!"

Delphick's attention was caught by the flash of another rocket, soaring into the cloudy heavens from the west. There followed a pause, while he pondered; and Bob, shifting from one huge foot to the other, shuffled dry leaves in an agony of frustration. Like Brinton, like Foxon, he longed for action: but there was no sense in going off half-cocked. The Oracle—all of them—had gambled on Foxon's, or rather Potter's, list of likely local houses—and they'd lost. But the Oracle had spent a fair old while talking with Princess Georgina; he'd heard what she'd had to tell him about Miss Seeton, and he'd tried to make her remember everything she could, and more. Now he'd had time for it to pickle in his subconscious, maybe—just maybe—he could tie it all in with those sketches they'd seen back at the cottage, back in Plummergen . . .

"Back to Plummergen," said Delphick, and Bob jumped as the others gasped: had he spoken the thought aloud, or was the old man a mind reader? Or perhaps it was—he grinned, as Foxon and Brinton made *if-you-say-so* noises—the logical thing to do: except that with Miss Seeton, logic was about the last word anyone would use.

"You are entirely correct, Sergeant Ranger." Delphick's dry tones informed his startled sidekick that he *had* spoken that particular thought aloud. "There is," continued the Oracle, above Bob's muttered apology, "no logic whatever to my proposal that we adjourn to Miss Seeton's village—no logic, that is, beyond the perpetually illogical premise that where her ambience is most strong, perhaps there will be found some means to guide us towards the, ah, personification of that ambience. Towards, that is, Miss Seeton herself. Another examination of her sketchbook would not, I believe, in these perplexing circumstances come amiss . . . ''

In Plummergen, Sir George—huffing through his neat moustache, conscious (despite his hidden concerns) of the importance of the occasion—struck the ceremonial match, and held it to a strategically-placed wisp of straw. It was thought an omen of good luck for next year's harvest if the fire caught at the first time of striking; and everyone watched intently as the tiny flame licked its way into life, scarlet and crimson and rich, ripening gold . . .

In Buckingham Palace, Georgina slipped from the window-seat, and turned slowly in the direction of her bedside table. On that table were a reading-lamp and a selection of books, a small tin of biscuits, a box of paper handkerchiefs (Royalty is far more practical in its lifestyle than many people realise), and a telephone.

Her hand reached out to the receiver; hovered; and fell back. With a sigh, she shook her head, and quietly scolded herself for her folly—or, perhaps, for her lack of conviction. Had she had a ridiculous, exaggerated idea—or an inspired brainwave? She took a step closer to the telephone—reached out again—paused . . .

From outside, the distant sound of exploding fireworks—the whine of Catherine wheels, the overhead crackle of rockets, the cannon-fire of Roman candles—broke for the first time into Georgina's consciousness.

"Guy Fawkes," she murmured. She smiled. "Guy Forks!"

She made up her mind. Better to appear foolish than, if she was too late proved right, afraid of *seeming* foolish—a coward. Generations of Saxe-Coburg ghosts looked on, and nodded their approval.

"And anyway," said Her Royal Highness Princess Georgina, with her index finger poised and her eyes dancing, "I've always wanted to do this—and it's probably the best excuse I'll ever have in my life!"

Whereupon, with no more hesitation, she began to dial.

Into Plummergen swept the two-car cavalcade, Foxon in front, Bob close behind. From over the marsh they came, racing across the narrow bridge and ready to roar up The Street to the bonfire to find Martha, or Stan, or someone with Miss Seeton's front-door key . . .

But Brinton and Delphick, keen-eyed passengers, spotted the light in the Bloomers' cottage as they passed, and both ordered their drivers to slam on their brakes and stop.

Foxon's reflexes were quick: mercifully, so were Bob's. Four car doors swung open; eight booted feet pounded up the short front path, and only Brinton's barked command for some common sense, dammit, prevented four urgent hands reaching out to seize one brass knocker.

The unorthodox arrival of these clamorous guests brought the Bloomers to the door before anyone had time to knock. It was Stan who opened to them; Martha, the corner of her apron to her reddened eyes, could only stare in dismay at the four official faces on the step, dreading what news they might bring.

"It's not bad news," said Delphick, before either of Miss Seeton's friends could speak. "In fact, it's no news at all, I'm afraid, and I don't propose to insult you with the bromide about no news being good news, because we have absolutely no way of knowing, at present. What we *do* know is that we should very much like to borrow the key of Miss Seeton's cottage—we want to take another look at her sketchbook. I have an idea . . ."

He hadn't; he was hoping, that was all. But the worried Bloomers knew nothing of this, and welcomed his suggestion with relief. Stan, almost before the tall policeman had finished his request, was hurrying down to the kitchen for

Miss Seeton's spare key, safe in its usual place on the board beside the Bloomers' own front, back, shed, and greenhouse keys; he was back as Martha was still only halfway through her sad little speech about not having the heart to go to the fireworks tonight, no matter what folk might say about poor dear Miss Emily not wanting to spoil anyone's Guy Fawkes fun, when they were both so worried about her, and those who said they'd no need to fret on account of her always turning up in the end just didn't understand, did they?

"They don't, indeed." Delphick deemed it wiser (and faster) to agree with Martha rather than waste time trying to explain that neither he nor his colleagues would ever insult the finer feelings of the Bloomers with such a suggestion. "We're as worried as you, Martha, but we are, as I said, still hoping. It's only an idea, I'm afraid, but there just may be something in the sketches that we missed first time around . . ."

And within three minutes they were all in Miss Seeton's sitting-room, poring over the sketches which stubbornly refused to give up their secret. Nobody spoke. Above the tense breathing of the four policemen, the sound of fireworks from outside masked the rustle of pages as Delphick flipped them back and forth, back and forth between the first cartoon—the guy with his battered hat, his cutlery limbs—and the last, the princess in her distant castle with the forces of law and order rushing to the rescue.

"Rapunzel," muttered Delphick, staring yet again at this final drawing as Catherine wheels screamed and whooped somewhere in the distance. "The helicopter flight back to Buck House—well, she was certainly right about that."

"Y-yes . . ." Brinton wouldn't normally have put himself forward as an interpreter when the Oracle was on the case, but when even the Yard's own Seeton expert seemed flummoxed by her drawings, he supposed he ought to be willing to give it a try, if nobody else was prepared to risk it. And he'd crown Foxon if the lad laughed at him afterwards . . . "Overdid it a bit, though, wouldn't you say? I mean—they'll have kept it quiet, won't they, as far as possible? None of this fire-engine-and-squad-car business the way she's shown it, I mean. She'll have thought the sirens were fireworks, most likely," he added, as a rocket howled low overhead and exploded in a high-pitched clatter at the bottom of the garden. "And with all the Guy Fawkes business as well . . ."

It made no sense: he knew it didn't: but somebody had to say something, do something to get the Oracle thinking along the right tracks—and as nobody knew what the right tracks were, it was a case of kicking ideas around until it all came together and he headed off in the right direction.

"Sirens," said Delphick thoughtfully, still staring at Rapunzel. "And Guy Fawkes . . ."

Foxon stirred; but it was Bob who spoke. "Sirens, sir," he said, breaking into the oracular thought process without apology. "Hear them? Heading this way—"

"No," said Foxon, "that's the bells—fire engines, if you ask me. But those others sound like police sirens, all right," and now his superiors could hear them as well. The whooping two-tone constabulary wail, the frantic tintinnabulation of the fire brigade—this last growing ever louder, nearer, speeding past the cottage with a roar . . .

"The playing-field, or I'm a Dutchman," said Delphick. "The Guy Fawkes bonfire—come on!"

# CHAPTER 25

Although Miss Seeton's closest friends had been concerned about her disappearance, they were of that class and generation which seldom permits its deepest feelings to show. The Colvedens were not the only people to attend the Grand Bonfire Celebrations determined to put a brave face on things; and more than one person that evening found that thoughts of their missing friend inspired them to follow her excellent example and—the sky being overcast, the outlook uncertain—to carry an umbrella, just in case.

Children in gumboots squealed with excitement as they hurtled through the churned-up mud around the base of the bonfire, around which Nigel and his friends had thrown a stern cordon, remembering Murreystone and the contretemps of the previous night. Only now Plummergen was out in force could the Village Watch relax its vigilance: the bonfire and the guy were safe, their one visible enemy being the low, dense, menacing cloud. Sir George—one eye out for the weather, one for the starter's signal—stood by with the ceremonial matchbox; Admiral Leighton, Dr. Knight, headmaster Martin Jessyp, and other village elders coordinated the distribution of sparklers for the opening extravaganza. Lady Colveden and Miss Treeves (sister to the Reverend Arthur, nominally in charge of cocoa) supervised the jacket-potato detachment and the Hot Spiced Punch. Many were anxious about Miss Seeton; in none was that anxiety evident.

Sir George—huffing through his neat moustache, conscious (despite his hidden concerns) of the importance of the occasion—struck the ceremonial match, and held it to a strategically-placed wisp of straw. The tiny flame licked its way into life, scarlet and crimson and rich, ripening gold; good luck for next year's harvest was assured. Adults stamped their booted feet and clapped; children cheered, and waved sparklers in wild, serpentine coils of burnished light against the dark.

Nigel snatched a brand from the merry burning, and set it to the blue touch-paper of a giant rocket, which coughed, sputtered into life, and roared into the heavens with tumbling silver glitter in its wake, and a series of jewel-hued explosions at the apex of its flight. A deafening cheer went up with the rocket: now, at last, the festivities proper could begin.

Enthroned at the bonfire's summit, the huge guy awaited its doom. Sir George, with a sigh, removed his pork-pie hat and gazed mournfully upwards, bidding a last farewell to his favourite armchair, sacrificed for the good of the village and for the sake of domestic harmony. He cleared his throat emphatically, and blinked.

"Good gad!" He blinked again, and rubbed his eyes, into which tendrils of acrid smoke had been blown by a mischievous breeze. "I could have sworn . . . "

He'd spent many a pleasant hour in that armchair: first in state by the sitting-room fire, then (after too lively an encounter with a wayward spark) in the comfort of his study; then—at her ladyship's decree—in the earthy bohemia of the potting shed. Woodworm, dry rot, and a virulent strain of fungus had finally worked their evil way on both the frame and the horsehair stuffing: even Sir

George could not deny that his chair had long since passed its prime, but he couldn't help feeling a little sentimental about that one piece of furniture—although surely that was no excuse for him to—

"Good gad, I was right!" It hadn't been any whimsical notion of the chair's making one last, wriggling attempt to escape its fiery fate: the thing really had moved. Rather, not the chair, but the guy seated in state upon it . . .

"Stop!" Sir George, hurling his hat aside, bellowed the command even as he ran across to where Major Matilda Howett had mustered a small group of wheelchair-bound patients from the nursing home. "The guy—the guy! Get it off!"

Wasting no time on explanations, he snatched from her startled grasp the Howitzer's umbrella, and galloped with it back to the bonfire, where he began raking furiously at the bottom branches.

"Help!" he cried, coughing. "Here—help, here!"

The major, like the major-general, had been trained by the military to respond promptly in an emergency. Her quick eyes saw what Sir George had seen; her quick wits urged her to seize a stout walking-stick—his favourite, but that couldn't be helped—from old Mr. Meredith's knees. Within seconds, she was at Sir George's side, tugging at the branches, shouting for more people to join the rescuers.

Lady Colveden, Miss Treeves, and other friends of Miss Seeton found their brollies wrenched from them by urgent hands. The smoke and flames were thicker now. Few could see what Sir George and Matilda Howett had seen; but if two such common-sense types thought the guy had to be got off the fire, then got off that guy would be, or they'd burst in the attempt. Those without umbrellas followed the Howitzer's example and indulged in a bout of stick-napping; Lady Colveden and the rest of the catering committee dragged the emergency buckets—woefully inadequate, never intended for more than a spark-caught coat, a careless match—to the bonfire and hurled their contents—"Don't!" cried Sir George, but too late—into its very heart.

Smoke surged out in a dense, acrid cloud. A fusillade of coughs, a cataract of tears from smoke-stung eyes. From above—from the guy—a feeble croak, a convulsive wriggle as smoke and heat enveloped its bulky form . . .

But no flames. Not yet. The wild water had suppressed, though not extinguished, the flames: the mischievous breeze was fanning them again into life, but it was at the same time blowing away the smoke. There was, after all, a chance . . . and those who had brought pocket flashlights pointed them towards the centre of operations, and prayed.

The guy croaked again, and jerked back and forth on the chair, which swayed and rocked as, settling a little on the first fire-weakened branches, the top of the bonfire slipped sideways and down—no more than an inch or two, but an inch or two closer to the red-hot peril still beneath.

"Stand back!" The words came in a bellow as loud as any Sir George could command: heredity will out. Nigel Colveden—soaked to the skin, his face cut and bleeding—erupted like a fury from the shadows with, close behind him, Jack Crabbe and Len Hosigg, carrying a ladder. "Mind out!"

"Nigel!" cried his mother, then clamped her lips in Spartan fashion together, and said no more. Sir George was too breathless now for speech, but his heart swelled with pride as he saw his son and heir plunge into the flames and smoke, swarming up the ladder which Jack and Len had thrown against the bonfire's side, stationing themselves— they, too, were soaked and dripping—at its base to catch whatever, whoever might come down, no matter in what condition.

Everyone fell silent. Moved away, if they feared they would be more hindrance than help; moved closer, ready to seize the guy from Nigel's hands and bear it out of range of the still-smouldering fire—if once he brought that guy to safety. But could he do so in time?

Only a muted crackling, the hiss and spit of green wood, was heard as Nigel neared his goal. Some watchers were so tense, they could almost swear they heard bells ringing. As he laid his hand in triumph on the sacking foot, there came a muted outcry, a release of pent-up breath, a groan of general excitement, almost a cheer: and the sound of bells was audible to all.

"It's okay," they heard Nigel say, as he tried to scoop the still-struggling guy into his arms. "Don't worry—try not to fidget . . . "

A swirl of smoke hid him from view, and they heard him cough. Heard, too, above the bells, the sudden swooping two-tone approach of sirens . . .

Torch-beams wavered through the smoke as—cautiously, but as quickly as he dared—Nigel began his descent. Over his shoulder, the sacking guy drooped, without movement: had rescue come too late? Jack and Len, steadying the ladder, reached up; were shouldered out of the way by big Dan Eggleden, head of the human chain organised by the admiral and PC Potter while Dr. Knight and Major Howett, with anxious faces, stood by to administer first aid. Deaf old Mr. Meredith—who'd always been suspected of leading a secret life behind his deafness—released the hot-wire safety switch on his wheelchair, and hurtled across the grass towards the gate, and the road, and the nursing home, where the alarm must be raised, emergency beds prepared.

As he rattled out of the playing-field, he was almost run down by the high-speed scarlet jubilation of a fire engine, its bell clamouring, turning gleefully in through the narrow gateway. As he whizzed up The Street, in his haste ignoring the Highway Code, he narrowly missed being flattened by the panda car approaching from the north. Old Mr. Meredith shouted something rude, and scorched onwards . . .

The crew of the fire engine couldn't believe their luck. A nine-nine-nine call to put out—of all conflagrations—the Plummergen bonfire? It was the best Guy Fawkes message the retained men of Murreystone had had in years.

"Stop!" thundered Sir George, as the oilskinned rivals from over the marsh leaped from their appliance and began to uncoil their hoses. "Stop! No need—panic over. She's safe!" And even in the heat of the moment, he couldn't help the hint of paternal pride as he imparted this information.

"Alarm call to Plummergen playing-field," said the chief officer stoutly. "Bonfire out of control, believed to have caused injury to an elderly party—it's got to be put out, and put it out's what we're a-going to do, so stand aside!"

"She's safe, I tell you!" Sir George almost choked on the words. "Look!"

Had they cared to follow his pointing finger, they would have seen a tumult of sacking and straw on the ground and, in the middle of this tumult, a small woman in tweeds. Her grey hair was rumpled, her eyes seemed out of focus in a pale, drawn face: but she was blinking up at the two persons chafing her limbs, and smiling her feeble thanks to somebody trying to wrap an overcoat about her shoulders.

"Look!" instructed Sir George: but Murreystone did not care to look. This, at last, was their chance, which they had no intention of missing.

"The hose, lads!" commanded the chief officer.

And the lads of Murreystone rushed to obey.

And Plummergen began to murmur . . .

And blue, flashing light filled the sky: light not from an errant firework, but from a police car . . .

Which swept, its siren yodelling, across the grass, and bumped to a halt just as Plummergen's menfolk were flexing their muscles and rolling up their shirtsleeves . . .

Official eyes quickly assessed the situation. And an official voice calmly remarked:

"Hello-ello-ello, what's all this, then? Did we get here too late—or just in time? Pity to spoil our moment of glory, if you ask me. When we've never had a nine-nine-nine call dialled direct from a palace before . . . "

# CHAPTER 26

"And neither," countered the Murreystone man at once, "have we." Through the glowing bonfire darkness, punctuated as it was by torchlight beams and the vivid, rhythmic blue of the official beacon, he glared at the glinting buttons and beady eye of the Ashford policeman. "So never you mind *moments of glory*," he went on, with a sneer. "We've a job to do, with this bonfire here reported out of control all the way from *Buckingham Palace,* no less. So there's nobody going to stop us a-doing our—our loyal duty by extinguishing it, I tell you straight!"

"That bonfire," said the driver of the panda, as Plummergen began to expostulate, "looks as safe as any I've seen, and then some—except," with a cough, as the wind changed, "for the smoke. But even then it's not that near the road it's a hazard to passing traffic, so—"

He broke off—or, rather, was drowned out: partly by the swelling murmurs of discontent from Murreystone (who saw themselves about to be thwarted of revenge by this uniformed jack-in-office), partly by swelling murmurs of annoyance from Plummergen—but mostly by the rumble and roar of two fast-approaching cars across the grass, and the urgent pip-pipping of their horns as they drew near.

The Ashford bobby looked round, in some relief: the cavalry was coming! He thought he recognised the sound of the closer of the two cars . . .

He was right. Headlights blazing, both vehicles came to a screeching halt, and four doors opened as one. Four large men—no, one was a giant, the others merely tall— leaped out, rushed towards him—and past him, though he tried to catch Superintendent Brinton's eye—rushed on towards the bonfire which was the subject of such heated discussion . . .

And all four, as they ran, clamoured severally: "Police! Stop! Put that fire out! Is Miss Seeton safe?"

"Hey!" cried Sir George, while PC Potter shouted, and the admiral view-hallooed. "Delphick—hold hard, man!"

But it was left to Major Howett to announce, in tones of utter triumph which halted the four in their headlong rush: "Perfectly safe, thank you! What this poor woman needs more than anythin' right now is *peace and quiet*—and she isn't," with a glare, "goin' to get that with you people makin' such a dashed noisy racket all around her."

The Howitzer could be a regular dragon where her patients were concerned. These draconian tendencies were given full rein as she supervised the loading of Miss Seeton— weakly protesting that she hated to be a bother—into the most commodious of the three official cars; after which Major Howett gave firm instructions that the invalid was to be treated with the utmost care during the half-mile trip to the nursing home, and herself followed in the second car, assuring Dr. Knight that she and his wife could cope very well between them, with the night staff and everythin', and that he must stay and keep an eye on the bonfire, just in case, as they'd previously arranged.

The major's forceful eye had not only quelled the rescue rush of Delphick, Brinton, Foxon, and Bob to the bonfire; it had also—at least temporarily—stemmed Plummergen's fermenting defensive attack upon devious Murreystone, the fire crew being all too ready to take advantage of a situation about which everyone kept trying to insist there was no further cause for alarm. Before the full effects of Major Matilda's personality had worn off, PC Potter remarked— at some volume—on the presence of official reinforcements. Sir George and Admiral Leighton loudly restrained their troops, then muttered sage promises of opportunities yet to come; Dr. Knight, examining the cuts on a now-shivering Nigel Colveden's face and the burns on his hands, expressed himself far too busy to bother with anybody else, adding that if people proposed committing wholesale slaughter on one another he was dashed if he was going to waste good bandages and sticking-plaster on a single man from either side.

"And this wreck here," he concluded, giving the sodden Nigel a jovial buffet on the shoulder, "is in danger of death from double pneumonia, never mind tetanus and blood-poisoning and multiple bruises." Nigel's teeth chattered, but he grinned even as he winced. "To jump," continued Dr. Knight, "head first through a cricket pavilion window, in my opinion, suggests less an urgent requirement for a shower than a sudden outbreak of rampant exhibitionism. Judging by the, ahem, dramatic results of his action, this patient is suffering from a previously unsuspected circus performer complex of considerable intensity. My prescription would be a booster jab, a hot bath—which should satisfy any latent craving for cleanliness—and a warm bed, in that order, to be followed by a stiff tot of whisky and a sleeping-pill, which together should serve to banish all thoughts of an acrobatic career. Such treatment to be administered," he added, with a nod for Jack Crabbe and Len Hosigg, lurking damp (but relatively undamaged) close by, "to anyone else in the throes of a similar complaint. Immediately."

The doctor's voice was a carrying one, and full of authority. Delphick and Brinton hesitated, exchanged looks, and then nodded. Brinton thereafter rolled his eyes in the direction of PC Potter and the panda man, who meekly signalled back their obedience to his unspoken command. Sir George and the admiral did not allow their eyes to meet, but they cleared their throats, and otherwise said nothing.

"I believe," said Delphick, "that our wisest course of action is to set a guard around Miss Seeton before another attempt can be made upon her life, and so that a statement may be obtained from her at the earliest possible moment. In the circumstances, those who are already conversant with the complexities of this particular case must be best suited to the task of bodyguard: and, as there are several persons here in obvious need of medical attention, I suggest that we combine two duties in one by giving them all a lift to the nursing home. This will, of course, necessitate the use of more than one official vehicle . . . "

Quite how it happened, Murreystone could never afterwards decide. One minute there were six policemen and three police cars keeping the peace in the bonfire field; then the cars—and the policemen (even Potter, who lived, as everyone knew, so near he had no need to drive)—were gone. The women of Plummergen hustled the children out of the way, and muttered reminders about not spoiling the kiddies' treat; the men of the village closed ranks, and once more rolled up sleeves the untimely arrival of the Law had encouraged them to roll back down.

"Now then," said Sir George, as the leader of the fire crew prepared to renew the offensive, "just what was it you were saying about hoses?"

"I doubt," said Delphick, as they drank coffee and waited for news of Miss Seeton, "whether worse than a good soaking is likely to befall them—and I also doubt they'll seek refuge here with Nigel and company. Once the fire tender has been thoroughly emptied, I imagine they will be allowed to make their escape—whereupon the celebrations may begin in earnest."

"Let's hope we've got something to celebrate, as well." Glumly, Brinton stirred sugar into his cup. "Potter's a good man: he'll keep an eye from behind the hedge to see things don't get out of hand—but what about Miss Seeton, poor old biddy? In her case, they've already got—out of hand, I mean, or pretty damned serious, at any rate. She looked more than peaky, I thought, and there's got to be a first time she doesn't come bouncing back . . . "

An indignant chorus from Foxon and Bob—privilege of rank be blowed—drowned out the rest of Brinton's remarks. Delphick smiled.

"There, I think, you have your answer, Chris. Miss Seeton, thank heaven, is a born survivor. The yoga, of course, will have helped—being drugged and bound without food for twenty-four hours must come as less of a hardship to MissEss than it would, say, to young Georgina."

"What a girl!" Brinton forgot lamentation in his amusement. "Something she's always wanted to do, she says— like pulling the communication cord on a train, except I don't suppose royal trains have emergencies, really—but to dial nine-nine-nine all the way from Buckingham Palace like that . . . The kid's made history, I should think."

"A worthy recipient," agreed Delphick, "of the Order of the Gold Umbrella, should such a decoration exist. Perhaps we might have a word with the relevant authorities."

"Awarded to people who've survived one of MissEss's adventures." Brinton grimaced. "In which case, young Georgy'd better be the first person to get it, or I'll—I'll—"

The door opened before he could find words to frame the threat, and Major Howett marched in, rubbing her hands.

"Give her a few hours," she said, "and you can pop up for a quick chat—just one of you, that is. The poor woman needs a natural sleep now, and to wake up in her own good time without people explodin' rockets in her ear or half chokin' her with smoke. Try around mid-mornin' tomorrow—though don't be surprised if she's still a bit woozy.

After a sensible breakfast, mind you, if she can keep it down, she could well surprise us all.''

"In the past, she frequently has," Delphick agreed, as his companions expressed their relief at the major's advice. "If we must wait," he went on, "then naturally we will. But if you could tell us whether Miss Seeton has said anything about how she came to be in her recent predicament . . . ''

Matilda Howett shot him a shrewd look. "She hasn't said much at all." She paused. "Not much that made sense, that is . . . '' She seemed to be considering his request for information very carefully; and nobody made any attempt to hurry her to a decision. The sound of late-night fireworks filtered through the curtained windows of the comfortable little room; a sudden loud bang overhead made everyone jump. The major frowned at the noise, then coughed. After a further contemplative pause, she continued:

"But then, she was very fidgety, don't you know. Twitchin' a good deal—and we were tryin' to calm her down, so we could well have missed it even if she did. Say anythin', that is.''

"Twitchy," repeated Delphick. "Her fingers?" He knew a hint when he heard one.

"Dancin'," replied the major at once. "Almost as if the poor soul was playin' the piano in her sleep. And mutterin' about . . . '' For the first time in their acquaintance with Matilda Howett, the four policemen saw her blush. "About," repeated the Howitzer firmly, though her maiden cheeks were pink, "about drugs, and—and about havin' to—to go to the powder-room . . . ''

"Aaah," said Delphick, as light, at last, dawned: and he heaved a great sigh of triumph.

"These are from Bob, these from Chris Brinton, these from my humble self. And Foxon''—Delphick hid a smile— "has been revealed as possessing a far more practical streak than I'd ever given the boy credit for—he sent you this.''

Gravely, he handed Miss Seeton in turn three bunches of flowers, and a bronze chrysanthemum in a decorated pot. "I observe," he went on, as Miss Seeton blushed above her woolly bed-jacket, "that you have some truly splendid floral specimens here—let me guess," as Miss Seeton blushed still more. "By Royal Command, perhaps?"

Miss Seeton murmured in some embarrassment of the great kindness of Her Royal Highness, then perked up to say how very, very glad she was that the poor young thing had been restored in safety to her family.

"And all thanks to you—to your umbrella, anyway," amended Delphick, as Miss Seeton voiced a muted, but startled, protest. "Has Georgina explained that it was . . . a little damaged during her escape attempt, and that it will be returned to you as soon as it has been repaired?"

"So very kind," said Miss Seeton, still muted and pink. "Indeed, most gracious, when really, there was no need— to go to so much trouble, I mean. I can only be thankful that, even if I could be of no particular help or comfort to Her Royal Highness during her—during our, that is, I suppose I should say, although I can hardly feel that it can have been in the least deliberate, in my case . . . during the incarceration, if that is not too melodramatic a term . . . that it should have been of use. My umbrella, I mean. Thankful. Except, of course," blushing with sudden, dreadful realisation, "that I would naturally have arranged for it to be repaired just as soon as I could—and it would have been no trouble at all, Mr. Delphick, I assure you."

"I believe you," Delphick said quickly: he couldn't bear any longer to see her blush and fluster her way through this tortuous apologia. "And you must believe me, Miss Seeton, when I say that I feel every bit as—as honoured as yourself to think that in some small way the umbrella I gave you has served a purpose of which neither of us, in the beginning, could ever have dreamed."

"Indeed not." At the chief superintendent's matter-of-fact tone, Miss Seeton was almost her old self again, with a smile in her voice and the beginnings of a twinkle in her eye. Only the pallor of her face, and a slight hollowing of her normally smooth cheeks, showed that she had so recently passed through the grim experience of being drugged close to death, then set still closer to death—by combustion—than even the drugs could contrive.

"An honour," said Miss Seeton, in the assured tones she would use when teaching, "for us both, Mr. Delphick—but oh, dear," and assurance turned to anxiety. "I fear I had forgotten, in the pleasure of being allowed a visitor—though the dear major—and the Knights, of course—have been more than kind, and I was most certainly not suggesting that she—I mean they—had forbidden . . . "

At this point, Miss Seeton's innate honesty brought her to a blushing halt. Ever since the marriage of Anne Knight to Detective Sergeant Bob Ranger had installed Major Matilda Howett in Plummergen's private nursing home, the Knights—whose names were on the mortgage as owners of the property, whose signatures were on the cheques which paid wages and rates and running expenses—had bowed to a far superior force, and acknowledged themselves the merest ciphers. The whole village knew that Major Howett was—to mix naval with military metaphor—the captain of the ship, if not the admiral of the fleet. Her word was law, her command absolute. Under the old regime, Miss Seeton would have been permitted without argument to discharge herself and go home straight after breakfast, as she had on more than one occasion in the past. The bed (she had insisted) should be left for others in greater need, the nurses freed to continue with more pressing work . . .

"I had forgotten," said Miss Seeton, recovering herself with a gulp, "that you might reasonably expect to be at work today, rather than waste your time—not, of course, that it is not always a pleasure to see you, Chief Superintendent, but when there are so many demands on . . . "

"Not as many as there were," he told her cheerfully. "Nor on Superintendent Brinton's, either. Things have been happening while you were, shall we say, sleeping it off under Major Howett's, ah, protection. The kidnappers have been found—thanks to you, Miss Seeton, as I said earlier. And it may not come as any great surprise to you that it was, indeed, they who were responsible for the death of the caterer Donald Bragbury—and, I'm sorry to say, for the subsequent death of one of their own employees . . . ''

"The KarriKlozzet company," said Delphick, above Miss Seeton's shocked exclamations of dismay, "has been in financial difficulties for some time. Caroline Kelshall did wonders, mind you, with the firm she inherited from her husband Caradoc—put it on the map, built it up to the third largest portable powder-room supplier in the country—but Caroline isn't growing any younger, and she hasn't been in the best of health." He smiled. "Not everyone, Miss Seeton, is blessed with the stamina and physical fortitude which your yoga has imparted to you—nor, I might add, does everyone possess your strength of character and your high moral scruples." He sighed. "Few, alas, do. I only wish they did—except, of course, that if they did, I'd be out of a job." There was a wry twist to his lips as he spoke. "Human nature, however, being what it is, I rather think I'll be in gainful employment for the rest of my working life . . ."

Miss Seeton, likewise sighing, said with regret that she feared the chief superintendent was right. She clicked her tongue, and shook her head. For anyone to—to contrive the death of another was bad enough. Wicked, indeed: but the added wickedness of the—the betrayal of trust in causing the death of one's own employee . . .

"Luke Hadham," Delphick said. "He'd started with Kelshalls when they were just an ordinary builders' merchants, and he went along with old Caradoc when he branched out into KarriKlozzet. He knew pretty well as much about running it as Caradoc himself. He watched the children grow up, watched Caroline take over when Caradoc died, offered advice from time to time, especially when things started to go wrong—advice which sometimes she took, and sometimes she didn't. The layoffs, for instance: he was very much against that idea. He would have preferred reducing overall hours, so that everyone would at least keep some regular income, to reducing staff numbers—but Caroline wouldn't listen. She considered herself the ultimate boss, you see, even though Caradoc left more shares in the company to his children than to his wife: but the children have always been completely under their mother's thumb. So what Caroline Kelshall said, went—with everyone except Luke.

"Poor chap." Delphick shook his head. "He'd begun to think of himself as an éminence grise, which in some ways he was—but he was also, once the Kelshalls decided to turn to crime as a way out of their difficulties, a danger to them. He knew them all so well, you see. Not just the everyday work routines, but their personal foibles, their nervous habits—and some of them grew very nervous, in the course of their illicit activities. He knew enough, in short, to know when they were up to something, or at least to have strong suspicions that something wasn't right. He noticed when they kept sneaking away for their secret meetings to plot the abduction of young Georgina; he went on noticing whenever one or other of them took time off to give their prisoner her food; and maybe he said something, or perhaps tried a little blackmail—they're not saying—but it's clear the Kelshalls decided that he had to go."

In other circumstances, he would have smiled. "Killing

two birds with one stone, it might be said. By the so-called bomb attack on their premises they not only removed the threat of Luke Hadham, they also removed—reduced to smithereens, in fact—all evidence of their original scheme for Georgina's kidnap. A scheme which . . . ''

Miss Seeton began blushing once more. Delphick hurried on: '' . . . which your encounter with the radiation meter only served to bring forward, Miss Seeton. Believe me, they would have gone ahead anyway: their plans were all laid, and it was just that they were sufficiently quick-witted to take advantage of the—the inevitable confusion which resulted from the setting off of the alarm.''

''Oh, dear,'' breathed Miss Seeton, falling back on her pillows in guilty dismay. ''Oh, dear . . . ''

''Their original scheme,'' he went on quickly, ''would have been far less dignified for the princess than the actual quick sack over the head and subsequent hustling to a nearby car. Peter Therfield, the husband of Caroline's daughter Cleopatra—Caroline might be the lady boss herself, but she didn't hold with other females going into the business world, or taking too much responsibility upon themselves; that's why she recruited her son-in-law to take Cleopatra's place—anyway, Therfield, acting as a substitute for his wife, either bribed, or blackmailed, Donald Bragbury into spiking young Georgina's drink at the opening reception.'' He grinned. ''Blackmailed, probably—Bragbury's wife, or rather widow, is hardly . . . ''

Delphick, himself happily married, shuddered in sympathy for the marital burden borne by the late Mr. Bragbury. ''Let us say, Miss Seeton, that Mrs. Bragbury does not give the impression of having been the most affectionate of helpmeets. For Donald to take a mistress would have been hardly surprising: almost predictable, indeed.'' Once more, Miss Seeton sighed. Delphick nodded.

''Caroline Kelshall is a shrewd woman. She must have looked for a weak point in the caterer's armour, guessed at the likelihood of another woman in his life, and instructed

Therfield to arrange to have the wretched man slip a diuretic in Georgina's lemonade.'' Miss Seeton clicked her tongue, and murmured with great disapproval of royal dignity. Resting on the bedclothes, her clasped hands gave a sudden twitch.

Delphick nodded again. "That, of course, was the basis of their plan. Where else should a poor sufferer from waterworks trouble go to relieve her sufferings than to the lavatory? And when Royalty visits, it is not necessarily subjected to the indignities of the common cloakroom, particularly in a place which hasn't long been open, where all the niggling little problems of the plumbing haven't been entirely ironed out. The country-wide supplying of de luxe portable toilets for royal occasions is a serious business, or so I have been given to understand.''

Miss Seeton's fingers had begun to dance, despite their owner's clasping them tight, during the latter part of the Oracle's explanation. Kindly, he ignored the way she tried—and failed—to still them. "The particular closet the Kelshalls had supplied that day was altered to have an extra door, camouflaged very cleverly in the wall behind the wash-basin, and connected by a most ingenious system of levers to the ballcock in the cistern. As soon as the princess pulled the chain, the noise of rushing water would cover the sound of the levers unlocking the hidden door. When she turned on the tap to wash her hands, the door would open—and bingo.''

"Ingenious," agreed Miss Seeton, as Delphick came to a temporary halt, "but—but discourteous, in the extreme, and hardly a—a responsible attitude . . . ''

Her disapproval had, for the moment, quietened her restless fingers: a quietening which Delphick remarked with interest, though he still said nothing.

"To be fair to the Kelshalls," he continued, "they did their best throughout the remainder of their, ah, involvement with the princess to ensure that her washing and sanitary arrangements were of the highest standard that could, in the circumstances, be achieved. Kidnappers, believe me, are not often so considerate. Perhaps if we had paid more attention to this unusual fact once Georgina had been safely recovered, we would have found you rather more quickly than we did." His smile was apologetic. "I must tell you, Miss Seeton, that we—that the police—are only too sorry you had to be subjected to such . . . unpleasantness. We're deeply thankful that the outcome of your adventure wasn't a good deal more serious than it proved, in the end, to be."

"Oh, dear." Miss Seeton turned pink with mingled guilt and dismay. "Poor Nigel—he has already been in to see me this morning, and his face—such a dreadful shock. And his hands, with their bandages . . . I remember so little, I fear, of what occurred at the time, although dear Major Howett has since explained . . . Nigel himself told me almost nothing, beyond the fact that"—the embarrassed note gave way to a hint of amusement—"the major had refused to allow him to go home before breakfast . . . "

"Nigel," said Delphick, "is a born knight-errant. When there is a lady in distress, would you suppose his courage to fail him? As of course last night it did not. But," he added, as Miss Seeton blushed again, "does it surprise you that his courage *did* fail him when faced with Major Howett's . . . professional resolution? In order to resist the major in, let us say, full cry, one would need to be more than courageous. One would have to be rash beyond belief, as well as totally lacking in common sense."

"Nigel," said Miss Seeton warmly, "is a very intelligent young man, besides being"—a little sniff escaped her, and she blinked rapidly several times—"a true gentleman."

"Indeed he is." Delphick grinned. "And bright enough to know when he's beaten by superior odds: so I'm not surprised he stayed here overnight. He wouldn't have dared do anything else." He chuckled. "Not unless he was quite out of his mind, that is; and Nigel is far from crazy."

Miss Seeton's fingers suddenly twitched again. Delphick couldn't help glancing at them; then he dragged his gaze away, and prepared to go on with his exposition.

There was no need to upset Miss Seeton by telling her that it had been the media notoriety she so greatly disliked which had made the Kelshalls suspect her of knowing more than she in fact did. They might, without that notoriety, have been able to ignore the several uncanny coincidences which had occurred: Miss Seeton's having been in charge of the child who presented the bouquet to their victim; her insistence on searching, as they'd seen it, the booby-trapped lavatory; even her waving of her umbrella in what anyone less guilty must have recognised as an innocent signal for assistance—that same umbrella which had provided so convenient a distraction after the alarm went off that they had been able to swoop upon the princess so much sooner than they'd expected . . .

They *might* have ignored all this: but, in fact, they hadn't. The newspapers' insistence on coupling the name of the Battling Brolly with Scotland Yard, the local knowledge that the soubriquet concealed Miss Emily Dorothea Seeton of Plummergen, had pricked the uneasy consciences of the Kelshalls, leading them to case the village joint under the pretext of admiring the many penny-for-the-guy displays along The Street. One of these guys had worn a hat which could only have belonged to Miss Seeton: try as they might, they couldn't escape her.

Had they balked at killing her outright? Had they left it to chance—to the strength of the barbiturates in the doctored tea? The same devious mind (thought Delphick grimly) as had planned the diuretic spiking had planned *that,* he'd wager. Miss Seeton was a small woman; the post office guy had been an unusually fine specimen, sufficiently large to accommodate easily two bound, living limbs within one sacking leg, one pinioned torso within its enormous body. It had been a close-run thing. Though the clues towards her ultimate rescue had been plain in her sketchbook, the police—he himself, renowned throughout the force as the Seeton expert—had failed to interpret them in time. It had been the quick wits of Nigel Colveden which had saved her . . .

Plus her own undoubted stamina, of course. The yoga: how many people of her age could have gone as long as she had without food or drink, yet still have the strength to move and cry out when the effects of the drug had finally worn off?

"Worn off," muttered Delphick, and caught Miss Seeton's curious eye. *Had* it been intended that it should wear off in time—should give her a sporting chance? They'd have the truth out of the Kelshalls, sooner or later. He wouldn't tell Miss Seeton, of course; there was evidence enough to convict them without that last knowledge—but for his own satisfaction he needed to know whether it had been a deliberate gamble on the kidnappers' part, or an honest-to-badness in-the-heat-of-the-moment mistake . . .

"A mistake," Miss Seeton broke into his thoughts with a nod and a smile, startling him: he hadn't realised he'd been thinking aloud. He wondered how much he'd said: she didn't seem too worried—but then, she never did.

"A mistake," said Miss Seeton, smiling. "Naturally: why should anyone, especially someone I have never met, wish to harm me? And, as you implied, it is most fortunate that my knowledge of yoga enabled me to overcome the discomfort and inconvenience rather more easily than, for example, might have been the case with Her Royal Highness. Except, of course, that she is so much younger—but one must be thankful that she was spared the experience. After all," she explained, with a smile, "I was, remember, among friends—a most fortunate circumstance. So very alarming for the poor child to have woken up surrounded by complete strangers, no matter how well-disposed towards her—as, of course, they would be. Nevertheless . . . "

Only Miss Seeton could regard her abduction and drugging and narrow escape from death as a positive advantage. One day, Delphick mused, there would be some occurrence which even she couldn't fail to regard as dangerous, unpleasant, and deliberately aimed against herself: one day. But not, he hoped, just yet . . .

"And more than fortunate," he told her, "that you'd set us on the right track with your drawings—the powder-puff, in particular, encouraging us to look at those who had provided the portable powder-room." Once more Miss Seeton's fingers danced on the bedclothes. The chief superintendent kept a fascinated eye upon them as he continued:

"I really must apologise again, Miss Seeton, for having failed to understand soon enough what you were telling us—me, that is. The catering arrangements, the Karri-Klozzet connection—they were all there, but we were, I fear, much too slow in a proper interpretation of them, with the result that we had to rely on everyday police work when these were far from everyday crimes. The gamble paid off, but it was a crazy risk to have taken . . ."

That twitch again. He couldn't bear it. "Miss Seeton, is there something you feel you should be telling me—us? The police, I mean—ah, there is. I thought so," as there came another convulsive leap. "I see that you have been the recipient of several get-well cards: would it disturb you to rough out a few ideas on the back of that monster there, for instance?"

Miss Seeton, across whose face a look of relief for her friend's understanding had flashed at his words, now looked regretful. She murmured of dear Mr. Potter, or rather Amelia and her mother, who had so kindly brought . . .

"The wrapping from my bunch of flowers, then." Without waiting for her to demur, Delphick seized his bouquet and deftly unrolled the patterned paper, disclosing blank whiteness on the other side. "My ballpoint pen," he said, "and a firm surface, that's what you need—as these flowers," with a quick gesture pulling the over-the-bed table towards her, and collecting the floral assortment with one hand as with the other he dug his pen from his pocket, "as

these flowers need water. I'll just have a word with Major
Howett . . . ''

"I apologise for troubling you, Mrs. Potter." Delphick
stood on the doorstep of the police house with a roll of
paper in his hand. "But if I might have a quick word with
your husband, I'd be most grateful."

"Why, he's not here." Mabel Potter seemed astonished
that anyone should think her spouse neglectful of his duty.
"Bin gone these twenty minutes or more, he has, doing his
rounds. Course, there's the radio"—she saw the involun-
tary shake of his head, and went on quickly—"but if it
might be something I could help with . . . ''

Delphick hesitated. While he had been talking to Miss
Seeton, Bob had kicked his heels downstairs, too much in
awe of the major to grumble at being denied the bedside
of his adopted Aunt Em. It was Miss Seeton herself who
had broken the impasse. She'd been dressed and waiting
by the time Delphick had returned to see what manner of
sketch it had been to set her fingers dancing; and Major
Howett, with stern warnings about overdoin' it, had con-
sented to her patient's discharge on condition that she went
home by car rather than on foot, as she'd wanted. A delighted Bob had done the honours in the Yard's unmarked
car, leaving Delphick to puzzle alone over the wrapping-
paper sketch his ballpoint pen had produced . . .

"It's this drawing of Miss Seeton's," said Delphick, as
Mabel Potter closed the door and led him into the office,
realising that he came on police business. "Even with hind-
sight, I can't for once quite make out what she's trying to
express, and I wondered . . . ''

Together, he and Mabel Potter gazed at the image of a
hospital bed, neatly made. The corners of its sheets were
mitred, its counterpane was crisp and smooth—apart from
that part beneath the long-armed table, on which stood a
large and ornate vase of flowers, and a bowl of what had
at first appeared to be mixed fruit, but which closer in-

spection showed was an assortment of nuts. Directly under the table, the folds of the counterpane were scooped back by a man's hand: a man who, in police uniform except for the helmet, crouched under the bed and peered out, his face wild and working—peered out from beneath, not a helmet, but an enormous, upturned china chamber-pot . . .

And the man had the face of Police Constable Potter.

Delphick looked at Mabel. Mabel looked at the drawing. For some while, she did not speak.

Neither did Delphick. Then, as Mrs. Potter seemed to be struggling with herself, he sighed. "It's my fault, I dare say." He took the sketch and rolled it up again. "Preferring all the loose ends to be tied up, I mean—one can't, every time, have everything. I believe that, while I was talking to her, I said something about someone-or-other being, well, crazy . . . It was she who spoke of your family's kindness in sending her a card—and the vase of flowers is obvious, of course, though I confess I didn't notice any nuts, or even fruit, while I was there. We must, I think, assume it is the shock of her recent experience which has—has somewhat distorted her usual good sense. I do hope you aren't too offended . . . ''

But Mabel wasn't in the least offended. Her struggle had been not to erupt into giggles rather than not to explode in anger; and now the struggle was lost. She laughed out loud. "Bless you—sir," she added, "Potter's used to it—and so'm I, being married this long. What else could we expect? *And* young Amelia, now she's started school." She saw Delphick stare, and giggled still more.

"He," said Mabel, indicating ballpoint Potter under the bed, "looks barmy, don't he? Potty, you might say—and that's what she's drawn, see? Grew up with 'em making jokes like that at school, he did. Water off a duck's back." She twinkled at the chief superintendent. "Why," she quizzed him, "does a madman hide under the bed?"

Delphick struck himself lightly on the forehead as she waited, grinning, for his reply. "Of course! Because he thinks he's a little . . . oh, dear, to be caught out by that old chestnut. I haven't heard it in years—but what, in a case like this, could be a more apposite conclusion?'' He joined Mabel in her laughter. ''Why, she's even drawn the blessed chestnuts for us, to tell us it's a joke . . . ''

Delphick and Bob—leaving Brinton to charge the Kelshalls and begin the laborious task of getting the paperwork in order—returned to London, confident that they had tied up every loose end.

But they weren't, for once, altogether right.

It was some days later that—unknown to anyone directly concerned with the case—the true meaning of Miss Seeton's final sketch was made plain: although those who made it so, being no great friends to Miss Seeton, would have been most annoyed had they realised the truth.

''Too clever of Eric, I think.'' Mrs. Blaine beamed, all sulks and tantrums forgotten. ''No, Eric, don't blush—you shouldn't hide your light under a bushel. I'm willing to admit,'' said Mrs. Blaine bravely, looking about the post office to make sure her magnanimity didn't go unnoticed, ''that I was wrong. Though you must admit that to use my best sieves and buckets to wash the clay—''

''Body,'' corrected Miss Nuttel, in knowledgeable tones.

Mrs. Blaine tittered. ''I'm sorry, Eric. Body. That's the technical name for it,'' she explained, whether or not anyone wished to know. ''To rinse all the stones out of *the body:* clay from deep in our garden, of course, because Eric keeps the topsoil in such splendid condition—''

''Heart,'' came the next correction from Miss Nuttel. Mrs. Blaine scowled, then quickly recovered herself.

''Keeps the soil so splendidly,'' she amended, ''that she had to dig positively *yards* down before she reached the subsoil. And then all the straining, and rinsing—''

''Slurry,'' said Miss Nuttel.

''And drying in great plaster-of-Paris beds,'' said Mrs. Blaine, ignoring her. ''And then having to cut it with wire over and over and over again to squeeze all the air out—''

"Wedging."

Bunny shot Eric a very nasty look. "And then to have our own—that is, a home-made potter's wheel, *and* a kiln—and Eric taught herself all about electricity from the book, which I think too clever for words . . . ''

Somebody sniggered, remembering how all the lights had gone out in Lilikot, and the Nutty outcry there had been.

"Anyway," said Mrs. Blaine, proudly, "to think we might never need to buy a plate or a pot or a vase ever again!"

And, on this note of triumph, the Nuts departed.

There was a pause. The sniggerer sniggered again, more loudly. "Make your own plates—they're mad," she concluded. "Nutty as fruitcakes, they really are!"

But another conclusion—had the speaker but known it— was even more apposite: providing, as it did, the punchline to Delphick's—to Miss Seeton's—last little joke.

"Potty," she said: and nobody disagreed.

**Hamilton Crane** is the pseudonym of Sarah J(ill) Mason, who was born in England (Bishop's Stortford), went to university in Scotland (St. Andrews), and lived for a year in New Zealand (Rotorua) before returning to settle only twelve miles from where she started. She now lives about twenty miles outside London with a tame welding engineer husband and two (reasonably) tame Schipperke dogs. Under her real name, she writes the mystery series which stars Detective Superintendent Trewley and Detective Sergeant Stone of the Allingham police force.